CLAIMING THALIA

Blood Maidens of Karthia – Book 1

REGINE ABEL

CONTENTS

CLAIMING THALIA

She was a pawn coveted by kings.

From the moment of her birth, Thalia has been groomed to become a Blood Maiden to a vampire. As a human born in one of the colonies of Karthia, Thalia's extremely rare blood type is her ticket out of the life of poverty and hardship that normally befalls her species. During her first Blood Fair, she intends to entice the Vampire Lord Konstantin into claiming her. But unable to resist an unexpected offer, her long years of hard work and carefully planned future are derailed by the stunning, silver-eyed Lycan named Drogo.

Struck by a rare but deadly illness, King Drogo's only chance of survival relies on securing some golden blood. Yet, the moment he sees Thalia, the rabid emotions the clever female awakens in him surpass even his thirst for her unique blood. But the Lycan King's efforts to claim Thalia as his mate revive a century-old rivalry with his nemesis, Konstantin.

As the realm braces for a cataclysmic event, the clash between the two most powerful males of Karthia escalates. Will the battle to claim Thalia bring about her ultimate demise?

DEDICATION

To all those born with little who never stop fighting to achieve their dream of a better tomorrow. To all those who use their good fortune to make the world a better place for everyone.

To Ronika Williams. Thank you for always being there when I need you the most and for helping me overcome my bouts of insecurities. This book would have never seen the light of day without you.

CHAPTER 1
DROGO

My heart swelled with pride as I observed Darya training the next generation of Iron Maidens. The young females leaped with grace and power, swiping their weapons with deadly precision against their holographic enemies. Despite their young age, they already mastered their wolf form enough to battle partially shifted.

"Magnificent, aren't they?" my mother's soft voice said next to me.

"They are," I concurred without taking my eyes off of the teenage girls. "Darya is an amazing trainer. But then, her mother was the greatest Iron Maiden of the past three generations."

"She was. And her daughter does her proud. Unfortunately, Darya's pack wants her back," Mother said.

"She doesn't want to go," I countered, knowing it was a moot point.

"We both know she has no choice." Mother placed her hand on my shoulder to make me look at her. She tried to keep a neutral expression, but I knew her too well not to see the distress she felt at my appearance. "You need to speak with Viktor and convince him to let her stay longer."

"No, Mother," I said in a gentle but firm tone. "Right now, what I need to do is choose my heir and rally the pack behind him. Otherwise, we're going to end up in a massive succession war that will leave the Lycans far too weak when the Moon Well opens."

"You're not dead yet," my mother hissed, her anger flaring.

I cupped her beautiful face in my hands and gave her a sad smile.

"But I will be soon. We both know it," I said without bitterness, having already come to terms with my fate. "Look at me. I am wasting away. I'm not worthy of Soren."

"No, *you* listen to me," she said, her silver eyes—which I inherited from her—locking with mine. "The Great Sun Wolf's Spirit chose you right after your father passed. You are the Lycan King. What's eating you from within isn't Soren, but the Blood Starvation—the scourge of the trueborn."

"Nothing sates the hunger," I argued. "Ever since Soren claimed me, no blood I have consumed has satisfied him. I'm eating myself from the inside out. Ulia has scouted every town and village for Blood Maidens with the purest bloods and rarest types. None have helped. The more I drink, the faster I wither."

Mother covered my bony hands with hers, hiding the wretched appearance mine had taken over the past few weeks. The skin had darkened then taken a leathery texture before sinking in on itself, outlining each bone like I'd been mummified —the clear signs of Blood Starvation.

"You need golden blood," Mother said.

I huffed in exasperation and rolled my eyes while pulling away from her. "Where the fuck am I going to find golden blood?" I asked angrily.

I hissed and took a step back, pulling on the hood of my robe to better hide my face from the sun. In my anger, I had stepped too close to the edge of my private terrace and out of the shade. Even that had been taken from me. What was left if I, the Apex of the descendants of the Sun Wolves, could no longer run with my pack in broad daylight in either my Lycan or wolf form?

"Careful, Drogo," my mother said in a concerned voice.

Clenching my teeth, I cast a final glance at the maidens training below before turning back inside towards my private suite.

"The Blood Fair is only three weeks away," my mother's gentle voice said to my back as she followed me in. "The word is that a Golden Blood Maiden will attend."

I froze and turned around to stare at my mother. She smirked and flicked her long reddish-brown hair streaked with silver over her shoulder.

"How reliable is that rumor?" I asked, not daring to hope or think of all the obstacles we would face trying to lure such a maiden—if she actually existed.

"Every high-ranking Vampire Lord will be in attendance," she said with a triumphant glimmer in her eyes. "Konstantin, Vladimir, Vasska, and Morana have all confirmed their presence."

I whistled through my teeth.

"Exactly," Mother said with a smug grin.

She strutted her way to my minibar to pour herself a glass of Karthian wine. She raised the glass of silver liquid to ask me if I wanted some, but I shook my head.

"Konstantin can't have her," I reflected out loud. "He will grow too powerful and will challenge the Lycan rule over Karthia. Humans will get slaughtered, and he'll bring wolves to the brink of extinction."

"He won't have her because *you* will," Mother said with a certainty that I would have found amusing under different circumstances. "She will save you, and then everything will go back to normal."

I gave her a sad smile and shook my head while pulling down the hood that covered my features.

"She can't save me," I said in a tired voice. "The Blood Fair is still over twenty days away. I will not make it through the week." My mother's beautiful face blanched. Her silver eyes widened with disbelief and a quickly hidden fear. I opened my robe to show her the desiccated body it sheltered. "It's growing exponentially. I'm out of time."

My mother approached me and ran her fingertips on the leathery, sunken skin on my chest and the protruding bones of my ribs. Her face hardened with an angry resolve as she closed my robe.

"I am *not* letting you die," she said, her gaze boring into mine. "Time can go fuck itself. We will put you in stasis if needed, but you *will* get her blood."

I snorted. "And how am I supposed to court that maiden with my 'sexy' appearance and while unconscious?" I asked mockingly.

"You leave that to your mother, sweetheart," she said smugly, tapping the tip of my nose with her index finger. "No one can resist me."

I chuckled, ignoring the bone-deep pain it provoked. "True enough. But I doubt even your charisma and mesmerizing charm can convince a human to come to Hundilinn. They fear the Lycans."

"And whose fault is that?" Mother replied in a stern voice. "I warned both you and your father to put a stop to the vampire's anti-Lycan propaganda. I told him we needed to get closer to the humans. Neither of you ever saw the wisdom of my words. And now, look at us?"

I pursed my lips but didn't challenge her statement. What could I say besides acknowledging that, although she was right, the situation with the human colonies was far more complicated than most people realized? As much as I sympathized with their plight, *they* needed to initiate the much-needed changes. If we did, we'd only come across as the new thugs taking over where the previous ones had left off.

"There is more you should know," I said grimly. She gazed at me inquisitively. "The same day my bloodlust began acting up, I felt the stirring of the Moon Well."

My mother gasped and recoiled. "It's finally reopening?"

I nodded.

"When?" she insisted. "This moon cycle?"

"No," I said, running my hand over my bald head. The absence of the glorious, dark brown mane that once graced it made my throat tighten. "The pull is still weak. It won't be for another two or three months."

"That's perfect. Between the maiden's golden blood and the serum from the Well, you will be whole again," Mother said with enthusiasm.

"It's been three hundred years, Mother," I said in a harsh voice. "Three hundred years since the Well has opened. Can you imagine what kind of Guardian has grown within? Last time, the Well opened after one hundred and thirty years, and Father—in his prime—barely survived it. Even assuming we manage to heal me with some golden blood, the battle may be impossible to win."

"And that is why Soren chose you," Mother countered as if it was self-evident. "The Spirit of the Great Sun Wolf came to you now to make sure you have no choice but to claim the Blood Maiden before Konstantin. He's also making sure that you have time to master the increased power he's infusing you with before the battle of your lifetime. Like me, he knows *you* will reign over all of Karthia for at least the next millennia."

"Mother—"

"I will not hear it," she interrupted, raising her palm in an arresting gesture. "If it makes you feel better, do what you must to ensure the ruling continuity in Hundilinn. And I will do what I must to see that it remains in your hands. Now, if you'll excuse me, love, I have much plotting and scheming to do."

She absentmindedly kissed my cheek, before hurrying out of my quarters, her wheels already spinning. I affectionately watched my mother leave. When the door closed behind her, I heaved a sigh and gazed at my shriveled hands. Queen Mother Raina Volkov would stop at nothing to save me, her only son. Despite her delicate and sophisticated appearance, one would be foolish to underestimate her. After all, she had been a fierce Iron Maiden in her own right before becoming Queen.

Even now, I could feel the Wolf Spirit within me express his approval of my mother. But I couldn't rely on wishful thinking. While I still held hope for a miracle, the future of my species and, by extension, of the entire population of Karthia, depended on Lycans maintaining the rule of the planet.

With another painful sigh, I forced myself to put one foot in front of the other, ignoring the debilitating hunger that nothing could sate and that was eating me from within. I entered my private council chamber where my closest, most trusted friends had begun trickling in. The time had come to choose my replacement, should fate turn its back to me.

CHAPTER 2
THALIA

I clasped my mind-control protection necklace behind my neck before giving myself a final, critical once over in the standing mirror. Tonight, the Blood Fair was finally happening, and my entire future depended on its outcome. Here in Verelinn, the vampire capital of Karthia, my attire would be deemed elegantly sexy and naughtily seductive. I just called it slutty.

Granted, my black lace neck corset properly covered my nipples, but the cut out between my breasts and the standup collar still provided an eyeful. The sheer lace between the boning of the corset and the narrow strip of lace that shaped my skirt left little to the imagination. But then, that was intended. After all, I was a Blood Maiden on my way to sell myself to the highest bidder.

If nothing else, it allowed me to flaunt my second-best asset after my unique blood. My body was phenomenal. God knew I had worked my ass off for it, too. My face, though, I had no power over. I wasn't ugly by any stretch of the imagination, but I was no beauty either. I was pretty enough, in a girl next door kind of way. However, my light makeup and the elaborate messy bun I'd bound my hair in, flattered my high cheekbones and big green eyes. I only hoped my freckles wouldn't turn anyone off. While my face would not make heads turn, my tits, my narrow waist, the sexy curve of my hips, and my ass certainly would. I wasn't selling my body, but when it came to vampires, the line between feeding and fucking blurred very quickly.

Heaving a sigh, I turned on my sky-high heels to pick up my cup of basil tea and down its contents. Although I knew my blood to be perfect, one last cleansing before the most important night of my life couldn't hurt.

Before heading out, I double-checked that I hadn't forgotten anything vital. Despite the narrowness of my skirt, its ingenious design allowed for a hidden pocket which contained the phials I would need for tonight's tasting. I verified that the testing wand inconspicuously inserted in my intelligent bracelet was also in good working order.

I tapped on the silver pattern on top of the bracelet. It parted to reveal the interface, allowing me to call the hover cab at the entrance of my hotel. It was neither the fanciest venue in the city nor the worst. As a human from one of the many colonies of Karthia, I had to count every penny. Being at the bottom of the food chain sucked the big one. Thankfully, my unique blood offered me the ultimate ticket to a better life. I had busted my ass for the past twenty-five years to get to this moment, and I intended to make the most of it.

I donned a long cape to cover my barely-there outfit then made my way down. Keeping my head straight and my chin up, I ignored the intense, envious, hungry, or resentful stares of the patrons and staff—humans and vampires alike—I encountered on my way out of the hotel. It was common for Blood Maidens, but even more so in my case as a Golden Blood Maiden. Many felt that we didn't earn the better life our blood types entitled us to. I could understand the bitterness of other humans. Their common blood made them nothing more than peasants in a world where we'd initially been brought as chattel and slaves before the liberation.

However, they had no idea how many years of hard work were involved in becoming a Blood Maiden. They only saw our lavish life of comfort, our full bellies, our fancy clothes, and the fact that those like me indulged in living alongside the elite simply because we lucked out in the DNA lottery. But a Blood Maiden's life wasn't as rosy as they might think. Nevertheless, I would milk mine for as long as possible to ensure myself a comfortable retirement rather than being forced to continue toiling when my body was no longer in its prime.

I gazed at the tall buildings of Verelinn, enchanting in their mix of gothic design and alien structures that seemed lit from within. It always fascinated me how the vampires' love of dark colors both in and outside of their buildings still managed to look spacious and luminous. Black, shades of grey, gold, and every possible gradient of dark red dominated. With lots of stone, metal, and wood—all intricately carved and detailed—and little to no plants, Verelinn was as elegant, mysterious, cold, and hard as its masters.

Here, no one could question who sat at the top of the food chain. Everything in the city made sure to highlight one's status. The richer and the more powerful you were, the bigger the dwelling, the more luminous and obnoxious the size of the coven's symbol on the structure. The poorer and the lower class you were, the smaller and the darker your dwelling was, not to mention the further it stood from the city center.

Still, from the bird's eye view of the hover cab, it made a beautiful effect from the darkness of the outskirts to the soaring lights of the city center. And elevated at the northern edge of the city, the glowing castles of the Vampire Lords, the most powerful and most ancient on Karthia, looked down upon Verelinn. Those nobles were my targets tonight. Then again, they represented every Blood Maidens' ideal patron. Lucky for me, I had an edge none of the others possessed—my blood was RH null.

Too soon, the hover cab began its descent towards Verelinn's Great Hall. Gawkers already crowded the magnificent plaza in front of it, hoping to get a glimpse of the elite that would be attending tonight. Lower rank vampires, who would only be allowed in after the nobles and Lords had made a grand entrance, also stood in that crowd.

Even though the other maidens and I were the main attraction, we didn't get to come in by the main door. The cabbie dropped me at the side entrance, away from prying eyes. It suited me just fine. I wasn't here for the attention of the public, and it reduced the risks of foul play. Shit was about to get real. I needed to get my head in the game with as little distraction as possible.

I waved my bracelet before the screen embedded in the backrest of the passenger seat in front of me to pay the driver. One glance at my balance made me cringe. My funds were nearly depleted. If I didn't secure a great position in the next three days of the Fair, I would be forced to make some very unpleasant decisions.

The large cathedral-style doors parted before me upon my approach. A tall, lithe, slightly stern-looking vampire greeted me. By his burgundy, long jacket, with black velvet cuffs and pants, I recognized him as one of the coordination staff of the Great Hall. It surprised me that it wasn't one of the security guards—the vampires with black leather tops—who granted us access. I raised my palm before him, and he scanned it with a wand-like device. The dark crystal end of the device swirled with a blood red energy-like light, indicating all was fine. A bright red color would have spelled trouble while a white one would have meant I was either dead or to be executed on sight.

The harshness melted from his features. Under different circumstances, I might have found him handsome, even though I liked men a lot less androgynous than he was. But his covetous expression turned me off. No doubt, the interface on his wand had stated either my name, or my blood type, or both. He waved me towards an impressive set of stairs which led to the antechamber where all the Blood Maidens would receive their final test. Then, we'd wait to be called in to finally be presented to our potential future patrons.

This was the part I dreaded the most.

As soon as I reached the top of the stairs, two guards properly clad in black this time were standing watch next to another set of doors. As I approached, their nostrils flared, and a predatory smile stretched their lips. Their blatant hunger made me want to squirm. My stomach dropped at this first glimpse of the future that awaited me if and when I moved here to serve my patron.

As soon as I walked in, a dozen pairs of eyes zeroed in on me. Nine of them belonged to other Blood Maidens—although rivals would be a more accurate designation in their minds. The other three belonged to the two other guards standing by the entrance door into the Great Hall and to the Master Coordinator of the event. He gestured for me to approach.

I complied, pretending to be totally unfazed by the heavy scrutiny I was under. He was standing behind a burnished gold table with a shiny black surface. A holographic screen floated above it although I couldn't read anything on it from this side.

"Welcome to the Great Hall, Blood Maiden," the vampire said in a polite but slightly cold voice. "I am Ulrich, the Master Coordinator of this Blood Fair."

"Thank you, Master Ulrich," I said with the same politeness but also with the right level of submission that the vampires considered their due. "I am Thalia Velky."

I said my name matter-of-factly, but the way his eyebrow slightly rose and the calculating glimmer in his purple eyes confirmed it had the effect I had hoped for. The shift in the tension inside the room was almost palpable. The fact that a

Golden Blood Maiden would be attending this Fair had been deliberately leaked by yours truly in the hopes of attracting the most powerful Vampire Lords in the realm. Naturally, the word had spread like wildfire throughout Verelinn.

Others had attempted a similar tactic, although they had not truly been RH null. That deception had seriously backfired. If I didn't prove myself to be the real deal, I would be blacklisted and reduced to a true life of poverty and misery. As punishment, I would not even be hired for the most menial labor anywhere.

Even though this was my first time participating in a Blood Fair, I knew exactly what to do thanks to the thorough training I'd received. I couldn't help the amused smile that stretched my lips as I pulled out the stinger embedded on the opposite side of the testing wand in my bracelet. Master Ulrich's eagerness and curiosity oozed out of him in droves. I presented my empty left hand to the Master Coordinator.

Despite my reluctance at having any foreign substances applied to my skin unless I controlled where it came from, I waited patiently while he cleaned the tip of my finger with some alcohol-free disinfectant. I then pricked my index finger with my stinger and let a drop of blood fall onto the small glass plate with my name on it that lay on top of the table. Within seconds, the glass edges of the plate lit up with a golden color.

Master Ulrich's lips parted, giving me a peek of his fangs, and his eyes widened ever so slightly at the confirmation of my golden status. He cast a swift glance at his holographic monitor, his eyes widening further before he turned back to look at me.

"Your blood is not only golden, but also 99.9% toxin free," the Master Coordinator said with undisguised awe and a blatant hunger, all prior coolness evaporated. "You, my dear, are going to be *extremely* popular tonight."

"Thank you, Master Ulrich," I said demurely, impatient to see how the evening would pan out.

He gestured at someone in the far corner of the room behind

me. By the somewhat contemptuous way he had performed it, Master Ulrich was addressing someone he considered inferior. Sure enough, a young human boy no older than sixteen who I hadn't noticed before, came running our way. He was no doubt both a servant and a familiar to a lesser vampire.

"He will take your coat for you," Master Ulrich said as the boy came to a nervous stop before me.

"Thank you," I said, smiling gently at the boy who seemed taken aback by it.

I removed my cape and extended it to him, feeling suddenly exposed and vulnerable. I had no problem with nudity, but I'd never been one to flaunt my assets. And, in this instance, my cape had felt like a shield against the inevitable fate that awaited me.

The Master Coordinator shamelessly undressed me with his eyes, making no mystery of his approval. I wanted so badly to slap him across the face, and yet, it reassured me that I should prompt this reaction from him. Over the decades, if not centuries, he would have seen plenty of candidates. He knew what would be well received by the Vampire Lords. As much as I hated my situation, it helped boost my confidence for what would follow.

"You will be very popular, indeed," Master Ulrich whispered as if to himself with a lecherous expression that made me nauseous. "Please, have a seat while we wait for the beginning of the event, Golden Maiden."

I nodded with a grateful smile and just the right amount of timid humility. I turned around to face the rest of the room. Only a handful of the other Blood Maidens were sitting on the comfortable-looking, fancy chairs that had been put at our disposal in the large room. A couple of them were standing next to a refreshment table propped against the back wall. While I could have used a glass of water to help steady my frayed nerves, I wouldn't go anywhere near any of those females.

Instead, I made a beeline for one of the most isolated chairs, separated by a table and with very little room on the other side for anyone to justifiably want to come hang there.

The rivalry between Blood Maidens was not only real, it could often be deadly—especially for one such as me. It was a basic rule for maidens not to come within one meter of another, but ideally to keep a distance of two to three meters. All it took was an 'accidental' bump into you for a convenient protrusion on their outfit to give you a little scratch that would poison or ruin your blood.

Having a rare blood type meant that the richest and most powerful would be interested in you. But many things could make your rare blood utterly unappealing, such as any type of infection, drugs, alcohol, too salty, too sweet, or too many toxins. Those factors determined how much a patron would be willing to pay to have you as his blood cow, and how many concessions you could wrest out of him—or her—to make your years of service more palatable.

I had spent the past twenty-five years following the strictest diet to ensure my blood was the cleanest and the purest one could find. I had also denied myself any relationships as a virgin Blood Maiden was even more prized. I had aced all the mandatory classes of the Blood Maiden Academy, from the most superficial ones of the perfect hostess, including languages, dancing, etiquette, social interactions, and fashion, to deeper ones such as politics, diplomacy, history, and economy. I wanted to be the perfect Blood Maiden, able to face any possible situation and please any potential patron.

The most awkward lessons had been the Seduction classes. Prostitution 101 would have been a more accurate name. Unfortunately, it was a highly probable aspect of the services we would be expected to provide as part of our role. The upside was that the majority of the vampires were in fact quite attractive. The downside was that most of them were tramps. I had no desire to be part of a harem. While Blood Maidens rarely had much of a say on that front, my unique blood type gave me leverage that I intended to use to the fullest.

Two more candidates arrived while we waited. One of them, a male. They were few and far between. The vampires generally wanted women, even the female vampires. Apparently, we were more malleable. However, if a male had a rare enough blood type, he would find takers.

At long last, Master Ulrich announced the beginning of the Fair. One by one, he would call out our names in order of blood rarity—the lowest first and the highest for last. We would then go through the large doors leading into the Great Hall, strike a few poses, then take position on the stage at the location indicated by a luminous spot on the floor.

Heart pounding, I rose from my chair as my name was finally called. My nervous fingers pulled down on the tight, lacy fabric of my skirt before I moved forward under the intense stares of the two guards and of Master Ulrich. Lifting my chin, I began to strut in the seductive way the matrons had taught me at the Academy. The men smiled approvingly as I walked past them and through the large doors where my destiny awaited.

As soon as I entered the Great Hall, the bright lights all but blinded me. Pretending not to be affected, I smiled as I walked to the front center of the stage. There, I stopped at a mark on the floor and took a series of poses meant to show me under my best angles.

Master Ulrich's voice resonated through the invisible speakers of the massive room.

"I present to you the final candidate, the Golden Blood Maiden Thalia Velky. She has a wonderfully low blood toxicity of 0.1%, and her overall health status is stellar. The maiden has never been touched by either male or female, and that stunning body is 100% natural."

Tears of humiliation pricked my eyes, but I fought them back as approving murmurs rose from the crowd, some of them on the raunchier side. It took all my willpower to continue smiling as if it was the greatest honor to be treated like cattle being auctioned off.

By the time Master Ulrich was done listing all of my attributes, including my height, weight, size of my tits, academic achievements—including high scores in Seduction—I had finally gotten my mind in the right headspace. I'd always known it would come down to this. It was a small price to pay to ensure I'd have a better future than the one other humans endured.

I strutted to my assigned position at the end of the stage. The hatred oozing out of my rivals as I walked in front of them was almost palpable. As soon as I reached my spot, the entire stage began lowering until it became flush with the floor level. Only then did the wretched lights blinding us finally dim, allowing us to see the faces of those who might decide to claim us.

But a single face held my attention, making me cold and hot, excited and terrified, thrilled and weak in the knees. Konstantin, the most ancient and most powerful of the vampires stood only a short distance away. And his eyes were locked on me.

CHAPTER 3
THALIA

I could hardly breathe as his gaze bore into mine. I had seen pictures of him before but had never met him in the flesh. He was stunning with his light blue eyes and curly, shoulder-length black hair. It was unusual for the vampires to have such short hair. Most of them had it down to the middle of their backs and sometimes even longer. He had a noble face that had something lethal, predatory, and extremely dirty. Konstantin exuded not sensuality but feral sex: raw, savage, and unapologetic.

I barely noticed all the potential patrons lining up before each candidate that had held their interest, so strong was the power of his hypnotic aura. It wasn't the effect of the vampires' mesmerizing ability that had me so enthralled. My necklace would have blocked it had he attempted to use it against me. It was just his irresistible, natural charisma, pure animal attraction, and awe. I blinked and forced myself to regain control.

The smug, knowing smile that stretched his sensuous lips stung, further knocking me out of my daze. This was *not* how I had wanted to initiate my first interaction with the potential patron at the very top of my list. Becoming Konstantin's Blood Maiden essentially guaranteed a comfortable future. I had no illusions that he would keep me forever or even make me either his concubine or his consort. However, being chosen by him would grant me a status that would make me very sought after once he was done with me. Every other lesser vampire would want the bragging rights of claiming one of Konstantin's ex women. On the opposite end, if my first patron was of low rank, no one of status would want their sloppy seconds. Your first patron determined your future.

Shifting my gaze away from that beautiful monster, I glanced at the other High Lords surrounding him and who were also headed my way. My breath caught in my throat at the sight of the breathtaking Resnik brothers: Vladimir and Vasska. Although their facial features could have almost made them pass for twins, Vlad's hair was the darkest shade of black while Vasska's was silver white, with blue eyes so pale they almost looked white. They were nearly at a level with Konstantin. I didn't know all the history with these ancient beings, only that the brothers were a few decades younger than the unofficial King of Verelinn.

Rumors had it that a certain rivalry existed between the brothers and Konstantin, fueled by the vampire factions wishing to steer their people in one direction or another. I didn't know enough of the real politics and power plays amidst the noble ranks. The Academy only taught us the well-known conflicts between covens. This transcended public knowledge. Choosing one of the brothers would be almost as beneficial to my future. I would have to tread carefully—assuming any of them actually made me an offer—and choose wisely. Should they go into open war, I would want to make sure I ended up on the winning side.

The three men stopped before me, Konstantin in the lead.

"Hello, Thalia," he said in a delicious voice that had shivers running down my spine. "The announcement of your presence has caused quite an uproar and made even the biggest snobs crawl out of their lairs," he added while casting a mocking glance at Vladimir.

"Hello, Lord Konstantin," I said in my most seductive voice. "My Lord Vladimir, my Lord Vasska…" I continued, nodding at each of them in turn. "Under normal circumstances, I would apologize that such an announcement would have inconvenienced any of you. However, it would be a blatant lie as it would have deprived me of the honor of meeting the High Lords of Verelinn—a once in a lifetime opportunity."

"So prettily said," Vladimir replied, stepping closer. Konstantin slightly frowned, clearly displeased to have a rival stand by his side rather than slightly behind him. "But please, call me Vlad. Only my mother and exasperated Ancients call me by my full name," he added tauntingly in a clear effort to needle Konstantin.

"You honor me, Vlad," I responded, timidly batting my eyelashes.

I was playing a somewhat dangerous game. Watching Konstantin clench his jaw comforted me that his interest was extremely high. But more than that, if my quick assessment of his personality was accurate, Vlad's interest would only push Konstantin further into taking all the means necessary to have me just so that he could claim victory. That would put me in a very good negotiating position. But I also needed not to overplay my hand and end up with nothing.

"I believe you are here for a sampling, yes?" I asked.

"That would be most appreciated," Konstantin said, his face taking on that same hungry look that made me weak in the knees.

I fished out one of my two 30 ml phials from my hidden pocket and extended my left arm before the men. The sleeveless cut of my top allowed them to see the port through which I would extract the blood. It allowed for frequent blood donations without risks of infection or of damaging a vein. Raising the phial to the port in the crook of my elbow, I pressed the tip to extrude the needle before inserting it. After years of repeating this process, I hardly felt a sting anymore.

While my blood filled the flask, I cast a furtive glance at the three men surrounding me. The same predatory look was etched on their faces. But Konstantin's made me uneasy. The man was too intense. Lips parted, his fangs peeking between them, his eyes had darkened, and his features had become strained like a man on the verge of losing control. I highly doubted he would, especially not in such a public setting with the dire consequences that it would bring down on him, but it still freaked me out.

Thankfully, although it felt like an eternity, it took only seconds for the phial to be filled, and the needle automatically receded. The way Konstantin stared at it, I almost expected him to snatch it right out of my hands. I turned the tip of the phial halfway. The nanites immediately reshaped it into a dropper while also softening the container to make it squeezable.

"I hope you like it," I said in a voice full of promise as I raised the phial towards Konstantin's face.

"I do not doubt it for a minute," he replied before opening his mouth.

I gave the phial a single squirt. As per the setting I had selected, it poured exactly the equivalent of twenty drops into his mouth. It wasn't much, barely a third of a teaspoon. And yet, it was three times the standard amount for tasting. Konstantin's pupils dilated. His entire body tensed while he rubbed his tongue on his palate. He took a hissing breath, his eyes closing as he tilted his head back. He looked like a man fighting the urge to give in to his orgasm. It was sexy as hell and did wonderful things to my ego and shaky confidence. Although I'd known my rare blood would give me a unique advantage, I'd still felt uncertain how it would fare in a real test by a true connoisseur.

"I'll have what he's having," Vlad said with a snort.

I chuckled and gave him the same dose, and then to Vasska as well. Their faces also dissolved in an expression of pure bliss.

But where Konstantin and Vasska both closed their eyes to savor my blood, Vlad's never strayed from my face. His light grey eyes smoldered, and his tongue alternated between rubbing on his palate and licking his fangs. When his eyes finally lowered, they didn't stare at my neck—which I had deliberately covered with that boned high collar to reduce temptation—but to my lips. I knew beyond the shadow of a doubt that he wanted to kiss me, and that seriously turned me on.

"Well, well," a feminine voice said to my right, startling me. "Looks like you've got the elite of the Verelinn enthralled."

My eyes widened upon recognizing the most powerful female vampire.

"Lady Morana," I said, bowing my head respectfully.

"You have a body to die for, love," she said, pushing Vasska aside to take his place next to Konstantin.

The male vampire merely seemed amused by her apparent rudeness.

"That is a tremendous compliment coming from you, milady," I replied, genuinely flattered.

Lady Morana was a true stunner. She had a fiery mane which fell down to the middle of her back, a luminous, milky-white skin, light-green eyes that lit up her long face, with a pointy chin and a wide, pouty mouth. Her form-fitting black leather dress with a plunging neckline hid nothing of the perfection of her body.

"Do you care for a sample, milady?" I asked, showing her the phial.

"Absolutely," she said before opening her mouth.

Her reaction after I gave her the same dose as to her companions left me speechless. Morana moaned before slipping a hand under the left panel of her plunging neckline to fondle one of her breasts, while licking her lips in a lascivious fashion. I stopped myself just in time from gaping, plastering a neutral expression on my face even as I felt my cheeks burning. Where Konstantin seemed annoyed and cast a hard, sideways glance at the female, Vlad smiled, visibly amused and winked at me.

For a reason I couldn't explain, it dissipated the awkwardness and embarrassment I felt, allowing me to see the comical side of the situation. I smiled back with gratitude.

"Would you consider a female patron?" Morana asked, looking at me through hooded eyes while her hand continued to fondle her breast.

"I—"

"I doubt Thalia saved her virginity this long only to have it popped by one of your strap-ons," Konstantin said, interrupting me.

"And I doubt she only saved it so that *you* could add another notch to your bedpost before moving on to greener pastures," she retorted.

In that instant, I realized that some sort of love-hate relationship brewed between them. With a certainty I couldn't explain, I knew Morana would do everything in her power to steal me from Konstantin. But, failing to do so, she would either try to use me to hurt him, or try to get me out of the picture. It didn't feel personal against me—I was likely far too insignificant in her eyes—but it definitely was personal against him.

"On this, I must concur," Vasska said with a mischievous glimmer in his gorgeous eyes. "Correct me if I'm wrong, Thalia, but I suspect you do not wish to be particularly free with that stunning body of yours."

"Indeed," Vlad said. "What kind of limits would you set to a contract if one wanted the exclusive rights on that divine nectar in your veins?"

My face heated a bit, and I licked my lips nervously. The intensity in the eyes of the four vampire nobles—royalty even—told me this was the moment of truth.

"I do not put limits, per se," I said carefully. "Naturally, I have my preferences. Should I be so blessed as to receive multiple enticing offers, the one that ticks the most of those boxes would certainly have a greater chance of being my choice."

"Such as?" Vlad insisted.

"I want to serve *one* good patron," I said, trying to find the right balance in being assertive without coming across as demanding. "I do not wish to be passed around for a taste as a trophy or to occasionally 'reward' a friend, a business partner, or a political ally. My blood is for my patron only. As far as intimacy goes, I do not wish to be a side piece, or a part-time bed warmer. However, the length and terms of the contract will definitely impact my willingness to be more flexible. Same with drinking from the source. I would not allow biting me for a short-term contract. The risks of contaminating my blood would be too high."

"You are demanding," Konstantin said with a frown, the disapproval barely veiled in his voice.

My stomach dropped, wondering if I'd been too bold in voicing my wishes.

"Hardly. They are quite reasonable expectations," Vlad countered.

My heart leapt upon both hearing his comment and at the sight of the speculative look in his eyes. He looked like a man attempting to decide how much he was willing to bid on a rare piece of art.

"You do not bed and discard a Golden Maiden," Vlad continued. "You make her a concubine or a consort. Are you willing to sacrifice your freedom for such a unique female?" he asked, his gaze boring into Konstantin's, challenging him. "Because I am."

My heart skipped a beat. I never would have dared dropping either of the C words, least of all 'consort' which was essentially a wife. But either status would have me set for life. Even after the vampire no longer required a concubine's services—for both sex and blood—he was duty bound to continue giving her alimony for the rest of her human life. Naturally, concubines and consorts were beyond few and far between.

Konstantin narrowed his eyes at Vlad. For a split second, I thought he was going to backhand him.

"You're not the only one who recognizes a rare treasure when he sees it," Konstantin said in a clipped tone before turning to give me a slow once over. "Some things warrant greater sacrifices."

Morana snorted in amusement, although I didn't miss the quickly dissimulated seething anger that flashed through her pale green eyes.

"Well, you can spend the rest of the evening pondering how much of your freedom you are willing to sacrifice before you commit to anything," she said in a taunting voice. "For now, we need to move aside. Others are waiting for a taste of golden blood, and time is ticking before the lesser groups are brought in."

"We have indeed hogged you long enough," Vasska said with a gentle smile.

Konstantin huffed and cast a glance over his shoulder to stare down the long line waiting behind them with growing impatience.

"What are they lining up for?" Konstantin asked in a disdainful tone, intentionally loud enough to be heard by the other vampires. "Do they really think a Golden Blood Maiden would go to them?"

"Of course not," Morana said in an amused tone. "But who can blame them for wanting a taste of a once in a century opportunity?"

"Her blood is wasted on them," Konstantin muttered.

It took every ounce of my willpower to hide my shock at such contempt and elitist behavior towards his own people.

"Whatever your feelings about it, Konstantin, they are entitled to it," Vlad said in a slightly clipped tone.

"As a Blood Maiden seeking a patron," I said, choosing my words carefully, "it is vital that I give a blood sample to as many interested parties as possible to increase my chances of getting a good offer. We only have thirty minutes to make the first impression that could determine the rest of our lives."

"Do you doubt you'll be receiving offers from us?" Konstantin asked in a somewhat superior and annoyed tone.

"I dearly hope I will," I conceded, biting back my growing dislike of him. "But it would be foolish of me to take a most sought-after Vampire Lord for granted and presumptuous to assume that the offer—should it be made—will be one I can live with. I'd rather err on the side of caution."

"Unique, beautiful, and smart," Vlad said with a warmth that only endeared him further to me. "Give the plebs a taste of paradise, and then await my offer. I do not doubt you will find it very much to your liking."

"*Our* offers," Konstantin snarled, glaring at him.

Vlad chuckled, utterly unfazed. "Come, old friend. We have overstayed our welcome," he said, slapping the back of Konstantin's shoulder. "Looking forward to seeing you again at tomorrow night's ball, my golden beauty," he added for me with a wink.

I smiled, genuinely smitten by Vlad's boyish charm.

"Until tomorrow," Konstantin said in a warm voice.

His gaze bore into the mine the same way it had when I first saw him after the blinding lights had dimmed. This time, however, the entrancing magic didn't kick in. I pretended to be as mesmerized while shyly batting my eyelashes at him. Morana waved at me, only wiggling her fingertips while giving me the naughtiest of looks. I was starting to believe she had an even greater sex drive than any of the three men.

Vasska stopped before me, a sweet and seductive smile on his angelic face framed by his waist-length, silver-white hair.

Although he invaded my personal space, I didn't feel threatened or offended in the least… quite the opposite.

"When the offers come in, choose mine," he said in a conspiratorial tone. "You don't want those old farts anyway. Plus, you know what they say about the stamina of youth."

I burst out laughing, and immediately slapped my hand over my mouth, embarrassed to have broken one of the implied rules of a Blood Maiden being discreet and demure. He winked at me mischievously, bowed with a flourish, then left to join Vlad and the others with a graceful gait. I had mixed feelings about the High Lords finally stepping away from me, part relief and part disappointment.

It's the brothers you miss.

They both had an undeniable charm that had my girly bits standing at attention. But naughty thoughts about the sexy Vampire Lords would have to wait. Although it shouldn't have shocked me, I still felt winded by the insane line of potential patrons that stood before me. A quick glance to the right at my 'rivals' showed some of them to have already run out of patrons. However, I suspected a number of those at the tail end of my line would rush to them before our time was up.

Speaking of which, I needed to make haste. Despite my total lack of interest in the vampires past the twelve front ones standing before me, it was wise to have a good and friendly reputation among even the lesser ones. I twisted the tip of the phial to reduce the doses to six drops, the standard amount for a tasting.

As expected, the first dozen potential patrons took a second to ask me if I was seeking a temporary or long-term contract, a couple of them wondering if I had inhibitions—which was a polite way to ask if I was open to being lent for sex and blood to specially selected friends of theirs. The other vampires didn't bother. They weren't here to offer me a contract, knowing they couldn't compete with the ones the wealthy nobles would make me. They just wanted a taste of golden blood. Thankfully, they merely approached, opened their mouths, received their dose, and moved on.

I finished with five minutes left on the clock before my group—the rarest blood types—would be excused to welcome the Blood Maidens of 'lesser' status. We were the first to come so that the High Lords would be free to leave and go on about their business.

I wanted to make a discreet exit before another straggler suddenly decided he or she also wanted a taste. However, seeing the three Vampire Lords still standing a short distance from my position, Morana having wandered off somewhere else, prompted me into a bold move. Vasska was the first to notice my approach. The surprised—but welcoming smile—on his face as he looked at me drew the other men's attention.

"Apologies, milords," I said with a slightly sheepish expression. "I do not mean to overstep but, I am about to depart and still have sixty-eight drops of blood remaining in my phial. I hope you won't find me too bold for offering it to you rather than throwing it away."

Right on cue, the same hungry look descended on their features.

"A most welcomed offer," Konstantin said.

"Sixty-eight. That means twenty-two drops for each of those old-timers, and twenty-four for me," Vasska said with a shameless grin.

"Why the fuck should you get twenty-four?" Vlad asked, casting a half-amused, half-outraged look at his sibling.

"Because I'm the youngest, and I'm still growing," Vasska responded, unrepentant.

I bit the insides of my cheeks to keep from bursting out laughing again. While Vlad snorted and shook his head as his brother, Konstantin huffed dismissively.

"As the Elder vampire, I claim that privilege," Konstantin said in an imperious tone.

Yeah, I really don't like that man.

There was something about entitled people that always rubbed me the wrong way. I cast an inquisitive look at Vlad.

He smiled and shrugged. "The Ancient one has spoken. He's welcomed to it," Vlad said with a strange glimmer in his eyes.

I bowed my head in gratitude that he didn't escalate things. I gave each of them their respective doses. Once again, where Konstantin and Vasska closed their eyes to savor my blood, Vlad's gaze remained locked with mine. I knew then with the utmost certainty that if I were to give him my virginity, he would look me in the eye as he broke my hymen.

That made me shiver… in the best of ways.

"An enjoyable evening to you, milords," I said respectfully, with a curtsey.

"And to you, Thalia," Konstantin said with a possessive expression full of promises.

The two brothers smiled, Vasska giving me another of his bratty winks. I repressed a grin and the urge to shake my head before heading out.

The stress that had temporarily left me while surrounded by the vampire elite came back with a vengeance when I made my way to the main entrance. I felt exposed and vulnerable with too many vampires and humans surrounding me. Until I had secured a contract, a split second could suffice to ruin everything for me. A toxic scratch, noxious air, spoiled food, or a questionable drink could end me. I wished I could have left through the side door again, but the next group of Blood Maidens were already waiting in the antechamber.

Despite its dark grey walls, dark furniture made of wood and stone, and dark polished stone floor, the entrance hall was a luminous room thanks to the many modern chandeliers and wall sconces. They made the gold highlights and accents on the bas-relief carved on the walls and furniture stand out. A significant number of stone benches with dark red cushions lined a series of nooks and alcoves alongside the walls. A few animated statues adorned the middle of each wall of the diamond-shaped-room. They represented the mythical Karthian Nymphs, ancient priestesses of the original, primitive people of the planet Karthia who watched over the sacred Moon Well. Each one was pouring the silver water from the pond surrounding the Well in a different fashion.

Trying to appear nonchalant as I made my way to the reception desk, I remained alert for any sign of possible trouble. The place was packed with far too many people scattered in small clusters around the entrance hall. Sadly, the reception desk was sitting right in the center, forcing me to keep watch from all angles. I loved having a wall behind my back to keep anyone from sneaking up on me.

I asked the guard for my cape, and he promptly sent a human servant to go fetch it for me. Just as I was thanking him, I noticed a hooded female looking at me intently. Even from the distance, her eyes seemed to glow in the shadow cast by her hood. My heart skipped a beat when she began advancing towards me with determined steps.

The shocked, outraged, and almost angry stares some of the guests cast her way as they noticed her presence did nothing to appease me. And yet, despite the intensity of her stare, I sensed no actual threat from her. The fact that she came openly towards me instead of sneakily also helped.

"What the fuck is that she-wolf doing here?" one of the guards mumbled.

I froze upon hearing those words, my eyes widening in shock. Sure enough, as she closed the distance between us, I recognized her stunning silver eyes as belonging to the Lycan breed. I had never met one in the flesh before. What in God's name was she doing in Verelinn? Although she legally had the right to do so, the Lycans never came to the vampire cities, and vice-versa.

By the exquisite quality of her black cape embroidered with a marvelous dark thread that shimmered like gems, I could tell she was no commoner. She pulled down her hood as she reached me, staying at a respectful distance. She was stunning with her reddish-brown hair streaked with silver, a straight nose, heart-shaped lips, and an aura of authority wrapped in kindness. At least, in appearance. There was no doubt in my mind she could turn into a vicious beast when crossed.

"Hello, Ms. Velky," she said with a polished voice. "My name is Raina Volkov, Queen Mother to the Lycan King Drogo. I have a proposal for you, if you would grant me a moment of your time."

CHAPTER 4
THALIA

My jaw dropped and my brain froze. Twenty-five years of training flew out the window in that instant. Facing a Lycan for the first time hadn't been enough; it had to be their flipping queen! She partially repressed an amused smile and raised an eyebrow when I failed to respond. I closed my mouth with an audible sound. Heat crept up my cheeks, embarrassed by my lack of self-control.

"Apologies, your Majesty," I said, snapping out of my daze. "This is a most unexpected encounter."

"No need to apologize. Your reaction is perfectly normal," she said with a gentle smile. "But please, call me Raina. Unlike other species, we Lycans are quite informal."

The less than subtle jab almost made me smile. Vampires had a disturbing obsession with hierarchy, status, and power.

"You honor me," I said in all honesty. "Then it would only be fitting that you should call me Thalia."

The Queen smiled, her features warming while her silver eyes shone with approval. Whatever she wanted from me, establishing an initial friendly rapport could certainly benefit our negotiations—should it come to that.

Just as she was opening her mouth to reply, Raina suddenly looked left, her body slightly tensing the way a predator does when bracing for a possible attack. My gaze followed hers, and I recognized two of the guards that had stood by the doors inside the antechamber. They were heading straight for us, one of them carrying my cloak. That he should take on such a menial task rather than leaving it to a human told me that someone had informed them of the presence of a Lycan 'bothering' me.

I took a step forward and smiled at the guards, drawing their attention towards me. For some strange reason, my protective instincts towards the she-wolf had sprung forth. It was all the sillier that she was definitely more powerful than I would ever be. I had never seen a Lycan in battle mode, but I'd heard plenty about their savagery.

"Thank you for bringing my cloak," I said preemptively as they closed the distance between us, forcing them to look at me.

"Our pleasure, Blood Maiden," he said, extending the garment to me, his gaze assessing. "Is everything okay?" he asked, casting a not-so-subtle glance towards Raina.

"Why wouldn't it be, *guard*?" Raina asked, answering in my stead, her voice filled with challenge and contempt as she stated his rank.

That should have made me cringe, but I instantly recognized this as a move to remind him he was dealing with a queen. Still, it concerned me that, informal or not, her people would allow their Queen Mother to venture into a hostile territory without an escort. However badass she might be, there was only so much one could do against severely uneven odds.

Just as those thoughts crossed my mind, movement at the edge of my vision caught my attention. I then noticed two males, a short distance from us, that were undeniably Lycans. Their hairy faces and pointy wolf ears were dead giveaways. They looked ready—if not eager—to jump into action.

"Everything is fine, thank you," I said quickly, wanting to

prevent the situation from escalating. "Raina and I are simply having a friendly conversation."

Both vampire guards stiffened, and their eyes widened, taken aback by the familiarity with which I addressed the Queen Mother. A smug smile settled on Raina's naturally pink lips as she gave the guards a defiant stare.

"Now, if you would excuse us, Thalia and I have important matters to discuss," Raina said. "This way, my dear," she added, gesturing for me to head in the general direction her guards were waiting.

I smiled stiffly and complied, wondering if I hadn't put myself in harm's way. Despite my instinctive liking of the Lycan female, looks could be deceiving. I didn't want to go converse with her in some dark corner where I could be killed, harmed, or abducted. My anxiety further increased when she rubbed with her index finger the large, yellow stone on the ring adorning her right hand.

"It is a disrupter," explained Raina, catching my concerned look. "The vampires' hearing is almost as keen as ours. I would rather avoid them eavesdropping. It will create a cone of silence around us for anyone more than a meter away. This way, we can discuss right here, with plenty of witnesses so that you can feel safe."

My lips slightly parted in shock, and my cheeks heated that she'd so accurately guessed my concern. Had I once again failed at hiding my emotions?

"I understand well the kind of terrible stress someone as unique as you must constantly be under," Raina said with a sympathetic smile. "I want you to feel at ease so that you may focus on the proposal I'm about to make you rather than worry for your safety."

"Thank you," I said with sincere gratitude. "It is very considerate of you."

And highly unexpected.

So far, the Lycan Queen Mother was nothing like the horror stories we'd been fed about her people's savagery and constant state of anger. This was certainly more consideration than the vampires had shown me. Normally, I should have had at least one bodyguard accompanying me at all times. But I couldn't afford it. I'd barely had enough to make the trip here.

We settled on a bench next to one of the animated statues. Her Lycan guards moved a few meters away, one on each side of the alcove we were sitting in. Raina sat at a respectful distance from me. It was considered highly inappropriate to touch a Blood Maiden in any way unless you were her patron. This further put me at ease.

"How much do you know about Lycans?" Raina asked without preamble.

"Hmm, not much to be honest. Only what is commonly reported," I said cautiously.

Raina chuckled. "So, basically, all the propaganda portraying us as rabid beasts, controlled by our primal instincts."

Heat crept up to my cheeks, and I gave her a sheepish smile.

"It's okay. I expected as much," Raina said in a friendly tone. "What I'm about to tell you is not common knowledge in the human colonies, but a well-known fact among the vampires. Lycans also experience bloodlust."

I recoiled, my eyes widening in shock and disbelief. "You're blood drinkers?!"

"We are the *original* blood drinkers—the ancestors of the vampires," Raina said matter-of-factly. "*They* are our descendants that either renounced their wolf or that never managed to connect with it or tame it. *We* chose to renounce our bloodlust and embrace our wolves."

I gaped at her, flabbergasted. It sounded completely farfetched, but I had no reason—at least for now—to doubt her word. Very little was ever said about the Lycans, but all of it was always negative. However, I'd often wondered how come they never attacked us or pillaged the colonies if they were as feral as the rumors claimed.

"You *renounced* it?" I asked. "As in, you no longer need it, or you're able to resist the urge?"

"We no longer need it, and the majority of us do not feel the slightest urge," Raina replied. "I'm six hundred and twenty-eight years old, and I've never had a single drop of blood. By then, my people had already tamed their bloodlust."

I looked at her beautiful face with undisguised envy. Most human females didn't look that good by the time they reached their mid-forties. The harsh life in the colonies aged humans before their time. Even I, as a Blood Maiden, would age prematurely from the toll frequent feedings would take on me. This was why we needed to score the best-paying contracts as soon as possible as our careers didn't last long.

"You look stunning," I blurted out, immediately kicking myself.

What the fuck was going on with me? My first Blood Fair seemed to have utterly messed with my mind. Where was the poised, controlled, and stoic Golden Blood Maiden I'd always prided myself to be?

"Thank you, dear," Raina said, looking genuinely flattered. "You look quite lovely yourself."

Although I knew her reply to have merely been the standard polite response, she still said it in a way that actually made me feel good about myself. Her charisma was off the charts, and the type every Blood Maiden aspired to possess.

"The 'majority' no longer feels bloodlust, but a minority still does," I said, getting the conversation back on track as I analyzed her words. "Is that where your 'proposal' comes in?"

She once more smiled with approval, the glimmer of respect in her silver eyes making me want to puff out my chest.

"Good catch, Thalia," Raina said. "Indeed, a few of our people still experience bloodlust. It is genetic, and not just a strong craving that could be controlled with enough willpower. Unlike vampires, it is not their main source of sustenance. A Lycan's bloodlust is sated with only 35 ml of blood per week."

"That's all?!" I exclaimed, flabbergasted.

A vampire needed three times that amount daily. It was unsustainable for a single human. The poorer vampires therefore settled for synthetic blood, which deprived them of day walking ability. Richer vampires had a harem of familiars which they paid a pittance for their commoner blood, and a couple of highly paid Blood Maidens whom they tapped once a week. Still, the Maiden gave every month more than the normally safe amount a human should give every three months.

Despite all the efforts Maidens did to compensate, the complications from the severe anemia it created usually resulted in an early death from heart failure. The only ones who managed to live to an old age were the ones who had scored a five-year contract with a high-ranking noble, then got out of the game after saving her generous wages. Better yet, the consorts or concubines had it made.

"Yes, that's all," Raina said smugly. "Our Blood Maidens aren't physically taxed in any way. Even at 35-40 ml a week, they stay well within the safety guidelines."

This was incredibly appealing, but I was still missing something. The Queen Mother wouldn't have come here in person to try to lure a Golden Maiden for such small amounts of blood, especially since she didn't even drink herself.

"So, who needs my blood? And why golden?" I asked.

Raina burst out laughing, the same glimmer of admiration burning in her eyes. "The rarest blood on the planet, beautiful, and smart; I like you, Thalia," Raina said, her words strangely echoing those Vlad had proffered a few moments prior. "I need your blood for my son, King Drogo. He's stricken with a rare genetic condition which manifested itself only a few weeks ago.

His status has devolved so quickly that we had to put him in stasis so he wouldn't die. Only golden blood can save him."

"Oh my God! That's terrible. I'm so sorry," I said in a commiserating tone.

"And for this reason, to save the life of my son and our King, I am here to make you what you should find a very generous offer," Raina said in a tone filled with tension.

"If you're asking me to come to Hundilinn—" I said, making no effort to hide my reluctance at the thought of moving to the Lycan territory.

"I am not," Raina interrupted in a reassuring tone. "I realized such a prospect might be a little too daunting for a human whose only exposure to our people is what propaganda has been spewed. My son is nearby, at the Kivilinn General Hospital."

That was already a relief, although it was in the neighboring city.

"Why not right here, in Verelinn?" I asked.

"Because I do not trust my son's welfare to vampire doctors," Raina said in a hard tone. "His death would make them far too happy and advance their agendas. Kivilinn is a human town. Lycans have always been well-treated by the medical personnel there. It is a very short ride from here."

I nodded slowly. In a hover cab, it would take us less than twenty minutes at high speed.

"So, this would be a one-time deal then, I presume?" I asked, seeing the upside of a quick money injection to get me out of my current difficulties.

Sure, I could walk into any blood bank and get a large amount of credits in a blink. But the word would spread quickly, and my value would tank accordingly. No high-ranking vampire would take a blood whore as his concubine, let alone his consort.

Raina hesitated, making my back stiffen.

"The first proposal would indeed be a one-time deal, tonight," she conceded. "However, should you be pleased with the outcome of this first deal, then I would most definitely like to discuss with you the possibility of a much longer-term arrangement. But let's not get ahead of ourselves."

"Very well," I said, more intrigued than ever by what she had to propose and especially eager to hear what kind of numbers we were talking about.

I hated feeling like such a money hungry tramp, but I'd sacrificed too much to spare myself the life of misery that was the lot of most of my peers.

"So, the first proposal, the only one I wish you to focus on right now, is to come with me to the General Hospital and give my son 250 ml of your golden blood. In exchange, I will pay you 300,000 credits, the equivalent of six years in salary of the highest paid Blood Maiden in our history."

I gasped. My jaw dropped, and my hand flew to my chest. My eyes flicked between hers, trying to assess if she was bullshitting me. She held my gaze unflinchingly, a satisfied smile stretching her lips. She nodded slowly to reaffirm that I had heard correctly. This by far exceeded anything I could have possibly dreamt of.

Sixty years ago, Patricia had set the all-time record of 50,000 credits per year for a Blood Maiden's services. However, on top of her rare AB- blood and her incredible beauty, she had also been open to the type of kinks and debauchery that very few would have consented to. I had hoped that despite my refusal to participate in these types of 'extracurricular' activities, my golden blood would have sufficed to earn me a similar salary, or close enough.

With this offer, if I lived on a very strict budget for the rest of my life, I wouldn't have to sell myself at all. However, I had also planned on the gifts in clothes and jewelry that a high-level patron invariably gave his Maiden to help pad my nest egg for the future.

"And should you consent to go as high as 500 ml, I would

pay you 750,000 credits instead, the equivalent of 15 years of wages," Raina pressed on. "You and I both know that very few maidens make it past the seven-year mark. You would be set for life without ever having to subject yourself to the inevitable abuse of such a life."

I felt faint upon hearing such an insane compensation. Who threw around such crazy numbers for such a small amount of blood, all things considered? Then again, it was to save the life of a King. The offer was obviously made to be impossible to refuse, but what did I know of this woman? This whole thing could be a lie, meant to con me into moving away from the relative safety of Verelinn. The enmity between the vampires and the Lycans was well known. What if this was only a trap to keep the vampire nobility from getting even stronger by drinking my blood?

"I see your wheels turning, Thalia," Raina said with a gentle smile. "It is wise of you to question my motives and the truth of the offer. One such as you can never be too cautious. If I can appease your concerns as to the honesty of my offer, would it be fair for me to assume that you would be willing to consider it?"

"Only a fool would refuse such a generous offer," I conceded with a shrug. "But I hope you will not take offense if I say that I have no reasons to trust you? My blood could sell for significant amounts on the black market. I must be very careful where I go, and who I trust."

"Understandable," Raina said kindly. "For this reason, I have retained the services of Master Elias, whom I understand you have done business with in the past."

"Master Elias Orlov?" I asked, my eyes widening.

My heart soared when she nodded in confirmation. Master Elias was a well-renowned and highly respected human business lawyer. He had overseen my contract with the Blood Maiden Academy and given me very wise advice while negotiating the terms, making sure I understood all the intricacies involved. I implicitly trusted him.

"The man himself," Raina responded smugly. "He drafted the contract of this proposal, and I've already transferred the maximum potential amount to him to be held in escrow. This way, once you hopefully agree, you can be certain there will be no default on you being paid your due. Should I call him?"

"Yes, please," I said, feeling overwhelmed by this unexpected turn of events. "Thank you."

She tapped a few instructions on the interface of her arm band—a stunning piece of jewelry that put my own bracelet to shame. She then lifted her head to look at me with warmth.

"I understand this must be a lot for you to take in but learning of your attendance at the Fair has given new hope to an entire species," Raina said. "My son is a wonderful man and a great King. I want you properly compensated for the great gift you could give us. Like I said earlier, I want you to feel entirely safe throughout the process."

The Queen Mother shifted on her seat and flicked her long hair over her shoulder, giving me a first glimpse of her adorable wolf ears.

"I realize that the largest amount of blood would be pretty much the maximum one should donate in a short period of time," Raina continued. "However, you could still choose to accept one of the countless offers I have no doubt you will be receiving. It is not uncommon for the Vampire Lords to have to wait a month or two before their new Blood Maiden can join them. So, accepting this offer only puts you in a much stronger negotiating position, should it come to that. But then, maybe we will make you another far more enticing proposition."

Before I could respond, the tall and lanky silhouette of Master Orlov walked in through the opened large cathedral doors of the Great Hall's entrance. He was clad in a midnight blue suit with shiny black shoes. His black hair streaked with grey at the temples gave him a noble air that even his very prominent nose couldn't ruin. His dark brown eyes lit up when he spotted us seconds after coming in. He made his way towards us with determined steps, a beaming smile on his face. I didn't miss the friendly nod he gave each of the two guards before reaching us.

I rose to my feet as he came to stand before us.

"Master Orlov," I said warmly. "What an unexpectedly nice surprise."

"I could not refuse the opportunity to help enable a business transaction between two of the ladies I hold in high regard," he said in a friendly tone. "Raina, looking as lovely as ever," he added with undisguised admiration towards the Lycan Queen.

To my shock, he leaned forward and kissed her on the cheek. Although it was purely friendly, it spoke of a far older friendship than I had presumed. That further reassured me. A part of me felt a bit of envy at this type of feel-good physical contact that I was deprived of as a Blood Maiden.

"I assume Raina has given you the details of her offer?" Elias asked, jumping right into business mode. "Excellent," he continued when I nodded. "I'm transferring the contract to you and can confirm that all the funds have been transferred to me to hold in escrow on your behalf until either one of the two tiers has been met."

"Yes, Raina was kind enough to inform me of such," I said with a smile.

I tapped the interface of my bracelet which displayed a small holographic screen allowing me to read the details of the offer. The standard technology nonetheless provided privacy, preventing anyone in front, behind, or next to me from seeing the contents on display. The contract was short, sweet, and straightforward, confirming all the impossible details of this heaven-sent offer.

"Everything seems in order," I said, struggling to rein in my excitement. I wanted to shout at the top of my lungs with unbridled joy; I had just won the lottery.

"If this offer is agreeable to you, I would only need your signature so that we can proceed," Elias said with enthusiasm.

I lifted my thumb, hovering it over the interface of my bracelet before hesitating. I lifted my eyes, locking gazes with the lawyer. He held it unflinchingly and nodded.

"It is all on the up and up, and a once in a lifetime opportunity for you," Elias said. "I wouldn't be involved if I didn't believe it could change your life for the better."

I smiled, grateful for his understanding and reassurance, then pressed my thumb on the interface, sealing the agreement.

"Wonderful!" Raina exclaimed, her excitement palpable. "I would like for us to proceed immediately. Master Elias has agreed to accompany you to the hospital while my guards and I travel in our own shuttle."

"Perfect," I answered, once more impressed with her foresight and thoughtfulness.

Naturally, I would have been quite reluctant to travel aboard a stranger's vessel. What would have kept them from just continuing all the way to the Lycan capital of Hundilinn with me captive onboard?

We left the Great Hall with hundreds of eyes burning holes in our backs. As much as I had welcomed the safety provided by holding this discussion in a public setting while still maintaining privacy as to its nature, I now worried that they might track us. I didn't need my business exposed to the whole world.

It was a short trip to the Kivilinn General Hospital. Master Elias and I had a friendly conversation while he piloted his personal shuttle—a top-of-the-line hover vehicle that very few humans could boast owning. Strangely, I had expected him to delve further into his obvious friendship with the Lycans, but he didn't. It wouldn't surprise me if he kept such details to a possible secondary offer. I didn't stress over it as I wouldn't be able to give any blood for at least a month if I gave 500 ml today—which I obviously intended to do. I would be set for life.

We landed near the underground parking entrance, and a valet took care of the shuttle while we headed inside. It was an impressive establishment, high-tech and fully staffed by the healthiest looking humans I had seen in a while. Most in my village of Ellisgrad were overworked, underfed, and crushed by stress.

We didn't even have to state the reason for our presence. A nurse immediately gestured for us to follow her. She took us down a series of long, white corridors to the easily recognizable VIP area. It had a few private rooms, all very spacious, and a fancy lounge with a snack bar for guests and relatives. The nurse nodded at her colleagues manning the nurse station at the entrance of this section. I smiled nervously at them when all their eyes settled in a speculative fashion over me. I would never get used to being viewed as a curiosity merely for the type of blood that ran in my veins.

My pulse picked up at the sight of the three hulking Lycans standing outside a room, giving away their King's location. I only recognized one of them as belonging to the pair that had accompanied the Queen to the vampire capital city. They perked up upon noticing our approach. The hopeful glimmer in their eyes as they gazed upon me increased my nervousness. What if my blood failed to aid their ruler?

Without a word, the guard on the left opened the door for us. The Queen Mother was already inside, talking to a middle-aged human doctor. Wiry, with dirty blonde hair and blue eyes, his thin lips stretched into an easy smile upon seeing us.

"Come in, come in," he said with warmth, in an oddly youthful voice.

I advanced further inside the room towards them. The smile that had begun to blossom on my lips froze when I cleared a privacy curtain only to see the desiccated form of the man I presumed to be Raina's son. My hand flew to my mouth, keeping in the gasp of horror that wanted to escape my throat. Eyes wide, chest constricted, I numbly advanced towards the bed, as if drawn by an invisible magnet. Despite the sunken skin that made him look mummified, the Lycan King was undeniably a beast of a man. At least 6'5", thick-boned and broad-shouldered, his atrophied muscles hinted at what a magnificent specimen he had previously been. Only patches of hair remained on his mostly bald head, and smaller ones of fur could be seen along the line of his shoulders and the sides of his arms. Raina hadn't been kidding when she said her son was dying.

"I had not expected him to be in this grievous a state," I whispered.

"Now you understand why we would resort to such a generous offer to ensure your cooperation," Raina said in a soft voice. She approached the side of her son's bed and gently caressed his head. "I would do anything for my son. And you, my dear Thalia, are the key to his salvation."

I nodded then turned to look at the doctor. He immediately moved forward and cast a glance at Raina, waiting for her to make the formal introductions.

"Dr. Tanner, this is Thalia Velky, the Golden Blood Maiden," Raina said. "Thalia, this is Dr. Tanner. I have already explained to him the agreement we have reached."

"Hello, Ms. Velky," the doctor said with enthusiasm. "It is an honor for me to meet a Golden Maiden. You are almost considered a creature of legend."

I chuckled, slightly embarrassed but mostly amused by his sheepish expression.

"The patient is already prepared," Dr. Tanner continued, this time reverting to a more professional tone. "I understand that you have agreed to a minimum of 250 ml. We could provide you with a 125 ml phial if you wish. But I understand that Blood Maidens usually prefer using their own devices."

"That is correct," I said with a nod. "Usually, it is safer in order to avoid any source of contamination. However, in a medical setting, we can be more flexible as we know you observe the highest standards of hygiene. I will use your phial."

The doctor puffed out his chest, honored that I should use their device. It was silly how little it often took to get people on your side. In this instance, I genuinely trusted the medical system. But I also knew my comment would prompt him into making extra sure that all precautions were taken.

His assistant—a petite brunette I had not noticed before now —fetched the phial while I removed my cloak. Dr. Tanner took it from her and made a show of disinfecting the needle although the nurse had just removed it from a sterile package. I bit the inside of my cheeks not to smile. Raina stared at my arm as if she expected something magical to happen as I inserted the tip of the needle into the port in the crook of my elbow. Golden blood wasn't actually gold-colored. It looked like any normal red blood. And yet, even the nurse was stealing glances my way while tapping some instructions in the strange looking equipment Raina's son was hooked to. She was likely bringing him out of stasis.

My blood flowed into the phial at great speed. It was awkward having so many eyes locked onto me as I did so. It was almost as unsettling as having someone stare at you while you were eating. As soon as I finished, Dr. Tanner took the flask with the care one would when handling a newborn child. Once more, I fought the urge to smile. But all hilarity evaporated as I watched him approach the tortured body of the Lycan King.

"Would you like to sit?" Elias asked, startling me.

I shook my head with a slight irritation. Although it had been very considerate of him, I wanted to see what was happening with the patient. It would take a lot more for me to become dizzy from blood loss.

To my surprise, rather than injecting the Lycan King with my blood, they opened this mouth and started pouring it in. For a split second, I feared he would choke as he seemed unconscious. In fact, if not for the very subtle movement of his chest as he breathed, he could have passed for dead.

He didn't react at first as my blood trickled into his mouth. Then I jumped, a yelp tearing out of my throat when his hand suddenly came to life, closing over Dr. Tanner's own hand holding the phial over his mouth. The Lycan King squeezed hard, almost crushing the poor physician's hand while increasing the flow of blood into his mouth. Dr. Tanner groaned, his face contorted with pain for the few more seconds it took his patient to drain the phial.

As soon as the Lycan released him, Dr. Tanner held his bruised hand to his chest and took a step away from the bed. The troubled expression that crossed his features made me extremely uneasy.

"Calm, Drogo," Raina said, caressing his head in a soothing motion.

His eyes snapped open, the same silver color as hers.

"More," he said in a deep, rumbling—almost growling—voice.

It wasn't a request, but an order that brooked no argument. I instinctively took a step back. The movement drew his attention, and his head jerked towards me. My breath caught in my throat as his wolfish eyes bore into mine, paralyzing me. His nostrils flared, and a low growl rose from his chest.

"Peace, Drogo," Raina repeated. "She will give you more, son. Be patient," she added, gesturing at the doctor with her chin to get a move on.

Dr. Tanner shook his sore hand and reached for the phial. Drogo didn't resist as the doctor took it from him. He didn't even seem to realize it, he was so intent on me. Dr. Tanner removing the tip of the phial to put a new sterile needle seemed to trigger Drogo. The Lycan froze, inhaling deeply as a savage expression descended on his features. Terror and an impending sense of doom washed over me. Yet, at the same time, my stupid brain oddly noted that his skin was quickly returning to a more natural color and texture, losing its leathery appearance.

Something seemed to snap inside him, and Drogo leaned on his elbow. Teeth bared, a vicious pair of fangs descended while the growling sound intensified.

"Oh God," I whispered, as panicked voices urging him to calm down rose all around the room.

The bedroom door burst open just as I was turning on my heels to hightail it. The four Lycan guards rushed inside—the fourth one having returned—a worried expression plastered on their faces.

I never made it to the door.

A dark shadow flashed at the edge of my vision. I felt myself being swept off my feet. The room spun, and then my back collided brutally against the wall. My breath rushed out of my lungs before a mountain of flesh flattened me. My scream of terror turned into one of pain as Drogo fisted my hair, yanked my head sideways, then buried his fangs in my neck. Panicked shouts ricocheted throughout the room with Raina begging her son to stop, while the guards yelled at him to let me go.

I tried to push him away. The countless hands of the guards attempted to pull him off of me, their faces inches from mine reflecting the horror I felt. But they all suddenly dropped to their knees, as if an invisible power had forced them down. My necklace warmed as it parried the compulsion Drogo was exercising over everyone in the room. At the same time, my pain suddenly dissolved, and a tsunami of liquid bliss flooded my veins.

I moaned in ecstasy while my hands, instead of pushing him away, were now clinging to Drogo. My nipples hardened, and my core throbbed with a terrible ache that had me pressing myself against him. I barely felt the Lycan King releasing my hair. He didn't need to keep my head tilted to the side. I was deliberately stretching my neck, holding his face against me to give me more of the divine nectar that had my body drowning in an ocean of pleasure. The odd texture of his hands slipped behind my knees, propping me up against the wall. My short skirt rode up, leaving nothing but the thin triangle of my panties between me and Drogo's thick, rock hard cock rubbing against my sex. I went off like a rocket. My shout of bliss as I climaxed buried the muffled sounds of the pleading voices behind him.

However, through the fog of ecstasy, I felt my heart stutter. My feverish skin tingled, and I fought the urge to let my eyes roll to the back of my head. He was drinking too much, too deep.

"I'm dying," I whispered in a barely audible voice, even as I tightened my embrace, wanting more, needing more.

"DROGO! YOU'RE KILLING HER!" Raina's voice shouted, finally piercing the haze that had swallowed me.

I didn't know if it had pierced through his as well, or if the odd electric flash on his chest made the Lycan King snap out of daze, but he stiffened against me. Drogo abruptly pulled his fangs from my neck, his head jerking up to look at me. My head swam as our eyes connected, and a horrified expression descended on his face.

"No!" he whispered. "What have I done?"

"Release us, my King!" a male voice shouted behind him, echoed by other voices.

But I couldn't hear them anymore. As a veil of darkness fell before my eyes, and Death pulled me into her cold embrace, the last thought that crossed my mind was that Drogo was stunning.

CHAPTER 5
DROGO

The blood of the ancient gods themselves flowed through me, filling me with divine power, driving me insane with a burning hunger and an insatiable lust for the delicate beauty in my arms. Her scent was maddening. My Spirit rattled and raged to claim her, but his intervention had saved her life. My chest still ached where he had zapped me. A sliver of rational thinking fought its way through the blissful haze, allowing me to regain control over my primal urges. I stared in horror at the Blood Maiden who had gone limp in my arms, then at the bleeding puncture wounds on her neck. I licked them, the healing properties in my saliva immediately sealing them.

Lifting her in my arms, I turned around to find my mother, Elias, the doctor and the nurse, as well as four of our Iron Guards getting back up on their feet. My compulsion no longer shackled them. As the Lycan King, I naturally had a powerful sway over my people. But since Soren had chosen me, that power had multiplied.

"She needs blood," I said in an urgent voice while carrying her to the bed I had previously occupied.

My mind still reeled as I laid her down on the mattress. I had never lost control this way. Even now, I still hungered to suck her dry, but my protective instinct kept the savage hunger at bay. Her skin had gone pale and clammy, her breath rapid and shallow.

"You can't transfuse her," Elias objected, his voice filled with grief. "It will kill her. Anything other than golden blood will kill her."

"Thalia, can you hear me?" the doctor called out, tapping her cheeks before lifting her eyelids.

"Doctor, she's going into shock," the nurse said as spasms began shaking the Blood Maiden, as if she was trying to dry heave.

"We must put her in stasis. It's her only chance," Dr. Tanner said.

Despite her divine blood coursing through me, I felt dizzy. I stumbled to a nearby chair, my gaze never straying from Thalia. My Spirit was howling for her while the doctor was swiftly hooking her up to my stasis apparatus. My mother came to my side to see how I was faring. I absentmindedly squeezed her hand, worry for the young female gnawing at me. Within seconds, Thalia's body went slack. But this wasn't a cure. She wouldn't be regenerating the blood I had taken from her. As long as she remained in stasis, Thalia was essentially frozen in time.

"She could drink from the Well," I suggested, seeing no other solution to the terrible thing I had done.

"You cannot turn her, brother," Ulia said. "Doing so without her explicit consent will start a war with the vampires."

"Her dying at my hands will also start an all-out war," I hissed, fighting another wave of dizziness.

"She must have a blood bank in her village," Dr. Tanner interrupted before things escalated. "Everyone with such a rare blood type would. It's a question of life and death."

"Oh God," Elias whispered, his eyes lighting up as if he'd been struck by an idea. "Dr. Tanner, check her bracelet."

"What?" the physician asked, although he complied. His eyes widened, relief and awe etching on his face. "Is that what I think it is?"

"I had advised that she acquire an emergency pod with the first compensation wages from the Academy," Master Elias said, his voice bubbling with excitement.

"What is it?" I asked, not daring to hope.

"People with extremely rare blood sometimes use this portable blood bank," Elias explained. "In her case, Thalia acquired the high-end model. It has a homing system which allows it to seek its owner in case of distress. The pod should normally be linked to the port in her arm."

"According to the interface on the bracelet," Dr. Tanner said, "it should reach us in the next fifteen minutes. We must open the windows to let it in as it will seek the most direct path to her."

While waiting for the pod to arrive, the nurse made Thalia comfortable, and Dr. Tanner seized the opportunity to check up on me. I hadn't received anywhere near enough blood, no matter how much I had stolen from her. And yet, her golden blood had worked magic on me. In the last couple of days before my mother had me put in stasis, I had been weak, in constant, horrible pain. Even the simple act of breathing had been excruciating.

My desiccated limbs were now already regaining their normal, healthy appearance. The dull throbbing I had experienced, despite the heavy painkillers they'd given me, was completely gone. My entire being thrummed with an insane amount of energy. I could see my body returning to its former glory in real time.

"This is simply amazing," Dr. Tanner whispered to himself as he stared at my chest and arms, filling up as if I was being inflated from within.

"I knew it would save you," Mother said, in a choked voice.

To my shock, her hand caressing my head was no longer

rubbing my scalp but my hair, which was growing back at an exponential rate. But even as those wondrous changes were taking place, I could feel the energy from Thalia's golden blood fading within me as my body consumed it to restore itself. And with that, a gnawing hunger tortured me. Within minutes, the healing process slowed and then stopped. I had no doubt used up all that she had given me.

"You need more blood," Dr. Tanner said with a frown. "Mine is in no way special. However, when you look at me or at my assistant, Sarah, do you feel nauseous at the thought of biting us?"

My gaze dropped to the doctor's neck, zeroing in on his pulse palpitating there. As my illness had progressed over the past couple of months, the thought of biting anyone had made my stomach queasy, even as it growled with hunger. I felt no urge to bite the doctor, but also no nausea, which was a great sign on both fronts. Although it guaranteed nothing, I wanted to believe the absence of revulsion meant I had received enough golden blood—for now—to allow me to tolerate common blood for a while. But more importantly, it reassured me that the blood-lust madness had abated.

"No, I don't," I said with undisguised relief.

"Excellent," he replied. "I'm going to give you a very small amount of synthetic blood to see how you respond. If all goes well, then we will give you as much as you need to get you back to your old self."

"Very well," I said. "But not until she's been taken care of."

The doctor opened his mouth to argue, but one look at my face sufficed for him to know there would be no arguing with me. He gave me a stiff nod and instructed the nurse to get a hover stretcher for me.

My mother fussed over me while the minutes trickled by. Just as the nurse was returning with the stretcher, and Dr. Tanner was finishing the preparation of the synthetic blood sample for me, Elias perked up.

"It's here!" he exclaimed, staring at Thalia's bracelet before looking out the open window by her bed.

I made to stand up, but my mother pressed down on my shoulder to keep me seated. Under different circumstances, I would have sternly told her not to interfere. However, not only was I still unsteady on my feet, but I would only get in the way. Dr. Tanner all but shoved Master Elias aside.

Although my extremely keen hearing perceived the hum of the device, I couldn't see the pod. The doctor removed Thalia's bracelet before turning her arm flat on the bed with the crease of her elbow facing up. A long, elliptical indent—almost rectangular with rounded edges—formed on Thalia's stomach.

My eyes widened, realizing the camouflaged pod had landed on top of her. The stealth system was clever. Whatever amount of blood it contained, that pod would sell for a fortune on the black market. Without the camouflage, anyone seeing the pod flying on its way to its owner would attempt to intercept it. Dr. Tanner tapped a series of instructions on the interface of Thalia's bracelet. At the same time a very discreet clicking sound reached my sensitive ears. A human wouldn't have heard it. Seconds later, the stealth cloak of the pod deactivated—no doubt thanks to Dr. Tanner's efforts.

Sleek, almost bullet-shaped, the silver pod had a luminous gauge on top indicating it was full as we couldn't see inside. The source of the clicking sound became apparent while I watched in fascination as a narrow tube appeared, protruding from the tip of the pod. It extended, homing in on the port in Thalia's arm, before connecting to it.

"That's fucking awesome," Ulia whispered, as he stared at the self-sufficient device, expressing out loud what we were all thinking.

Ulia was the leader of my Iron Guard. Although I considered

him a brother, he was in fact my blood cousin on my mother's side. My other three guards had gone back outside of the room to keep watch.

Thalia's blood started flowing in through the transparent tube. The memory of its exquisite taste on my tongue, of how it quenched the impossible thirst that had kept me parched for weeks and devoured me from within, came back to the fore. My stomach grumbled, reminding me I still needed more. Every head jerked towards me with a look of alarm.

"Relax," I growled. "I'm in control."

Despite their palpable relief, Ulia stood a little closer to me, ready to intervene. Dr. Tanner gestured with his head for Nurse Hindman to come give me the blood sample. I almost argued, but the gnawing hunger in the pit of my stomach was growing exponentially, and my Spirit was clamoring for it.

However, even as I accepted the blood ampoule from the nurse, my gaze never strayed from Thalia. My heart soared at the sight of her lips, that had taken a slightly bluish tinge, starting to regain their natural pinkish color. Her pale skin also started looking better. The whole time, the doctor was running a hand-held scanner over her. The tube of the pod suddenly retracted, having apparently completed its task. And yet, based on the luminous display, it appeared to still have a little less than a third of its contents left. Nevertheless, judging by the size of the emergency bank, I had clearly drunk a significant amount of blood from the poor woman.

While I swallowed the contents of the ampoule, the doctor deactivated the stasis device. The monitors tracking her vitals immediately responded as her body slowly returned to life.

"How are you feeling?" Nurse Hindman asked.

"Fine," I said distractedly, focused on the doctor and Thalia.

"Good. I'm going to need you to lie down on that stretcher for me," she continued in a soft voice.

I glared at her, annoyed by her constant distraction. It wasn't fair, considering she was trying to make me better. But, right this instant, my priorities lay elsewhere.

"Do as she says, son," my mother said in a soft voice. "In fact, should we leave the room before Thalia regains consciousness?" she asked the doctor. "The poor girl must be traumatized."

I winced, kicking myself for not having thought of it myself.

"She will not wake for a while," Dr. Tanner said in a reassuring tone. "She just went through a pretty severe shock. I want to monitor her for a couple of hours to make sure she's fine. Having her awake and panicked will not help me achieve that."

"Okay," I said, relieved.

"That's going to give us time to take care of you," the doctor continued, before squirming uncomfortably.

I didn't need him to speak to know what issue troubled him. "Do what you must, Dr. Tanner," I said in a firm but gentle voice. "I will not resist."

"No!" Ulia exclaimed. "We need to get you out of here before he reports you."

"No," I countered in a tone that brooked no argument. "If Thalia files a complaint, and the hospital staff allowed me to flee, Konstantin would have their heads."

Dr. Tanner swallowed hard, confirming that very fear was clawing at him.

"If you stay, Konstantin will have you executed," Ulia hissed. "You know he wants nothing more than to eliminate his one obstacle to the rule of Karthia."

"And if he flees against the human's consent, Drogo will be a fugitive," my mother snapped. "Konstantin will demand we hand him over. And if we refuse, his Red Guards will be entitled to storm Hundilinn to apprehend him. *That* will result in an all-out war. Fleeing is *not* an option."

"Agreed," I said, calmly. "He cannot execute me if I plead Blood Starvation madness."

"I can vouch for that fact," Dr. Tanner eagerly interjected. "It has already been noted in King Drogo's medical report. Speaking of which, how are you feeling?"

"I'm famished," I said in a grumpy tone. Hunger made me highly irritable. "I'll have more of that synthetic blood."

Dr. Tanner cast a glance at the Nurse who ran the handheld scanner over me. After a quick check of the results on its interface, she nodded.

"Give him as much as he needs," the doctor said. "But I want him on that stretcher first."

I reluctantly got up from my chair, grateful for Ulia's support as a wave of dizziness washed over me. My stomach cramped painfully with hunger, infuriating me. Like every Lycan, I had never been mastered by bloodlust. This would not do. I wouldn't be a slave to this new hunger like the vampires were.

I sat at the edge of the hover stretcher and gratefully accepted the one-liter flask of blood Nurse Hindman handed me. I immediately began gulping it down.

"The Blood Starvation case will be easy to make," Master Elias said. "However, Dr. Tanner, we need you to delay informing the authorities about the incident for a couple of hours."

"Why?" the doctor asked, his surprise reflecting mine.

"Ms. Velky will be very upset and distraught when she wakes," Elias explained. "If Konstantin is the first person she speaks to, he *will* make her file a complaint and push for maximum punishment for ruining her and her future. King Drogo didn't just drink her blood, he bit her. Her value as a Blood Maiden relied heavily on the purity of her blood. It has now been tainted, and by a Lycan no less."

"I did not infect her with the Lycan virus," I countered forcefully. "I may have been out of my mind, but I was still in my man form. She will not be turned. The virus must be activated by me going into my Lycan form."

"But you injected her with some sort of euphoria or aphrodisiac," Elias insisted.

"That will not taint her blood," Dr. Tanner said. "Although powerful, the Lycans' aphrodisiac dissipates much faster than standard opioids and without any of the detrimental addictive effects. It will be completely gone from her system within twelve hours. We performed a toxicity test right after we put her in stasis. I will perform another right before we wake her so that we can answer all the questions she will undoubtedly have."

Elias heaved a sigh, his shoulders sagging with relief. Although I had known this already, it still reassured me to have it confirmed by a human medical doctor. I handed over the empty flask of blood to the nurse who gave me another full one.

"Then that will help us appease her when she wakes," Elias said. "Give us two hours, Dr. Tanner. Do not call the Red Guards until she's awake. You can do so once I start talking to her."

Dr. Tanner gave him a stiff nod.

"Thank you, doctor," I said, my voice slurring a little.

I'd barely drunk a quarter of that second flask, but the toll my illness had taken on my body, including two weeks of stasis, was manifesting itself. Feeling groggy, I didn't resist when the nurse took the bottle from me, and Ulia helped me lie down on the stretcher.

The last thing I saw before darkness swept me away was the concerned look on my mother's beautiful face.

CHAPTER 6
THALIA

I woke up with a start, confused and my chest constricted by an impending sense of doom. The memory of what had happened came rushing back in a violent tsunami of images, sounds, and conflicting emotions of terrible pain and incredible pleasure. My hand flew to my neck as I jerked into a sitting position, shocked to find myself in the medical bedroom of the Lycan King and lying on top of the bed he had previously occupied.

"You're awake," Dr. Tanner said in a solicitous fashion as he turned away from the machine to face me.

It took me a second to realize he had hooked me to the stasis device previously used on Drogo. Too many questions swirled through my mind for me to be able to latch onto a single one, let alone to voice it. My fingers kept rubbing the side of my neck looking for the puncture holes or wounds that would testify to the assault I clearly remember sustaining but found none.

"Calm down, Ms. Velky," the doctor said in a soothing voice. "You're safe. You are fine. All is well."

"He… he bit me," I said in a trembling voice.

"He did," the doctor conceded in a gentle voice while pulling up a chair to sit next to my bed. "But you are safe, thanks to your foresight."

He looked over his shoulder, and I followed his gaze. The sleek curves of my emergency pod sat on top of the counter. I clasped the crease of my elbow where the port was still hooked, realizing what had saved my life.

"We have performed multiple tests on you to make sure, and I can confirm that you didn't sustain any damage from this," Dr. Tanner said. "All the tests came back negative."

"I'm alive but ruined," I said through my teeth, sorrow and anger filling my heart.

"You are *not* ruined, Ms. Velky," he countered.

When I opened my mouth to argue, the doctor launched into a quick explanation on how the Lycan virus worked. He then showed me the result of my blood toxicity tests. My eyes widened in shock, and my heart sank at the low percentage of 72.3% purity when only hours earlier I had been at 99.9%.

"Do not fret," Dr. Tanner said reassuringly. "You were at 45% only a couple of hours ago. The hormone he injected you with is dissipating quickly from your system. By this time tomorrow morning, it will likely be completely gone. It is no different than any other safe painkiller and analgesic you may have used in the past."

I heaved a sigh, relief flooding through me. I was so angry with myself for having put my own sorry ass in this situation. Greed had made me throw all caution to the wind. Even now, despite the good news on the quality of my blood, if any of my potential vampire patrons found out someone other than they had been the first to sink their fangs into me—worse still that it had been a Lycan—my worth would plummet. It wouldn't nullify my golden blood, which still guaranteed I would find a patron, but it could easily knock off a zero at the end of whatever figure would be offered for my services.

"I thought only vampires were affected by the Blood Starvation madness?" I said angrily. "If you knew Lycans were also subject to it, why wasn't he bound?"

Dr. Tanner recoiled in surprise.

"You know of the Blood Starvation madness?" he asked.

"Of course," I said, stunned he would ask such an obvious question. "Every Blood Maiden is warned of that possibility. It's the reason why we're strongly warned against meeting potential patrons in private settings or without a bodyguard. I thought I was safe with him being a Lycan and with all of you present, including his guards. So, I ask again, why the fuck was he not bound?"

"Honestly, Ms. Velky, we have no excuses other than we had not expected it either," the doctor said, his face burning with shame. "We had never seen a Lycan this old be affected by such a severe case of Blood Starvation. It usually happens to infants who rarely survive it."

That comment broke my heart. The thought of such young lives snuffed before they'd even started was terrible.

The doctor cleared his throat. "Master Elias wishes to discuss the situation with you, as well as the contract you entered into. But first, I will answer any other questions you may have regarding your current condition before I let him in—assuming you agree to speak with him."

My heart skipped a beat upon hearing those words. My instinctive reaction was to shout 'no'—a silly one at that. Master Elias had not been responsible for these events, even though he had convinced me to come here. That said, I had given the blood —or rather, it had been taken from me against my will. But it still had been given, which meant I deserved compensation. Maybe all wasn't lost after all. I looked at the doctor and then nodded before running nervous fingers through my hair. To my surprise, my messy bun had been undone.

"The only question I still have for you would be what is my ability right now to give blood again?" I asked.

This was not where I wanted my head to be. The mere thought of giving blood again was making me queasy. But if I did receive offers from the Vampire Lords, I needed to know what kind of delay would need to be negotiated if it came to me having to go through with any of them.

"Normally, since the totality of the blood lost was replaced within minutes of said loss, thanks to your pod, you should be able to resume almost immediately," the doctor said cautiously. "However, your body did go into shock. I would like to keep you here overnight and then give you a final verdict in the morning. For now, my recommendation would be to wait at least a week, and preferably not to exceed 100 ml per week for the next month."

I nodded. "Okay," I said, making no effort to hide my relief. "And yes, I would like to stay overnight to make sure everything is indeed fine with me."

"Perfect," Dr. Tanner said. "If you have any other questions, do not hesitate to ask for me. I am on the night shift and will be here until you wake. For now, I would like you to speak with Master Elias so that he can explain everything to you both regarding your contract and the legal ramifications of this incident. I have delayed as long as possible, but now I must alert the authorities."

"What?! No, you can't do that!" I exclaimed, my eyes widening with fear. "If the word spreads—"

"For all we know, it is already spreading," the doctor said in a commiserating voice. "If we do not report this incident and it reaches the Council, I will lose my license, both Nurse Hindman and I will face criminal charges, and the hospital will pay a heavy fine. I must report it."

"They will execute him," I argued, hoping to sway him.

For a strange reason, beyond wanting to protect my own ass, I didn't want Drogo to get hurt. I had seen the state he'd been in. The horrified sound of his voice asking himself what he had done as I lost consciousness still lingered in my mind. He hadn't meant to do this. His mother's and his guards' shocked and panicked reactions had been genuine.

"Only if you press charges," Dr. Tanner said with an unreadable expression. I recoiled, his underlying meaning sinking in. "Speak with Master Elias. And then you can make a decision. I will send him in."

Without waiting for my response, the doctor rose from his chair and headed towards the door. It suddenly struck me that I had no idea where Drogo and his mother had gone. Were they outside, only meters away from me? For the strangest reason, the panic that should have swept over me didn't.

If they had wanted to silence or dispose of me, they could have done so while I was passed out.

Would they have, though? After all, as I had intended, countless vampires had witnessed my departure with Master Elias and the Lycan Queen Mother. If I came up missing, they would be hard pressed to prove their innocence.

Master Elias came in alone, the guilty expression on his gentle face killing any desire I might have felt of chastising him. He took a seat in the chair Dr. Tanner had just vacated. I turned to face him, my legs dangling at the edge of the bed.

"How are you feeling, Thalia?" he asked in an almost paternal tone.

"Fine, I guess, all things considered," I answered. "He's going to inform the Council."

Elias stiffened before nodding. "He has no choice. But before we discuss that, there is something else I need to tell you."

He leaned towards the nightstand next to my bed. I was stunned to see my bracelet had been placed there instead of on my wrist. He picked it up and extended it to me.

"As Dr. Tanner no doubt explained to you, Blood Starvation can cause the unfortunate incident which occurred earlier," Elias said. "But that doesn't change that you have held *and* exceeded your end of the deal. I have therefore transferred to your account the agreed upon amount plus a bonus for the extra blood that was drained from you, and for your pain and distress. Please verify that everything is in order."

My heart skipped a beat as I took my bracelet with shaky hands. I had hoped he would say that. In fact, a part of me had believed it. But believing and seeing were two very different things. I placed the bracelet on my wrist before accessing the interface and logging into my account. I froze, feeling my blood drain from my face at the sight of the amount displayed. I blinked a few times and barely resisted the urge to pinch myself. Mouth gaping, I looked up at Master Elias, needing confirmation that today's incident hadn't messed with my brain. He smiled and nodded.

"Two million credits?" I whispered.

He nodded again, his smile broadening. "The agreement had been 500 ml for 750,000 credits. He drank a little under 1,200 ml, which is more than double. Drogo and Raina both felt it was a fair compensation, and I agreed."

It was more than fair, it was insane. I was set for life. It was more than double what I had hoped to earn in my Blood Maiden career, including the credits I'd have gotten for selling whatever clothes, jewelry, and gifts my patron would have given me over the years, and any potential pension had I been so blessed to become a concubine or consort. My eyes misted as the truth of my freedom dawned on me. I no longer needed to sell myself.

And then a thought crossed my mind. For a silly reason, it hurt.

"I wouldn't have filed a complaint against him," I said in a voice I hoped came out neutral. "Anyway, you can't win against a case of temporary insanity."

"First," Elias said in a slightly stern voice, "these credits are not to buy your silence. They are your contractually earned compensation for your blood. Second, I am pleased to hear you wouldn't have charged Drogo. Despite your terrible first encounter with them, the Volkovs are truly good people. Third, you *can* prosecute someone who attacked an innocent victim because of Blood Starvation. However, those cases are *always* settled out of court. The amount of the compensation is normally calculated based on a chart that accounts for the victim's blood rarity, the quantity of blood drained, multiplied by the aggressor's wealth score. In your case, the chart determined that amount to be set at 75,000 credits. The Volkovs have authorized me to offer you 150,000 instead."

My head spun to have such large amounts of credits being thrown around like it was nothing.

"Good God! Just how rich are those people?" I asked, flabbergasted.

Elias chuckled. "He's a King," he said, as if that explained everything.

"Well, either way, it is very generous of them, but they have compensated me enough through our original contract. And, anyway, I was not going to press charges against them for the attack," I said, even more shocked to hear myself turn down what, just this morning, I would have deemed an insane fortune.

He smiled, but it quickly faded as he regained a serious expression. I braced.

"I do not mean to seem crass, but would you be willing to sign that you waive the right to sue?" he asked in a firm and yet slightly embarrassed tone.

Although it rather displeased me, I understood his desire to protect his client. Words often meant nothing when the potential for credits loomed on the horizon, and even more so when someone in such a position of power as a King could be blackmailed.

"Yes. I am willing to sign," I said matter-of-factly.

The paternal look he gave me, full of gratitude, respect, and something akin to affection, turned me upside down. I had no recollection of my father before his untimely death. To him and my mother, I had been an investment for the future. Families were broken in the colonies. Humans bred like rabbits, couples interchanging freely in the hopes that one pair would produce a rare-blooded child.

After giving birth to me, my parents handed me over to the academy and immediately started working on a second child. My father also sowed his seed far and wide, some women even paying him in the hopes he was the one with the golden gene. But it didn't go down too well with the partner of one of those females—or at least, so it was presumed. My father's body was found in a ditch, his skull bashed in. As my mother gave birth to many other children after me, none of them with golden blood, we could only assume that my sire had been the one to grant me this gift.

Therefore, I had never known paternal affection and support. Master Elias had been the only male to have ever shown me some genuine, selfless kindness, and given me invaluable advice to increase my chances at a happier, safer, and more prosperous future. The emergency blood bank pod had been but one of his many, very wise suggestions.

He sent a digital copy of the agreement to me, which I signed through the interface of my bracelet.

"Thank you," Elias said, his shoulders sagging with relief. "Just so you know, and as per the Volkovs' request, the additional credits were transferred to your account the moment you signed the agreement."

"What? But I said—"

"I know what you said," he interrupted gently, "but my job is to execute orders. And trust me, child, one is never too rich."

Wise words if I'd ever heard any.

He checked his watch, a tense look on his face.

"You're worried about their Red Guards?" I asked, sensing what thoughts were troubling him.

"I am," he conceded. "Konstantin would like nothing more than to eliminate the one man that keeps him from ruling all of Karthia."

"Drogo is the ruler of Karthia? I thought Konstantin was!" I exclaimed, stunned.

"You have met Konstantin," Elias said in a hard voice. "If he ruled, do you think he would 'waste' his wealth wooing Blood Maidens and deprive himself from simply draining and bedding the ones he wanted whenever he felt like it? Do you think any of the 'plebs' would have gotten to taste your sweet blood tonight?"

I cringed, remembering all too well how uncomfortable his contempt towards his own people had been. If he treated lower-ranked vampires this way, how much worse would he treat humans without anyone to rein him in?

"They didn't strike me as all being bad," I argued. "Vlad and Vasska seemed pretty decent. I was actually considering Vlad as my patron. Vasska struck me as adorable but still a little immature... if that can be said about someone a few centuries old."

Elias chuckled, although I didn't miss the approving glimmer in his eyes. "You have a keen eye to assess people's character. An invaluable quality to have in these circles. The Resnik brothers are indeed fine men. Vasska is nowhere near ready to settle, and Vlad is not in power."

"Yet," I countered.

He smiled.

I glanced around the room, things becoming even clearer to me now. "No wonder Raina didn't want to bring her son to Vere-linn. I'm guessing Konstantin isn't... or rather wasn't aware of his condition?" I asked.

"Most certainly not, which is why we couldn't risk Dr. Tanner not informing him. If anyone ratted him out..."

I nodded in understanding. "So... how is Drogo doing?" I asked, far more concerned than I probably should be. "Is he still under treatment?"

"You should go find out for yourself and have a word with him before Konstantin arrives," Elias said in a mysterious way. "He's currently being held in the medical jail of the hospital until the Red Guards arrive. Anyway, the Vampire Lord will want to see you to make sure we haven't coerced you into anything."

CHAPTER 7
DROGO

I stopped mid-sentence when my ears perceived the sound of approaching footsteps. My mother's and Ulia's pointy wolf ears perked up at the same time. For a split second, I thought it to be the Red Guards. But how the fuck had they gotten here so quickly? The tension draining from my mother's shoulders hinted the newcomer wasn't an enemy. And then my nostrils picked up the maddening scent that had my Spirit in a frenzy.

I rose to my feet to get closer to the energy field that kept me imprisoned. As a wild creature, confinement didn't mesh well with me. The door opened to the antechamber of my cell. Elias entered first before gesturing encouragingly at his companion. Although I couldn't see her, the spicy, and yet lightly fruity, scent of Thalia wafting to me confirmed her presence.

She walked in, wearing one of the silky white robes the hospital offered to VIP patients. I could see why she wouldn't want to walk around wearing the very skimpy, yet tasteful, outfit from the Blood Fair. Although timid and understandably nervous, Thalia entered the room with a regal posture that awakened the most irrational sense of pride within me.

Her face lacked a bit of symmetry to be deemed beautiful, and yet, she was breathtaking to me. The minute our eyes locked, everything else seemed to fade away. Her steps faltered, and she stopped in the middle of the antechamber right in front of me. I doubted she had even noticed the presence of the others as we drowned in each other's eyes. At the edge of my vision, I felt more than I saw Elias gesturing for the others to grant us some privacy. I would have thanked him, but my tongue had turned to lead. I could feel my Spirit purring, wanting to edge closer to her—as did I.

Thalia was the first to break out of our trance, her gaze roaming over me with something akin to awe. A part of me wanted to believe it was also fueled by attraction and not just wonder at how much I had recovered. Her stare lingered for a moment on the mark of my Spirit, Soren, on my chest.

"This… this is amazing," she breathed out, waving at my body. "But should you be standing?"

I snorted and looked down at myself before locking gazes with her again. "I should be the one asking you how you are feeling and if you should be standing," I said, touched that her initial reaction to me would be compassion. "Please, have a seat. And thank you for giving me the opportunity to apologize in person. You saved my life. The last thing I ever wanted was to hurt you."

She nervously tucked a lock of her hair behind her ear before sitting in one of the two chairs that had been brought in for my mother and Ulia to sit in while conversing with me. I drew the chair on my side of the force field so that I could also be as close to her as possible.

"It is good to see you looking so well," I said sincerely. "Although, I expected you to be furious."

"Do you wish me to be?" Thalia asked, raising an eyebrow.

I snorted again, pleasantly surprised by this unexpected answer. "I would definitely rather you were not. Although, it would be justified. I am touched that your first words to me expressed concern instead. You truly are unique."

Her face heated, making her look even more adorable with her freckles standing out, and making me itch to draw her into my embrace.

"We were taught about the negative side effects of Blood Starvation," she said in an understanding voice. "Thankfully, you regained control before it was too late. All that matters is that we're both safe and sound. Thank you for honoring the agreement, and especially thank you for your generosity."

"It is hardly generous, merely deserved," I said gently. "No amount of credits is really too high when it comes down to saving one's own life."

She smiled, and my stomach tightened with the strangest sense of longing. The way it softened her face and lit up her eyes was mesmerizing. There was something about her that just soothed me and made me want... more.

"I can see that," she said, sobering. "It was the reason I had spent most of my meager earnings in acquiring that pod. Best investment ever," she added with a bit of a nervous smile.

"Indeed," I said, my chest constricting at the memory of the panic I had felt when I realized there were likely no compatible donors for her on the entire planet. "I am so very sorry..."

"Don't be," she said, leaning back on her chair and crossing her beautiful, long, and shapely legs. "And don't fret about the Red Guards. I have no intentions of pressing charges. Never did. But I certainly appreciate the very generous compensation you offered."

I already knew she had dropped the charges as my mother had immediately received a notification the minute Thalia had signed.

"Thank you, Ms. Velky," I said with genuine gratitude. "Just as you have given me a new lease on life, I hope these funds will also help you enjoy the life you want rather than the one you felt obligated to."

To my surprise, she clasped her hands on her lap, and her eyes misted as she gave me a shaky smile. "Please, call me Thalia. And yes, you have given me the greatest gifts. Freedom and security were things I never thought would truly be attainable for me. So, even if for that alone, this has all been worth it. But…"

She hesitated, her voice trailing off before she bit her bottom lip.

"What is it, Thalia?" I asked. "You can ask me anything. And please, call me Drogo."

"The doctor said bloodlust is a relatively rare occurrence in your people, and Blood Starvation even more so. Did my blood cure your condition? Are you still going to be affected by bloodlust?"

I was grateful for the opening she was giving me, leading into the topic I wanted to get to. However, the timing didn't quite feel right, especially with Konstantin's impending arrival.

"I will always be affected by bloodlust," I said calmly. "I am the Lycan King, a descendant of the purest bloodline. The need to drink blood isn't an addiction, but a genetic requirement. I would die without it. Before I had developed the illness that required increasingly rare blood, I was like every other Lycan blood drinker and only required a small amount once a week. The state you saw me in was the result of a few months of my body rejecting any type of blood, until yours."

She nodded slowly, her gaze roaming over my body, taking in the wonders she had done for me. I was still wearing nothing but my form-fitting, stasis shorts. Even though my body had not yet regained all the muscle mass it had lost over weeks of illness, I didn't miss the appreciative glimmer in her eyes as she examined me.

That pleased me tremendously.

But I also didn't miss the fact that her wheels were turning, analyzing my words. Mother had warned me that Thalia had a keen analytical mind. I let the words hang between us, letting her reach the conclusion I hoped she was reading between the lines. Seconds later, her body slightly stiffened, and her eyes jerked back up to me. I repressed a triumphant smile.

"But if your body no longer accepts regular blood, that means you'll be right back to square one in a week from now," Thalia said, her eyes narrowing.

I nodded slowly.

"That's what entailed the second proposal your mother had planned on discussing with me, isn't it?" she asked, understanding dawning on her.

"It—"

The rest of my sentence died in my throat as the loud sound of the boots of the Red Guards resonated down the hall. Thalia frowned in surprise seeing me stop so abruptly and gave me a questioning look. And then she heard it. Her head jerked towards the door. I rose to my feet, not wanting to be in any kind of 'inferior' position in front of Konstantin. Thalia followed suit, instinctively tightening her robe around her as if to shield herself from what was coming.

The door opened violently, banging against the wall with a loud sound. Accompanied by four Red Guards, the Vampire Lord barged in with a victorious, self-righteous expression on his face. Relief flooded me when Ulia and Gavril—another of my loyal Iron Guards—followed in their wake. Konstantin's malicious grin stiffened and then faded at the sight of Thalia alone with me in the room. His eyes widened before an expression of outrage descended on his features.

"Thalia?" he said, shocked. "Whose demented idea was it to put you in the presence of your aggressor? Has that beast not caused you enough trauma?"

"It's okay, Lord Konstantin," Thalia said with a slight frown. "I requested to see him."

The flabbergasted expression on his face upon hearing that unexpected response almost had me bursting out laughing. I didn't know if her answer was truthful, but I certainly liked that she seemed displeased, almost defensive, in her response to him. Konstantin was not only a stunning specimen of masculinity, his charisma and power had most females—and a large number of males as well—fanning themselves over him. I had expected Thalia to have been under his spell, whether naturally, or because of his mesmerizing abilities.

That she didn't—at least, at first glance—pleased me beyond words. It also gave me hope that convincing her to be mine wouldn't be the uphill battle I had initially expected.

"Hello, Konstantin," I said in a taunting tone. "It's been awhile. You're looking fine although a little pale these days. How's the sun treating you?"

"The sun is treating me just fine, Lycan," he hissed, taking a menacing step towards the energy field keeping me trapped in. "In your shoes, I would leave the cocky attitude to others. This time, you've done it, *King* Drogo," he added with all the contempt he could muster in stating my rank. "Let's see how smug you look once I lay down your pelt as a rug in front of my fireplace. How dare you come here and attack my humans? And not just any human at that, but my Golden Blood Maiden."

His possessiveness towards her made my hackles rise. An all-consuming jealousy erupted within me. It had nothing to do with the centuries-long rivalry between Konstantin and me, but everything to do with Thalia. I wanted her as mine in every way at a visceral level I couldn't explain. The mere thought of another man touching her or sinking his fangs into her made me burn with the need to shift into my Lycan form and ravage all in my path.

Thalia brisling at his comment slightly soothed my blossoming anger.

"He didn't come here to attack humans," Thalia said in a calm but firm voice. "Queen Mother Raina approached me on his behalf, seeking aid only I could provide. I came here willingly."

Konstantin recoiled, shock plastered on his face, and a sliver of disgust fleeted over his features so quickly, one might believe they had imagined it. But I knew the bastard too well to be fooled.

"You defend this animal who has ruined you?" he asked her, disbelievingly. "Who tainted you with his disease the rarest Blood Maiden of Karthia in generations? The beast who destroyed your chances at a lavish future of wealth, comfort, and adulation?"

"I am *not* ruined," Thalia exclaimed. Her hands fisted in anger, she lifted her chin defiantly. "Dr. Tanner has confirmed that my blood has not been tainted in any way. Should I return to the Blood Fair's Ball tomorrow, another test would show my blood purity to be the same as it was earlier."

Konstantin's eyes narrowed. "I am glad to hear it," he replied in a cold voice that actually sounded rather disappointed. "But what do you mean by *'should'* you return?" he asked, suspiciously.

Thalia crossed her arms over her chest and held his gaze unflinchingly. Pride in my woman skyrocketed... rather in Thalia. It was disturbing how possessive I already felt of her, but at a visceral level, I already knew she would stand by my side. It was... inevitable.

"My contract of assistance to King Drogo has been beyond generous," Thalia said in a casual tone. "It is far more than I could ever earn as a Blood Maiden to a dedicated patron, even should I match the longest career in this field. Now, for the first time in my life, I have options."

Konstantin gaped at her as if she'd lost her mind. His almost belligerent attitude appeared to seriously begin to rub her the wrong way. Of all the scenarios that had played in my head as to how this confrontation would go down, I never expected him to win the battle for me. Then again, Thalia's insightful evaluation of Konstantin's personality had helped shield her from his seduction. Had she been entranced by his charm, he would have gotten her to come after me with the full arsenal of the law. He would have seen me burn.

"Are you saying that you would not enter into a contract with a patron?" he asked slowly, as if she was so dumb he had to carefully enunciate to make sure she understood him.

I barely repressed a smile, loving how the fool kept digging his own grave. He wasn't used to people, especially human females, not being fully enthralled by him and subservient to him.

But then, he had never dealt with my Thalia.

"I'm saying that I no longer have to in order to survive," Thalia said calmly. "I no longer need to sacrifice my health with frequent draining that would have me age before my time or destroy my heart before I even reach the age of forty. It means that, should I decide to enter into such a contract after all, I am truly in a solid negotiating position."

"You'd be surprised how apparent wealth can quickly melt away when no new income sustains it. As a Blood Maiden, you will have no expenses. As an independent, you will drown under them. Plus, you have golden blood," Konstantin snapped. "You cannot possibly consider letting it go to waste."

"Listen to yourself," I interjected with contempt. "Centuries ruling over humans haven't changed you at all, have they? You still believe humans merely exist to sate your needs. But they don't. Whatever Thalia does with her blood is her choice, not yours. She's not a slave or prey for you to feast on whenever you crave a fancy meal."

"You are one to speak, dog," the Vampire Lord hissed.

"Careful, bloodsucker," Ulia said in a threatening tone. "You are speaking to your King."

The Red Guards tensed, ready to jump into action. But Konstantin merely glared with disdain at my cousin before turning back to me.

"You forced yourself on her, drained her to an inch of her life, and then brainwashed her into absolving you of your crimes. I respected her and was going to offer her a place as my consort. But you couldn't bear that thought, could you? You can't bear the idea that your time of keeping vampires weak and under your thumb might come to an end if my chosen Blood Maiden—my mate—makes me stronger than your parasite does."

I felt myself blanch, seething fury rising deep within. Although his words were pure lies, he gave them a ring of truth that brought a glimmer of doubt in Thalia's eyes. That wouldn't do. I took another threatening step towards the energy field, stopping barely an inch from it.

"You will never be stronger than me," I said in an icy cold voice. "You will never rule over Karthia. Soren rejected you once for a reason. You now call my Spirit a parasite, and yet we all remember how destroyed you were when he cast you aside. We both know why he chose me instead. Your plotting and scheming will never change that. You will never have full dominion over the humans."

A confused look descended on Thalia's face while her eyes flicked between my nemesis and me, trying to make sense of our semi cryptic exchange.

"Whatever you may think, Lord Konstantin," Thalia said at last, "there had been no malice or premeditation in his attack. King Drogo was under the effect of Blood Starvation. Dr. Tanner can confirm it. I thank you for coming so promptly to investigate this matter, but no crime has been committed. All parties involved are satisfied with the ultimate outcome. As I stated earlier, I am not filing any charges against him and have in fact waved any such intentions in a binding legal document, which Master Elias can share with you."

Konstantin clenched his jaw and stared at her with such anger, I feared for a second that he might raise his hand to her. Thalia clearly got a similar sense as she took an involuntary step back. That seemed to snap the vampire out of his seething rage.

"It is unfortunate," Konstantin said in a surprisingly controlled voice. "I believe that choice was a mistake, but it is done. As for the other matter, should the word spread that you were bitten by a dog, your value would greatly plummet on the market. Any other Maiden would have been completely ruined, even without any taint in their blood. Because I have such high regards and hopes for you, I will see that this unfortunate event remains hushed. And I will eagerly await your presence at the ball. I do have great plans for you… *and me.*"

The way he added those last words were sickening. I could hear a sliver of compulsion in the deep, sensual tone he used while speaking those words. I'd seen him use that technique centuries ago. Human females got so hot and bothered, the smell of their arousal all but slapped us in the face. He only would have had to speak a word and they would have ripped their own clothes off and sprawled on their backs, legs spread wide and heads thrown back with their necks exposed so that he could stick them with cock and fangs.

He was treading a fine line. A certain amount of compulsion was tolerated to the extent it represented no more than a nudge in a certain direction. But flat-out mind control would have dire consequences if one was caught doing so.

A troubled expression flitted over Thalia's face. Consort to Konstantin wasn't something one casually lifted their nose at. I would have to make sure to dissuade her from being lured into a trap. He had no love for her, only for what her blood could do for him.

"Have a good evening, Lord Konstantin," she responded,

noncommittally.

The Vampire Lord cast a last disdainful glance my way before turning on his heels and leaving, followed by his retinue. My own men locked gazes with me, a silent communication passing between us before they exited the room as well.

"Well," Thalia said, somewhat shaken, "there is clearly no love lost between the two of you."

I snorted. "It's a long story which I hope to have a chance to tell you about someday. Thank you again for dropping the charges. As you can see, Konstantin dearest would have made certain to give me the most unpleasant of times."

She nodded, the same concerned expression settling again on her delicate features. I gestured for her to resume her seat before doing the same with mine. Thalia complied, although she frowned at the energy field separating us. Technically, as I had been 'exonerated' of any wrongdoing, it should be disabled, and I should be free of movement. I would be, shortly. However, for now, I wanted Thalia to focus on what I was about to say and not be distracted by concerns for her safety.

"Despite all that, he made one very valid point," I said, choosing my words carefully.

"About my newfound wealth not lasting eternally?" she asked, casually.

My brows shot up, once more impressed by her analytical mind and capacity to discern the important tidbits from whatever people said.

"Yes," I replied with a nod.

"I do not need a lavish or extravagant lifestyle," she said with a shrug. "I only need basic comforts and the peace of mind that I will never want for anything anymore."

"That would be true for anyone else but you," I said in a gentle tone. She recoiled, a slight frown marring her forehead as she tried to guess my underlying meaning. "You heard his comment about letting your blood go to waste."

Thalia blanched, understanding dawning on her.

"Do you really believe he would allow such wealth to go untapped?" I asked, feeling like a shit for causing her any distress. "What you must understand is that your blood is far more than a mere delicacy. Drinking regularly from you would give him the power to overcome the one thing that keeps him in check: limited access to the water from the Moon Well."

Her expression confirmed she—like the majority of humans—knew nothing of the Well.

"The water from the Well makes those who drink from it immune to light sensitivity," I explained. "But it also enhances the bloodlust and physical attributes of the drinker, on top of rejuvenating them."

"The fountain of youth," Thalia whispered. I nodded. "And let me guess, you control it?" Although she framed it as a question, the Blood Maiden was actually making a statement. "But Konstantin is nearly a thousand years old and a Daywalker," she argued.

"Because he can drink enough human blood to keep him going until the next time the Moon Well opens, and I *allow* each vampire a sip or two to get them going for a few more centuries," I said smugly.

"You mean you could wipe them all out if you so choose by denying them access to the Well?" Thalia asked, shocked.

I hesitated. "It's a bit more complicated than that," I answered cautiously. "If they were deprived from it, they would slaughter the youngest vampires to reduce the number of mouths to feed. And then, once the lingering effects of the water had completely faded from their system, it would be open season on humans to keep them alive. It is a... complicated balancing act. But that's a discussion for another time. For now, what matters is for you to understand that without protection, you will not fare very well. Your blood is too valuable."

"I already planned on hiring bodyguards," she said, although uncertainty had crept into a voice.

"An average bodyguard, at the lower end of the spectrum, is paid 25,000 credits a year," I said calmly. "You would need a minimum of two to keep you safe around the clock. Spread that over ten years, and that's already a quarter of your wealth. By then, you'll only be thirty-five years old. At this rate, you'd be completely broke before you'd even reached the age of sixty. Don't forget that we haven't even yet factored in food, lodging, and basic expenses. And we're still talking about the lower end of the spectrum."

I heaved a sigh, as Soren—my Wolf Spirit—broadcast his displeasure at seeing her like this, while encouraging me to proceed. I rubbed his mark on my chest before continuing.

"If I were a vampire hungry for power and with mildly deep pockets, I would offer each of those guards four times their annual salary to simply turn a blind eye while I absconded with you. Actually, if I were your guard, I might lock you up in a cellar and drain you over decades to sell your blood in small amounts on the black market."

Thalia shuddered then hugged herself. I hated how each of my words had made her grow increasingly paler. However, beyond my selfish reasons, she needed a reality check.

"I'm sorry if I upset you, but there is a reason why Blood Maidens *always* seek a patron," I continued in an apologetic tone. "Only those that are already burnt out don't need one. It's not only because no one will bother with them, but especially because attacking them would be a disrespect to their former patron."

Her shoulders slumped. It wasn't surprising she hadn't thought of that aspect. The possibility of a life without a patron had never really been an option she would have contemplated. But Thalia had a lot of major decisions to make in the next forty-eight hours. I wanted to make sure she made the right one, both from a self-serving standpoint *and* for her own safety. I bit my tongue to remain silent and gave her some time to digest my words.

She straightened, her gaze boring into mine with the hint of a hard glint. "So," she said at last, "my newfound wealth doesn't actually set me free, but only gives me more negotiating power when picking who I'm going to sell myself to."

The bitterness in her voice clawed at me. My Spirit stirred, just as displeased as I was.

"It doesn't need to be that way," I said gently. "In the end, you need a protector, someone with the means to keep you safe. That protector needs to be able to instill enough fear in those who would seek to take advantage of you to keep them at bay. What you give that protector in exchange is a matter to be discussed. But it doesn't *have* to be blood."

She stiffened, and the intensity of her stare almost made me squirm.

"Really?" she asked in a dubious tone. "Pursuing our earlier conversation, which got interrupted by Konstantin's arrival, weren't you about to suggest that a Lycan protector with far tamer blood needs would be a good alternative to a vampire patron?"

I snorted and smiled, making no effort to hide my admiration. "That was not the suggestion I was going to make, although it certainly was the second offer my mother intended to make you on my behalf," I said matter-of-factly. "You know my situation, and the fact that I will need 30 to 40 ml of golden blood once a week for at least the next couple of months. So, yes, I will definitely try to convince you to enter into some sort of agreement with me on that front. But I don't need to be your patron for that."

She blinked in confusion, having not expected that answer. I could see how troubling it would be for her to be told exclusive rights to her precious blood was not a requirement. With recent events, she could fear her value had lessened as Konstantin had alluded to.

"Then, what other protectors are you referring to?" she asked, nervously clasping her hands on her lap.

"Someone who would rather you not enhance their enemy," I deadpanned.

Her eyes widened, first in disbelief and then in understanding.

"You would offer me your protection, no blood requirement involved, merely to keep Konstantin from having me?" she asked, flabbergasted.

"Absolutely," I answered firmly. "Right now, as powerful as he is, Konstantin is controllable. With you enhancing him regularly—and I promise you he would gorge on you—he would become a threat to all Lycans and to Karthia itself. Offering you a place to live, safe and unthreatened by anyone, costs me nothing while gaining me much."

Thalia licked her lips nervously and shifted in her chair. Her eyes flicked from side to side as she analyzed what I had just said.

"Just to be certain, if I were to move to Hundilinn, I would be allowed to get my own home, settle peacefully, and enjoy a normal life with no expectations of any kind from me?" she insisted.

"If you were to come to my lands, you would be given the choice between having your own quarters in the castle, or choosing one of the vacant houses near it to keep you safe," I answered. "Just like with a regular patron, lodging would be free. If you choose to stay in the castle, food and all basic needs would also be covered. Nothing would be expected from you in return."

"That sounds excessively generous," she argued suspiciously.

"That sounds like me making you an offer you cannot refuse,

which would cost me next to nothing," I countered. "A full contract has already been drawn by Master Elias. I would love for you to give it a look see, and sleep on it tonight. As I understand it, you will not be leaving before morning. No vampire will ever make you such an offer that essentially guarantees your freedom. In Hundilinn, you can choose to practice whatever career your heart desires, or none at all. You could just live off the interests from your newfound wealth. Or you can occasionally sell samples of your blood to a very generous customer," I added with a mischievous smile.

She snorted and shook her head at me as if I was hopeless.

"You have given me much to think about, Drogo," Thalia said, in a tone I could not define. "And you are correct in that I only have a couple of days to make a series of very important decisions. Thank you for bringing this issue to my attention."

"My pleasure, Thalia," I replied with a slight bow of my head. "You will find that Lycans do not play mind games. We are very straightforward in what we want and in our dealings. Speak with Master Elias, and review the contract. I hope you will get to discover the beauty of my lands. I even promise to play tour guide if you allow it."

This time, she didn't smile or chuckle. She tilted her head to the side, her gaze locked with mine as if she was trying to assess something or as if my features held the answer to a question or mystery plaguing her. She rose to her feet, and I instinctively followed suit.

"Maybe I'll take you up on it," she said in that same strange tone. "You should rest. And I will go do the same."

"Rest well. I hope to see you in the morning," I said, struggling with a strange sense of loss when she smiled before heading towards the exit of the antechamber.

When the door closed with a soft click, the only image that kept playing in a loop in my mind was her climbing the stairs to the castle by my side.

CHAPTER 8
THALIA

I woke up feeling surprisingly well-rested. In light of last night's events, I had expected to toss and turn for hours on end. I hadn't gone to bed immediately after my conversation with Drogo but instead had a long discussion with Master Elias. Too many conflicting emotions were pulling me in every direction. Who would have thought that my world would be so utterly turned upside down in the space of twenty-four hours?

In a quick visit, Dr. Tanner dropped by to give me a clean bill of health and confirmed that my blood toxicity had returned to its previous stellar level. He left just as breakfast was brought in. After my meal, I would be free to leave. Overwhelmed by too many thoughts swirling in my mind, I barely noticed what I ate. A first for me who was always so careful about anything I put inside my body.

I had become a pawn in a high stakes game for power and the rule of an entire planet and its people. Just a day ago, if anyone had asked me how I would respond to the great Konstantin offering me a contract to become his consort, I would have shouted 'yes' from the top of my lungs. And yet, now that I had indeed received such an offer less than an hour after the vampire's departure from the hospital, I eyed it with extreme reluctance. It was generous, insanely so, but it was the implied and unspoken expectations that made me cringe on top of the man himself.

I had fantasized about him for years. He was such a handsome and powerful male, wealthy and charismatic, and with that predatory aura typical of vampires that turned me into a puddle. Last night at the Fair, when I first laid eyes on him, he took my breath away. I was entranced, mesmerized by his undeniable appeal. At that very second, he could have asked me anything, even to let him have his way with me right there in public, and I would likely have said yes, so strong was his power over me. But in the few hours since, the fog of infatuation that blinded me had lifted. Now, whenever I thought of the Vampire Lord, a queasy, slimy sense of uneasiness took hold of me.

As per his contract, Konstantin would claim me as his consort right from the start, with full privileges. That meant he would expect me to share his bed and to feed from the source—meaning biting me to drink—from day one. There was a reason Blood Maidens rarely consented to such a thing. A vampire could easily lose control and drink too deep, especially at the beginning of a relationship.

In direct contrast, Vlad had sent me the type of offer I had dreamt of but not dared to hope for. Just like Konstantin's, it was very generous, although slightly less on the credits side. However, his contract started with a first six-month period as a standard exclusive Blood Maiden contract to get to know each other. After that, my status would be upgraded to concubine for another six-month period. If that also went well, then at the end of that first year, he would take me as his consort. However, whatever the outcome of the first two stages, if we didn't deem each other compatible for a more involved relationship, the contract would revert to that of a standard Blood Maiden for the duration of my career. Once I retired, a form of pension would be paid to me for as long as I lived.

This was a phenomenal contract. It not only showed consideration from the patron but also guaranteed my safety and comfort for the rest of my life. The additional notes also confirmed one of the factors that mattered greatly to me: I would not be shared around, be it sexually or for my blood. Konstantin's contract made no mention of any of that, therefore leaving it open.

Even before this whole mess went down with Drogo, I had already pretty much decided that I would go with Vlad if he made me at least a reasonable offer. I didn't need to be rich and powerful, I just wanted to be safe and comfortable. However, even that had raised some concerns. Konstantin didn't strike me as the type of man who could lose graciously. I feared if I went with Vlad that he could make our lives hell in one way or another, especially if my blood would indeed make another vampire more powerful than he was.

The rivalry between the two Lords was undeniable. Me belonging to Vlad would definitely tip the scale in his favor. While my gut said he would make a far better vampire leader, I didn't know enough about the underlying political intricacies to risk tipping the scales in such a radical way. I would need a lot more time to make an enlightened decision—which, in many ways, the Lycans had now afforded me.

I had received a large number of other offers, including from Morana and Vasska. The female vampire creeped me the heck out. Her offer was not only fueled by her personal hunger for power, but I also believed by her jealous need to keep Konstantin to herself. That mere thought alone reinforced my decision not to accept his offer. I didn't doubt for a moment that she would make my life unbearable. As for Vasska, his offer had felt more like an acknowledgement of attraction while knowing he never stood a chance.

Which brought me to the Lycan King's offer. Even now, it felt too good to be true. And yet, it was in writing, a binding contract that would guarantee the *normal* life of *freedom* I had always wished for but never believed possible. I'd gone over it with a fine-tooth comb, grilled Elias with a billion questions, poked at any potential hole or loophole. He not only had a satisfactory answer for each of them, but also gladly amended the contract to spell out things that might even remotely be subject to interpretation whenever I raised concerns about them.

The second contract was just as sweet, 40 ml of blood once a week, from a phial, and way too many credits as compensation. It was a permanent contract, although I—and only I—had the right to put an end to it once every three months. Between these two contracts, I was set for life with a steady stream of income, and at a minimal cost to myself. One might ask why I hadn't already jumped all over it.

The truth was that the vampires were a danger I knew. Before yesterday evening, the only thing I had ever heard about Lycans had been negative propaganda. The idea of transplanting myself into their world, their capital, away from anyone and anything I'd ever known scared the living daylights out of me.

And then there was the Lycan King himself. Drogo was a magnificent beast. I was still reeling from the sight of the stunning male that had stood before me when I'd entered the antechamber of his medical cell. Gone was the shriveled-up mummy that had made my heart break with compassion. Even though he had clearly lost some mass following his illness, Drogo was bigger, broader, and far more imposing than any man I had ever seen before.

Vampires tended to be more on the lithe side and with very little body hair. Drogo's wolfish genetics were undeniable. While his hair had initially been all but gone, with flimsy patches of fur along his arms and shoulders, my blood had restored them to their former glory. I suspected his wavy dark brown hair would grow longer still into a magnificent mane once he had fully returned to his old self. Short hairs encroached on his cheeks and forehead and around his jaw with that adorable dimple in his chin. I would have expected it would make him beastly, but it made him incredibly sexy and deliciously manly.

My fingers had twitched with the urge to caress and pinch his pointy wolf ears, and to roam over the dark brown fur that ran in a straight line along the side of his arms, up the curve of his shoulder blade, and around the back of his neck. There, it formed a small, furry mantle that tapered off in a V-shape between his shoulder blades. The very sparse fur on his chest also taunted my eager hands. The powerful attraction I felt for the Lycan was quite disturbing as I had never been drawn to hairy men.

The memory of his hard body pinning me against the wall while he rubbed his stiff manhood against my core had me throbbing all over again with need. I'd never been with a man or even been held so closely by one before. Any pleasure from sexual gratification I've had in the past twenty-five years had come at my own hands, curious about my body. But that orgasm he gave me simply with the friction through our underwear, and that hormone he injected into me had been mind boggling. If that had sent me so violently over the edge, what would the real thing be like?

I shivered as his deep growl of pleasure while he fed from me replayed in a loop in my ears. I'd felt trapped, helpless, caged by his powerful body, and set ablaze by his burning skin. Despite the terror I'd initially felt, I now ached for his embrace again. Even in his cell last night, the way his beautiful silver eyes had darkened as he looked at me made me believe he, too, wouldn't have minded a repeat. However, where *I* was drawn to the man himself, *he* was likely only drawn to my blood.

The pathetic story of my life.

A knock on my door startled me out of my wandering

thoughts. To my surprise, it wasn't Dr. Tanner or Nurse Hind-man, but the very man who had been occupying my thoughts.

"Drogo," I said in greeting, with a slightly surprised tone.

He remained in the doorframe, visibly reluctant to enter. Although it was normal for him to be fully dressed, I couldn't help but bite back my secret disappointment. At least, his light grey shirt clung to his muscular body enough to give a girl some nice eye-candy to drool over. It made his gorgeous silver eyes pop even more.

"I have been given the all-clear health-wise to return home," he said in a gentle voice. "I wanted to see you one last time before I did to ask if you had given my proposal further thought?"

"Right," I said, before gesturing for him to enter. "Please, come in."

He hesitated, eyeing me warily. "Are you certain? I do not wish you to feel uncomfortable."

I tilted my head to the side, uncertain how to interpret his words. I would have expected him to jump at the opportunity to prove that he was indeed in control and not a threat. That would go a long way into convincing me that coming to his city wouldn't be dangerous for me. On the other end, I like that it signaled his concern for my well-being, and the fact that I was in control.

"Are you afraid you may go crazy on me again?" I asked teasingly.

He snorted, a strange glimmer appearing in his eyes. "Not a chance," he said with confidence. "Should I ever once more get the honor of drinking directly from you, it will be with your blessing or not at all."

My stomach flip-flopped upon hearing those words, and not only because of the sexy way his voice dipped when he said them. My excessively vivid imagination was already picturing it happening, and how it would feel to deliberately yield to his embrace. I could almost feel the soft warmth of his lips on my neck, the sting of his fangs piercing my skin, and the unyielding hold of his body around me.

"Then all is fine," I said matter-of-factly, relieved that I was already dressed and presentable.

The Queen Mother, having guessed at my discomfort with the revealing dress I'd worn to the Fair, had bought me a fresh set of clothes from a local store in Kivilinn. The black leggings were stunning, made in a stretchy fabric that could have passed for leather in appearance. The thigh-length, sleeveless, black tunic crossed over my heart in a neckline deep enough to make me look enticingly sexy, but not slutty. Decorative strips of the same stretchy leather on it, made it casually chic. She'd nailed my taste in clothes.

"You look beautiful," Drogo said, taking me by surprise. "I'm glad to see you're doing so well."

The approving way Drogo's eyes discreetly slipped over me confirmed he genuinely liked what he saw. That made me hot and cold all at once.

"Thank you," I said, sincerely flattered. "You don't look too shabby yourself, my King," I said teasingly to hide how much he was affecting me.

Drogo snorted, amusement lighting up his stunning eyes. "Why, thank you Golden Maiden Velky. You honor me," he said, taking a few steps inside the room to come stand a short distance in front of me.

"I had a lengthy discussion with Master Elias last night and reviewed both of your offers," I said, sobering.

The mirth faded from Drogo's eyes, the intensity of his stare testifying just how important my next few words would be to him.

"Yes," the Lycan King said in a cautious voice. "He has informed me of your concerns and the amendments he had effected to assuage them while you pondered the matter."

"He has, which I greatly appreciated," I said with a nod. "Once again, you are proving extremely generous."

"But?" he asked in a tense voice when I paused for a split second.

I smiled, amused by this involuntary display of impatience on his part. "But nothing. All my concerns have been addressed, and you are giving me an opportunity to enjoy the life of freedom and security I always hoped for. Therefore, it is my honor to accept both of your offers."

For some inexplicable reason, my throat tightened as I pronounced those words. Instead of the triumphant expression I anticipated from him, Drogo's face melted into an expression of tenderness and joy I never would have expected from one with such visible wolfen DNA. My breath hitched when he closed the distance between us and cupped my face between his hands. His thumbs gently caressed my cheeks. My hands instinctively closed around his wrists, but I didn't attempt to pull away from his touch.

I should have been offended, outraged even. You didn't touch a Blood Maiden without her express consent. But right here and now, Drogo wasn't touching a Blood Maiden, but me, Thalia Velky. For the first time in my life, I felt like a person instead of a valuable commodity.

"You will love Hundilinn and its people," he said in a voice so full of emotion it twisted me from the inside out. "I will endeavor to make sure you *never* regret this decision. On my honor, for as long as I draw breath, I promise to make you happy and keep you safe."

I stared at him, robbed of voice. His words went beyond a thank you for a successful deal, they constituted a pledge the likes of which a groom would make his bride. He seemed about to speak more but froze, his wolf ears perking and slightly shifting towards the door. He suddenly let go of my face and moved a couple of steps back. A shocked and embarrassed look descended on his gorgeous features as he realized he'd touched me—again—without my blessing.

"Apologies!" he said, mortified. "I—"

A knock on my door interrupted him. It was certainly the person whose approach he had heard before pulling away from me.

"It's okay," I said in a gentle voice. "Come in!" I called out.

Once again, it wasn't Dr. Tanner entering but Queen Mother Raina. She seemed pleasantly surprised to find her son alone with me.

"Oh, I'm sorry," she said. "I didn't mean to interrupt. I'll come back later."

"No, it's all right, Mother," Drogo said with affection. "I was leaving anyway. Thalia just gave me the great news that she has accepted both of my offers."

Raina gasped and clutched her chest over her heart with both hands. Her eyes misted as she beamed at me. Once again, this felt more like a son telling his mother that his girlfriend had accepted his marriage proposal rather than me merely accepting their protection. Then again, my blood would keep Raina's son alive. Therefore, I could understand what a huge relief this news had to be for her.

"That's wonderful!" Raina exclaimed while taking a few steps towards us.

"Thank you," I said, feeling self-conscious.

"Actually, now that I think of it, you could travel to Hundilinn with my mother," Drogo said. "Except, of course, if you want a few days to pack your things and handle your personal affairs before relocating. There's no pressure."

"That's a great idea," Raina said, turning towards me with an inquisitive expression on her face.

"Technically speaking, no, I don't really have much to handle," I said carefully. "I had already closed and packed my things before coming to the Fair since I had hoped to start serving my patron as soon as possible. I only have my luggage to recover from the hotel and to inform the movers where to bring my belongings, which are essentially clothes and a few personal items. All my furniture belongs to the Academy."

"That's perfect then," Raina said with a smile. "We could make a detour to pick up your things before heading towards Hundilinn."

I nodded slowly, suddenly feeling overwhelmed by how quickly things were moving.

"Well, it's up to you," Drogo said, probably sensing my blossoming distress. "If you want to take a few days before joining us, I can leave a couple of guards to protect you until you are ready."

I immediately felt silly for my hesitation and nervousness. Although it was a beautiful city, I didn't feel welcome or at ease in Verelinn, just constantly stressed and paranoid with so many hungry vampires.

"That won't be necessary," I said in a decisive tone. "Nothing keeps me here. I'm beyond ready for a new start."

This earned me an approving smile from the Volkovs. We spent the next few minutes discussing arrangements for our departure before Drogo finally parted ways with us. Apparently, some important meeting awaited him back in his capital city. Although he didn't go into any details, I suspected it had something to do with reverting the rule of his people to him now that he had recovered from his debilitating illness.

It was odd how moved I felt saying goodbye to the doctor and his assistant. During my very short stay, Dr. Tanner had acted more like a friend than a physician, and with a concern that wasn't self-serving. It was very different—and extremely refreshing—from my usual experience with people.

I traveled aboard a private Lycan shuttle, accompanied by three guards. The Queen had remained in Kivilinn to run a few more errands in the city but also to avoid unnecessarily exposing herself to danger in Verelinn. It proved to be a wise decision in light of the accrued hostility expressed by the vampires when they saw my escort on my way back in and out of the hotel. I wouldn't miss this place or its people.

However, it was the outraged expression of the handful of Red Guards that conveniently happened to be lurking in the vicinity of my hotel that made me uneasy. They contacted someone about seeing me under the protection of the Lycans. I remained tense until we finally crossed back into Kivilinn where we rejoined Raina.

CHAPTER 9
THALIA

Raina was nothing like what I had pictured a Queen to be. No stiff and haughty attitude from her, but a healthy, laid back personality that I really connected with. When we picked her up and the other guards in the human city of Kivilinn, she had all but robbed the local stores... for me. Thanks to her and Drogo, I was no longer poor. Therefore, I could have acquired all that I needed myself. But she waved a dismissive hand saying that she only acquired the basic necessities so that I wouldn't be caught unaware when the need arose. It was merely to help me out until the rest of my personal belongings arrived.

When we got aboard the shuttle to head towards my new home, Raina decided to pilot the vessel herself while I sat next to her in the copilot's chair. The couple of guards with us piled up in the passenger seats at the back. They chuckled at my flabbergasted expression when the Queen casually dragged me to the front. The look on their faces pretty much stated that this was the least of the Lycan female's 'eccentricities' if that word could be used.

Despite that, I was grateful for the unhindered view of the land during the flight. Strangely, instead of bombarding me with the list of do's and don'ts of her world, Raina launched instead into a retelling of the legend of Soren, the first Lycan of Karthia.

"It all started two millennia ago," she said in a mysterious voice. "Soren, the ancient Sun Wolf—and rebellious son of Selene, the Moon Goddess—had fallen in love with a mortal female. The beautiful Skala was one of the daughters of the primitive people that originally inhabited Karthia. Soren was so taken by her beauty that he renounced his place among the stars for a mortal life at the side of his beloved."

"How sweet and romantic," I said, already sensing the making of a tragedy. "Let me guess, his divine mother did not approve."

Raina smiled. "Of course, not. She was all the more livid that five hundred of his Sun Wolf brothers followed him. Skala and Soren were to be married at the Altar of the Moon, which is now known as the Moon Well. A Karthian Priestess led the ceremony under the light of the Blood Moon in the presence of Skala's entire tribe and the five-hundred brothers."

"They held a wedding at night?" I asked, stunned.

She nodded, casting sideways glance my way before looking back at where she was piloting. "There are very few original Karthians anymore," she explained. "Most of their villages are located in Hundilinn and in the vicinity of the Moon Well. They are a very photosensitive species. Since the dawn of time, the ancient tribes have sought a cure for their condition. They do not interact much with the other species that have now populated Karthia, since they mostly live at night."

"Oh wow, I thought the original inhabitants of the planet had been completely wiped out by some sort of plague brought by the settlers," I said, blown away.

"There are many falsehoods spread in the 'history books' passed around to humans in the vampire lands," Raina said with an undisguised contempt for the rival species. "You will learn much now that you are coming to Hundilinn. You will discover many truths."

"I look forward to it," I said sincerely. "So, what happened to the newlyweds?"

Raina's smile broadened, pleased by my interest in the tale.

"The wedding had been a trap," the Lycan female continued. "As soon as Soren and Skala finished exchanging their vows, she slit her husband's throat with a silver blade. The whole ceremony had been a Pagan ritual to allow their priestess to steal his light so that they, like him and his brothers, could walk in broad daylight without burning. Half of the other Sun Wolves were slaughtered, and it turned the surrounding holy silver water into a river of blood."

My hand flew to my mouth, covering it as I stared at the Queen Mother in horror. I had expected a curse from the scorned Moon Goddess, not such a betrayal from the bride and her people.

"With their powers bound by the ritual, the surviving Sun Wolves were taken prisoner and forced to mate with the local priestesses, and those of neighboring villages," Raina continued. "The Sun Wolves who attempted to resist were tortured and then drugged to force them into compliance."

"They had all been in on it? Not just Skala's village?" I asked, even more stunned by this turn of events.

"It had been a concerted effort," Raina confirmed with a nod.

"Wow, talk about cold and calculated."

She snorted. "Indeed, and Selene punished them for it," Raina said with a hard glimmer in her eyes that gave me pause. "The Karthians all drank from the bloodied pond after the carnage and for a couple of years thereafter until its water became silver again. During that time, they enjoyed a short period of normalcy where they could walk in the sun without harm. But as the water cleared, so did its magic."

"And they reverted back to being photosensitive again," I concluded, seeing where that was headed.

"No," Raina said, shaking her head with a harsh grin. "They didn't get off that easy. The sun didn't simply blister and burn their skin as it used to, it now flat out incinerated them into ashes in seconds."

"Oh God!" I whispered. Although I couldn't muster any sympathy for them in light of their deception, I could only imagine their horror realizing how much worse their cruelty had made their already difficult plight.

"To make matters worse, many of the offspring conceived with the wolves either died in the womb or in their infancy. They were withering like my son had until you saved him. In despair, the priestesses begged the goddess for forgiveness. But Selene had no mercy for the Karthians. They had bled the wolf, so they would live on blood. Only the offspring who became the wolf would be spared if the child drank once a month from the pond, but even more so if it could find the roaming spirit of a Sun Wolf willing to embrace it."

"Wait," I said, confused. "You mean the young had to drink from the pond and hope to become possessed by the spirit of a dead Sun Wolf?"

Raina burst out laughing. "Not possessed, no, but welcome the Spirit within themselves. It's difficult to explain. But each of the original Sun Wolves has a symbol. When they choose to embrace a Lycan, that mark appears on their chest, like a tattoo. The Lycan can feel the Sun Wolf Spirit's presence but is not controlled by him. The Spirit makes him stronger, can give warning and insights about a situation—usually danger—but it's a sensation, not a conversation. However, it didn't apply back then as none of the offspring were chosen."

I nodded slowly. Although she was presenting this as a legend of the Karthian folklore, I was beginning to suspect there was a true story with a more scientific explanation behind the events.

"The silver water saved the children's lives. Unlike their mothers, they were able to walk in daylight, and drinking from the pond silenced their bloodlust. But the original Karthians had no such luck. Anyone without Lycan DNA or at least carrying the Lycan virus who tried to drink from it, systematically died of a horrible death within hours."

"So, the Karthians also lost access to their fountain of youth," I reflected out loud. A sliver of sympathy finally took root in my heart for them, even though they had brought all of this pain onto themselves.

Raina's eyes widened in shock, and she stared at me questioningly.

"This morning, your son hinted at the properties of the water from the Moon Well, although he didn't go into too many details," I explained. "However, I thought the water increased the bloodlust?"

The Queen Mother's brow shot up, having clearly not expected this, although she seemed pleased by it.

"Indeed, it increases it in vampires, but dampens it in Lycans," she said with a shrug. "But yes, the Karthians lost their access to long life, not that it would have mattered in the end. The surviving Sun Wolves took their offspring and founded Hundilinn while bloodlust decimated the Karthians. Villages would raid each other at night, so much that entire tribes all but vanished. Until the birth of Oleg, the first Lycan to find grace in the eyes of Soren's spirit, and the first true Lycan King to bear the Sun Wolf's mark."

"Wait," I said suddenly struck by a thought. "Soren's mark, is it the same as the one on Drogo's chest?" I asked, remembering how it had drawn my attention despite Drogo's delicious nakedness.

"Yes, Soren has embraced my son," Raina said, puffing out her chest with pride.

The urge to ask then how come he had become sick since carrying a Sun Wolf's Spirit was supposed to cure them, but I held my tongue. I had certain suspicions and didn't want to derail the story by launching into a debate.

"How did Soren's embrace change the fate of the Lycans and Karthians?" I asked.

"Oleg begged Selene to lift the bloodlust," Raina said. "But the Goddess said that what was done couldn't be undone. However, as long as the Spirits of her sons continued to find the Lycans worthy, she would bless the water of the Moon Well. Once every little while, she would refill the Well. If a worthy king spilled his blood for his people, they would thrive. Otherwise, they would perish."

"And what determined the worthiness of that king?" I asked, intrigued.

"His ability to defeat the Guardian of the Well," Raina said with a mysterious smile.

My jaw dropped as the pieces all began to fall into place. I frowned and licked my lips nervously before turning to Raina. "So, the Well is currently dry?" I asked.

"Not so much dry as inaccessible," Raina corrected. "The entrance of the cave that shelters it is closed. It will open on its own when it's ready. According to my son, it should be within the next two to three months."

"And that's why you cannot afford for Konstantin to have me," I said, understanding finally dawning on me. "My blood would make him stronger, more even than Drogo. If Konstantin defeats the Guardian, *he* becomes the new King of Karthia."

Raina turned to face me, a serious expression on her face. It wasn't threatening but made me instead think of that of a mentor about to impart some invaluable knowledge to her pupil.

"You are a very smart young woman, Thalia," Raina said

softly. "You have an amazingly analytical mind and an uncanny talent for understanding people, what makes them tick, and for making the connections between actions, motivations, and their fallouts. These are invaluable talents in our world. Konstantin seeks to use you as a pawn to win this war. But when properly played, a pawn can become a Queen. And the Queen is the most powerful piece on the board."

My breath caught in my throat. I couldn't believe she meant what her words implied, and yet, there could be no other explanation. Surely, she didn't mean…?

I gasped when an alarm sound went off, startling me. The navigation board lit up. Raina cursed then brought up a holographic screen. My blood turned to ice at the sight of two dozen mercenary vessels on an intercept course with us. The three shuttles that accompanied us—each one carrying four guards—peeled off to delay our pursuers.

"The bastards are coming for you," Raina said, an angry expression on her face as she accelerated. "But they will *not* get you. Tighten your seatbelt. It's going to get rocky."

A shimmering wave flowed over the vessel as Raina activated the shuttle's stealth shield. She sent a distress signal to Hundilinn then made a sharp turn right while lowering our altitude. I wanted to believe it was to make it harder for them to guess our location and not to ensure we'd crash from a lesser height if we were shot down.

We'd only been flying for forty minutes, with still about the same amount of time to go before reaching our destination. By now, Drogo and his guards would already be in their capital city. I doubted any rescue would get here in time.

Heart pounding, I watched helplessly while our escort fought an impossible battle, outnumbered eight to one. Despite that, they put on a valiant effort managing to take down a handful of the enemy vessels with all three of our shuttles focus-targeting one ship. But too soon, they all started going down. Before they were even defeated, six enemy ships left that battle to give us chase.

The interior of the shuttle shifted, a section of each side wall extending into a battle station nook. The guards immediately manned them but didn't open fire yet as that would give away our position. To my relief, our downed shuttles hadn't been destroyed, despite being forced to perform an emergency landing.

However, in spite of our great speed, the enemy vessels were gaining on us. They were undeniably of vampire make, but the ships bore no clear markings that would identify which coven they belonged to. My gut said Konstantin had hired mercenaries to make me 'disappear' and spare himself the inconveniences of a contract. No doubt, the Red Guards that had been staking out my hotel informed him that I had left with the Lycans. I couldn't begin to imagine how livid he must be that I'd chosen 'a beast' over him. I believed he would seek to make me pay dearly such an affront.

"Fuck!" Raina muttered before pulling up sharply and then making another hard turn, left this time.

My stomach churned with motion sickness. I gripped the arms of my seat with such force my hands hurt. A volley of dots on the display screen flew in every direction at mind boggling speed. They canvassed the sky while still closing in on our position.

"What are they?" I asked in a trembling voice.

"Heat-seeking rats," Raina answered while trying to take us out of range from them.

"Rats?" I repeated, confused.

"They are creating a net to trap us in," Raina explained. "Those missiles have an EMP charge that will knock our stealth shield offline. They've already latched onto the traces of our energy signature."

My heart sank, and my stomach knotted. Once we'd lost our camouflage, all would be lost.

"Do not despair, child," Raina said in a firm tone. "They will not get you. Drogo is on his way. We will hold them off until he arrives."

The unshakable certainty in her voice gave me hope even though I saw no possible positive outcome. But I could fight and had a few tricks up my sleeve. Under normal circumstances, I wouldn't have stood a chance against a vampire. However, they wouldn't want to harm me, as my blood was too valuable. That gave me an edge I intended to exploit.

Seconds later, the first missiles started going off blindly, each one getting distressingly closer to us. And then one detonated right in front of us. I screamed as the blast knocked us off course. The shuttle rocked violently while Raina struggled to regain control. Only a couple more seconds and the damn thing would have exploded right on top of us. We started falling, and our shield collapsed. Had the charge been stronger, instead of this light version only meant to ferret us out, our ship might have been ripped apart or its systems been completely fried.

Without missing a beat, the guards manning the battle stations of our vessel opened fire. They blew up the missiles that were now converging on our position. But there were far too many. Despite Raina boosting the defensive shields of the shuttle, the electromagnetic impulses of a few more missiles going off next to us wrecked it. Much too soon, they quickly forced us into an emergency landing before we completely lost our propulsion system.

My blood roared in my ears, drowning the erratic beating of my heart as I watched the ground rush towards us.

"Brace!" Raina shouted.

In spite of the terror choking me, I didn't scream and merely braced for impact, my hands gripping the arms of my seat. I owed this semblance of calm to the Queen Mother's in control demeanor, despite the tension in her voice. She oozed confidence in her ability to land the shuttle safely. Even her guards seemed unconcerned on that front, their entire focus having shifted from blowing up the missiles to targeting the ships pursuing us.

Although we struck the ground with non-negligible force, the impact was nowhere near as brutal as I'd expected. The shuttle rocked and slid over a considerable distance before coming to a full stop. The guards continued firing from their battle stations while the Queen all but ripped off her seatbelt before jumping out of her seat. I followed suit, more grateful than ever for the leggings she had bought me instead of the skimpy dress I'd worn last night.

"Do you know how to shoot?" Raina asked me while rushing to the back of the shuttle.

"Yes," I said, proud of the firmness of my voice under the circumstances. "I'm also a rank five Ketunji fighter."

Raina stopped dead in her tracks and turned to look at me, eyes wide, mouth gaping. I shrugged, feeling self-conscious.

"I have golden blood. I have to be able to defend myself," I responded in a defensive tone.

She snorted and shook her head, a glimmer of admiration in her eyes. Under different circumstances, I would have basked in that maternal blessing, I who had never known a mother's love and affection.

Raina turned away and pressed an inconspicuous-looking section of the back wall. It opened onto an impressive armory. She picked a badass pair of blasters which she extended to me. To her shock, I shook my head.

"I have my own guns in my bag," I said, matter-of-factly. "But I would like a couple of these blades," I added, pointing at a fabulous arsenal, from small knives, to daggers, to swords.

She gave me a strange, speculative glance, while a mysterious smile stretched her lips. "Take what you need, my dear."

We simultaneously reached for a weapons belt, making quick

work of tying one around our respective waists before hooking our weapons of choice onto it. I picked a few daggers and a longer blade, which I strapped to my back.

"We're going in," the two guards told Raina while I retrieved my special guns from my bag.

The men had already prepared for battle the minute the alarm had gone off. But they each still grabbed a couple of the heavy duty, two-handed assault rifles that looked like they could fire hundreds of bullets in seconds—although I suspected them to be some sort of lasers.

To my shock, they kicked off their shoes, and a growling sound rose from the two males' throats as they began to shift. They grew even taller by a good head, their muscles bulging, their jaws expanding and lengthening into a lupine maw filled with dagger teeth. Their skin took on a leathery texture reminiscent of the one Drogo had during his illness—but without the sickly appearance to it. Then a thick fur covered parts of their arms and all around their necks. Their uniform prevented me from seeing the full extent of their transformation, beyond their increased mass, especially in the upper-body area. Vicious, talon-like claws grew at the tips of both their fingers and toes.

I swallowed hard, memories of all the propaganda about the mindless savagery of Lycans coming back to the forefront. And yet, there was no feral rage burning in the guards' eyes despite their terrifying beast form. Intelligence, fury, and the cold determination of the predator screamed that our stalkers had fucked with the wrong people. Without a word, they stormed out of the shuttle.

While I gaped at the Lycans' receding backs, Raina filled the pouch on her hip with a series of strange, luminous balls I had never seen before.

"Let's go," Raina said, grabbing a long staff with nasty-looking bladed tips, and a massive assault rifle. Although it looked like it weighed a ton, she casually held it with one hand.

"You want us to go outside?" I exclaimed, taken aback.

"Staying here is a trap," she said, casting a tense glance towards the display screen showing our enemies closing in on us. "They will dock us with their grappling hooks and carry us to whatever destination they have in mind. We have better chances outside. We just need to hold them off long enough for Drogo to get here. Come on, trust me."

Although this was not what I'd wanted to hear, Raina's arguments made sense. Silencing the fear knotting my innards, I followed her outside. The wide, open field stretching before us on all sides made me feel even more exposed and vulnerable. A thick forest northeast of our current position could have provided us with some shelter, but it was still at least two miles away.

The guards were running, guns blazing, towards the first vampires to have landed behind us. Far in the distance beyond them, dark shapes were approaching. I could only assume it was the Lycan guards from our downed escort shuttles trying to get back to us. More enemy vessels were landing, three of them flying overhead to go settle two hundred meters in front of us. We were effectively sandwiched. As the Queen Mother had predicted, one of the larger enemy vessels made its approach with grappling hooks ready. It slowed down before continuing on to join the other three vessels blocking our path forward. The pilot had likely spotted us both outside the vessel.

"This way," Raina ordered, indicating those new ships.

She picked one of the luminous spheres from her pouch and threw it violently at the ground about ten meters in front of us. To my surprise, it created a large energy wall, about four meters wide and three meters high. Raina threw a couple more of them on each side to widen our cover before casting a second row in front of us.

"You can shoot through them from this side," Raina explained. "But they will stop anything coming from the opposite direction."

She stabbed her staff into the ground next to her before holding the assault rifle with both hands. I set my blaster to lethal, while trying to come to terms with the fact that, this time, it was no longer practice. I would truly take a life... likely multiple ones.

The vampires poured out of their vessels like a malevolent swarm of insects. In reality, maybe only six or eight disembarked from their respective ships, but it looked like an endless multitude to me. Had it not been for the flowy way in which they moved and their supernatural speed, I couldn't have sworn they were vampires. Half of our attackers were clad from head to toe in black outfits, including a black mirror helmet. The other half all had the exact same face.

Clones.

If nothing else, it confirmed they weren't the Red Guards. The elite law enforcement unit—which served both as police and army—were all Daywalkers. Receiving sufficient blood on a regular basis was one of the perks of joining the force. New recruits received lesser amounts and worked the night shift. The good news was that these vampires running towards us were therefore weaker—which didn't mean feeble. And the clones were expendable meat shields sent on dirty missions when one wanted to remain anonymous.

Raina opened fire on one of them. My jaw dropped at the sight of the thick laser beam that shot out from her weapon. The first vampire failed to raise his shield quickly enough. At first, I thought his suit had absorbed the damage. Then the material started melting away, as if eaten by some acid and exposing the vulnerable flesh beneath.

The vampire screeched and collapsed to his knees, ashes pouring out anywhere the sun touched skin. The effect of the beam wore off, leaving him split in two. His lower body from pelvis to toes as well as his upper body, from his clavicles to his head—including his arms—were still intact within the shelter of his armor. As his heart appeared to have also turned to ash, I could only surmise he was dead, even though his head was intact.

Raina turned to slay more of the fully clad vampires, but with their shields raised, she had to target one longer to make the shield collapse before she could strike him—time we didn't have. They were coming too fast, all of them throwing some sort of star blades to take down our shields. Each star that made contact sent an electric shock at the point of impact, weakening it. That they weren't firing blasters at us while we were killing them reinforced my belief that they wanted us alive.

I fired at the vampires whose faces were exposed, taking headshots. But the bastards were moving too fast. Zigzagging at insane speed, they made it impossible for me to follow. Still, I got a couple of lucky shots in, but they were already almost on top of us. At least, the horrified look on some of the clones when they saw their brothers turn to ash from a single bullet was beyond satisfying. In that instant, I didn't feel like I was taking a life, but wiping out a threat.

"Stand back!" Raina shouted to me while throwing a few more shield walls around us.

She began shifting into her Lycan form, while the vampires clawed at the energy fields. A couple of the clones—more daring than the others—used the momentum from their run to jump over the shield. I shot one of them in the head mid-jump, the UV round in an armor piercing casing turning his head and part of his neck to ashes. His corpse collapsed to the ground in front of us.

Raina, still in the midst of shifting, grabbed her bladed staff and impaled the second vampire just moments before he would have landed on her. She immediately rotated on herself before swiping the staff towards the swarm, sending the severely injured vampire flying through the shield and into his acolytes.

The impact knocked down a number of them. I shamelessly

used the opportunity to shoot them. To my relief, even the fully armored ones proved vulnerable to my UV rounds. Raina went into a feral frenzy on them. She threw herself at our enemies in a flurry of reddish-brown fur peeking through her off-white tunic and dark brown leggings. Raina moved with the grace of a dancer and the savagery of a wild beast.

Her staff blurred as it twirled and swiped incredibly fast around her. She stabbed them with the bladed tips, bashed them with the staff, crushing skulls and breaking limbs, and slashed throats with her claws. The Queen Mother almost appeared to fly when she jumped over the group of vampires simultaneously attempting to pin her down, landing right behind them to continue wreaking havoc.

While it was wise of them to try and eliminate the bigger threat first, three of them realized catching the weaker one—me —and using me as bait might be more effective. I successfully shot one and roundhouse kicked the second while drawing my blade. Although the kick did make the vampire stumble back, my foot felt like it had struck a brick wall. Before he could recover, the third one was upon me. He caught my wrist, preventing me from shooting him, and his other hand closed around my neck. Fighting the urge to panic and to pull at his fingers choking me, I stabbed him in the gut twice in quick succession, enough to make him release his hold before I shot him in the face.

The one I had kicked never got a chance to get at me again. Without even looking behind her, Raina stabbed backwards with supernatural precision, the bladed tip of her staff piercing right through the vampire's skull to protrude out of his gaping mouth. Without missing a beat, I slashed his throat with the Lycan dagger I had taken from the armory. The blade was so sharp, it sliced effortlessly through skin and bone, nearly beheading him. Raina yanking her staff back out finished the job, the head turning to ash before it ever hit the ground.

And then, as if in slow motion, I saw one of the clones raise a strange-looking weapon towards Raina. I screamed her name at the same time as the flash of the muzzle went off. The Queen Mother stumbled, her body jerking as at least three bullets found their mark. One of the vampires she'd been fighting brutally backhanded her, and another kicked her square in the chest, sending her flying back. She landed hard with a thud a few meters away, the wind knocked out of her. On instinct, I threw myself on top of her, stopping the shooter from firing again. I'd barely reached her before a multitude of hands were already trying to grab me.

"LIGHT SHIELD!" I shouted.

My bracelet immediately responded to my vocal command, and a cylindrical shield formed around me with a two-meter radius. The vampires who had been reaching for me screeched in agony as the light shield severed their limbs, and in some cases, part of their faces as well. The high lumens of the shield—blinding even for me—inflicted severe burns to the clones standing too close from it. The survivors backed away in shock.

I was in a total panic. The silver bullets fired at Raina had thankfully only struck her legs but were slowing her Lycan fast-healing abilities.

"I'm fine," Raina ground through her teeth, although visibly in pain.

There were still at least seven or eight vampires outside our shield, and I didn't dare shoot at them through it for fear it might collapse. I'd designed that shield for emergency situations where a vampire might get out of control with bloodlust. As it had fortunately never happened—until the incident with Drogo—I never got to test that scenario. The assumption had been that any vampire attacking me would have been sent packing by the luminosity. If they started attacking it, I had no idea how much damage it could sustain before it crumbled.

Before I could respond to Raina, the powerful roar of an enraged beast startled the living daylights out of me.

"Drogo!" Raina whispered, joy and relief seeping through her voice.

The vampires started, their heads jerking towards the direction from whence the roar had emanated. The howls of countless wolves resonated before and behind us. The vampires, their faces contorted with terror, tried to run back to their vessels, but the pilots took off, having realized their men would never make it. In the distance, moving at an insane speed, the dark silhouettes of giant dire wolves were running towards us. However, the significantly bigger one leading the pack held all of my attention.

I would have recognized that dark brown fur anywhere, as well as those silver eyes. The vampires attempted to flee towards the other vessels. To my shock, the vampires behind us were also being overwhelmed by the Lycans.

In a dash of dark fur, Drogo effortlessly jumped over our shield and landed right behind one of the clones. His massive jaws closed around his neck, and he yanked left while his huge paw raked his target's back. The vampire's head tore right off, turning to ashes, while his body collapsed to the floor. Not a single drop of blood fell from the gaping wounds his claws had made, the visible flesh also turning to cinders.

Without pausing, Drogo chased after his next victim—a fully armored vampire—all the while shifting into his Lycan form. He stood on his hindlegs, with a strange additional segment around the ankles. In a savage movement, he sank his claws through the helmet and inside the skull of his victim before ripping him in two, as one would tear up a sheet of paper. He tossed each half to his sides—the empty rags of the armor landing on the ground in a shower of ashes—before resuming running on all fours towards the remaining vampires. It was a strange run as, in his Lycan form, his body was more humanoid. The rest of his companions also shifted out of their wolf form into their Lycan forms.

One of them stopped before us. I dropped my shield, recognizing Ulia despite his transformation.

"We're fine," Raina said, in a strong, firm voice, devoid of the pain I'd expect to hear from someone injured as she was. "Go have fun."

Ulia's savage and toothy grin should have frightened me, but a single thought crossed my mind: 'Give them hell.'

In the distance, the vampire vessels having abandoned their men on the ground, went into stealth mode. As if that had triggered some sort of self-destruct sequence, the handful of enemy ships that had been downed by our Lycan escort all exploded, leaving nothing but debris. Seconds later, a bright light detonated at the nape of the surviving vampires fighting the Lycan, ripping down the length of their spines. It affected even the corpses of the vampires that had only partially turned to ash, leaving nothing behind but empty armor.

"The bastards didn't want to leave any evidence that would let us track them back to the mastermind behind this," I said angrily.

"We both know who did it," Raina said in a hard voice. "And that's just the first salvo. He will stop at nothing to get you back. We had underestimated his resolve. It won't happen again. Help me up, child."

I wanted to argue, but the look she gave me kept me quiet. Still, she required little of my help, standing up mostly on her own power. I extended the staff back to her, which she gratefully accepted.

"You did beautifully, Thalia," Raina said, with undisguised pride that touched me deep within. "You just keep impressing me, more and more."

I smiled in gratitude, my throat too tight to speak. A small fleet of Lycan vessels making their approach saved me from my embarrassment. At this point, as Drogo and his troops were coming back towards us, it all felt like overkill. But then, they were coming to defend their Queen Mother.

As the adrenaline rush from battle began to wane, the reality of what had just happened—and of what could have happened—sank in. Suddenly feeling numb, my ears filled with white noise as Drogo came to stand before us. I watched him place a hand on his mother's cheek with a concerned look on his face as he spoke to her. His lips moved, and the rumbling sound of his voice filled my ears, but my brain couldn't register the words.

I have taken a life… Many lives…

I'd had no choice. It had been them or us. And yet, it distressed me. Drogo turned to me and spoke. Once again, I didn't hear his words, just the lovely sound of his voice. Instead, my brain just decided to notice random things. For example, Drogo had shifted back to his human form, and someone had given him some kind of loincloth for the sake of modesty. Raina was the only one with any blood on her, and the amount was far too minimal around her leg for receiving three bullets. There was an almost equal number of males and females still in Lycan form, probably not to shock me with their nudity as their fur hid the naughty bits. Despite her clothes being intact, except for the bullet holes, Raina was still in her Lycan form.

I couldn't tell if it was some sort of coping mechanism, but the more seconds lapsed, the more things I noticed. Drogo pulling me into his embrace snapped me out of my daze.

"You are safe, Thalia," Drogo whispered in my ear as he held me tightly against his hard body. "They didn't get you, and they never will."

I closed my arms around him and buried my face in his chest. He tightened his embrace with one arm, his other hand gently massaging my nape while he rested his head on top of mine. To my shame, my body trembled from the excess of emotions, stress, and fear I'd tried to keep under control during the attack.

I didn't know how long we remained like that, with him

speaking soothing words in my ear, but by the time I lifted my head, the other Lycans had dispersed, including Raina. A couple of them were busy fixing our crashed shuttle to get it airborne again. Others were picking up the remains of the vampires or rummaging through the carcasses of the blown-up vampire vessels.

I gasped when Drogo lifted me in his arms to carry me towards one of the new Lycan vessels that had come to our rescue.

"I can walk," I exclaimed in a whisper, embarrassed by the amused looks we immediately received. "They're all going to think I'm weak!"

With reason, too, after the way I'd just made a spectacle of myself.

"No, they will simply think I'm excessively protective, as it should be," Drogo said matter-of-factly. "If it's any consolation, my cousin Ulia carried my mother. And you've probably noticed by now that she isn't one to want pampering."

That did pacify me. Resting my head against his shoulder, I let him carry me to the ship, reveling in his warmth and strength, silencing the troubling thought gnawing at me.

CHAPTER 10
DROGO

I was livid, my blood still boiling with the need to slaughter more of those wretched bloodsuckers. The nerve of that bastard to have launched an attack in broad daylight, on my lands, and against the Lycan Queen Mother, spoke volumes about how emboldened Konstantin had become. While some of his rivals could have orchestrated such an attack and lay the blame at his feet, they never would have had time to mount it so quickly—failed though it was. It also spoke of fury and desperation. He would never forgive Thalia for choosing me over him.

Once the word spread that he had lost the first Golden Blood Maiden in centuries to 'an animal,' his detractors would never let him hear the end of it. The humiliation would only further fuel his rage and determination to strike me down and punish her. If *he* couldn't have her, he wouldn't allow anyone else to do so. I would need to seriously ramp up security around her.

This was *not* how I had envisioned the beginning of her new life among us. I'd swayed her with the promise of a life of peace, freedom, and safety. Yet, on day one, I'd utterly failed her. And in the upcoming days, weeks, and maybe even months, I'd ask her to forfeit some of her freedom to increase our ability to keep danger at bay. I could still feel her slender body trembling against me once her battle focus had shed. They had terrified my woman and harmed my mother. There would be hell to pay.

I cast a sideways glance at Thalia. She had regained her composure and was fussing over my mother while Darya was removing the bullets from her leg. An instant affection had formed between my mother and the lovely Maiden. It pleased me all the more that it was genuine and had nothing to do with what her blood could do for me. I knew exactly what thoughts were crossing my mother's mind as she stole appraising glances at Thalia. She'd be pleased to know I shared her thoughts. The mix of innocence, strength, intelligence, and compassion in the Blood Maiden appealed to me beyond words. Thalia wasn't a classic beauty, and yet she was stunning to me. I couldn't take my eyes off her, and let's not talk about my hands.

I loved that she didn't seem disturbed by my mother's Lycan appearance. The awe in Thalia's eyes when Darya finally removed the last bullet from my mother's leg, allowing her to shift back into her normal form, pleased me tremendously. The way the Blood Maiden had been conditioned to despise and fear Lycans, I had worried about how she would respond to us shifting. She'd seen me in both my wolf and Lycan forms, and yet, I'd perceived no fear from her, just relief and gratitude when she'd trustingly returned my embrace earlier. My arms ached to hold her like that again.

"Thank you, Darya," my mother said, hopping off the stretcher in the small infirmary of the vessel and back onto her feet. "Since you two haven't been officially introduced, please meet Thalia."

I groaned, annoyed with my mother. I had planned on doing the formal introductions after we'd looked after her and returned to Hundilinn.

"Thanks for stealing my thunder," I mumbled.

She sniffed haughtily at me. "You took too long," she said

dismissively before turning back to the other two females. "Thalia, this is Darya, the head trainer of our Iron Maidens."

"It's a pleasure to meet you," Thalia said warmly. "Thanks for coming to our aid. You Iron Maidens are quite badass. Then again, so is the Queen Mother," she added, glancing at my mother with undisguised admiration.

Darya snorted and flicked her silver white hair over her shoulder. Her pale blue eyes—that contrasted sharply with her dark brown skin—sparkled with pride. "Thank you for the kind words, but you two did a lot of the work for us. I shouldn't be surprised, considering that before she became Queen, Raina was one of the top duelists of the Iron Maidens."

"She was *fantastic*!" Thalia exclaimed, her eyes lit up with awe. "The way she spanked those vampires with that staff, it's like she was everywhere at once. I've never seen anyone move so fast and so gracefully."

My mother's cheeks flushed with pleasure. "Pfft, you were pretty badass yourself," she countered. "In fact, I think she might end up challenging you as the best Iron Maiden of this generation," she added while giving Darya a teasing look.

Thalia snorted in disbelief. "Hardly. I've taken enough self-defense training lessons to not be helpless, but I will never be able to rival you ladies. Your strength and speed alone guarantee it."

"You can fight?" I asked, pleasantly surprised. "That's wonderful. You and Darya should spar."

"If by spar you mean her training my sorry self to be less pathetic then, yes, I'm your woman," Thalia countered, looking slightly intimidated.

"I would love that!" Darya said with a grin.

"She's also pretty impressive with a blaster," Mother continued.

"And seems to have some interesting technology," I added,

eyeing Thalia with a questioning look. "That was a spectacular shield you'd both sheltered in."

"More impressive than you know, son," Mother intervened.

My jaw dropped when she recounted the effects of the special bullets Thalia had fired at the vampires, and how that high-tech shield had saved their lives at the last minute.

"Where did you get those?" I asked with undisguised curiosity.

"I made them," Thalia said, with an embarrassed shrug.

"You *made* that shield and those bullets," I asked, incredulous, while the two other females gaped at her.

"I just combined some existing technologies and tweaked them," she said in a defensive tone. "I couldn't afford bodyguards. So, for all the study hours not reserved for compulsory classes at the Academy, I took subjects that were ideal for self-defense, in one form or another."

"I didn't realize the Maiden Academy offered combat and engineering classes," I mused out loud.

"They'll offer whatever classes you want if they benefit enough from it," Thalia retorted with sarcasm laced with bitterness. "You see, for the duration of our training—which ends at the earliest on our eighteenth birthday, or at the latest on our twenty-fifth—we are expected to pay our tuition with regular blood donations. As you can guess, the rarer the blood, the higher the perks and privileges, and the more savings we make."

"Savings?" I asked, unsurprised by this 'exploitation' of the Maidens, yet still angered.

"We receive a small fraction of the proceeds from the sale of our blood as spending allocation," Thalia said. "Naturally, as mine brought in more substantial revenue, I was able to demand less traditional training and receive it."

"That's how you were able to buy the pod and fund your weapons craft," I said, understanding dawning on me.

She nodded.

"Well then," Mother said, staring at Thalia, "maybe we'll need to try and sweet talk you into another contract, but this time as a weapons designer."

"Agreed," I said, pleased with any way I could bind Thalia even more to us. Making her feel like a valued member of our society, giving her purpose and a career all her own that didn't rely on her genetics would go a long way.

"I'm not *that* advanced," Thalia argued, embarrassed. "I just hacked my way through things."

"Then we'll just have to provide you with the assistance and additional training you may need, should you choose to follow that path," I said casually.

Thalia smiled then nodded. "Okay. I would like that."

We finished the trip back home having an amiable conversation. I lured Thalia back to the front of the ship so that she could admire the bird's eye view of Hundilinn as we began our descent. My chest swelled with pride at the sight of our capital city. Its light colors and organic shapes were in direct contrast to the dark shades and hard lines of Verelinn. Thalia's beautiful green eyes sparkled as she gazed upon her new home, her plush lips parted in excitement.

Hundilinn sprawled organically on a large plateau. The buildings of varying heights were all made of pale stones, a plethora of woods, light metals, and an abundance of vegetation. From a distance, the canopy of the trees could almost make one believe that there were far fewer buildings than in reality. Roof and terrace gardens further reinforced that illusion. Yet, countless defensive walls, guard towers, and moats had been cleverly weaved into the design of the city in the most inconspicuous fashion. A large lake sprawled on the northwestern side of the city with a massive forest on the northeastern side. North of the city, partially carved into the rocky face of the Ion Rise mountain, Novik Castle stood steadfast, watching over its inhabitants.

"This is amazing," Thalia whispered, enthralled.

My smile widened. "Wait until you see inside!"

It was silly how excited I felt about showing her the city. At last, Gavril set down the vessel on the landing pad next to the castle. I cast a quick glance at Darya. She nodded to confirm she'd stay with my mother to make sure her Lycan healing had fully handled the bullet wounds. I gave her a grateful smile and turned back to Thalia.

"Come on, little human," I said teasingly. "Time to see your new home!"

She smiled, her eyes lighting up as she followed me to the exit doors. They parted with a soft hiss. On instinct, I grabbed Thalia's hand and pulled her after me as I went down the ramp. Halfway through, I realized what I had done and cast a worried sideways glance at her. Thalia was looking at our clasped hands with an unreadable expression. No anger or outrage emanated from her.

"I will not apologize for my unintended boldness," I said, matter-of-factly. Thalia's head jerked up, and she stared at me in shock. "You will soon discover that Lycans are very physical and affectionate. We hug, touch, cuddle, and kiss all the time. Occasionally, you will also stumble on a group of pups—sometimes also adults—all cuddled together in their wolf form."

"Really?" she asked, fascinated. "Just in random spots?"

"Sometimes random, but rarely," I explained. "This usually happens in front of a fireplace, or on the hot stones—by a garden or body of water—after the sun has warmed them. You'd be amazed just how soothing and relaxing it feels under the belly."

She burst out laughing, the delightful sound washing over me.

"Now, I'm stuck with an image of you, in that humongous wolf form of yours, sprawled on your belly, your tongue lolling, and purring with content. Or is it growling?" she asked teasingly.

I chuckled. "We don't purr. It would be more like a chuffing sound or a short growl. Then again, it's often a whimpering sound to express playfulness or happiness."

"Why do I have a hard time picturing you whimpering?" she asked, making a face at me.

"Don't you question my whimpering, woman!" I said with false outrage. "I'll have you know that I'm a proper wolf."

"Apologies, Wolfy," she deadpanned, with the most insincere air of contrition I'd ever seen.

I snorted and shook my head at her, delighted by this playful side of her. I had feared the strict grooming of her Blood Maiden upbringing might have made Thalia stiff and uptight, just the way the vampires liked their trophies. I gave her hand, that I still held, a gentle squeeze. She returned the gesture, her smile taking on a slightly timid quality.

Fuck me, I was falling hard and fast for this woman. And my Spirit approved.

The sound of voices ahead made her tense as we approached the guard post protecting access to the entrance of the castle and the rest of the city. The Iron Warriors manning it saluted me with a nod and a grin, before bowing their heads with friendly deference at Thalia. She returned the gesture, visibly intimidated but putting up a brave front.

I doubted she had noticed that she'd moved closer to me. It took all of my willpower not to slip my arm around Thalia's slender waist and pull her close against me. We passed the gate, leading to the large plaza sprawling in front of the castle's entrance. As always, it bustled with activity, between the children running around in their wolf form, the staff going about their business, and visiting Lycan clans starting preparations for the Summer Solstice celebration two weeks from now. A few of them, probably waiting for some shipment to arrive, were relaxing in their wolf form, under the warm rays of the sun.

I still reeled at the thought I would host it once again. Without Thalia, the three-day long event wouldn't have been a celebration of light, of the legacy of the Sun Wolves, and of the unbreakable friendship between the wolf packs of Karthia. Instead, the packs would have attended my funeral and then borne witness to the ascension of my appointed heir to my throne. Now, my beautiful Thalia would stand by my side. If only we'd had more time before then, I would have introduced her as my mate, not my Blood Maiden.

But that would wait until the next gathering of the packs when the Moon Well opened.

Four children in wolf form came barreling down on us. Thalia gasped, a sliver of fright fleeting over her features. I barely managed to repress a frown at that reaction. At least, there had been no disdain or disgust. She had shown no fear in front of my mother and my Iron Guards in their Lycan form. Why would she fear pups?

The young rubbed themselves against my legs and hers. Little Milos, ever the troublemaker, playfully nipped at my foot.

"It's okay, Thalia," I said in a reassuring voice. "The pups are not going to hurt you."

Her cheeks turned crimson, and she looked mortified, which further increased my confusion.

"I know," Thalia said sheepishly as she tried—but failed—to fully relax. "It's... It's a reflex. I've been trained to avoid anything that could possibly damage me in any way. I couldn't have a pet for fear it would accidentally claw or bite me. Any cut has the potential of resulting in a blood infection that would devalue me."

"Ah yes," I said, relieved. "Well, all that is in the past now. You no longer have to torture yourself with strict diets and a hyper sheltered life. Nobody here gives a fuck about the purity of your blood, least of all me. I promised you a normal life, and I will see that you get it, even against yourself. So, lose that reflex. You *will* have pups climbing all over you at the most unexpected —and often worst possible—times. Get used to it."

As if to prove my words, Milos literally started climbing her like a tree. Thalia yelped and, releasing my hand, she picked up the pup and held him at arm's length with bulging eyes. Milos wiggled in her hold, leaning his head forward towards her face. Understanding what he wanted, Thalia hesitated for a second before bringing him closer to her. The little brat immediately began licking her face. The poor female couldn't seem to decide whether to cringe or giggle. I wanted her to drop her guard and start enjoying life, but I realized it wasn't simply a switch she could turn off.

"That's enough out of you, pup," I said, grabbing Milos by his scruff.

Thalia gladly let go, looking somewhat traumatized. I fought the urge to laugh as I put the whimpering brat on the ground. He immediately started running circles around us. I didn't know if the Blood Maiden was actually a germaphobe, or if she was just fighting her instinctive panic. Then again, if you weren't used to getting your face licked like that, I could see how she'd be distraught to have some strange pup slobber all over her. Even now, her freckled face still glistened.

"It's okay to wipe it off," I said, failing miserably to hide my hilarity.

She gave me the oddest look, half-glaring, half-grateful, before pulling out of her pocket the tiniest case. It looked no bigger than a card but flipped open to reveal a thin sheet of white fabric the size of a hanky. Thalia picked it up and eagerly wiped her face with it. Although subtle, the scent of the sanitizing solution on it wafted to me. The Blood Maiden relaxed as she folded the hanky and put it back in the casing. Judging by the purplish-blue light inside the container, I assumed it to be UV rays that would kill any bacteria, making it usable again in the future. I intended to enjoy curing her of that phobia.

As she was putting the casing back in her pocket, Milos finally stopped his antics. Standing in front of her, he began shifting to his human form. Thalia stared in awe at the adorable little five-year-old, with his shaggy, dark brown hair, light brown eyes, heart-shaped mouth, and slightly upturned nose.

"Thank you for making King Drogo better," Milos said to Thalia with his baby voice. "We were very sad."

My heart seized then melted with love for the little rascal.

"Aww, you're very welcome, sweetheart," Thalia said, looking both moved and embarrassed. She gave me a shy sideways glance, before turning back to the boy. "I'm happy I was able to help."

"You did, and you made us all very happy," Milos said, coming to Thalia to hug her legs.

The poor female seemed unsure what to do. It dawned on me then how utterly deprived she had been of any type of displays of affection. I couldn't begin to imagine a life where I'd never given or received a hug. I ruffled the boy's hair. Thalia observed what I had done, then tentatively caressed his head after I removed my hand. Milos looked up at her and grinned with gratitude.

Letting her go, he took a couple of steps back then gave me a mischievous look that spelled trouble.

"I think she's very pretty. When I grow up, I'm going to take her as my mate," the boy said matter-of-factly.

Thalia snorted in disbelief. I glared at the brat.

"What you're going to do is run off before I spank that bare bottom of yours," I said.

Milos gasped, his eyes widening in pretend fear while protecting his behind with his hands.

"Okay, okay," he said submissively, while taking a couple of steps back. He then cast a glance at the other pups still in their wolf form, chasing each other around the plaza. "Let's go to the lake! Last one there has fleas!" Milos shouted with his high-pitched, childish voice.

The little brat made a face at me then immediately dashed

off. The other pups yipped or growled, initiating the shift back into their human forms. Stark naked, they took off, giving chase while shouting that he was cheating. Two of the adults from the Rock Plain Pack—a male and a female—lounging in their wolf form on the plaza, began shifting into their human form as they followed the children. While our young were all competent swimmers, we always had at least one or two adults supervising in case they played too roughly, and someone got hurt.

The adults both ran past us in their glorious nakedness. Thalia gaped at them, her eyes all but popping out of her skull. Her head jerked back towards the rest of the people on the plaza. Finding them all totally unfazed by that 'unexpected' display had her even more flabbergasted. She turned back to me with a disbelieving look on her face, waiting for me to explain what the heck had just happened.

I chuckled. "So… Nakedness is another thing you will need to get used to," I explained sheepishly. "We are all quite comfortable with nudity. We cannot remain dressed while in our wolf form, and we often shift in and out of it."

"I see," Thalia said, trying not to sound horrified.

"However, throughout the city and the surrounding woods, there are countless caches with clothes made of that same stretchy fabric your leggings are made of so they can fit pretty much anyone," I amended quickly. "People are rarely naked for more than a few minutes at a time."

"Well… You did say life here would be different," Thalia said, shock giving way to amusement. "Seeing how you shifters all seem amazingly fit, I guess I might as well enjoy the eye candy."

I couldn't repress a jealous growl. "Don't enjoy it too much," I grumbled.

Her eyes widened. "Am I hearing jealousy?" she asked, playfully.

"Yes," I said, matter-of-factly. She slightly recoiled, taken aback by my response. "Come on, let's get you inside," I continued without giving her a chance to respond.

I took her hand again and led her up the short flight of wide stairs to the entrance of the castle. To my relief, she came willingly and even closed her own hand around mine. I didn't want to come on too strong, too soon. But I was glad for this initial opportunity to plant the seed of my genuine attraction to her.

On our way to her quarters, I walked at a slow pace to allow her to gaze upon the beauty of her new home. Once again, pride swelled within me at the obvious awe plastered all over her delicate features. Her eyes flicked this way and that to take in her surroundings. Here as well, white and beige stones, exposed dark wood beams mixed seamlessly with forged metal railings and accents in a rustic-chic style.

"This corridor at the front leads to the first barracks. Through these large doors, you will find the gathering hall where we all usually hang out," I said, gesturing at it with a wave of my hand. "This other set of doors further down leads to the dining hall—which can also be accessed through the gathering hall. On the other side, you can see the meeting halls, and the gallery. The armory and the larger barracks are located at the back, next to the training grounds and opposite to the kitchen."

As I led her up the majestic central staircase leading to the second floor, Thalia let her finger run over the smooth carvings of the wooden top of the wrought iron railings.

"Most of these rooms are the personal quarters of relatives or high-ranking members of my Council," I explained as we reached the landing. "There are quite a few additional rooms here reserved for honorable guests. However, as our visitors are usually other packs, they often prefer a large cabin in the city, which they can share with their pack members instead. Your quarters are here at the back, in the most secure section of the castle."

We reached a large set of intricately carved wooden doors

with white gold accents weaved into them. I took a second to configure the biometric lock to her, drawing out the suspense, before finally opening the door.

I held my breath as she took her first step inside. Once again, I felt silly for being so nervous about her reaction. If she didn't like the décor, it would be very easy to rearrange and redecorate the space just the way she wanted. And yet, I wanted her to be amazed and to feel like she had just stepped into a fairy tale. I wanted her to have no regret about choosing a life here... with me.

And her reaction did not disappoint.

Mouth agape, she entered the room with slow steps, entranced by the luxurious suite that had been prepared for her. In the same tone as the rest of the castle, the large space included a massive four poster bed, a spacious living area with a three-cushion couch and a series of huge cushions to relax in, as well as a reading nook with a chaise lounge. On the opposite side, a small eating area complete with a minibar occupied the left corner by the window overlooking the terrace.

I followed her quietly as she made her way to the large set of glass doors leading onto the balcony. It, too, was immense. It gave a breathtaking view of the gardens and of the lake a short distance away. While it didn't have as direct a line of sight on the training grounds as in my room, you could still get a glimpse of the Iron Maidens training if you stood at the right angle at the right spot.

Thalia turned back to look at me in disbelief. "This is too much!"

"No, it's not," I said gently as I closed the distance between us. "This is your new home. I want you to be happy and fulfilled. Have you made a decision whether to stay here in the castle or have your own home in the city?"

"I hadn't really decided," Thalia admitted, tucking a lock of her light brown hair behind her ear. "I figured I would spend a few days here first while looking around at what was available."

"Good," I replied. "In truth, after this morning's incident, I would prefer you remain in the castle for the next couple of months until I have secured the Moon Well again. It would reassure me to have you in the most secure area of Hundilinn. I have no doubt that Konstantin will continue to seek a way to get to you."

To my relief, Thalia didn't argue, but nodded instead.

"A couple of months is actually good," she said in a soft voice. "It will allow me to decide for sure what I would prefer. Considering how posh this place is, you'll be hard pressed to get me to complain," she added with the most adorable shy laughter. "And yes, it will also make me feel safer."

All amusement faded from my face. I took a couple more steps towards her before taking her hands in mine.

"I am sorry I failed you this morning," I said in a contrite voice, anger and shame boiling within me. "I promised you would never be afraid anymore, and yet you almost got abducted. I will never underestimate him like this again."

Thalia smiled gently and squeezed my hands. "You have nothing to apologize for. You did hold your end of the bargain. You saved me. You saved *us*. Granted, you were a little late, but I'm sure I can find a few ways for you to make it up to me."

I snorted, loving the mischievous look in her eyes. "Why do I have a feeling you're going to put me through the wringer?"

"Maybe because I am?" she replied with a falsely evil grin.

"Looking forward to it," I said, my voice dipping deeper.

Her eyes slightly darkened, and I didn't miss the subtle shiver that ran through her. I was loving Thalia's physical responses to me. She was drawn to me, and I fully intended to nurture that sentiment until it blossomed into something far greater. Fighting the urge to kiss her, I let go of one of her hands. Pulling her after me with the other, I led her back inside towards the one section I hadn't shown her yet.

"This is your en suite bathroom," I said, opening the door to the large spa-like room. "And right there is your walk-in closet. Someone will soon bring up the bags of clothes Mother bought for you. As for your personal belongings still back at the colony, please let Master Elias know what needs to be done so that he can handle it on your behalf."

She nodded absentmindedly, her eyes glued to the four square meter mini pool that served as her bathtub.

"Are all your guest suites this insanely lavish?" Thalia asked disbelievingly as she turned to look at me.

I hesitated, which immediately had her narrowing her eyes at me with suspicion.

"No," I confessed somewhat sheepishly. "This is one of the royal suites."

Thalia stiffened. "What do you mean?"

I gestured for her to follow me outside of the bathroom and back into the main room. I crossed the room to an inconspicuous section of the paneled wall near the seating area. I pressed the center of the pattern, which depressed with a soft click. The panel slid open, revealing a small antechamber leading to another door two meters down.

"This door leads to my personal quarters," I said carefully. Right on cue, Thalia recoiled, an outraged expression descending on her face. "Relax," I said, lifting my palms in an appeasing gesture. "I know what it looks like, but it is not what you think. Your quarters would normally be given to the king's concubine or consort. In your case, it would have naturally been your suite as my Blood Maiden so that I may easily have access to you, regardless of the nature of the relationship between us."

I turned and tried to open the door to my room. It didn't open. I then closed the door to her room, locking us within the narrow space before trying to reopen it. It also didn't budge.

"As you can see, no one can enter either room simply because they want to," I explained carefully.

I then held my hand next to a discreet bio scanner that one would easily overlook without knowing the camera was hidden in the pattern carved on the wall framing the doors. A red light blinked, indicating access was denied.

"Now, wave your hand in front of it," I said in an encouraging tone.

Thalia licked her lips nervously and then complied. The light turned white and the door unlocked with a soft click. Her eyes slightly widened, and she tentatively turned the door handle, which gave in easily, allowing her back into the room.

"So, you see," I said gently, "I will never enter without your explicit consent. You do not yet know me enough to blindly trust me, but time will show you who I am. Hundilinn is the safest place for you. I have attacked you once when I was out of my mind with bloodlust. That will never happen again. No man will ever be more devoted to your well-being than I."

"I… I'm sorry for doubting you," she said sheepishly. "It's just—"

"I know," I said with understanding, interrupting her. "But do not apologize. With your upbringing and the way everyone you've ever met has treated you, your reaction is natural. Had you behaved differently, I would have given you a stern talking to about self-preservation."

She snorted and smiled shyly at me. Once again, I fought the urge to pull her into my embrace and kiss her.

"Whenever I want to see you, I will knock," I said. "Feel free to tell me to piss off."

She laughed. "If you come knocking in the wee hours of the morning because you're afraid of the monster in the closet, I definitely will. Any other time, I might allow you inside my fancy new place, if you're nice," she replied playfully.

I laughed and shook my head at her. "Then I guess I'll just

have to sit on the floor and scratch on your door, whimpering for hours until you finally take pity on me. I did warn you my whimpering skills were unrivaled."

"I actually believe you *would* do it," she said, eyeing me suspiciously.

I smiled noncommittally before sobering. "All kidding aside though, should you ever need me, don't hesitate to come in. While the door to my quarters is locked, the bio scanner will authorize you, my mother, and Ulia to enter through this secret door."

Thalia gaped at me. "Why would you authorize *me*?" she asked, winded.

"Because I have pledged myself to your safety and to your happiness," I answered matter-of-factly. "And because I know that you will never abuse this privilege."

She opened her mouth to argue, but a knock on her bedroom door silenced her. I closed the door to the secret passage and went to see who was calling. Gavril stood outside with Thalia's bags.

"I'm sorry to interrupt," Gavril said in an apologetic tone. "I'm bringing the Blood Maiden's bags. But I must also inform you that your presence is needed."

"Of course," I said in a friendly tone while suppressing the urge to frown in annoyance.

I had walked out of an important meeting to go rescue Thalia and my mother. However, right now, the last thing I wanted was to go deal with Karthian politics instead of enjoying the presence of my woman.

"That's fine," Thalia's soft voice said behind me. "I'm sorry for pulling you away from your other duties. Thank you for this wonderful room and for giving me a tour."

"My pleasure," I replied with a wink. "Take your time to settle in, then feel free to explore the castle to your heart's content. There are very few restricted areas, and they will be easy to recognize. Do not hesitate to ask anyone questions or directions. They will be happy to assist you. Lunch will be served in an hour from now. Do join us then. If you're hungry before then, don't be shy to raid the kitchen. We all do. I will see you soon."

"See you soon," she replied with a mysterious smile.

CHAPTER 11
DROGO

L eaning back in my stone throne at the head of the Council Chamber, I let my gaze roam over the pack leaders gathered in the room. They sat in a circle in front of me—although ellipse would be more accurate—as we resumed the discussion before Mother's distressed call had pulled me away.

Viktor's ears perked up, and he waved a hand over the light stone on the arm of his chair to claim the right to speak. Forcing myself to keep a neutral expression, I nodded for him to proceed while bracing for more of his doubts as to my ability to reclaim my role.

"Before Drogo was called away to rescue Raina and the Blood Maiden, I had presented a motion demanding that we still proceed with the appointment of an heir despite our Alpha's phenomenal recovery," Viktor said with a booming voice while he stared at me with his silver eyes that stood out starkly against his dark brown skin. "While I stand by my opinion that such an appointment should be done in all haste to avoid any upheaval in case something unfortunate would happen to our King, I am retracting that motion."

I recoiled, and my eyes popped, unable to hide my shock in

the face of such a sudden reversal. The twelve other pack leaders also gaped at him.

Viktor chuckled, his silver white hair—typical of the wolves of the Rock Plain Pack—bounced slightly on his broad and muscular shoulders. "I saw you in action during that rescue," he said with a shrug. "You have recovered far beyond what I would have deemed possible. I am therefore satisfied—at least for the time being—that you are able to fully resume your duties."

"Well, that's a relief," Axel said with his legendary sarcasm. "And here I thought we would endure your nagging for the next few hours."

The other Alphas snorted their agreement with the Holman Pack Leader.

"Oh, but you still will," Viktor said smugly, with an obnoxiously sweet smile. "The Queen Mother and the King's Blood Maiden were attacked on Lycan soil. This demands a swift and exemplary retaliation. Konstantin cannot be allowed to think he can strike at us like this and get away with it."

Many approving murmurs welcomed his comment. As one of the Ancients, and even a few years older than my father had been, Viktor held a huge sway over the Pack Council. Although I would never question his loyalty to the Lycans, he and I often butted heads. His old ways didn't mesh with the more modern direction I wanted to take our people and our role with the inhabitants of Karthia as a whole.

"Believe me, I want nothing more than to avenge this affront," I said in a growl. "The bastards shot my mother."

"And yet, I can already hear a 'but' in your voice," Viktor snarled with a sliver of disdain.

"BUT," I said, glaring at him, "we have no proof he's behind it."

"We don't need any fucking proof," Viktor shouted, rising to his feet in anger. "We all know damn well who is behind it. He's been coveting the rule of Karthia for centuries. That Maiden by your side ensures he will never rule. He will *not* tolerate that."

"Sit down, Viktor," I said, my voice dangerously low, my ears standing straight in dominance.

He held my gaze defiantly, the thick muscles of his arms bulging under the white fur that lined his forearms. Without shifting from my laidback position in my seat, I bared my teeth. My fangs descended while a low growl rose from my throat. Viktor's fingers twitched, his claws no doubt itching to come out. The other pack leaders watched silently, tension gradually building in the room. Viktor clenched his teeth and swallowed hard—not out of fear, but to silence the growl that wanted to rise in his own throat. With visible effort, he flattened his ears on his head in submission, lowered his gaze, and emitted the briefest of whimpers before resuming his seat.

A part of me wanted to show him my ultimate dominance by using compulsion to make him kneel before me, but I reined myself in. As the Alpha of his pack and as one of the Ancients of our species, it had to be extremely difficult for him to submit to the will of one he still considered a pup in many ways. I had no desire to humiliate him, but I also couldn't allow him to simply challenge me at every turn and undermine my authority. By his own standard, I *should* be making a show of my dominance to make him earn my forgiveness for this affront.

I kept my icy stare on him for a few seconds while the silence thickened, growing almost into a living entity. I then nonchalantly crossed my legs, while resting my hands on the arms of my throne.

"Retaliating without proof will only start an all-out war, which we cannot afford right now," I said in a neutral tone, indicating I considered this temporary rift settled.

"We would easily win that war, if it came to that," Andrei argued. "We would overwhelm their limited Daywalker numbers and obliterate the Fledglings once the sun goes down. As proven during your Golden Maiden's rescue mission, the Daywalker vampire clones are not a challenge."

Once again, the others expressed their agreement except for Axel and, surprisingly, Viktor.

"The idea is *not* a massacre of the vampires," Viktor said reluctantly. "But this insult to the Queen Mother, to the King, and to the human female who has saved his life cannot be simply ignored. Konstantin must feel our wrath."

"He will feel it soon enough," I said, calmly. "For now, his humiliation will have to do. According to my mother, Konstantin made a show of monopolizing Thalia's time during the Fair, letting the others know they didn't stand a chance at claiming her. When she fails to show at the ball tonight, there will be plenty of questions. And that's not mentioning that she is sending out rejection letters to the multiple offers she received. The word will spread like wildfire. Konstantin will be the laughingstock of Verelinn to have lost the first Golden Blood Maiden in centuries, not to Vlad but to a Lycan."

That comment had quite a few evil chuckles resonate through the room. Viktor pursed his lips, somewhat mollified but far from satisfied.

"But beyond the fact that we will *not* commit a vampire genocide over Konstantin, we cannot afford to waste any of our troops or risk a single one sustaining serious injuries in the upcoming weeks," I said in a serious tone. That caught everyone's attention, and they all stared at me questioningly. "When Soren claimed me slightly before my illness began, I felt the Moon Well stir."

The males all straightened in their chairs, eyes widening with awe, excitement, and disbelief.

"It's opening?" Viktor asked, a thrill in his voice.

I nodded slowly. "In two, maximum three moons, it will open," I said with a slight tension. "We need everyone in their finest physical shape, and in top-notch combat readiness.

Konstantin *will* try to steal the Well." The men nodded with grim expressions on their faces. "But that is a secondary concern. The last time the Well opened dates back three centuries ago."

"Fuck… The Guardian…" Viktor whispered, understanding dawning on him.

"Yes," I replied. "Something has been growing in the depths of Karthia for three hundred years. When it comes out, it will be devastating. So, this Summer Solstice, we will dance, drink, be merry, and give thanks for our countless blessings and the unity of the Lycan Packs of Karthia. But the morning after the end of the celebrations, everyone is to begin an intense training regimen until the Moon Well opens."

The leaders all agreed. In the next half hour, we discussed training and ironed out a handful of other pack and territory-related issues before the meeting ended. Everyone left but Viktor. I rose from my throne and descended the three steps to the floor level while he approached me.

"I meant no disrespect," Viktor said without preamble in a matter-of-fact tone. "I admit that I do not often share your views on the way of handling things. But while I enjoy challenging you, you have been a good ruler for our packs. I appreciate you showing more restraint than I did."

I smiled tauntingly. Although he only looked to be in his late forties, Viktor was even older than Konstantin, and nearly three times my age. This was the closest he would come to an apology. It made me all the happier that I hadn't humiliated him as I'd itched to. His last comment confirmed he'd been aware of it. But no good would have come out of it, for either of us.

"It was not out of any consideration for your mangy old pelt, Ancient," I said mockingly to defuse the situation. "I only did it so that I could demand Darya remain here longer to train my Iron Maidens as reparation."

Viktor frowned and glared at me. "I need my daughter back

to train our own troops," he grumbled. "You've hogged her long enough."

"There will never be such a thing as enough," I said dismissively. "Plus, I need her to train my female. Thalia already has strong combat skills, but she's been trained to fight other humans, not vampires. Darya is best suited to teach her how to overcome her human limitations."

Viktor tilted his head to the side, his eyes narrowing at me. "Your woman?" he asked.

"I plan on claiming her. She stirs me like no other, and even Soren clamors for her," I said, suddenly feeling awkward and hating my defensive tone.

Viktor's brow furrowed, and his silver eyes almost seemed to glow against his dark skin as he stared at me with great intensity.

"As the lore of the Sun Wolves states so clearly, Soren is the worst possible reference when it comes to choosing a female partner," Viktor said with a warning in his voice. "Be sure whose feelings are drawing you to her—yours or his? The Maiden's blood saved your life, but it could just as easily take it away, too."

Before I could respond, Viktor nodded in goodbye then walked out of the room. Soren rattled inside me, enraged by the Pack Leader's very valid comment. The brand of the Sun Wolf on my chest throbbed with my Spirit's discontent. I absentmindedly rubbed it, feeling it shift under my fingers as I exited the room as well.

CHAPTER 12
THALIA

The castle continued to take my breath away. Everywhere I looked, everywhere I turned, something new jumped at me that left me mesmerized. I could definitely see myself living here for the rest of my life. My suite exceeded the fanciest accommodations I had hoped for as a potential concubine. The bed was beyond divine, unlike the stiff cot I'd been sleeping on at the Academy. Having the staff making my bed for me, cleaning my room, and handling my laundry was a huge bonus. Waking up to a large buffet breakfast served in the dining hall every morning was also a perk I would gladly get used to.

Last night, I'd been both relieved and disappointed that Drogo hadn't come knocking at the hidden door connecting our respective rooms. I was torn by conflicting emotions as far as the Lycan King was concerned. The shameful truth was that as much as I'd dreaded becoming some vampire's property, I had been rather curious—if not eager—about finally exploring my sensuality. Since our contract wasn't that of a 'traditional' Blood Maiden, Drogo had not included an intimacy clause. A part of me wished he had.

I caressed the back of my hand, remembering how it had felt

when he'd held it to lead me around the castle. I loved the possessiveness and tenderness of it. And yet, I couldn't tell if it was attraction, brotherly affection, or merely his protective instincts that prompted this behavior. After our first brutal encounter, Drogo was going out of his way to prove to me that I had nothing to fear from him. I also suspected he wouldn't make any romantic moves towards me to avoid me thinking he was trying to pressure me into anything I didn't want.

But I *wanted* to get frisky, now that my virginity no longer weighed on my 'worth' in the market. I loved that I could freely choose who would be my first, not based on what they'd be willing to pay for it, but purely on mutual attraction and compatibility. However, losing my hymen wasn't my true priority. I just wanted to finally be able to touch and be touched, to be hugged and kissed, to cuddle with someone who cared about me as a person.

All evening yesterday, as we feasted in the dining hall, I'd seen so many children enjoying their parents' loving embrace, lovers exchanging passionate kisses or tenderly fiddling with each other's hair and fur. I'd felt so envious of one couple with the female in her human form petting her mate in his wolf form as he rested his head on her lap. I had glanced at Drogo, sitting next to me at the head of the table, and my fingers had hitched with the urge to sink them in the patch of dark brown fur on his nape.

Yeah, I wasn't necessarily ready to go all the way, but I wouldn't mind doing some serious cuddling and heavy petting with him. Maybe if I let him drink directly from me, he wouldn't be able to resist the urge to cop a feel.

Chasing away my wandering thoughts, I made my way down the stairs to head towards the gathering hall with its massive windows, a number of which were actually large doors that gave access to the garden and to the nearby training grounds. Darya would be giving me my first training session—or rather assessing my current combat skill level. I'd never felt so intimidated.

Back in the colony, I'd felt proud of my unrivaled talent among other Blood Maidens. On top of my golden blood setting me as different, I'd further been considered an oddity for my choices in training. Unlike the others that had mainly focused on disciplines that would make them the perfect hostess, companion, and lover, I had leaned towards self-defense. From combat, to weapons engineering, to basic biology, each of these tools had allowed me to get at least some illusion of control over a life that had never truly been mine until now.

But the Lycans' head trainer was nothing like the human female that had trained me. Darya could make mincemeat out of me without breaking a sweat. At least, the kindness she had displayed yesterday when I first met her, and the gentle way she had handled Raina while removing the bullets gave me hope she wouldn't rough me up too much for this first assessment.

However, just as I was stepping off the stairs, Ulia's voice calling my name startled me. My head jerked towards him as he closed the door of the gathering hall behind him then hastily approached me. At 6'4, Drogo's cousin was almost at a comparable height with him, though they didn't resemble each other much. Still, he had the dark brown hair shared by most of the Lycans of the Hundilinn Pack. He was ruggedly handsome with a square jaw, stunning pale blue eyes, and adorable dimples on his cheeks that softened his otherwise predatory expression. Like his cousin—and frankly most of the Lycan males—he was broad shouldered and with muscles for days. But I constantly wanted to brush aside the rebellious lock of hair that stubbornly kept falling over his right eye.

"Yes?" I asked, my friendly smile fading at the sight of the tension stiffening his shoulders.

"Unexpected visitors have just landed in the city and have requested an immediate audience with you," Ulia said with a clipped tone that expressed a mix of contempt and anger aimed at whoever those mysterious guests were.

"Visitors?" I asked, although I immediately suspected who it might be. Then again, Konstantin wouldn't be so foolish as to show his face here after yesterday's attack.

"A vampire and human delegation is demanding we release you at once from captivity," Ulia spat out with barely repressed anger.

It struck me as odd how unafraid I felt in the presence of such a powerful being, clearly angered. And yet, I felt safe, knowing his anger wasn't aimed at me but also sensing his protectiveness of me. In truth, since my arrival, every single Lycan had made me feel the same. It was wonderful.

"Well then, let's go reassure them that all is fine," I said in a lighthearted tone despite the tension I felt rising within.

I understood why they were here. Under different circumstances, had I heard about this situation happening to another Blood Maiden, I would expect—if not demand—that the Grand Council of Verelinn intervene at once. The Grand Council was constituted of representatives of the vampires, the humans and—in theory—of the other alien species also established on Karthia. But all of those seats had fallen to the wayside as most otherworlders usually left within a few months or a few years of their arrival here. The few stragglers that remained on the planet were much too few in numbers to justify having a seat. And, until yesterday, I hadn't even known that original Karthians still lived.

In truth, the Grand Council was essentially controlled by the vampires—and more specifically by Konstantin—with a token bone thrown at humans to keep them in line. However, Elmund, the human Ambassador, had all but sold us out in exchange for a life of comfort for himself.

Ulia nodded and gestured for me to follow. He had almost touched the small of my back to nudge me forward but caught himself at the last minute. I was once more reminded of what a physical people the Lycans were. It would take me a bit of getting used to in order to not be so instinctively jumpy whenever someone came a little too close to my bubble. However, I was genuinely looking forward to it.

I loved how laid back and informal everyone was here. At first, it had shocked me to see how rarely Drogo was referred to by his title and the lack of deferential behavior towards him. It would have greatly disturbed me if not for the obvious respect and affection his people bore him. Truth be told, this lack of pompous and self-aggrandizing behavior was quite a turn on.

Ulia opened the doors to the gathering hall and held it for me. To my shock, Vlad, another vampire, and Ambassador Elmund were standing in the center of the room in front of the massive stone fireplace. It was framed on each side by three-meter-high sliding windows that gave access to the gardens. The tables, benches, and variety of seats alongside the walls of the imposing rectangular room with slightly rounded corners, all sat empty. On the balcony circling the room, a handful of guards watched us. Standing a few meters in front of the delegation, a very angry Drogo was glaring at them.

Looking completely unfazed by his host's anger, Vlad's features softened, and he gently smiled at me as soon as I entered the room. Just like in my memory, the Vampire Lord looked beyond scrumptious in his form-fitting, gothic black clothes mixing fabric, leather, and silver detailing around the straps on his chest. With a certainty I couldn't explain, I felt the elder vampire's relief at seeing me unscathed. He had genuinely been concerned for me.

"Hello, Thalia," Vlad said with that delightfully seductive voice of his. "I am pleased to see you well. You were sorely missed at the ball last night."

"Hello, Vlad," I said in a friendly tone laced with guilt. "I am sorry but, as you can see, my plans changed at the last minute."

"Indeed," he said in a neutral tone.

The Vampire Lord turned to look at Drogo. His gaze was firm but not hard and, thankfully, devoid of the contempt Konstantin had displayed and that I had feared Vlad would as well.

"If you wouldn't mind, we would like to speak with the Blood Maiden in private," Vlad said politely.

"I do mind," Drogo said in a growly tone, his back stiffening.

"We cannot speak freely with the maiden to assess her current situation with your presence intimidating her," the second vampire said with a haughty attitude that made me want to punch him in the throat.

"I can show you intimidation," Drogo said, taking a menacing step towards him.

I instinctively placed my hand on his forearm and gave it a gentle squeeze. Drogo immediately stopped, his eyes flicking towards my hand before looking up at my face.

"It's okay," I said in a gentle voice. "They wouldn't be crazy enough to try anything inappropriate while surrounded by your guards and while standing within your very castle. I also happen to trust Vlad."

The Vampire Lord and the Lycan King both slightly recoiled upon hearing those last words. I'd surprised myself as well by speaking them out loud. And yet, I realized I genuinely meant them. Which was odd considering I barely knew him. Vlad's features further softened, and the strangest expression crossed his features.

"If you are certain," Drogo said reluctantly.

"I am," I said with a smile, hoping to soothe him a little.

He gave me a stiff nod, glared at the delegation—with an extra savage glint in his eyes when they stopped on the second vampire—then headed to the other end of the gathering hall, near the large doors connecting with the dining hall. He leaned against the wall, arms crossed over his muscular chest, while staring at us with a grumpy expression. I barely repressed a smile, feeling both flattered and amused by his protectiveness that felt borderline possessive—not that I minded in the least.

Vlad rubbed the stone on one of the three large rings that adorned his hands. Having seen Raina do it before in Verelinn's Great Hall, I didn't panic this time as he activated the cone of silence around us. With their keen hearing, Ulia, Drogo, and his guards on the balcony would otherwise be able to hear everything.

"Thalia, please allow me to introduce you to Ambassador Yakov, representing the covens, and Master Elmund, the human Ambassador who I assume you are familiar with," Vlad said.

I nodded politely at each of the two males. They returned the gesture, Elmund with the eagerness of a starstruck fan, and Yakov with the superior air of the excessively rich and entitled assessing the worthiness of someone they considered inferior. And yet, the hunger in his eyes was undeniable, reminding me all too well what I had avoided by coming here instead of becoming the Blood Maiden of a vampire.

"I admit that I was extremely disturbed when I received your message yesterday informing me of your decision," Vlad said in a gentle tone. "As you can guess, Konstantin is livid."

I barely managed to repress a smile at that last comment, especially hearing the amusement in Vlad's voice as he said it. I actually wished I had been a fly on the wall spying Konstantin's reaction when he had been informed of me leaving with the Lycans. His tantrum must have been of epic proportions.

"As you can guess," Master Elmund said, "we were extremely concerned that you had been enthralled or taken against your will. Why else would a Golden Blood Maiden reject the offers from the High Lords of Verelinn in favor of the beasts of Hundilinn? Have the Academy's Matrons not warned you of the nature of the Lycans?" he asked, looking both shocked and outraged.

"First of all, they are far from being mindless animals," I

replied in a clipped tone. "Would beasts have constructed such a magnificent dwelling, and allowed you to walk in here unscathed to discuss with me?"

"You're oddly defensive of the Lycans for someone who had never interacted with them until a couple of days ago," Yakov countered. "Such devoted loyalty in so short a time reeks of compulsion."

Elmund nodded slowly in agreement, while Vlad merely studied my reactions to their words.

"I am not under any compulsion," I said in a firm tone, hoping to convince them. "King Drogo made me an offer I simply could not refuse, and I gladly accepted it. No one coerced me into coming to Hundilinn. I am here of my own free will. I cannot be compelled."

I no sooner spoke those words than my protective necklace began warming against my skin. The spindly tingle at the back of my skull confirmed an attempt at compulsion. I immediately knew who it came from. My head jerked angrily towards Ambassador Yakov.

"Cut it out!" I hissed. "How dare you try to control me?"

His two companions turned to look at him: Elmund with outrage and Vlad with fury. Yakov flinched, and yet lifted his chin defiantly.

"It was the only way to make sure you are indeed free of any mind-control," Yakov said stiffly. "Why else would a Blood Maiden in her right mind refuse an offer from Lord Konstantin? Even if the wolf had made you a nice offer, you should have given the High Lord the opportunity to counter it. Credits are not an issue for him."

"Or me," Vlad added.

I softened as I cast a glance at him, feeling a sliver of guilt where he was concerned.

"While there is no question that credits are important, they aren't everything. On top of a very generous compensation, King

Drogo has given me what vampires can't; peace of mind and a normal life." I hugged my midsection and paced a few steps away from them before turning back to face them. "You don't know what it's like to constantly live in fear, having to watch over my shoulder to check if someone is about to abduct me, or a jealous rival is attempting to poison me. Everywhere I walk in the streets of Verelinn, countless pairs of eyes are staring at me like I'm their next meal."

"They wouldn't have dared, Ms. Velky," Edmund scoffed as if I'd said something ludicrous.

"No one would risk a High Lord's wrath," Vlad said softly. "If anyone disrespected or threatened my Blood Maiden—and I can speak for Konstantin as well on that front—we would decimate their entire coven."

"And I believe you," I replied in all sincerity. "That still wouldn't have changed the fact that I would have walked around constantly feeling like prey."

"That is a minor concern," Yakov said dismissively. "If it can reassure you, the High Lords will have no problem providing you with extra security. After all, you are a Golden Blood Maiden."

"That is a kind offer, but the other reason, and probably the main one for my choice is my long-term health," I said sternly. "You don't need me to tell you what toll feeding vampires takes on our bodies. Most Maidens are used up in less than five years, the luckier ones stretching it for six or seven years. And then they keel over from heart failure in their early forties. King Drogo has offered me a contract that will put no strain on my health. Here, I get to live a full, normal, and healthy life. No vampire will offer me that."

As I spoke those words, my heart tightened at the sight of the expression on Vlad's face. Despite his efforts to hide his sadness, I could clearly read it on his noble features.

"Those other Blood Maidens are expendable," Yakov said

disdainfully. "You have golden blood. Lord Konstantin will want to keep you healthy for decades. So—"

"My decision has been made, Ambassador," I interrupted, starting to get seriously annoyed.

"Then you need to revise it and state your terms. Lord Konstantin—"

"Enough with Konstantin!" I shouted with exasperation. "Even without the Lycans, he would *not* have been my choice."

I kicked myself as soon as the words left my mouth. And yet, a part of me rejoiced to have finally put it out there and shut that aggravating vampire ambassador up. While Yakov and Edmund gaped at me, Vlad took a few steps towards me, his gaze hypnotizing me.

"Because I would have been your choice," he said, matter-of-factly.

I swallowed hard as I gazed upon his beautiful face, then nodded. My throat tightened as the same sad expression fleeted over his features.

"Leave us," Vlad said over his shoulder at his companions.

"What?" Edmund exclaimed.

"We can't leave like this!" Yakov countered with outrage.

Vlad partially turned to look at them, the feral expression on his face both thrilling and terrifying. "Argue with me again. I dare you," he said in a chilling voice.

The human Ambassador Edmund didn't need to be told twice, and immediately started moving towards Ulia, still standing by the door. Yakov pinched his lips, visibly fighting the urge to retort something. Clearly, Konstantin had sent him as his envoy, and that was making him dangerously cocky. Still, he wisely kept his mouth shut and stiffly walked towards his human companion. Vlad continued to glare at him until Ulia let both males out of the room.

The Vampire Lord then turned back to me, his face melting into a soft expression. To my surprise, he extended both his hands towards me. On instinct, I placed mine in his without hesitation. His palms were incredibly soft and surprisingly warm. I'd always assumed vampires would be cold. His thumbs gently caressed my knuckles, while his gaze bore into mine.

"I understand all the arguments you have laid out, and do not dispute their merit," Vlad said in a soft voice. "I am willing to revise my offer to match the amount of blood you agreed upon with the King and triple your security. You tell me what you want so this will work for you."

"Oh, Vlad. This would never be enough for you," I said apologetically, my heart breaking for him. "Drogo only needs my blood once a week for a couple of months until he's fully attuned with his Spirit," I said, not wanting to mention the imminent opening of the Moon Well.

"So, you will be free in a couple of months?" Vlad asked, perking up.

I licked my lips nervously, hesitating before I answered. "Well, yes. But I may remain here afterwards, under his protection, and live off of the extremely generous compensation he has given me."

"Come to me instead," Vlad pleaded, taking a step closer to me. "You feel the chemistry between us. We hit it off the minute we met. Tell me I'm wrong."

I bit my bottom lip, unable to deny the truth of his words.

"I wish to make you my consort because I believe we can be happy together. You know I will do all in my power to give you the life you've always wanted. While I do want your blood—like any other vampire—I don't *need* it. Unlike Konstantin, I'm quite satisfied with synthetic blood, and I only drink once a week from my familiars to preserve my Day Walking ability. Think about it. Finish healing the King, then come to me."

I stiffened, my eyes slightly widening at his words. How did he know?

A smug smile stretched Vlad's sensuous lips. "I have eyes

and ears where it matters. I know of Drogo's 'illness' and of the 'incident' between you. I suspect the Well is opening soon. And if I'm correct, the Lycan King will need to be at his best."

I neither denied nor confirmed his claims, shifting the topic instead.

"Konstantin would never allow you to have me," I countered.

"Fuck Konstantin!" Vlad hissed. "He doesn't control me, and I am far stronger than he realizes. If concerns over him are what's making you hesitate, wipe those fears from your mind. His time is running out."

"I... I don't know, Vlad," I said, shaking my head in confusion.

A part of me really wanted to explore what could happen between us, but Hundilinn, and especially Drogo, felt like home. As much as Vlad attracted me, when I thought of a man embracing me, it was the Lycan King's face that floated before my eyes. In a way, even though he'd only dry humped me in the hospital, Drogo was technically my first—the first man to have ever held me so intimately and given me an orgasm.

"It's him, isn't it?" Vlad whispered with a sad smile. "You've been smitten by all that lustrous fur," he added in a teasing tone.

My face heated, giving me away. "He's a good man," I said apologetically.

To my shock, Vlad nodded slowly. "He is," he conceded. "But he's not me." The Vampire Lord released my hands and caressed my right cheek with his knuckles. "I would see you happy, Thalia. Once your duty here has ended, should your heart still waver, know that I'll be right here waiting. In the meantime, if you ever need anything, do not hesitate to call me."

He didn't wait for me to answer, not that I would have known what to say. After a light bow of his head, Vlad made his way towards the exit with that incredibly fluid gait of his. I felt Drogo approach long before I heard his footsteps. I turned around to face him, taken aback by the strange expression of his face. He looked troubled.

"Are you all right?" he asked with concern.

"Yes," I said with a nod. "I made it clear I came here by choice and of my own free will."

Drogo studied my features as if they held the answer to the questions swirling in his mind.

"Without my offer, he would have been your choice," Drogo said, matter-of-factly.

I flinched internally, suddenly feeling guilty. There was no reason for me to feel that way, and yet, I couldn't help it.

"Yes," I admitted. "He strikes me as a really good man."

"He is," Drogo conceded, the same way Vlad had done for him. "Do you regret accepting my offer?"

I recoiled and stared at him in shock. "No, not at all," I said in all sincerity. "Vlad is a charming man. I believe he could give me a good and happy life. But Verelinn is not for me. I've only been here for a couple of days, but I've never felt so welcomed and so at peace anywhere else before. This feels like home."

Drogo beamed at me.

"Good answer," he said, tension bleeding from his broad shoulders. "You cannot see it right now, but my wolf form is wagging its tail."

I burst out laughing and gave him a playful tap. "Silly man."

"Come," he said, taking my hand as was his wont. "Now that your vampire boyfriends are done pestering you, let me take you to Darya for your training before she loses her shit. She's a real slave driver, that one."

I snorted and grinned at him, while reveling in the warmth of his strong hand holding mine. Yes, this man, this place, felt like home.

CHAPTER 13
DROGO

I watched Mera shyly approach me as I stood by the massive fireplace in the gathering hall. I suppressed an amused smile as she strutted in that typical seductive style of hers whenever we were alone. I didn't understand why she persisted in her attempts at luring me into her bed. I had made it clear to all of my Blood Servants that there would be no physical involvement between us.

She was a fourth-generation human from Zima, a Karthian village southeast from Hundilinn. Pretty, with the very pale skin of the original Karthians passed down to her, she used to come once a month to give me some of her blood, in rotation with my other four Blood Servants. Over the ten days since my return from the hospital, and for the next month, I'd increased that frequency as I needed a significantly higher amount of blood for me to fully recover and complete the bond with my Spirit. Truth was, Soren was consuming all of what I was getting from my Blood Servants. The synthetic blood that Dr. Tanner had given me at the hospital and the small amount that I continued to drink daily served to restore me.

"Hello, King Drogo," Mera said demurely, while batting her eyelashes.

I fought back the urge to snort in the face of her behavior in such direct contrast with the incredibly revealing second skin of a dress she was wearing. Dark blue—my favorite color—with a plunging neckline and a very short skirt, the dress left little to the imagination. It also greatly invited gropey hands to explore what was on full display. However, beyond the fact that I had made it a rule not to have affairs with the females from the Karthian villages, Mera never appealed to me. We had nothing in common personality-wise, and I didn't believe she particularly cared for me beyond seeking me as a way to climb the ladder.

Still, I believed she was physically drawn to me. But now, even more than before, her chances of luring me into her bed were beyond nil. The only female that my hands itched to touch was a lovely Blood Maiden who I would be taking on a visit to the Moon Well in the next twenty minutes or so. Darya should be done with her training by now, and Thalia had requested time to freshen up first.

"Hello, Mera," I said in a friendly voice. "Thank you for accepting my request to come in sooner to accommodate my change of plan."

"That is not a problem, my King," Mera said with a soft smile. "I am always at your disposal, whatever your needs. It is my honor to please you."

This time, it was the urge to roll my eyes that I needed to fight back. I never quite understood why some people would repeatedly throw themselves at someone that had clearly expressed, on multiple occasions, that they were not interested. I couldn't decide if it was a lack of self-respect or because they genuinely believed that, with enough persistence, they would eventually get what they wanted.

"That is most kind of you," I replied in a polite tone.

Raising her left hand at the back of her head, Mera pulled her long, light-brown hair behind her shoulder. She then tilted her head to the left, exposing the pulsing vein on the right side of her neck. My Spirit stirred with hunger, although with far less enthusiasm than when I thought of drinking from Thalia again. Four more days to go before I would once more savor her divine golden blood.

I closed the distance between Mera and me, then slipped my hand around her neck to hold her nape. She pressed the palm of her free hand to my chest. She'd always done that in the past. In fact, most of my Blood Servants did as well, some of them nervously gripping my shirt while waiting for the sting of my bite. It had never bothered me before. But right this instant, specifically with Mera, it took all of my willpower not to tell her to take her hand off me. For some silly reason, it felt like cheating on Thalia.

Like most blood drinkers, I didn't like using a phial. I never had before with any of my Blood Servants. I hated that Thalia and I would be using them. But, right now, I'd give anything to be using one with Mera. Silencing my unease, I leaned forward and gently sank my fangs in her neck. She gasped, her nails digging into my chest under the initial sharp pain of my bite.

As her blood flowed into my mouth, its metallic taste exploding over my taste buds, I injected the female with some of my aphrodisiac, giving it a few seconds to take effect. It was nowhere near enough to actually get her aroused, let alone as mad with lust as I'd made Thalia in the hospital. But it would suffice to numb the pain caused by my fangs.

I sucked in her blood in nine long pulls, gulping down the 100 ml agreed upon. Just as I was pulling my fangs out, the discreet sound of the gathering hall's main door opening reached my sensitive ears. My eyes jerked up to see who it was. My stomach dropped at the sight of Thalia. She froze, shock and something akin to betrayal fleeting on her features before she plastered a neutral expression on her face.

"Stay!" I called out when Thalia made to leave.

She complied, back stiff and the soft lines of her jaw hardened by her clenched teeth. The Blood Maiden discreetly pinched her lips when I licked Mera's bite wounds to seal them before straightening and taking a step back. My gaze shifted to Mera, who stared back at me with hooded eyes. I gave her a strained smile then quickly tapped a few instructions on the interface of my bracer. She cast a glance behind her. At the sight of Thalia, her shoulders drooped.

"There," I said, cordially to Mera. "Your payment has been transferred. See you in two weeks?"

She nodded with a forced smile, her disappointment plain to see. "Good day to you, King Drogo," Mera said in a small voice before turning on her heels.

"And to you, Mera," I said, watching her walk towards the exit.

Thalia moved a couple of steps to the side to make way for my Blood Servant. She gave her a polite smile devoid of the usual warmth she expressed towards everyone else. I extended a hand towards her. She hesitated for a split second before complying. I half expected her to ignore my hand but, to my great delight, she placed hers in mine.

"What you just saw upset you," I said in a gentle voice. "Why?" Her face heated, and she squirmed with embarrassment. "This is not a reproach," I continued in the same appeasing tone. "As you have probably noticed in the ten days since your arrival here, Lycans are very blunt. We speak our minds and discuss issues openly."

Thalia licked her lips nervously and chose her words carefully before speaking. "I'm not upset per se," she said hesitantly. "I... I didn't realize you had other Blood Maidens. I thought you only needed to drink once a week."

"I don't have other Blood Maidens," I said firmly. "Mera is one of my Blood Servants. There are no contracts like with a

Blood Maiden, no exclusive bond or relationship. Her blood is common. Before you, she was one of the five Servants I used on a rotation—a different one, once each week. But for the next month or two, I need 100 ml of blood three times a week to fully recover from my illness. I may seem back to normal to you, but my regular self is bigger and far more muscular than I currently am."

Her eyes widened, and her lips parted in shock while she gave me a slow once over. I loved the way her gaze roamed over me. I loved even more that she was jealous of me drinking from another female. I hadn't meant for her to witness it, but I was glad it allowed us to have this conversation.

"Wow, you will be quite the beast," she mused out loud.

"I hope that doesn't scare you," I said, only partially kidding.

She absentmindedly shook her head, her gaze still lingering on my chest. Thalia frowned then examined my features before her eyes locked on my lips.

"You drank from the source," she said pensively. "How do you know you haven't drunk more or less than 100 ml?"

"Practice," I said with a shrug. "One pull—or mouthful if you prefer—is between 10 and 12 ml for me. I pull nine times on her, so that puts me either right under or barely over."

"You prefer that way?" she asked.

"Of course," I said, matter-of-factly. "No blood drinker likes phials, but they make perfect sense when interacting with a Blood Maiden. With Blood Servants, it is unnecessary. The purity of their blood is irrelevant, the amount drawn from them is usually small, and the frequency is low."

"You didn't ask it of me," Thalia said with a certain tension in her voice.

I tilted my head to the side and smiled. "You are a Blood Maiden, and we do not have an exclusive contract. I am in no position to make such a request from you."

Thalia held my gaze for a few seconds with the most indecipherable expression on her face. I was no longer hungry, but my mouth watered at the thought of biting her.

"I see," she said at last. "Well, I'm happy you are getting what you need to make you better."

"So am I," I replied teasingly. "But come, we have some sightseeing to do!"

I gave her casual outfit an approving glance. Her comfortable hiking shoes, dark grey leggings, and casual shirt were perfect for where we were headed.

Thalia smiled, the lingering tension bleeding from her shoulders as I tugged on her hand for her to follow me. We exited the gathering hall through the large sliding windows that opened onto the garden. The packs were busy setting up the huge banquet tables, the pit for the bonfire, and the even bigger ones where some of the meat for the feast would be roasted.

People waved at us as we walked past them on our way to the garage, a short distance from the landing pad. Initially, I had planned on taking a shuttle to the Moon Well but thought better of it. I wanted Thalia to discover the beauty of my territory—her new home—and for her to learn a bit more about us.

Gavril had already prepared the hover bike we would be riding together. I didn't have to ask Thalia to know that, as a Blood Maiden, she wouldn't have learned how to ride such a 'dangerous' vehicle. She eyed it with a mix of worry and excitement. But the latter dominated. I loved that about her. Even though she continued to struggle with shedding her old habits indoctrinated over her entire life—and probably would for weeks, if not months, to come—Thalia was making real efforts to embrace new things. And the best part was that it wasn't forced. The prospect of trying new things and taking risks genuinely thrilled my female.

We didn't mount the bike right away. I set it to follow, and the vehicle simply hovered alongside me as we made our way to the Wisdom Trail. It was an immense passage carved through the

Ion Rise mountain range to provide Hundilinn with a ground shortcut to the northern forest and the Moon Well. I loved that no sooner was I done with the bike than Thalia gave me her hand again. It had become the norm for us whenever we walked side by side.

The giant doors were located at the northern end of the garden, on the left side of the castle. The doorframe had been carved directly into the rock of the mountain. It depicted the profile of two Sun Wolves facing each other, with one hand extended towards the fat moon that floated overhead in the middle of the two doors. A blue light shot out from the moon as we approached the five-meter-high doors, scanning me.

"Welcome to the Wisdom Trail," I said, waving at the entrance.

The massive doors parted almost silently. Thalia's eyes widened, curiosity and surprise etched on her lovely face.

"I had expected quite the ruckus and lots of grinding noises as they opened," Thalia said with a bit of awe.

"They used to," I said with a grin. "Technology has come a long way since the primitive days when this had first been constructed."

Indeed, over the years, while we had maintained most of the original designs and architecture, both inside the castle and in the dwellings surrounding the city, we had performed many technological upgrades. Greater ease of function had naturally been a factor. However, security and defense had been an even bigger one.

I walked quietly next to Thalia as her gaze flicked this way and that, taking in the beauty of the intricately carved murals that covered the long passage to the other side of the mountain. Everything from Soren falling from the heavens and the five hundred Sun Wolves that had followed him, to the Bloody Wedding, the curse Selene cast onto the Karthians, and Oleg's ascension. The work was exquisite. Despite being stylized, each character depicted was easily recognizable.

At the top of the murals, in one long strip on each side of the cave, a series of portraits were lined up in a cameo with its symbol above it. Thalia stopped dead in her tracks in front of the first one. Her head jerked towards me, her eyes staring at my chest as if she could see it through my shirt before looking back up at me.

"That symbol above that portrait is the same as the one on your chest. Isn't it?" she asked with a look of wonder on her face.

I nodded then lifted my shirt for her to see it. She took a step closer, examining its lines. Soren stirred in approval. Thalia slightly recoiled, then blinked a few times before staring at it again.

"Did it move?" she asked, flabbergasted.

"I don't know," I said teasingly. "You tell me."

She held my gaze for a moment, her face taking on that slightly tense expression she always did when her wheels began turning in earnest. She had been forming a number of theories about my people and the vampires ever since my mother had told her about the legend of Soren. I couldn't wait to hear what conclusions my clever little female had reached on that front.

Without a word, she looked back down at my mark then glanced back up at the carving on the wall. She pursed her lips then slowly nodded to herself. I would have given anything to hear the thoughts crossing her mind.

"So, I'm guessing the symbol above all the other portraits are the marks of each of the Sun Wolves depicted on those carvings?" she asked, although it was more of a statement.

"That's correct," I replied in a factual manner.

"Which means that if anyone has been 'claimed' by one of them, they would bear their mark on their chest like you do," she mused out loud.

"Yes," I said. "During the Summer Solstice celebration, some of the tribal dances will be performed mostly naked—but with the naughty bits covered," I added teasingly. "You will see quite a few of them bearing the mark of their respective Sun Wolf."

She nodded again with a pensive expression on her face before starting to walk again. I loved the fascination with which she examined each of the scenes, asking intelligent questions here and there about what she was seeing. And then she froze when she reached one of the more recent sections—although recent was a relative term.

"Is that Konstantin?" she whispered, her voice filled with shock.

"Yes," I answered in a neutral tone.

She took a step closer to the carving and ran her fingertips over it, her index finger lingering on the marking on his chest.

"That's the mark of Soren," she said, turning to look at me questioningly. "How can there be two?"

"There aren't two," I replied gently.

"What happened?" she asked.

"Soren rejected him," I said calmly. "At the time, Konstantin had been a magnificent, natural leader. He was smart, charismatic, and full of ideas to take the packs to the next level. Except he didn't have a wolf. Back in the early days, many of the offspring of the surviving Sun Wolves were failing to connect with their Lycan nature, unable to shift in either form. And yet, they were able to drink from the pond around the Moon Well, so they thrived."

"Lycans and vampires used to live together?" Thalia asked.

"Yes," I said, running my fingers through my thick mane. "They weren't second rate citizens and enjoyed all the same privileges as everyone else. However, they were smaller, weaker, and far more limited in what they could do since they didn't have a wolf. Many were angry, feeling left out when the pack would run in their wolf form through the woods, howl together at night, or lie around under the sun while it hung at its zenith. But above all, they couldn't be pack leaders. The Apex Alpha must be able to lead the pack in a hunt. They couldn't. Blood wasn't as abundant then as it is now. Most of them were forced to limit their exposure to the light."

"So, while they were accepted, their physical limitations effectively made them outcasts," Thalia reflected with a slight frown marring her forehead. "I can't see that sitting too well with Konstantin."

I snorted. "That is quite the understatement. But things radically changed one fateful day when Konstantin went to drink at the Moon Well. As soon as he started, he suddenly began to choke, as depicted by the scene right here," I said, pointing at his image, kneeling by the water holding his throat with one hand and raising the other one in a pleading gesture. "At the time, our ancestors believed he had an adverse reaction to the water, like all of the pureblood Karthians and many of the hybrid offspring. It had been a shock as he'd been seventeen at the time, and no one had ever manifested an adverse reaction so late."

"But he wasn't choking, was he?" Thalia said. "Soren had just taken him over."

"Not taken over," I corrected with an indulgent smile. "He had joined with him."

Thalia pursed her lips, clearly in disagreement of my statement but held her peace.

"What happened then?" she asked.

"In the days, weeks, and months that followed, Konstantin became incredibly powerful, just like Oleg had been in his prime before his death. From what I've been told of this era, all the vampires had rejoiced, hoping their turn might come. For the first time, one of them was slated to be the heir to the throne of Karthia. Apparently, there had even been talks of him challenging Ciril—the King that had succeeded Oleg—to take over his throne."

"He wanted to usurp the throne of his own king?" Thalia exclaimed.

I chuckled at her outrage. "The leader of a pack is the strongest Alpha male. The King is the most powerful among all the Alphas of all the packs. If another proves stronger than he is, the King must step down. With him benefitting from the blessing of Soren, Konstantin was in fact becoming the strongest among our people."

Thalia let her gaze roam over the carvings further ahead, the glowing stones that had been added over the years of maintenance helping to highlight the important elements of the fresco.

"I see nothing here referencing a battle or Konstantin becoming the Lycan King," Thalia challenged. "And yet, this seems to show him back at the river, losing Soren."

"Correct. Konstantin potentially becoming the next Apex Alpha stirred a great deal of dissent among the Lycans," I explained. "He didn't… think like us. What isn't depicted in these carvings is the arrival of humans on Karthia. Pirates and mercenaries looking for primitive species to enslave had come here. We spanked them raw, took their loot, and sent them packing," I said with no small amount of smugness.

"And that's how Karthia received its first human slaves," Thalia correctly deduced.

"Yes. Since most of us resisted the bloodlust, we were content to use the humans as manual labor. But the blood drinkers wanted to use them as chattel, breed them as quickly as possible, feed mostly on the males, and keep the females as broodmares… and entertainment," I said in an apologetic tone.

"Why does that sound familiar?" Thalia said bitterly.

"But more importantly, Konstantin was promoting ideas that would effectively break the hierarchy system of the packs to allow the blood drinkers to become the dominant breed of our species," I said before pointing at a couple more figures on the carvings. "This is Vlad and Vasska. They were some of his staunchest supporters. But where they could be reasoned with, Konstantin couldn't. Vlad understood that the changes they wanted weren't possible. We are wolves. Our pack instincts cannot simply be turned off to accommodate the vampires."

"And since they don't have wolves, following your hierarchy and your instinctive customs was impossible for them," Thalia concluded in my stead.

"Correct. Vlad was the first to suggest that the blood drinkers should go their separate ways, create their own city, and follow their own rules," I said wistfully.

"Vlad?!" Thalia exclaimed, taken aback.

I nodded. "It was a valid suggestion," I said with a smile, amused by her disbelief. "They were a different people, with different needs, aspirations, and ways of thinking. A friendly separation would have allowed both of our breeds to thrive. After all, they are family."

"But?" she asked.

"But Konstantin wanted to rule over ALL Lycans, not just the wolf-less blood drinkers. As the Apex Alpha, he considered it his due," I said with a sliver of contempt. "The packs never would have followed him. Even though he was technically the strongest, his style of leadership clashed with our inner-wolves. It made him an enemy, a threat to the pack."

"I guess Soren agreed," Thalia said with a snort.

I chuckled. "Yes. No one knows what actually happened," I said, turning back to the fresco. "Konstantin had gone to the Moon Well but didn't return that day. When he failed to show up the following day, we went looking for him, fearing he'd met with foul play somehow. Many of the Lycans were growing increasingly belligerent towards him."

"Instead, you found him by the pond, with Soren gone," Thalia said.

"We found him by the pond, Soren gone, but surrounded by

the corpses of a dozen humans that he had completely drained," I said in a harsh voice.

Thalia placed her hand over her mouth and stared in shock at the fresco depicting those events. "I thought this was a group of vampires becoming ill after drinking from the pond, not a slaughter," she said with a frown. "Why the massacre? Rage? Blood Starvation?"

"We don't know," I said with a shrug. "There was a trial, but he refused to answer any questions. He didn't even try to defend himself. Many wanted to execute him, but King Ciril decided to show clemency. He believed that the loss of Soren—which also meant any hope Konstantin held at ruling the packs—had temporarily driven him insane."

"And I bet he wanted to keep the peace with the remaining vampires," Thalia added teasingly, crossing her arms on her chest.

I smiled and nodded. "Yes, I believe it was, and maybe even the main reason for that decision," I conceded, once more impressed by her analytical skills and ability to discern what motivated people. "But that was the catalyst to the vampires' exodus."

"They followed Konstantin?" she asked.

"No. They followed Vlad," I said, my gaze boring into hers.

She looked at me in disbelief, then a strange expression crossed her features. A sense of unease—of jealousy as well—washed over me. I was still seething about the vampire delegation that had come to see her over a week ago. The connection and chemistry between my Thalia and Vlad had been undeniable. He genuinely cared for her. I hadn't questioned her about their discussion, but I knew beyond any doubt that he had tried to sway her into going with him… and that she'd been tempted.

The thought of Thalia in another man's arms had my blood boiling with rage. Worse still, I suspected that had Vlad been the ruler of Verelinn instead of Konstantin—unofficial though that title was—she might have never accepted my offer to come here to begin with.

"So, why doesn't he rule?" she asked, as I expected.

"Because he had no such ambitions," I answered truthfully. "Being an Alpha himself, Vlad chafed at the Lycan hierarchy that demanded his submission to the Apex. He didn't wish to impose it on others. He just wanted freedom."

"But Konstantin wanted to dominate," Thalia continued in my stead, understanding dawning on her. "Therefore, Vlad became the stop-gap to Konstantin's ambitions while allowing him a certain illusion of dominance."

"Clever as always," I said with undisguised admiration.

She smiled and lifted her chin proudly, basking in my compliment. But her smile quickly faded, replaced by a frown.

"I'm assuming this last fresco represents the creation of Verelinn," she said, her gaze then shifting to the other side of the stone passage. They only depicted giant and monstrous beasts—the defeated Guardians of the Moon Well. "I see nothing of us, humans, the Liberation, and the creation of the colonies."

I scratched the short fur at my nape which blended in with my hair—a telltale sign of embarrassment for me. "Humans were not deemed important enough to be recorded in the annals of history," I said sheepishly. "As you can see, there are extremely few here in Hundilinn. The only reason we had taken them from mercenaries and slave traders that had come to Karthia had been to sustain the needs of our blood drinkers. Once the vampires left, we released the humans—we had no use for them."

"But *you* still drink blood," she countered.

"True, but we had already developed artificial blood, and the few among us who occasionally needed true blood had made arrangements with local Karthians or the few humans that had either remained in Hundilinn or mated with Karthians. And that's how the colonies were born. Humans migrated to Verelinn where what they had to offer was actually needed and wanted. By the way, the name 'vampire' was given to the blood drinkers by your ancestors. It is an Earth word."

"Well, that explains a few things, even though we got screwed over in the end," Thalia said stiffly. "And now, you are the King of the people Konstantin wanted to rule. You have been chosen by the Spirit of the leader of the Sun Wolf that has abandoned him. AND you have claimed the Blood Maiden he coveted. You sure know how to make friends."

I laughed. "So it seems. I can't help that he wants things that are meant for the loveliest Lycan of Karthia."

Thalia snorted and gave me the "Oh please" look. "Well, King Lovely, what do you think will go up next on this fresco?" she asked teasingly.

"On this wall, you and me, once I'm fully recovered from my illness," I said, sobering. "The sketches have already been made."

"US?" Thalia exclaimed, flabbergast.

"Yes, Thalia," I said with a soft chuckle. "You are about to be immortalized in the Lycan history for saving the life of the first King to have been chosen by Soren since Oleg and to have survived Blood Starvation."

"Did Soren kill Oleg the way he almost killed you?" she asked with a tense expression.

I flinched at that comment, and Soren stirred, displeased by it.

"Oleg did develop the same symptoms that were slowly killing me," I replied, carefully choosing my words. "I became ill around the same time Soren chose me. But Oleg only became ill nearly a century later. Soren left him halfway through his illness. King Oleg continued to live for many months, his health steadily deteriorating until he died. I deteriorated very quickly and would have died with Soren still with me had my mother not put me in stasis."

"Hmm," she said pensively. "I see."

I suppressed a smile. I'd come to realize that Thalia needed to rationalize everything. She'd be like a dog with a bone, poking and prodding at the problem in the back of her mind until she found a satisfying solution.

"On the other wall, the Guardian of the next opening of the Moon Well will be sculpted right there—assuming we defeat it," I said, pointing at the location and trying to sound lighthearted, despite the concern that gnawed at me at that prospect. Who knew what kind of three-hundred-year-old beast would rise from the depths of Karthia? "But enough history for now. I promised you a visit to the Moon Well, and I'm a man of my word."

Thalia smiled, her gaze lingering once more over the magnificent carvings on the walls while I mounted the hover bike. She turned back to me, her eyes flicking nervously towards our means of transportation. Her pink tongue peeked between those plump lips of hers I was dying to kiss, moistening them in that typical fashion she always did when intimidated or worried. I encouragingly gestured with my head for her to hop on in front of me.

Normally, the rare times I had an adult passenger with me, they sat behind me. Teens and young pups I sat in front of me to make sure they didn't lose their grip. It also helped me keep them from leaning in the wrong direction, which made it harder to control the bike at high speed. However, in this instance, it was only partially to reassure her, and mostly to give me an excuse to hold her in my arms again. I'd been aching for it for the past ten days.

Thalia timidly settled in front of me. My arm instinctively wrapped around her midsection and pulled her closer to me. I barely repressed a moan at the feel of her warm body pressed against my chest. I could hear the beating of her heart picking up the pace and her breathing becoming faster and shallower.

"Do not be afraid, Thalia," I whispered in her ear. "I've got you, and I'm never going to let go."

She turned to look at me over her shoulder, her eyes searching as she examined my features. I'd made my underlying meaning less than subtle. Thalia was smart enough to have understood it. I held her gaze unflinchingly to make it clear she got it right. To my surprise, her shoulders relaxed, and she gave me a radiant smile.

"I'm happy to hear it," she said softly before leaning back against me.

This time, it was my turn to wonder if she'd meant more by those words than merely expressing gratitude. Her display of jealousy earlier made me want to believe she appreciated my hint about claiming her. My arm tightened around her, and I pressed my cheek against hers. Thalia all but melted in my embrace, and the delicious scent of her blossoming arousal wafted to my nose. The maddening aroma had blood rushing to my groin.

"Although you don't need to, you can hold on to these smaller handles if you wish," I said softly, pointing at them with my free hand. "Or you can put your hands on the main handles if you don't mind having mine on top of yours. It is a good way for you to start getting familiar with eventually piloting one on your own," I added shamelessly to incentivize her to hold those ones instead.

I placed my free hand on the left handle. Thalia licked her lips again, making me burn with the need to devour them in a hungry kiss, then boldly placed her left hand on top of mine. I turned my face towards her ear, my cheek caressing hers in the process.

"Good girl," I whispered in her ear before pressing my lips against it in a gentle kiss.

Thalia shivered, her hand unconsciously squeezing mine. I briefly tightened my hold around her, my thumb caressing her flat stomach before reluctantly letting go to hold onto the second handle. As she also held onto it, Thalia turned slightly to look at me sideways. With my cheek pressed against hers, our lips were centimeters from each other. In that instant, I believed she wouldn't balk if I kissed her. I almost did, but then changed my mind. The first time I kissed her, I wanted it to be with us face to face, not sitting on a hover bike next to a fresco depicting the construction of Verelinn.

I gently rubbed my cheek against hers, a common gesture of affection between Lycans, and also a way to mark our scent on our mate or offspring. Whether or not Thalia knew its meaning, she leaned into it and returned the gesture. Despite the lust bubbling inside me, my tenderness for the female dominated.

"Let's ride, my beauty," I whispered, switching the hover bike from follow to manual control.

"Lead the way, Wolfy," she replied, playfully.

I chuckled, loving the sound of that nickname on her lips. This time, I nipped at her ear while a clear protective dome formed all around us. Thalia looked at it in awe but didn't question it. I rarely traveled into the woods alone. As King, I normally had a couple of Iron Guards with me, be they Maidens or Warriors. But Lycans in general didn't venture alone outside of the protection of the city. The Karthian flora and fauna could be quite lethal to both the unwary traveler and the well-aware one. With Konstantin all up in arms about Thalia, we had to be all the more vigilant about potential foul play. But the path leading from the city, through the mountain cave, and to the Moon Well, was well defended. Many Iron Guards were patrolling nearby to catch potential intruders.

We took off, the bike rapidly achieving a dizzying speed. To my delight, Thalia didn't squirm or whimper, quickly enjoying the thrill of the solo race. The large doors at the other end of the tunnel parted before us so that we could exit into the woods where the packed dirt path continued to stretch deep into the forest.

The Blood Maiden gazed at the woods with wonder. Naturally, she'd never been so immersed with nature due to her sheltered life. The way she tilted her head all the way back, resting on my shoulder to look up at the giant Teramon trees, exposed her vulnerable neck to me in the most enticing fashion. The trees' huge, tear-shaped leaves flapped in the wind in a musical rustling that was both soothing and hypnotic. From our vantage point, you'd almost believe you were looking at a flock of giant birds, flapping their wings in slow motion as they hovered in place.

"The sap of these trees is used in the fabrication of that stretchy fabric your clothes are made of," I explained as we zipped past them.

"Why are some of their leaves a different color?" she asked.

"The yellowish-green ones indicate the sap has been harvested," I said, pleased by her keen sense of observation. "The blueish-green ones are ready to be harvested. The black ones indicate a clothes cache. Normally, we run through the woods on all fours in our wolf form."

"You will have to shift for me one of these days," Thalia said. "I didn't get a good enough look at you that one time. I'd been too busy freaking out about the vampires trying to grab us."

"I will be more than happy to," I said, genuinely pleased. "Just be warned that it comes with nudity first, and that I can't be held responsible if my instincts make me frantically lick you."

"I call bullshit on the 'instinct' part," Thalia said with false outrage while playfully elbowing me. "Good thing I always carry some sanitizing wipes with me."

"Good thing, indeed, my beauty," I said, rubbing my cheek against hers again. "We're here," I said, rounding the winding curve of the path.

The trees appeared to part before us, revealing the Moon Well.

CHAPTER 14
THALIA

I stared in awe at the large pond in a perfectly circular shape that sprawled before us. It was too symmetrical to have been a natural formation. The shiny silver liquid that filled it was no natural water. Behind it, a massive rock formation carved in a half-moon hugged the pond's northern edge. On each end, similar giant statues of the Karthian Nymphs I had seen in the Great Hall of Verelinn adorned the mountain face. In the recurved section of the rock wall, luminous symbols that reminded me of some sort of alien language, glowed in a slow pulse on each side of what looked like the sealed seam of a doorway. At the foot of what I presumed to be the entrance to the actual Moon Well, a number of rock plateaus could have almost passed off as a series of multi-level altars. Their slightly raised edges made me believe they could contain a certain amount of liquid.

The blood of the sacrificed?

A single, narrow stone bridge led from the end of the path to the altar-like plateaus. No vegetation whatsoever grew at the edges of the pond. Instead, the dirt and small rocks surrounding it had turned into shimmering little pebbles that shone like crystals under the sun. The entire structure dated back to a couple of millennia ago. However, beyond the high level of maintenance it had benefited from over the years, the central part of the wall was clearly a more recent upgrade, although still dating back a few centuries.

Drogo stopped the hover bike on the path, next to the grassy clearing surrounding the shimmering pebbles by the pond. The protective dome dissolved around us. A soft breeze caressed my skin and the oddest scent wafted to me. It wasn't unpleasant, but it would also never qualify as perfume. It had an earthy quality to it, laced with something metallic and slightly acidic. I surmised it emanated from the pond. To my shock, I realized that while the protective dome had allowed sound through, it had blocked out the scents from our surroundings and the heat from the burning sun overhead.

With much reluctance, I let go of Drogo's hands on the handles of the bike. He immediately got up, leaving me feeling bereft. A chill ran down my spine as I lost the soothing warmth of his strong body wrapped around mine. Drogo extended a hand towards me to help me up. I gladly took it and let him lead me to the small bridge. It was too narrow for us to walk side by side while holding hands. To my shock—and total delight—the Lycan King released my hand and slipped his arm around my waist instead, drawing me against him. On instinct, I wrapped my own arm around his waist. Although he didn't comment, his embrace tightened ever so slightly.

We stopped at the first and largest of the plateaus. From here, they almost looked like random stairs to the stone entrance. Some terrible claw marks could be seen here and there on the stony surfaces.

"This is the exact spot where Skala and Soren were married, before it all turned into a bloodbath," Drogo explained. "The Sun Wolves were standing in the water on each side of the bridge. A few high priestesses were standing on these plateaus, while the rest of the villagers stood on the bank."

Essentially, they had surrounded them and trapped them in water to make it harder for them to flee.

"But this isn't water," I said, pointing at the silver liquid in the pond with my chin.

Drogo smiled. "No, definitely not traditional water. Apparently, it has thickened since the massacre. But it was always this silver color."

I walked to the edge of the plateau and crouched to get a closer look. It truly resembled liquid silver. It didn't quite ripple but also didn't remain still. There was no current to stir it, and the breeze struck me as too tame to disturb the sleek surface. Looking over my shoulder, I glanced at the rock formation.

"Do you know if this rock mountain was once some sort of volcano, or something else along those lines?" I asked, annoyed that so many pieces of the puzzle still continued to elude me.

Drogo chuckled and shook his head. He was amused by my need to analyze everything, but he also knew far more than he was letting on. A part of me believed he wanted me to figure it out on my own. I couldn't say why. Was it a test? Was it just to entertain me since he'd guessed I loved puzzle-solving? Or was he just not at liberty to share freely some information he would otherwise really want me to know?

"No," Drogo said with certainty. "There are no… traditional volcanoes on Karthia."

I seized on his hesitation, and my eyes narrowed at him. "Not traditional but volcanoes nonetheless?" I insisted.

"I guess, if you really get loose with the definition of volcano. But I don't really see it applying to the Moon Well. It would be a *huge* stretch. Why?"

"Volcanoes are known to change the acidity of the water around it," I mused out loud. "There's clearly something within this small mountain that is affecting the chemical composition of this water. If you could identify what it was, you might be able to reproduce and market it in a pill as the fountain of youth," I said in a playful tone, although I wondered why they hadn't already explored that possibility.

Drogo smiled in a non-committal fashion. That alone told me they'd not only already thought of it but were likely in the process of studying or researching it.

"I must drink," Drogo said without answering my question. "I normally do it in my wolf form. I don't mind you watching as I strip," he added in a taunting fashion. "But if you prefer to avert your eyes to protect your innocence, I'll be quick."

My cheeks burned, and a ball of fire exploded in the pit of my stomach. My instinctive reaction was to turn around and close my eyes as hard as possible. But something about the taunting glimmer in his eyes prodded the rebel in me.

"You did say I had to get used to nudity in Hundilinn," I said nonchalantly. "Might as well start small and work my way up."

Drogo gaped at me for a split second. He had not expected me to call his bluff. Frankly, I couldn't believe my own boldness. But he quickly recovered. His silver eyes darkened, and his face took on an expression that I couldn't define. It wasn't lurid or overtly seductive in that vulgar way males often ogled females. It was intense and sexy as hell. Butterflies took flight in the pit of my stomach as Drogo removed his shirt. Although he took his time doing it, he didn't make a show of it. That would have made it feel cheap instead of deliciously enticing by its normalcy.

He kicked off his shoes. I forced my gaze to remain locked with his while he removed his pants. Even before he had begun undressing, the front of his pants had started straining. The now familiar throbbing between my thighs came back with a vengeance. The memory of his hard shaft rubbing against my core when he had lost it at the hospital was so strong, I could almost feel him again. As was apparently common with the Lycans, Drogo had no underwear. His eyes never strayed from my face while he slightly bent forward to slip each of his legs free from the garment.

He then straightened and casually tossed his pants in the same general direction his shirt had gone. Drogo stood proudly in his glorious nakedness before me, totally unfazed by his impressive cock loudly broadcasting his state of arousal. He had every reason not to be ashamed. Despite my burning cheeks, I allowed myself to openly examine the masculine perfection on full display before me.

The Lycan King was truly a magnificent beast, with bulging muscles crisscrossed by ropey veins and a strong chest with well-defined abs carved with surgical precision. Although scary in its girth and length, Drogo's cock had plenty for him to brag about. It looked eerily similar to that of a human male except for the slight bulge towards the base of the shaft. I realized then that like all canines, during sex, he most probably knotted with his mate. I felt hot and cold all at once, wondering how it would feel to be locked with him in post-coital bliss while he filled me with his seed.

To my surprise, considering the delicate patches of fur on the other side of his arms and at his nape, I had expected quite the furry bush around his crotch. To my delight, his wasn't at all. For a split second, I wondered if he shaved. But then, I remembered that most canine breeds had little to no fur either on their entire belly, or in their crotch area.

"You are a stunning male," I said in all honesty.

For the first time, Drogo looked genuinely shy and self-conscious. His wolf ears twitched, and he shifted on his feet.

"Thank you, Thalia. I am glad my appearance pleases you," he said in a somewhat grumbling voice. "I also find you quite breathtaking."

With my rather unremarkable face, I always took compliments about my appearance—that wasn't specifically related to my body—with a grain of salt. But the sincerity in his voice and in the way he looked at me, messed me up in every possible way. I therefore resorted to humor to hide my embarrassment.

"I certainly can *see* that," I said, casting a meaningful glance at his pelvic area. "I'm flattered."

Drogo snorted and stared at his erect shaft with a bemused expression. "Your presence always does quite a number on this poor guy. But it's a different tail I'm supposed to be wagging at you. Here it goes."

That comment turned me upside down. With these words, Drogo had essentially confirmed that his attraction to me was more than just fleeting. I liked that… *a lot.*

A low growl rose from his throat as he crouched with the fingertips of one hand resting on the ground between his legs. Dark brown fur the same color as his beautiful hair spread rapidly over his body. In a series of cracking and snapping sounds, Drogo's limbs and face gradually reshaped themselves. His body mass grew as did the sound of his growl. It looked painful, terrifying even. And yet, I stood there, transfixed, observing this impossible metamorphosis with wonder and fascination.

Drogo completed the process in seconds that felt like the most amazing forever. His wolf was beyond massive, his head reaching my chest. He slowly approached me and bared his teeth. Despite the impressive rows of dagger-like teeth with crazy fangs, I knew instinctively that he was grinning, not threatening. Throwing his head back, Drogo emitted a long and sustained howl. Seconds later, at least six voices at a non-negligible distance, scattered around our location, responded in kind.

Although beautiful, this place spooked me a little. Knowing other Lycans were within calling range greatly reassured me. Truth be told, it had worried me a little that they'd allowed their King to wander off in the woods without escort.

Drogo moved close to the 'water' and began lapping at it. For a brief moment, a sliver of fear flashed through me as the image on the mural of a defeated Konstantin, hunched over the pond after Soren had abandoned him crossed my mind. What if Soren abandoned Drogo, too?

A violent shiver shook the Lycan King, as if in response to my thoughts. He whimpered, then emitted a brief bark—a rare occurrence in a wolf—then whimpered again. My blood turned to ice, and my heart pounded in my chest as I watched him pant over the pond, his canine body wracked by an occasional spasm like he wanted to wretch or was fighting a dry heave.

Feeling helpless, I tried to rein in my growing panic. Was he having a negative reaction to the water, or was this the normal behavior after drinking? The spasms suddenly subsided. Drogo licked his snout then turned around, taking a few steps towards the center of the large plateau we were standing on. He looked at me with the strangest look in his wolf eyes. He was trying to tell me something, I had no idea what. Then, when I least expected it, he dropped onto his belly, legs sprawled, head facing me, and his tongue lolling out.

"Drogo!" I shouted in a panic.

But even as I was taking my first step to rush at his side, I suddenly froze. Staring at him, I recognized the tableau I had pictured in my mind the first time he had mentioned wolves warming their bellies on stones heated by the sun… stones like the ones that formed these plateaus.

"You little shit!" I exclaimed, torn between outrage, relief, and the need to laugh. "You scared me!"

Drogo emitted a series of little growls that were undoubtedly laughter. I wanted so badly to kick his ass, but he was so beautiful. To make matters worse, he made the most adorable puppy face and began crawling towards me with the most epic whimpering sounds.

"You have no shame," I said chuckling, before crouching in front of him.

With a will of their own, my hands buried themselves in the

thick fur around his face. He stretched his neck, emitting the cutest mix of short growls and whimpers as I scratched his neck and the back of his ears. It was strange how natural it felt to pet him, even knowing that despite that temporary animal form, a real man hid behind this wolf body—a real man that I was technically caressing. And yet, here I was rubbing my face against his as I would with a pet.

He knocked me on my back and began licking my face and rubbing his temples on me, marking me with his scent.

"Stop! It tickles!" I exclaimed between two giggles. I still was nowhere near comfortable with being slobbered on, but after so many assaults by the young pups over the past week and a half, it no longer freaked me out. Drogo naturally didn't listen. "You're going to make me all sticky!"

Eventually, he relented. For a split second, I thought of taking out one of my sanitizing wipes but didn't. I actually liked the thought of being marked with his scent, of being claimed by him. He lay down on his belly next to me, freeing me. Kneeling next to him, I wrapped my arms around his neck, rubbed my face against his nape, then snuggled against him. Drogo did that cute whimpering sound again and licked my hand. We remained that way for a few more seconds before I released him.

I rose to my feet and Drogo imitated me, turning towards his clothes. He suddenly froze, his head jerking towards the forest. I perceived nothing unusual. The birds were still chirping in the distance, and no odd movement caught my attention between the trees. And yet, the way Drogo peeled back the flaps of his jaw to bare his teeth was an undeniable sign of aggression. Throwing his head back, he emitted the strangest howl, with short interruptions that reminded me of some kind of morse code.

A cold shiver ran down my spine when no howls responded this time. I inwardly cursed myself for not bringing a weapon or wearing my anti-compulsion necklace. At least, I had my light shield integrated in my bracelet, which could be both manually and vocally activated.

Drogo shifted back and began dressing before he was even fully done morphing. While a part of me would have felt safer with him in his beast form, being able to speak to him also had its advantages.

"What's going on?" I asked, my voice slightly trembling.

"I don't know," Drogo said, shoving on his pants. "Soren warned me of an imminent danger."

"He spoke to you?" I asked, my head jerking around, looking for any signs of an incoming attack.

"He doesn't speak with words," Drogo said in a tensed voice while clasping his armband around his left wrist. "He just communicates through emotions."

He didn't bother putting his shoes or shirt on. That's when I noticed his toes and fingers still had claws. It made sense that he would rather battle in his Lycan form, which was essentially humanoid, but with the enhanced strength of the wolf. I wished he would fully shift into it rather than remain in this partial form. But my impatience was silly. I remembered well how quickly he'd done so when he had come to rescue us, shifting in a blink from wolf to Lycan while fighting.

"Let's get you back to the castle," he said with urgency, pressing his hand on the small of my back to nudge me forward.

"Are the others okay?" I asked, complying. "They didn't respond."

"They are fine and heading here," Drogo said. "Responding would give away their position to any potential—"

Drogo never finished his sentence. Splashing sounds resonated around us as enemies in camouflage rushed us from all sides. I clasped Drogo's wrist and opened my mouth to activate my light shield. But only a gasp of shock and pain escaped me as something—or rather someone—tackled me. Terror swept over me as the impact knocked me off the bridge. I flew back, feeling the firm grip and weight of an invisible person wrapped around me as I fell into the pond. Drogo shouted my name, horror etched on his face as he tried to reach for me while multiple assailants also attempted to tackle him. The last image I saw was Drogo managing to remain upright and blindly fighting his camouflaged foes.

Then the silvery water of the pond closed over me. It immediately irritated my skin as if it contained some strong or concentrated chemicals. But I failed to close my mouth quickly enough following my scream of terror. The strange substance rushed down my throat, burning like acid. Thankfully, the pond was fairly shallow. I placed my feet at the bottom and tried to push myself up, only to be pushed back down by my aggressor. On top of the acid eating me from the inside out, my lungs were also begging for air as I'd expelled what I had with that scream.

Trying to think straight despite my growing panic, I latched onto his pinky finger and yanked it back so hard it dislocated. Through the murky water, I heard the muffled sound of his shout of pain. He loosened his hold enough for me to kick up from the bed of the pond. I shot out of the water, breaking his hold, and inhaled loudly. My attacker viciously grabbed me by the shoulders, his thumbs painfully digging into the sensitive muscle right above my clavicles.

I shouted and, grinding my teeth through the excruciating pain, I blindly reached for where I believed his face to be. Although I still couldn't see him, aside from the splash of silver water trickling down his camouflaged body, my fingers connected with flesh. One hand appeared to be near his forehead while the other felt like it was touching part of his nose and his cheek. I didn't give a shit. With a war cry, I raked my nails down his face with as much strength as I could. The male roared, clutching his face as he stumbled back.

I turned for a split second to see Drogo in his full Lycan form fighting at least four vampires out of stealth mode on the bridge.

I suspected a few more were still camouflaged nearby. There were two corpses at his feet and a third partially immersed in the water, with one leg stuck on the bridge. My heart soared at the sight of a pair of white wolves dashing our way from the tree line a short distance away.

Swallowing painfully through my tortured throat, I tried to ignore the violent cramps in my stomach, rejecting this unholy water. But as I began to wade out of the pond that was chafing my skin, a vampire clone similar to the ones I'd previously encountered came out of stealth right in front of me. Unable to speak due to my damaged throat, I reached for my bracelet to activate my shield. But moving at lightning speed, the vampire closed his hand around my neck.

"Surrender!" he ordered in a calm voice but with an irresistible tone of command.

Mesmerized by his voice and the intensity of his gaze, my will to fight dissipated. As the tingling sensation of the vampire's compulsion spread from my nape outward, my shoulders slumped, and all tension left my body.

"Drink," the vampire commanded, his hand still holding my neck bending me backward to submerge my head.

I didn't resist, submitting to his will even as a small voice at the back of my head screamed for me to fight. But fight for what? This was so much simpler. So much easier. I closed my eyes as the silver water engulfed me. Opening my mouth wide, I swallowed a huge gulp. The pain in my throat multiplied a thousandfold, but I swallowed another mouthful.

Fleeting sensations rubbed all over my exposed skin. You'd think a bunch of fish were rubbing against me. It was silly. There were no fish in this pool of acid. The thought that it was chunks of my flesh peeling off from my body under the assault of the silver water crossed my mind. It didn't matter. I was dying anyway. If not the water, the burning pain in my chest from my air-deprived lungs would see to it.

As I swallowed down what would likely be my last gulp before my ultimate demise, something slipped inside my mouth. Thick and organic, it slithering down my throat. At the same time, the fleeting sensations on my skin turned into tangible things—algae crossed my mind—that settled on my face. At least two or three of them sealed my mouth shut, another covered my nose, closing my nostrils, while a couple settled on my eyes.

The burning in my lungs, in my throat, and on my skin faded. A tingling sensation spread over me along with a sensation of intense cold. As Death cast its dark veil over me, Drogo's face danced in front of my mind's eye.

I wished I had kissed him at least once.

CHAPTER 15
DROGO

I shouted with rage and fear as I helplessly watched the clone drowning my woman. I needed to get her out of there, but the vampires were pinning me on the bridge. She'd already swallowed too much of the silver water. A single sip would suffice to kill her. She didn't have the Lycan gene that would allow her to process it. Her only chance was for me to infect her with the virus, but even that was a long shot.

Soren's brand on my chest had grown so hot it burned. I didn't know what was going on with him. I no longer felt worry from him; only an intense concentration. He cared deeply for Thalia and was both extremely protective and possessive of her. Therefore, his current reaction confused me. However, now wasn't the time to dwell on this. Whatever the Spirit of Soren was up to, the enhanced strength he bestowed me was all that mattered.

With a vicious swipe of my claws, I nearly beheaded one of my foes. His head would have come right off if not for the two vampires behind me holding me back. I had quickly come to the realization that they weren't trying to kill me, only restrain me long enough to kill my woman. It baffled me that Konstantin would go to such an extreme rather than abduct her.

I headbutted one of the attackers behind me with the back of my skull, while snapping the neck of another standing in the water and clinging to one of my legs. But even as the wretch went limp, two more vampires launched themselves at me, one pulling on my left arm, the other immobilizing the same leg I had just freed. The vampire at my back wrapped his arm around my neck. Before he could tighten his hold, I tucked my chin in then bit clean through skin and bone.

He didn't turn to ash any more than the others I had defeated. Konstantin had upped his game by only sending Daywalkers. Then, in a flash of white fur, Viktor knocked out two of my attackers, nearly making me fall on my back in the process. Darya, also in her white wolf form, threw herself at the vampire in the water that was holding my arm. Her massive jaw closed around his shoulder, shattering his clavicle and breaking his scapula. I spun around, and with a single swipe of my claws, I eviscerated the wretch that had tried to chokehold me.

Wasting no time, I turned towards Thalia. As I jumped into the water to go rescue my woman, the dark silhouettes of Ulia and three others of my Iron Guards in wolf form ran into the clearing. They initiated their shift into Lycan form without slowing their advance. I rushed towards Thalia and the clone holding her under the water when a series of electric shocks went off in various parts of his body. Shaken by violent spasms, the clone let go of Thalia. I reached for her and pulled her out of the water, while another series of violent shocks erupted on the vampire.

Under different circumstances, I would have stared in disbelief once I realized the electric pulses were set off by the Spirits that had attached themselves to the clone. The white flash illuminated their translucent forms, matching their respective symbol, then electric tendrils spread outward over the clone's skin. But Thalia's unnatural stillness had me on the verge of panic.

To my shock, at least half a dozen Spirits slid off Thalia's face and back into the silver pond. Judging by the paler outlines on her skin, otherwise reddened by the prolonged contact to the water, the Spirits had protected her mouth, nose, eyes and ears, preventing more of the silver liquid from entering her system. Thankfully, this fluid didn't behave like standard water. It didn't cling to her skin, her hair, or her clothes, slipping right back into the pond instead.

While the Lycans finished dispatching the vampires, I lay Thalia belly down on the bridge, her face resting near the edge, over the pond. She wasn't breathing anymore, and I couldn't hear her heartbeat. I began applying pressure on her sides and her back in an upward movement to purge the fluid filling her lungs. But even as I worked on my female, my throat constricted, and my heart broke. The light-grey tinge of the veins visible through her pale skin testified of the large quantity already coursing through her system.

When what seemed like an endless flow of liquid silver finally stopped pouring out of her mouth, I turned Thalia onto her back to perform CPR. Tears pricked my eyes as I alternated between mouth-to-mouth and pumping her heart. Concentrated acid flooded my veins as I worked on the lifeless body of the one female that had been created for me. I should have told her how I felt. I should have wooed her right away instead of wasting what precious time we'd been given. I had failed her. Once again, I had failed her. What the fuck kind of protector was I that I couldn't keep my woman safe? She'd saved my life, and I'd let her die.

"Please, Thalia. Please, fight," I whispered.

"Bite her," Ulia suggested, startling me.

I'd been so focused on my mate that I hadn't noticed the end of the battle or my people gathering around us. The change had never been initiated that way. It was always the other way around. First, we infected the person with the Lycan virus and let it perform the initial changes in their body. Then we stabilized the change by making them drink the water. Thalia drinking it first had caused internal damage that the virus would have prevented.

But there was no other option. I couldn't lose her.

I took back my full Lycan form—having previously partially shifted back to human to be able to properly perform CPR. But as I leaned forward to bite her neck, a sharp pain exploded in my chest, and my heart stuttered. I gasped and clutched at my chest while my friends recoiled.

"What the fuck was that?" Viktor asked, the confusion on his face reflected on those of our companions.

The disapproving anger emanating from Soren further increased my confusion. I made to lean forward again, and a sharp pain radiated from my mark.

"What the fuck are you doing?" I asked Soren. "She's dying!"

"Your Spirit is blocking you," Viktor said, understanding dawning on him.

"But why?" Darya asked.

"Maybe your virus is too potent," Viktor reflected out loud. "You have the purest Lycan blood. She's only human. Yours might be too much for her to handle. Maybe another should turn her."

"You?" I snarled as an irrational anger and jealousy took over me.

His argument had merit, but a special, unbreakable bond was always formed between a fledgling and his creator. Thalia should have that bond with me, not with some other male.

"No," Viktor said in an appeasing tone, sympathy in his silver eyes. "I am an Ancient. My blood isn't as strong as yours, but not that far behind. Ulia, or better yet my daughter, could turn her."

Shame burned in my gut over my petty jealousy when my focus should be on saving my beloved.

"Darya should do it," Ulia said, rightly guessing that it would hurt me less to have a woman turn her than another male in his prime.

"Gladly," she said, shifting into her Lycan form.

But mid-shift, she clutched at her chest, a troubled expression descending on her beautiful face.

"My Spirit does not approve of this either," she whispered, before gaping at me with shock.

"Look!" Ulia said, just as I was about to lose my shit.

It took me half a beat to notice, but then I stared in disbelief as the silvery color of her veins rapidly drained, as if something was sucking the pond's water out of her system. Soren broadcast soothing waves that calmed me while confusing the fuck out of me.

Then a flash of light went off under Thalia's shirt, startling all of us. Her back arched off the bridge, and she gasped, taking a large and loud breath. She immediately started coughing, turning to her side before retching. More silver water trickled out of her mouth.

"Thalia!" I shouted, snapping out of my stupor.

I held her head over the edge until the last drop of silver water had fallen out, before cradling her in my arms. Her eyes rolled in her head, but she lost the battle and fell unconscious. I would have panicked again if not for her steady pulse and breathing, not to mention the pleased emotions from Soren. I carefully parted the V-shaped collar of her shirt and stared transfixed at the elegant curves of Zabek's Spirit on her chest.

"How is that possible?" I whispered. "She's human."

"A human with golden blood," Viktor countered. "Zabek will thrive."

"He will drain her! Kill her! He must come out!" I exclaimed.

"The Spirits joined forces to save her, just like she saved you. They didn't do all of this only to slowly murder her," Viktor said in a stern voice. "His presence is a blessing. Look at how the water has damaged her skin. How much more damage has the water she drank done inside? Zabek keeping her unconscious is sparing her the agony she would otherwise feel right now. Do not question the gifts of the Spirits, my King," he added gently. "Trust them to look after your Queen."

Soren confirmed the Ancient Lycan's words with more soothing waves. Throat tightening with emotion, I placed my palm over Zabek's mark on my woman's chest.

"Thank you," I said with sincerity. "Thanks to all of you." Soren warmed in my chest while Zabek shifted under my palm in acknowledgement. I looked up at my companions, gratitude giving way to anger. "I'm going to take Thalia back to the castle for immediate medical attention. Two of you will accompany me in case we encounter more foul play. But I want to know how the fuck they got so deep in our territory without anyone noticing them. This should have been one of the safest places in Hundilinn!"

"I've been wondering specifically about that," Ulia said with a frown. "We have scouts patrolling the entire area. Even using stealth, the vampires would have been detected by tripping one trap or another. They didn't come from the south, the east or the west. They came from the north."

"There's nothing but the Karthian villages up north," Darya argued. "They wouldn't be so foolish as to turn against the Lycans again after what happened the first time. And least of all to ally with the blood suckers!"

"You are right, daughter. But the Karthians could have been compelled," Viktor said, echoing the thoughts crossing my mind.

"Agreed," I said before turning to my cousin. "Ulia, I want

you to organize the search. I want to know who was compelled, and how the vampires knew Thalia and I were here alone at this specific time. They must have set up some surveillance somewhere. I want it all taken down, and those who were compelled released of their thrall. Then we're going to pay a visit to the vampires. This time, Konstantin went too far."

"Darya and I will escort you, my King," Viktor said with a predatory grin. "Then we'll start preparing our trip to Verelinn."

I nodded, then carried my woman to the hover bike. I was done playing nice.

I marched into Verelinn's Council Hall, flanked by the two Ancient Pack Leaders Viktor and Andrei. On each side of us, ten of my finest Iron Guards escorted us: five Iron Maidens on the left led by Darya, and five Iron Warriors on the right led by Ulia. Usually, I avoided pompous and flamboyant displays of my rank and authority. But this time, I came fully decked in ceremonial outfit and crown.

Unlike the vampires who normally covered themselves from head to toe—a habit derived from the need to protect themselves from the sun—Lycans preferred to show skin. In this instance, I'd chosen to come shirtless, settling on a pair of black pants and an embroidered and bejeweled, black leather pauldron over my right shoulder. The strap which held it fastened to me crossed over my chest in a manner that only made the mark of Soren stand out. Similarly, the fancy bracers clasped on both my wrists not only screamed opulence, but also possessed some of the highest end technologies, and especially personal defense features.

According to the vampire rules, weapons were forbidden inside the Council Hall. One of the Red Guards said as much when we marched in with blasters and blades. One look from me suffced for him to step aside.

The room was beyond packed. Located one block east of the Great Hall where the Blood Fair had taken place, the Council Hall was the senate of Verelinn. The rectangular Council Chamber had a large public section able to accommodate ten thousand guests spread over one floor and two balconies. At the front of the house, the chair of the President of the Council sat smack in the center of the back wall, with a perfect view of the entire room.

On the right side of the room, the four High Lords of Verelinn—Vasska, Vlad, Konstantin, and Morana, in that order—sat in a row at a level with the seat of the President. Below them, a row of twelve chairs seated the Vampire Lords. Across from them, spread over three rows of twelve, the thirty-six representatives of the people—twelve of which belonged to the human ambassadors of the various colonies—looked both excited and baffled by this once-in-a-lifetime occurrence.

My escort stopped at the base of the stairs leading up to the President's chair, a large open area where citizens could come voice their grievances to their representatives. I climbed the short flight of stairs to the elevated dais in front of the chair then turned to face the crowd.

"King Drogo Volkov and sole ruler of all the citizens of Karthia blesses you with his presence. Stand for your liege lord," Viktor shouted, his booming voice resonating through the massive chamber.

As one, the people in the audience rose from their seats. I didn't even try to hide my mocking smirk as I stared at Konstantin. He scrunched his face as if he'd bitten into something foul while forcing himself up on his feet.

"Hail, King Drogo!" Viktor shouted.

The crowd immediately echoed him, although many faces expressed a certain degree of confusion, mainly the humans and the fledgling vampires. Mother was right. I—and my father before me—had allowed Konstantin to spread his propaganda for much too long. The rightful place of the Lycans had fallen too deep into obscurity in the vampire lands. This needed to be rectified. And it was starting, with me enjoying seeing Konstantin all but choke while repeating the words Viktor had spoken. It had to scorch the fuck out of his lips to hail me.

Initially, I had not planned on sitting, but this was a display of dominance. By the time we left this place, I wanted the word of what had happened here to spread like wildfire. Today, I was planting the seed of change.

Taking my sweet time, making a show of it, I walked up to the large chair—that could have passed for a more subdued version of a throne—and sat down. I crossed my legs and leaned back in my seat, my forearms resting on the wide, cushioned arms of the chair. My gaze roamed slowly over the thousands of souls standing before me before settling on Konstantin again. I stared him down until he clenched his jaw and lowered his eyes. And even then, I continued to stare at him until the tension became palpable in the room.

"You may sit," I said at last. Relieved, the audience resumed their seats, more confused than ever. "Except you," I added for Konstantin.

Anger flashed through his features, and he fisted his hands. For a brief instant, I wished he would defy me so that I could unleash my wrath on him. And yet, I was relieved when he complied. A battle to the death wasn't part of my plans tonight. I wanted to set the bastard on the road to a prolonged journey of humiliation that would slowly but surely erode his status among the vampires.

As I turned back towards the crowd, I didn't miss the baffled frown on Vlad's face, the worry on Morana's, and the amused expression on Vasska's. If nothing else, it reassured me that they had no idea what Konstantin had been up to.

"Right now, you're all wondering why would the King call an emergency session out of the blue," I said. The discreet microphone system and perfect acoustics of the place clearly broadcast my voice throughout the room. "I am here because twice over the past ten days, one of your leaders has committed vile, and heinous acts. Had the Lycans been the mindless beasts depicted in the propaganda regularly fed to you, Verelinn would currently be bathing in your blood and ashes as retribution."

Troubled murmurs rose from the crowd, many cast worried or inquisitive glances towards Konstantin. The Red Guards scattered through the room also seemed highly uncomfortable. I didn't doubt for one minute that many among them were aware of some of his plans.

"That is a grievous accusation you make," Konstantin touted with arrogance. "What proof have you?"

"Silence, vampire!" Viktor snapped. "You have not been given leave to speak!"

Konstantin bared his fangs at Viktor, his temper ever swift to flare.

"You dare?" I said in a dangerously low voice.

Konstantin closed his mouth, then lowered his eyes again, fury pouring out of him in droves.

"The day of the Blood Fair Ball, the Golden Blood Maiden Thalia Velky turned down all the contract offers she received from the vampires and *freely* chose to come to Hundilinn instead," I continued. "Naturally, those who had hoped to become the patron of such a rare Maiden were quite disappointed by her decision. But one arrogant bastard decided she would be his, willing or not. He therefore sent a fleet of vampire clones to shoot down the shuttle she was traveling in on her way to the Lycan capital—a shuttle she shared with Queen Mother Raina!" I said in a seething voice.

Outraged cries resonated throughout the chamber. The

genuine shock on the other three High Lords erased any doubts I may have held about them being in any way involved.

"My Council wanted me to exact a swift and exemplary retribution in response to such an offense that could have cost the lives of my mother and my mate," I said harshly.

It was a bold statement as I had not made my official claim, and Thalia had obviously not given her consent. However, I knew in my bones that we would be together.

"But I didn't," I said in an icy voice. "Why, you ask? Because as Lord Konstantin so eloquently put it, we had no tangible proof. And yet, everyone in this room knows exactly who would be so arrogant, so motivated, and with the financial means to stage an impromptu kidnapping. He would have kept her caged somewhere, slowly draining her to enhance himself, without her well-deserved compensation. All this because he was always an entitled little bitch."

I clasped my hands on my lap and tilted my head to the side as I stared at Konstantin, daring him to lose his shit. While speaking, I'd changed my mind about actually fighting him. The bastard was strong. However, in spite of my recent illness, thanks to both Thalia's blood and Soren's blessing, my strength by far exceeded his. I wouldn't kill him, but I would derive great pleasure from publicly trouncing him. It was time for Vlad to take over the rule of Verelinn. Undermining his rival would further help his cause. Judging by the muttering and shocked glances of the crowd as Konstantin quietly took his licks, that process was already underway.

"Now, you all wonder why I'm here, publicly airing my grievances if I had let go of that first offense," I said, turning back to the crowd. "Because the vermin, emboldened by the absence of reprisal after his first trespass, launched a second attack at the Moon Well itself."

This time, the outraged gasp that rose from the vampires in the crowd were not aimed at my words but at the culprit himself.

All eyes turned towards Konstantin, glaring and condemning while I pursued my tale.

"Spite can make people very petty," I continued with contempt. "Since he couldn't have her, he decided that no one else would. He sent clones to the northern Karthian villages, who used compulsion on their inhabitants so that they could infiltrate Lycan territory unseen. And for what? So that they could try to drown the Golden Maiden in the sacred water of the Moon Well. Instead, they sullied this holy shrine with their blood."

This time, angry shouts erupted throughout the crowd. Vlad's eyes were throwing daggers at his rival. Even the ever-laidback Vasska had lost his perpetual amusement to look at Konstantin with a hard glimmer in his eyes. I couldn't say if the fury etched on Morana's face stemmed from her former lover's outrageous behavior, or jealousy that another female should have triggered such a powerful reaction from him.

"You can't prove this either," Konstantin hissed.

I discreetly raised my palm to stop both Viktor and Ulia from tearing into him for speaking again without leave.

"I don't need to, as this time again, no punishment will be exacted against the culprit," I said with a shrug.

The shock on his face and on everyone else's in attendance would have been comical under different circumstances.

"So then, what's the meaning of this entire circus?" Konstantin asked, as if he'd been the one wronged. "You came here simply to lay unproven accusations at my feet and make a display of your rank?"

"I came here to make clear to all vampires the reason why from this day forward and until the Moon Well next opens, no vampires will be allowed anywhere on Lycan territories, including the pond."

Shouts of dismay and anger rose from the crowd. My Iron Guards turned outwards to face the public, ready to take down any fool that might get overheated. The silver water was required to complete the change both in Lycans and Vampires, and to lengthen their lifespan. But for the younger blood drinkers, it was also necessary to allow their bodies to better process artificial blood, which was all that most of them could afford.

"You cannot do this!" Konstantin shouted. "This is genocide. You want to punish every vampire over crimes whose author you cannot identify! That's unconscionable."

"Conscience?" I exclaimed with a snort. "That's rich coming from you. As you stated so well, I cannot prove the identity of the vampire able to send so many expensive clones on such 'unconscionable' attacks. Therefore, I am forced to presume that any of you could be the culprit. As such, I must protect the Karthian villages, the Lycans, and the humans under my protection—including the Golden Blood Maiden."

"King Drogo," Vlad intervened. "It could be decades if not centuries before the Moon Well opens again. It has already been three hundred years. I do not challenge your right to protect your people, but the fledglings—who will be the most negatively affected by this royal decree—are also your people."

"Not decades, nor centuries, but weeks," I replied matter-of-factly while holding Vlad's gaze. The lack of surprise in his reaction made me believe he had been suspecting it. Or had he felt it as well? "The Well is stirring. Until it does, I will suffer no more disturbance because of the unrealistic ambitions of a would-be usurper," I added, my gaze hardening as it turned towards Konstantin. "Should *any* other incident occur, if I get even the slightest wind of a threat towards the Golden Maiden, my revenge will be swift and unforgiving. I will raze Verelinn to the ground and wipe out every single vampire, from fledgling, to Ancients, to clones."

"King Drogo!" Morana exclaimed, shooting to her feet with outrage while the crowd erupted in violent protest.

"SILENCE!" I shouted, rising to my feet as well.

In a display of power—fueled by the blessing of Soren—I

used my compulsion to numb the entire audience's vocal chords, robbing them of the ability of uttering the slightest sound, without impairing their ability to breathe. Many clutched at their throats in shock or panic. Morana, too, held her throat, but it was true fear that descended on her stunning features. She realized for the first time the extent my power had grown since the last time she had seen me battle a couple of centuries ago.

"ALL vampires, Morana," I said in an imperious tone. "However strong the vampires may believe themselves to be, it would take the Lycans no more than seventy-two hours to exterminate every single one of you while our ranks would sustain minimal losses. Remember that you live by *our* mercy."

I let my gaze roam over the public, completely unmoved by the anger and resentment visible on their faces. I lifted my chin and clasped my hands behind my back while allowing my words to sink in.

"To keep the pack strong, the wolves kill their defective pups," I continued. "Some even eat them. You were all born with a weak or non-existent Lycan gene. And yet, we spared your lives, nurtured you as kin, and helped you thrive. Still, even after discontent and ambition drove you to exodus, we let you leave with our blessing. For centuries, we have not meddled in your affairs and allowed you to seek your own destiny. We've even developed artificial blood to ease your life. And this is how you thanked us? By slandering the Lycans and rewriting history with an absurd narrative? By abusing the humans we have entrusted in your care to increase your chances of survival in light of your genetic defects? By trying to usurp the ruling of Karthia with cowardly attacks?"

This time, many of the vampires had the decency to look a little embarrassed, but still nowhere near enough.

"No vampire will ever rule Karthia," I said in a hard tone. "That role will *always* fall to the Apex Alpha of the Packs. The one time one among you was considered for that honor, he proved himself unworthy. You are your brother's keeper. See that the culprit of the recent aggressions against the crown stays in his place, or you will all face my wrath. There will be no mercy."

I turned towards the thirty-six vampires and humans of the Grand Council, sitting across the dais from the High Lords.

"And as for you, Councilors of Verelinn," I continued, "see that you get your own house in order if you want us to continue to stay out of your affairs. *We* protected *you* when you were the weakest links of the packs. See that you treat your fledglings and your humans better. Forty years is *not* an acceptable lifespan for a human. You have one year to show concrete improvements, or we will take charge and set the rules for you."

I walked down the couple of stairs to the dais where the High Lords sat, and Konstantin still stood.

"As per Pack Rules, anyone who wishes to contest my authority is welcomed to challenge me to a naked duel, no fabricated weapons, only the physical ones you naturally possess," I said, staring tauntingly at Konstantin. "As it seems you've grown quite foolish, if you have a death wish, you know where to find me."

With a final smirk, I marched down the stairs to rejoin my escort on the ground floor. In a final display of power, I forced the entire attendance onto their knees. For a split second, I feared Soren might take offense at me leveraging the additional power he bestowed upon me, and which allowed me to control such a massive crowd. Thankfully, I only perceived approval from him.

They had hurt our mate. They needed to be reminded that peace could be taken away even more easily than it had been granted.

CHAPTER 16
THALIA

I swayed gently in my liquid tomb. My lungs no longer burned. My throat no longer ached. The magical water surrounding me no longer abraded my skin. Instead, it tingled in an oddly pleasant fashion, like a million tiny kisses soothing what was now the fading memory of an old pain. A powerful wave of love, tenderness and protectiveness lit up in my chest and spread outwards, engulfing me in a cocoon of comfort and happiness. To think I had feared death. I curled up in a fetal position so that this endless love wouldn't be washed away by the water surrounding me. As I surrendered once more to oblivion, I could have sworn Drogo's beloved voice whispered softly to me, his words muffled by the water.

I smiled.

I woke up to the blissful sensation of silky blankets on my skin, the cloud-like softness of my cushiony mattress, and the fluffy support of divine pillows under my head. I felt wonderfully rested and utterly disoriented. My eyelids fluttered, reluctantly opening. I blinked as my eyes opened onto the familiar opulent décor of my suite. I frowned and tried to prop myself up on my elbows. But I fell back down, my limbs appearing to be boneless. They weren't numb, just comatose, like they hadn't been informed that it was time to wake up and get to work.

I stretched to get my muscles going again. They whined a little, wishing to continue enjoying this wondrous cocoon. But I'd never been one to linger in bed. As I pulled back the blanket to sit at the edge of my bed, memories of the recent events came rushing back to me.

I gasped and abruptly raised my hands before me, turning them this way and that to examine my skin. To my shock, my skin was flawless: no redness, no peeled off patches, and no damage of any type. And yet, I clearly remembered the abrasive sensation of the silver water nipping at my skin. And what of the acid-like burn in my throat as it had invaded my mouth?

My hand flew to my throat, and I swallowed hard. There was no pain, and yet it felt odd, as if it had internally been coated with something smooth. Beneath my palm covering my neck, my pulse picked up as post-traumatic stress over the attack washed over me. Where was Drogo? Was he all right? There had been so many attackers…

"The white wolves…" I whispered, the memory of their silhouettes breaking the tree line as they rushed towards us flashed through my mind.

Had they saved him? Had they saved me? They must have, or I wouldn't be here. I was drowning.

No, I didn't drown. I suffocated. The parasites killed me.

Heat exploded on my chest, followed by a strong wave of sadness. I instinctively pressed my hand over my heart. Beneath my palm, through the thin silky fabric of my ivory nightgown, something moved. I yelped, yanked my hand away, and stared at my chest in horror. For a split second, I tried to convince myself that I had imagined that sensation. But familiar soothing waves and an infinite love radiated from my chest. I had felt all of this before while submerged in water—pleasant water.

Raising a trembling hand to my chest, I carefully parted the spaghetti string attached to the low, V-shaped top of my night-gown. Beneath my skin, right above my heart, the elegant lines of a Wolf Spirit, different than Soren's, graced my chest. The panic and horror that I expected to take a hold of me never did.

Since the first time I'd spoken to Drogo in the Kivilinn General Hospital, with the force field keeping him trapped in his medical cell, I'd believed his 'Spirit' to be a parasite leeching him. Everything else he had told me about their history and Konstantin's adventure with Soren had reinforced that belief. But now that I felt one of them inside me, I realized the extent of my mistake.

This 'Spirit' was a sentient being, capable of thought, of deep emotions, and of coordinated action. As more memories of the attack came back to me, I remembered the sensation of the Spirit entering my mouth and going down my throat. Of the others covering my face. They hadn't been suffocating me but preventing me from swallowing more of that harmful water I'd been gulping down under the clone's compulsion.

With my fingertips, I gently caressed the Spirit's outline over my skin. I immediately felt its pleasure, like a fat cat purring at getting its tummy rubbed.

"You saved me, didn't you?" I asked in a whisper.

A wave of love exploded in my chest, radiating from him, and bringing tears to my eyes.

"Yes, he did," Drogo's voice gently said from my right.

Startled, I gasped, and my head jerked towards the main door of my suite. I hadn't heard him open the door in my fascination with the Spirit.

"Drogo," I breathed out, joy and relief washing over me.

I rose to my feet, surprised by how steady I felt when only

moments before my body had been utterly comatose. Drogo met me halfway as I all but ran to him before throwing myself into his arms. Fisting his hair at the nape, I drew his face to mine and pressed my lips against his. I hadn't meant to do that, but Drogo took over what my instincts had initiated. I gladly yielded control to him as he lifted me up, one arm behind my thighs and the other around my back.

For years, I had fantasized about what my first kiss would feel like. I never expected the raging inferno that erupted in the pit of my stomach, the rabid hunger for... something more, and an insatiable thirst that could never be quenched even as I drank at the divine fountain of his mouth.

Drogo's tongue teased the seam of my lips, demanding entry. Once more, I eagerly yielded. Although I had never been with a man—or woman—I wasn't clueless... far from it. Our Seduction classes had seen to it. Nevertheless, there was a huge difference between theory—and practice with toys for things such as deep throat—and reality.

I had never imagined how addictive the soft warmth of the Lycan King's mouth against mine could be. The rough texture of his tongue caressing mine sent delicious tingles through me that had my nipples pebble in seconds. The spicy-sweet taste of him, laced with the lingering taste of the Karthian wine he'd recently drunk made me dizzy for more. And the searing heat of his hard, muscular body holding me tightly had me melting against him. Despite the little amount of fabric covering me, I wished there had been no obstacle whatsoever between us so that I could feel all of him.

In my lustful daze, I hadn't noticed Drogo had carried me back to my bed. I gasped against his mouth when he started lowering me backwards. My fingers instinctively dug into his shoulders, only relaxing once I felt the soft cushion of my mattress against my back. To my disappointment, instead of joining me in bed, Drogo sat next to me at the edge. Supporting himself with his right hand on the mattress near my shoulder, he leaned forward to caress my face with his left.

"My beautiful Thalia," he whispered tenderly. "How are you feeling, my love?"

"Like I wish you hadn't stopped," I blurted out with a boldness that left me reeling and that had his gorgeous silver eyes widening with surprise.

Recovering quickly, Drogo chuckled and bent down to kiss me again. I immediately cupped his nape to keep him from pulling away. The light fur there and over his shoulders felt incredibly soft to the touch. Once more, he devoured my mouth while his left hand caressed my body more daringly. His palm settled over my breast and gently fondled it. I moaned against his lips, wetness pooling between my thighs as my core began to throb.

He broke the kiss, his mouth grazed my jawline and settled on the pulse in my neck. My inner walls clenched, and my pulse picked up with a strange mix of fear and anticipation. Drogo grazed his teeth over the palpitating vein, the sharpness leading me to believe his fangs had descended. My breath shortened, coming in quick, short bursts. His hand slipped under the short skirt of my nightgown and boldly settled on my sex, over my panties.

My breath hitched as he slowly rubbed his palm over my drenched underwear. His body tensed, and a growl rose from his throat as he nipped at my neck.

"Please," I whispered in a needy voice.

I didn't know what I was begging him for. For him to bite me? For him to touch me even more intimately? For him to make me his? With a will of their own, my legs parted to make more room for his large hand stroking me. I felt his hesitation in light of my blatant invitation. He lifted his head to look at me. The naked hunger on his face turned me into a puddle and further fanned the flame raging inside me. And yet, through my lustful haze that was setting my body ablaze, I didn't miss the worried glimmer in Drogo's eyes. He either believed I wasn't ready, or that I had not recovered enough.

"Please," I begged again, this time lifting my face towards his. However, instead of kissing him, I buried my face in his neck and, for some irrational reason, gave the crook of his neck a stinging bite.

Drogo emitted a sharp growl-grunt, and something seemed to snap inside of him. He fisted my hair and yanked my head back, forcing me to lie back down. My yelp of surprise was muffled by his lips crushing mine. At the same time, his hand wormed its way inside my panties. His thick fingers parted my wet petals to scissor my little nub. Once more, I moaned against his mouth, my pelvis lifting to get greater friction from his wanton fingers.

While pleasure steadily built in my nether region, Drogo's mouth explored my body. Annoyed by my nightgown that kept getting in the way, I all but ripped it off me. But my arms and hair got tangled in the wretched thing. The delicious torment of Drogo's fingers on my sex, his voracious mouth sucking and nipping at the hard nub of my nipple made it harder for me to free myself of my garment.

I finally succeeded at the same time the searing heat of the Lycan King's mouth settled on my core. I cried out his name, and my fingers gripped the silky locks of his long, dark brown hair, to maintain his head's position. My hips gyrated under his sensual assault, and my legs began to shake with my impending orgasm.

It then struck me with a suddenness and a violence that made my body stiffen almost painfully. Head thrown back, my mouth opened in a silent O, I felt as if the slightest breeze would snap me in half. My body collapsed onto the mattress, shaking as I rode the waves of ecstasy. Only when my spasms began to subside did Drogo's sinful tongue relent.

As he climbed on top, the possessive caress of his hands

along my body made me realize I was fully naked. I knew for a fact that he hadn't removed my underwear from me. And I couldn't recall him snapping it off either. And yet, here I was fully bare beneath him while he was still fully clothed. I gazed at him through hooded eyes, ready to complain about such unfairness. But the words died in my throat at the sight of the nearly feral expression on his face.

"You are mine, Thalia," Drogo growled, his tone menacing. "You belong to me, body and soul, now and always. You are my mate. MY mate."

He crushed my lips with a savagery that left me reeling. In a movement reminiscent of our very first encounter in his hospital room, Drogo slipped his arms behind my knees, spreading me wide open. I barely felt the thin fabric of his pants between us as he frantically rubbed his erect shaft against me, reigniting the inferno that had just abated. The powerful friction against my engorged little nub sent lightning bolts of pleasure through me, pushing me towards the edge.

Before my brain could fully register the stinging pain of his fangs sinking into the fleshy part of my neck, liquid ecstasy invaded my system. A blinding white light exploded before my eyes. For a split second, I felt as if the violence of my orgasm had kicked me right out of my body as I floated in a sea of bliss. I lost all sense of time and space, or even of self. Every inch of my body, every nerve ending, was overwhelmed by a maelstrom of sensation, casting me into an endless ocean of pleasure. Drogo's panting grunts mingled with my moans as I surrendered myself to him.

My Lycan's body seized, and he shouted my name, his arms tightening around me in a bruising hold. Still floating on the wings of bliss, I barely reacted as he gathered me in his arms. Rolling us over, he rested my head on his chest. I curled up against him, and slipped my hand under his shirt, settling it on the feverish skin of his abs. We remained silent, just savoring each other's presence. As I listened to the erratic pounding of his heart, mine seemed to synchronize with his, they slowed down to a more normal pace.

"I'm sorry," Drogo said at long last.

My head jerked up to look at him. I frowned at the guilty expression on his face. Surely, he wasn't regretting what had just happened between us? That would kill me.

"For your sake, you better be apologizing about the fact that you're still dressed," I said in a harsh tone to hide my vulnerability and lack of confidence.

Drogo recoiled, taken aback by my response. He cast a brief glance at himself and then snorted.

"Right," he said, looking mightily embarrassed. "I... I shouldn't have touched you like this."

Heedless of my nudity, I pulled away from him, hiding none of my sense of betrayal and of the stabbing pain of rejection his words had inflicted.

"No!" Drogo said, urgently, placing a possessive hand on my hips to keep me from further moving away from him. "I do not regret what has just happened between us. I meant every single word that I said. You are mine, Thalia. You were created for me. I knew you were my mate from the moment I laid eyes on you. I want you as my mate, my consort, my wife, whatever term you wish to use, for however long as we both draw breath. I am crazy for you. You're all that I think about, every minute of every day."

Each of his words soothed the pain while making my heart soar. I had felt the same about him from the moment we'd sat together in his medical cell.

"But you are still recovering from a serious physical trauma," Drogo added in a soft voice. "I shouldn't have so easily surrendered to my hunger for you. That said, that's not what I was apologizing for."

I blinked and gave him an inquisitive look. As soon as guilt took over his features, I realized what was gnawing at him.

"I promised to keep you safe, and I failed, once again. You—"

"Enough," I said, placing two fingers on his lips. "I'm here, aren't I? I'm whole. Had you failed me, I wouldn't be here."

"But—"

"No buts!" I interrupted again. "Okay, I got roughed up, but it wasn't out of negligence on your part. Frankly, I can't believe they attacked us at the Moon Well. From all accounts, it's also a sacred shrine for the vampires. Konstantin has gone too far. If the Great Council hears of this…"

"They know," Drogo said, smugly.

He then launched into a fairly detailed retelling of his speech to the Grand Council of Verelinn. My jaw dropped upon hearing the humiliation to which he had subjected Konstantin. As much as I would have given anything to witness this, worry settled in the pit of my stomach.

"You have made yourself a lifelong enemy," I said with concern.

"Konstantin has hated me for being born the heir to the throne of Karthia and knowing that he could never win a challenge against me for it," Drogo said dismissively. "That Soren chose me after rejecting him only further increased that hatred."

"And now me," I added.

"And now you, my love," he said before caressing my cheek.

"But… You… you wouldn't truly slaughter all the vampires if that fool attacks me again, right?" I asked, hesitantly.

My stomach dropped when his face took on a hard, unforgiving edge.

"I meant every single word I said in their Council Hall," Drogo said in a clipped voice. "The vampires know well that Lycans do not bluff. They also know that should an all-out war break out between our species, they will be wiped out in only a few days with minimal losses to us. With nearly half of them unable to withstand daylight, it would be a massacre. War isn't clean and ethical like dueling. It is dirty, ugly, and merciless."

"But everyone knows who is behind it," I argued.

"Exactly, and they will therefore keep him in check," Drogo deadpanned. "Out of self-preservation, the vampires will do the work of thwarting his nefarious plans on our behalf. This way, rather than spreading our troops thin to keep an eye on him, we can focus on our packs. If Vlad is wise, he will seize this opportunity to shift a greater number of Konstantin's allies to his side instead. While they play their little power games, we can focus on preparing for the opening of the Moon Well."

Heat radiated in my chest, drawing my attention back to my Spirit that had made himself discreet for the last short while. My face heated, realizing he had borne witness—probably even felt —some of what had just happened between Drogo and me. Affection and appeasing waves emanated from him.

I placed my hand over my Spirit and gently caressed him. "I think he agrees with you," I said softly.

Drogo smiled as he looked at my brand, but the slight frown marring his forehead as he did so worried me.

"His name is Zabek," Drogo said, delicately tracing the lines of my Spirit's shape with his index finger.

"Hello, Zabek," I whispered, smiling when he sent out another wave of love through me. "But you're not really a Spirit, are you?" Drogo said nothing, listening attentively while I lifted my head to lock gazes with him. "When your mother first told me about the Spirits of the Sun Wolves, I assumed she meant their soul. Then I thought they were parasites. But now, I real- ized they are symbionts. And each of the wolf-shifter aliens called Sun Wolves who visited Karthia, hosted one of these symbionts. But to the primitive Karthians, they were fallen stars with magical powers."

Drogo smiled and nodded.

"By the way, I still think you're far too dressed," I said in a pouty voice.

Drogo burst out laughing, and only met me halfway by removing his shirt. It wasn't much, but better than nothing. I nearly moaned at finally feeling the warmth of his naked skin against mine.

"The Lycan form… Did they also have that ability?" I asked, while my fingers fiddled with the light fur on the side of his left arm.

"No," Drogo responded, shaking his head. "It is a mutation following the mating between Karthians and Sun Wolves."

"I see…" I said, chewing my bottom lip. "Who was Selene? Obviously not a goddess. Was she their boss? The captain of their ship? An expedition leader?"

"We don't know," Drogo said with a shrug. "The Sun Wolves were clearly not warriors or hunters. They were too easily defeated and subdued by the primitive Karthian tribes. I believe they were settlers looking for new worlds to colonize. I also believe that Selene did not agree with this plan, but that Soren insisted because of Skala. Others followed Soren and the rest of the settlers left with Selene."

"Then what happened?" I asked. "Did King Oleg manage to get in touch with Selene to get her to help them with the children?"

"Oh no," Drogo said, shaking his head as if I'd said something ludicrous. "We have no means of contacting her or whatever home world we hail from. Selene came back probably to check up on the settlers, then found out what a mess had occurred here. Did it ever strike you as strange that I haven't introduced you to a single one of the original surviving Sun Wolves?"

"It did," I conceded. "But I assumed they had died. They may be long lived, but not immortal. I figured illness from the abuse at the hands of the Priestesses, or accidents had ended them."

"Nope. They left with Selene."

My hand plucking at his fur froze, and I stared at him with disbelief. "They just abandoned you? They abandoned their children?" I asked, my voice pitching up.

"We were too… different," Drogo said, choosing his words carefully. "We would have become medical experiments in their world. We didn't know how many more mutations would still happen, or what kind of strange illnesses we'd bring about—like the one your blood saved me from. They believed we would have a better future here."

"But what of the Spirits? Why didn't Selene take them, too?" I asked, still feeling like the Sun Wolves had actually abandoned their offspring. Then again, according to Raina's tale, generations had already been born, with some of them dying, by the time Selene came back.

Drogo's face softened, and he glanced at the brand on his chest. "History repeated itself. Soren refused to leave."

"And the others followed," I finished for him.

He nodded and watched my hand as I lifted it to caress Soren's outline on his chest. My own mark heated, and a wave of discontent flared from Zabek. I looked at my bare breast and caressed my Spirit as well.

"Don't be jealous. Me being grateful towards Soren doesn't make me love you any less," I said gently. "You did save my life."

Zabek's satisfied reaction filled me with the sweetest sense of well-being. No wonder all the Sun Wolves had hosted one. They were quite addictive. I looked back at Drogo, but my smile faded before his frowning expression.

"What is it?" I asked, feeling worried. "It's the second time you make that face."

"You cannot keep him, Thalia," Drogo said softly.

"WHAT?!" I exclaimed, flattening my palm protectively over Zabek's shape on my chest. "Why? He chose me!"

"You can't hold him," Drogo explained in a reasonable voice. "Genetically speaking, you're not made for that."

"I'm holding him right now without pain!" I countered, feeling irrationally betrayed. "So, clearly, I can!"

"Your golden blood is the only reason you can currently hold him," Drogo countered. "Any other human or Karthian would have died. The Spirits can process golden blood to sustain themselves and repair defects in the host. While you were submerged in the healing tank, Zabek used some of your blood to repair the internal damage you had sustained. But your body doesn't naturally produce what he needs to survive. You lack the Lycan gene."

The wave of sadness from my Spirit confirmed Drogo's words.

"Okay, but you said my blood allows him to compensate," I argued, being deliberately obtuse because I didn't want to accept that I would have to let him go.

"But he would need to drain it, to consume it in order to survive," Drogo said with a slightly stern tone. "Zabek is currently starving himself to protect you. He took a huge risk by joining with you. He had no way of knowing if this would work. He's thousands of years old, and yet, he risked death for a chance to save you. He must go back to the pond."

My throat tightened, love and gratitude overshadowing the terrible sense of loss that clawed at me. It was stupid, but I'd never been selflessly loved before. For my parents, I'd only been the jackpot in the blood DNA lottery. I'd been immediately handed off to the Academy, which had paid them monthly a fraction of the proceeds from sales of my blood during the twenty-five years of my training. When my father had died, Mother had demanded to receive his share.

"But… What if… what if you turned me?" I asked in a last,

desperate effort to keep Zabek. The other wave of tenderness the symbiont gave me in response to that comment only increased my desire to keep him.

"Turning someone is a permanent change that will affect many aspects of your life," Drogo said in a calm voice. "It isn't a decision that can be taken while you're in such an emotional state. And especially while under the influence of a Spirit's affection. AND, it wouldn't work," he added quickly, when I opened my mouth to argue some more.

"What do you mean?" I asked, my heart breaking.

"Once infected with the Lycan virus, it will take a certain amount of time for your body to change enough to be able to host him safely," Drogo said.

It was silly how heartbroken I felt. I caressed Zabek again through my skin. "Would... would he want to be with me again after I turned?" I asked in a small voice.

Drogo's face melted in a tender expression that did funny things to me. "I cannot speak on his behalf. But he did risk his life to save yours."

The thought that Zabek saved me only to ensure I'd be around long enough to give Drogo my blood until he was fully healed flashed through my head. But I immediately dismissed it. My whole life, I'd experienced the artificial kindness of people who only coveted my blood. Zabek's affection for me felt as genuine as Drogo's—although different in nature. Clearly pleased by my conclusion, my Spirit rewarded me with another affectionate nudge.

"All right," I said piteously.

Drogo chuckled and nipped at my pouty, bottom lip. "Stop fretting so much, my love. All will be well. Trust me."

I nodded and wrapped my arms around him as he leaned in to kiss me again. It was gentle and tender, unlike the previous wild passion that had possessed us earlier. But as he deepened the kiss, I felt a slight pinching sensation in my chest. And then my skin tingled as if I was about to pass out. By the time I felt a tickling in my throat and realized what was happening, it was too late.

"No!" I exclaimed when Drogo broke the kiss and pulled away from me.

My hand flew to my chest. Tears welled in my eyes when my palm met nothing but my skin. Zabek had left me. I had not been ready. I stared at Drogo, feeling betrayed, tricked even, as he spoke soothing words that I didn't want to hear.

And then Soren shifted on his chest as the outline of another Spirit began to form next to him. My anger flared; irrational, savage, and all-consuming.

"You bastard!" I shouted, slamming my fist on his chest, on the opposite side from the Spirits. "You fucking stole him from me!"

"Hush, my love, hush!" Drogo pleaded, catching my wrist before pulling me into an unbreakable embrace.

I fought in vain to free myself, but the strain of my recent injuries finally manifested itself. Feeling weak, I collapsed against him, and bawled my eyes out.

"Do not cry my love," Drogo said, his voice laced with sorrow in the face of my distress. "I didn't steal him. He had to leave because he was in pain and didn't want to leech your blood. Zabek didn't abandon you. He left to protect you from himself. He loves you very much, like I do."

The rational part of me understood that... *knew* that. Hearing it said out loud did act like a balm on the open wound of my messed-up emotions. And yet, I couldn't stop crying. It wasn't just the toll of having lost that wonderful Spirit, but all the shit from my entire miserable life that I had internalized for years. The indifference of my parents, the rigorous Blood Maiden training at the hands of cold Matrons, the constant fear of being kidnapped and attacked, whoring myself out at the Blood Fair, the endless stress of my uncertain future, and Konstantin's attacks all melded into one big, festering ball of slime that had been long overdue to be cast out.

I don't know how long I ugly cried on Drogo's shoulder. He held me patiently, speaking gentle words to me, and caressing my back in a slow, soothing motion, giving me exactly what I needed. My tears finally receded, leaving me completely wrecked and exhausted. I drifted to sleep to the gentle sound of Drogo's voice.

CHAPTER 17
DROGO

The Summer Solstice celebrations were in full swing. My heart had never been so full seeing all my people under my roof, joyful, thriving, and more united than ever before. I couldn't help grinning at the antics of the pups. There were so many of them now, strong, healthy—all of them full Lycans. It had been fifty-six years since the last vampire had been born to a Lycan couple. And the percentage of pups born defective or dying of Blood Starvation had dropped to 12% while it had been slightly over 62% in days of old. I hoped this was a sign that the DNA of the Lycan breed was finally settling and stabilizing. It was high time for us to stop living in survival mode and fully focus on our cultural and technological growth.

My smile broadened as I gazed upon my mate. Sitting on the grass near the massive bonfire, and surrounded by a handful of pups in their wolf form, she was playfully begging for mercy while the young pretended to devour her. What a long way she had come in such a short time.

Thalia still had certain manic behaviors when it came to interacting with potentially harmful things. But those responses were usually instinctive, and she quickly snapped out of it.

However, with food, she continued to be very picky. It had disappointed me at first, but her justification shamed me—I should have thought of it myself. After an entire life eating only the leanest and healthiest foods, she couldn't simply start indulging in spicy, fatty, rich, or extremely sweet foods. Her stomach would rebel.

But her near-death experience had broken some of her mental chains. Although Dr. Tanner had confirmed that the silver water had slightly altered the toxicity levels in her blood, Thalia no longer cared. Ditto with whatever toxins or bacteria could be introduced into her system by one of the pups scratching her. She no longer cared because I genuinely didn't either. It had been hard for her to reconcile the fact that the purity and taste of her blood was no longer important. But almost dying reminded her how quickly what you had could be taken away. My mate was now hellbent on living life to the fullest.

And I couldn't agree more.

However, that also meant protecting Thalia from herself and her excess of enthusiasm. I'd already yielded too much yesterday when we'd finally exchanged our first kiss. I hadn't meant to let things go that far, but I could never regret that it had officially sealed our status as a couple. Even now, the taste of her lingered on my tongue, making me ache with need.

Technically, I would be able to turn Thalia tomorrow if she still wished it. And she did—too much. For that reason, I would delay it for a while. First, I wanted to give her a few weeks of truly enjoying life as a human before the change forever altered the way she perceived and interacted with the world. Second, I wanted her to embrace life as a Lycan for its own sake, and not just as a means to get Zabek back.

Although I couldn't deny feeling a certain jealousy for how attached she had grown to the Spirit, I genuinely empathized with her loss. I couldn't fathom Soren leaving me. I'd only carried Zabek for a short while after he'd migrated into me upon leaving Thalia. And yet, I'd felt terribly bereft when I'd released him back into the pond less than an hour after my woman had fallen asleep. As much as I disliked Konstantin, I could only imagine the depth of his distress and pain when Soren had eventually rejected and abandoned him. I couldn't fathom what horrible things or thoughts the vampire had entertained to drive away such a loving and protective being as a Spirit.

The delicate scent of my mother tickled my nose seconds before her soft hand caressed my shoulder blade and then settled on the small of my back. I instinctively wrapped my arm around her shoulders when she came to a stop by my side.

"You have chosen the perfect Queen, my son," Mother said gently. "Your people love her."

I turned my face towards her and gently kissed her temple. "As do I."

Mother smiled, love and pride shining in her silver eyes. "Darya says Thalia is a fierce warrior and a fast learner, in no small part thanks to her previous combat training. The only thing keeping her from being true competition to your Iron Maidens is the limited speed and strength of her human body."

I snorted and cast a sideways glance at my mother, letting her know I wasn't even remotely fooled by her less than subtle hint.

"All good things come to those who wait," I said matter-of-factly. "It will happen when she's ready."

"What makes you think she's not?" my mother asked, a serious expression descending on her features as she turned to face me. "Dr. Tanner says she's physically sound for it, and the change won't affect her blood type. Sure, the virus will affect her purity and toxicity ratings, but that's irrelevant for you."

"I am well aware of that, Mother," I said patiently. "But her body and her mind have gone through enough shocks already. She deserves a little reprieve before I subject her to another traumatic experience."

My mother's face took on that mulish expression I knew too

well. That look expressed loud and clear that she believed I was being unreasonably obtuse, and that I should listen to her, since she always knew better.

"Drogo, you know that I make it a point not to meddle in how you run your affairs," she said with a seriousness that took me aback. I had expected a playfully chastising behavior instead. "Twice, Thalia faced terrible attacks without the proper means to fight enemies possessing ten times her speed and strength. Making her a Lycan—especially in light of her already great combat skills—will give all of us, including her, great peace of mind should something else occur. I know you will do everything in your power to keep Thalia safe. But bestowing upon your mate the means to protect herself is the greatest present you can ever give her. Just think about it, okay?"

"I will," I said with a nod, troubled by her argument.

I still didn't want to rush the process, but my mother's words had hit a nerve. I didn't believe in living my life based on the fears of what ifs. But indeed, what if Thalia found herself in a dire situation that she otherwise could have easily extricated herself from if only I had turned her already?

"I didn't mean to trouble you with unpleasant thoughts," my mother said sheepishly, scratching the back of my left ear as she often used to do in order to soothe me as a child. "I was coming here to tell you to open the ball. The men's bellies are full. They're starting to excessively indulge in Karthian wine and are boasting a bit too much about their skills. Your Iron Maidens—with Darya in the lead—are about to spank them raw. Unless you want to have your Iron Warriors tucking their tails in shame for the foreseeable future, I suggest you give them something to do."

I chuckled and cast a glance at my Iron Warriors mixed with various males from the visiting packs. Chests puffed out, some of them standing in their Lycan forms, they were flaunting their skills and attributes to the females who couldn't have looked less impressed.

"Good idea," I said to my mother.

I kissed her forehead and headed towards my poor woman, still being assaulted by far too many pups.

"That's enough, you bunch of fleabags. Release my woman at once. She and I have a date with the dance floor," I told the pups in an imperious voice.

They all made faces at me before obeying and stepping aside to observe us. I extended a hand towards my mate, but she looked at it sadly.

"I would have loved to dance, but Milos and Anya ate my legs," Thalia said with a crestfallen expression.

I gasped in fake outrage and pretended to glare at the two four-legged culprits. The pups immediately flattened their ears on their heads and tucked their tails between their legs. They both made heart-melting sad faces accompanied by an award-winning harmony of whimpers. I had to bite the insides of my cheeks not to burst out laughing. Anya, even more shameless than her older brother, discreetly pointed her back paw at Milos.

"Milos did it?" I asked sternly, looking at the little male.

His head jerked up towards me, then abruptly towards his sister, who was nodding her small wolfish head without the slightest remorse. Milos emitted a short warning growl at her. Anya took off a split second before Milos would have tackled her to the ground. Laughing, I helped my mate up while the little brats were off chasing each other.

I pulled her into my embrace and gently kissed her lips. She melted against me, oblivious to the approving stares leveled on us.

"I want at least a dozen of those," Thalia said against my lips.

"A dozen? No less?" I asked, tightening my arms around her.

"Minimum, for starters," Thalia said with a sharp nod.

"Anything you want, my Queen, you shall have," I replied,

my voice dipping lower. Now that Dr. Tanner had deemed her fully recovered, I was done holding back my passion.

"Good answer, Wolfy," my woman said, rubbing her nose against mine.

It was a silly nickname, and yet, I fucking loved it.

The band started playing even before Thalia and I hit the large dance floor built out of multiple hover platforms to avoid damaging the grass in the garden, and located a few meters away from the bonfire. Although our steps had evolved in a slightly different direction than the vampire dances, they had all stemmed from the same Karthian folk dances of ancient times. Thanks to her Blood Maiden training—which included dancing —Thalia was quickly able to adjust to our variation. Either way, it wouldn't have mattered.

Lycans were naturally gifted with anything that involved physical activity. My brothers and sisters could therefore move with the best of them. However, between those a little too tipsy, and those a wee bit too horny, the dancing became less a matter of following steps and more a question of how much you could grind against your partner. By the time the first song had ended, at least a dozen of the couples that had joined us on the dance floor, had vanished to go scratch that itch.

The scent of my people's arousal around me only fanned my hunger for my own mate. For all our open-mindedness and laid-back approach to nakedness, we were very jealous of our intimate moments with our significant other. Contrary to the propaganda spread about us based on the sometimes lascivious dances during the Summer Solstice, they never turned into massive outdoor orgies. However, if one didn't pay attention, you could run into isolated couples getting frisky in the woods, or by the lake.

My own erection was painfully straining against my pants, and Thalia was making a point of rubbing herself against it in a way that looked innocent yet was far from it. She was displeased with my insistence on waiting until Dr. Tanner had given us his blessing to go all the way and seized every opportunity to drive me mad with lust. A distant chime saved me from this torture.

"I will punish you later for this," I growled in her ear before nipping her earlobe.

"For what, Wolfy?" she asked, opening her eyes wide and 'innocently' batting her eyelashes.

"You know very well, female," I said, baring my teeth at her. "Come on, I want you to meet some people."

"Oh?" she said.

She followed as I led her by the hand to a series of vacant tables on the opposite side of the dance floor. If not for the dim blue spheres of light set in the center of each table and embedded inside the staves planted along the northern road leading away from the castle, the tables would have been pitched in complete darkness. Thanks to my wolf night vision, I could perfectly see everything, but my woman had to squint a little.

Thalia's hand tightened around mine when she finally spotted the large delegation approaching. I cast a sideways glance at my mate and was pleased to see her expression held the right level of stoicism despite the curiosity and awe that she currently felt. As much as I hated the lonely and difficult life she had had, Thalia's Blood Maiden upbringing had groomed her to become the perfect Queen.

Escorted by Ulia and Gavril, close to one hundred Karthians—representing each of the remaining tribes—were joining our celebrations for a couple of hours. With their photosensitivity, they avoided traveling too far from their homes to make sure they always had plenty of time to return to their shelters before sunrise. Their long and opaque white garments, along with the large hood currently cast down around their shoulders, would protect them in case things went south. Among them, I counted a handful of their human or hybrid spouses or offspring. Being immune to daylight damage, they would look after the Karthians in case of an emergency.

They stopped in front of us. Fisting their right hand over their sternum, they covered it with their other palm before bowing their heads in respect. I slightly bowed my head in return and Thalia imitated me.

"Welcome to Hundilinn, sons and daughters of Karthia," I said in a booming voice so all would hear me. "Thank you for coming in such large numbers to celebrate the Summer Solstice with us. Eat, drink, dance, and mingle with the descendants of your ancestors. And may these celebrations mark the renewed and continued friendship between our people."

The relief on the faces of the Karthian tribe leaders upon hearing my words was almost palpable. Even though Ulia had informed them that no reprisal would come for their involuntary contribution in facilitating the attack against Thalia, they had continued to worry.

"We thank you for your hospitality, King Drogo," Sene said.

The Karthian Priestess repeated the greeting gesture by cupping her fist to her chest and bowing her head. The paleness of her nearly translucid skin looked almost blueish against the pristine white fabric of her robe. She turned her pallid face towards Thalia. Although Karthians possessed a sclera, pupils, and irises like Lycans and humans, a white veil covered them. From a distance, it gave the illusion that their eyes were completely white. With Thalia's limited human vision, I wondered if she could see it.

Sene smiled at Thalia, the slit that served as her mouth stretching in a way that softened the otherwise sharp line of her angular face. Like all Karthians, the Priestess' face was long, with a very pointy chin. High cheekbones, partially hidden by her long, silver-white hair, framed her very narrow nose.

"Sene, this is my mate, Thalia," I said, loving the way those words tasted on my tongue. I would never tire of shouting from the rooftops that this beautiful, smart, and courageous woman belonged to me. "Thalia, this is Sene, an Elder Priestess of the Karthian tribes."

"It is an honor to meet you, Queen Thalia," Sene said, saluting again, her gesture repeated by all of her people following her.

"The honor is all mine," Thalia said in a gentle voice. "I had always dreamt of meeting a Karthian in the flesh. I never imagined it would be one of the mythical Karthian Nymphs. Your people are even more beautiful than in all the carvings I have seen. Thanks to all of you for the pleasure of your presence."

The powerful emotion that crossed the Karthians' features had even me feeling a little choked up. I had not mentored Thalia on how to interact with the Karthians—a terrible oversight on my part. But with her almost supernatural ability to read people, my mate had known exactly what to say. The stigma of the Bloody Wedding continued to haunt their people.

"Such kind words," Sene said, her pale face all but turning crimson. She cast a nervous glance at one of the Karthian males behind her. He approached, holding a stunning, intricately carved, wooden jewelry box. "We… hmmm. We hadn't expected to meet you so soon, but all the tribes collaborated to bring you a gift as a sign of friendship and apology for the recent unfortunate events."

"Oh, there's no need for apologies," Thalia exclaimed. "No one can resist compulsion. You were used. You did no wrong," my mate continued with conviction. "I hold no grudges or resentment towards your people. The real culprit has been confronted about it. So, please, cast out any fears or worries you may harbor about this incident. The Lycans and I know that you were victims as much as I was."

I gently caressed my woman's hair. She looked up at me, and I leaned down to kiss her forehead, before turning back to Sene.

"She is correct, Sene," I said in a gentle voice. "As Ulia told your people, we do not hold you responsible. Our friendship with the Karthians is intact."

"It is a great relief for the tribes to receive this further confirmation from you and your Queen," Sene said, making no effort to hide that a huge weight had been lifted from her shoulders. The sentiment was reflected on the faces of each of her companions. "But please accept this gift nonetheless, as a sign of friendship and to celebrate your union."

Thalia and I hadn't officially married, but it was a technicality here.

"Thank you," Thalia said, accepting the box.

Although I didn't doubt the honesty of the Karthians, I cast a discreet inquisitive glance at Ulia. He briefly closed his eyelids to confirm that he had indeed checked the gift for any potential foul play. Despite being confident that Konstantin wouldn't try anything else, we would continue to take every precaution where Thalia was concerned. Booby traps and slow-acting poison were only a few of the methods that could be used.

When Thalia opened the box to find a huge necklace, earrings, and bracelet set in Helthan stones. For a moment, I thought she would faint. They were the rarest and most expensive gemstones on Karthia. Vampires made a show of displaying their wealth by having as much of it as possible embroidered in their clothes, jewelry, and accessories. They loaded them onto their Blood Maidens to further show them off. However, only the luckiest of the Maidens got to keep them at the end of their contracts. Their extremely high resale value often represented the bulk of their retirement fund.

These stones were one of the main sources of the Lycan's tremendous wealth on top of the production and sale of synthetic blood. The Karthians were not wealthy. For them to have created such a lavish, queenly present in such a short time implied all the tribes had pitched in to round up so many gems. On top of revealing the extent of the fear they had felt, it saddened me to realize that the Karthians still felt very insecure about their status here. Over the next few weeks and months, I would work on convincing them of my commitment to protect the tribes and to treat them as fairly as any other loyal citizen under my care.

"This is too much!" Thalia said. "It's beyond stunning but—"

"But it's a gift offered in sincere friendship," I interrupted, my gaze boring into her.

Although I agreed with her that it was excessively generous, refusing their gift would effectively be a rejection of their friendship and of them as a people. Thankfully, Thalia understood my subtle hint.

"I… I never expected such a generous gift, nor have I ever been given anything so magnificent," Thalia said with a slightly shaking voice. "I am deeply moved and will cherish it."

Sene beamed at her. "It was drawn and crafted by my niece, Vesna," she said, gesturing for a young hybrid to approach.

Like all Karthians, she almost looked albino. But having one human parent had spared her the translucent skin and whitish veil of the pureblood over her eyes. She could walk under the sun for short periods of time, longer with the application of a thick layer of sunscreen.

"You are incredibly talented," Thalia said with genuine admiration.

"More than you know, my love," I said, slipping an arm around her waist to draw her against me. "Vesna is the current artist from a long line of artistic geniuses who now carves the murals in the cave. She has been dying with impatience to start making more sketches of you to determine how you will be immortalized on the wall."

"I still can't believe you all want me on there," Thalia said, her cheeks heating.

"We do because it is deserved," I said with undisguised pride. "Now, we will hand you over to Vesna's good care after the Summer Solstice events are over. For now, our guests are here to feast and celebrate with us." I turned to Sene and gestured at the darker seating areas, the nearby buffet where the lights had been dimmed, and the dance floor where the intimate lighting also suited the couples getting a little friskier. "Please, enjoy yourselves."

CHAPTER 18
THALIA

The party raged on for many more hours. Drogo and I danced some more, Viktor even cutting in to have a twirl with his Queen. As much as he had intimidated me when I first met him, the pack leader had seriously grown on me. Despite his swift temper and being strongly opinionated, he held a genuine affection and respect for my man. With his daughter, Darya, quickly becoming a friend—on top of my combat trainer—Viktor seemed determined to adopt me as his own. Between him and Raina, I was finally starting to get a sense of what having a family—caring parents—felt like.

On a few occasions, Drogo and I tried to sneak back to our quarters. However, there was always something or someone dragging us to some other part of the festivities. In the end, we managed to disappear when some of the packs started talking about a midnight race in the lake.

Despite the eagerness to get down and dirty with my Wolfy, I lured him to the bathroom as soon as we managed to reach my personal suite. Tonight, I intended to go all the way with him; his lingering reservations be damned. But I wasn't going to do that with the scent of so many Lycans on me after all the dancing, hugging, kissing, not to mention the heavy slobbering of the pups.

The Lycans were a very grabby bunch. They'd genuinely tried to keep their hands to themselves when I first arrived, but that didn't last long. Although I'd gotten better at it, it still felt awkward whenever someone passing near me would randomly rub my back in a quick, affectionate gesture, give me a drive by hug, or rub their temple against mine before continuing on their way. As I understood it, physical contact was an instinctive method of sharing their scent with those they loved, either as a sign of possessiveness or affection. While I welcomed both, especially the sense of belonging it procured, when I got intimate with my mate, my scent—and his—were the only ones I wanted him to perceive on me.

Guessing my intentions, Drogo started peeling off his own clothes even as he followed me into the room. He discarded them so quickly, I'd barely managed to remove my shoes and start lifting up my dress. His impatient hands were all over me, stripping me in a blink. He was so fast I almost believed he'd simply torn them off.

Lifting me in his arms, Drogo walked down the few steps into my massive pool-bath. I barely had a chance to catch a deep breath before he sank us under the water. His lips immediately met mine and our bodies wrapped around each other's. After the attack at the pond, I had feared the potential of developing some PTSD that would keep me from enjoying swimming or taking a dip in any large bodies of water. But I had bounced right back from that. Thankfully, Drogo pulled us back to the surface within seconds.

I would never tire of kissing my man. As our tongues mingled, the rough texture of his reminded me how wonderful it felt on my clit, enhancing each sensation as he licked and sucked on my little nub. I immediately began to throb. My hands feverishly explored his muscular body. Drogo allowed it at first. Then, still carrying me and without stopping kissing me, he waded through the water towards the edge of the bath.

Taking some soap from the built-in recessed shelf at the edge of the bath, Drogo began to wash me slowly, methodically, and in the most sensually taunting fashion. I tried to return the favor, but something had taken over me. Like a bitch in heat, I kept rubbing myself against him, groping him with a hunger that verged on obsession. He chuckled a few times as my eagerness got in the way of his ministrations.

I finally stopped 'misbehaving' when he sat me at the edge of the pool and lifted my legs over his shoulders. The warmth of the heated floor beneath my wet back mingled with the fire spreading from my core as Drogo's masterful tongue went to work on me. That, too, I would never tire of. My man knew perfectly how to use his mouth on me to turn me into a writhing puddle of bliss.

Over the past couple of days, since waking up in my bed after the attack, Drogo's tongue had made me see stars more times than I could count. I felt embarrassed that he kept giving but denied me the opportunity to give back. By the time he was done giving me strings of orgasms, I was usually too much of a mess to reciprocate—not that he seemed to expect it, which was wrong.

Between his skillful mouth, expert tongue, and diligent fingers massaging my clit, my lover had me crying out his name in a heartbeat. To my shock, I felt the sharp sting of Drogo's fangs as they sank into my inner right thigh. His hormone flooded my system, setting my nerve endings on fire. However, it wasn't the all-consuming explosion of ecstasy I had previously experienced. I couldn't tell if it was due to the location of his bite or, more likely, a lesser dose of his aphrodisiac. Either way, my muscles relaxed, and a sensual haze took over me.

Drogo pulled me back into the water and into his embrace. I moaned at the feel of the searing heat of his naked body against mine. I languidly wrapped my arms and my legs around him. The wet patches of fur on his nape, between his shoulder blades, and along the side of his arms and shoulders tickled my extra sensitive skin.

He captured my lips, slowly, tenderly, pouring all of his devotion into it as a satisfied growl rose from his throat. While his hand behind my nape held my head in place as he tilted his to the side to deepen the kiss, Drogo pressed my core against his erect shaft with the other. He rubbed himself up and down in a slow, deliberate fashion that clearly broadcast his intentions. Each movement, rubbing against my clit, also sent electric sparks throughout my body. My inner walls clenched, knowing what was finally about to happen.

Drogo broke the kiss and lifted his head to lock eyes with me. "I'm crazy for you, Thalia," he said in a voice rendered even more gravelly by desire. "Will you be mine, now and forever, and will you claim me as yours for as long as we both draw breath?"

A bolt of fire exploded in the pit of my stomach and tears pricked my eyes as I nodded my assent. "Yes, Drogo. A million times yes. Take me, keep me, and let me keep you forever. You are my world, my mate, my happiness."

"I love you, Thalia," Drogo whispered, his arms tightening around me.

His lips reclaiming mine kept me from answering. My stomach fluttered when he slightly lifted me, and I felt the tip of his cock probing my opening. My pulse picked up, and I instinctively tensed at the prospect of the inevitable pain that would follow when my body was finally breached. And yet, my pelvic area remained relaxed, no doubt thanks to my lover's bite.

With shallow thrusts, Drogo began inserting himself inside of me. I couldn't tell if the water eased the penetration, or if it was because of how wet he'd gotten me on top of his hormone. In the end, all that mattered was that thanks to his careful possession of me, I only felt a slight sting and quite a bit of pressure as he gradually slipped deeper inside me. That sharp pain of my hymen breaching was further drowned by another small injection of my man's aphrodisiac in my neck. This small addition was enough to have me on the edge.

Something primal took me over. Instead of allowing Drogo to continue his careful movements to finish taking possession of me, I lifted my pelvis and impaled myself onto his massive cock. I hissed at the painful burn. My nails digging into his shoulders, I buried my face in his neck while my inner walls constricted around his shaft.

"You foolish woman," Drogo whispered against my hair.

He remained still while I adjusted to his considerable girth, his hand gently caressing my back in a soothing fashion.

Yeah, I'd been foolish in my impatience, and yet, I didn't regret it one bit. Sure, it burned, but I'd expected that. The incredible fullness of him within me, being one with the man that had swept me off my feet had definitely been worth it. Soon—probably too soon by Drogo's standard as he initially resisted—I began moving, encouraging him to resume. I lifted my head to stare at him. One look on my face apparently sufficed to convince him that I was ready.

Carefully pulling out of me, Drogo slowly thrust back up. My lips parted in a moan at the delicious friction. My mate repeated the motion, gradually accelerating the speed and strength of his movements. Before long, water was splashing around us, cooling my feverish skin as my man took me in a growing frenzy. A pool of fire was swirling around my nether region, the inferno fanned by each stroke of his cock, claiming me, branding me.

Growling sounds of pleasure flowed out of Drogo's throat and vibrated through his chest pressed against mine. The slight tremor further titillated the hard nubs of my nipples. When he suddenly changed the angle of his movements, the head of his cock struck a particularly sensitive spot. Lightning struck, and I went off like a rocket.

My inner walls clamped down on Drogo's cock. He shouted, the sound between a growl and bark. He seemed to lose control as the prickling sensation of his claws dug into my flesh, and his hold around me tightened almost painfully. Through the haze of ecstasy that was sweeping me away, I briefly wondered if he had shifted into his Lycan form. But his human mouth reclaiming mine as he savagely pummeled my sweet spot with his cock convinced me otherwise.

Before I was even down from my second climax, his relentless assault had me already cresting again. This time, Drogo embraced his own orgasm when I toppled over. To my dismay, he attempted to pull out as soon as his seed began to shoot out into me. I instinctively tightened my legs and my arms around him, preventing my mate from moving away from me.

Even as I trembled against him in the throes of passion, his cock swelling inside me at lightning speed startled me. Considering he already had me stretched to the max, I almost panicked. But as the fog of ecstasy began to dissipate, I realized it wasn't his whole shaft expanding, but only his bulbus glandis—the knot at the base of his cock. It had swelled, locking us together to increase the chances his seed flowing into me would take root. Drogo could no longer pull out unless he seriously maimed us both.

"Way to go, woman," Drogo growled, still panting, his voice barely recognizable it rumbled so much. "We're locked for at least thirty to forty-five minutes."

"And that's a problem why?" I asked, my words a little slurred as I reveled in the last tremors of pleasure, and the burning feel of my mate wrapped around me.

"Because I wanted to dry you first, make love to you again in bed, and then knot with you on a comfortable mattress under silky blankets. Instead, we're here in the water where you're going to get all pruned up," he mumbled.

My face melted with affection with him even as my inner walls continued to contract around his cock. "I don't mind getting pruned, as long as I'm with you," I said, drawing his face towards mine to rub my nose against his. "You can talk dirty to me while your little guy does his thing."

"Little?" he grumbled.

I chuckled and kissed the adorable dimple in his chin. "Stop being grumpy, Wolfy. I love knowing you're entirely mine for the next little while."

"For the next eternity, my mate," he said before capturing my lips again.

When he broke the kiss, I pulled aside the wet locks of my hair sticking to my right shoulder. "While we're at it, we're overdue for your first feeding."

Drogo's silver eyes darkened, and a hungry expression descended over his gorgeous features. He glanced at the pulsating vein in my neck. The image of the human he had fed from flashed before me, but I immediately dismissed it. My mate had not looked at her the way he was now looking at me. I was still considering having him use my phials with those 'Blood Servants' for the next few weeks that he still needed them. His lips, his fangs, were mine alone.

He wisely didn't mention using my phials for us. I'd probably have ripped out one of his fangs to teach him. Instead, my core throbbed, and my inner walls clenched around his shaft as his fangs slowly descended through his parted lips. Drogo gently cupped my nape and tilted my head to the side. His lips brushed against the curve of my neck in a sensual kiss, sending a shiver down my spine. The sharp pain of his fangs piercing my skin oddly turned me on, as did the moaning growl that rose from my mate. His cock throbbed inside me as he drank.

After only a few seconds, he pulled his fangs out and threw

his head back while grinding his pelvis against mine. God, my beast was magnificent with his stunning face dissolved in an expression of pure ecstasy. I covered his throat with kisses, and my hands roamed over his slightly shaking body, while more of his seed shot out inside of me. That my blood had made him climax again was an even bigger aphrodisiac than his hormone.

He fisted my hair to force me to face him. Drogo looked at me with a savage expression that had my stomach do a couple of backflips.

"My Thalia, you are my drug," he growled before crushing my lips in a possessive kiss.

Better believe it, Wolfy.

CHAPTER 19
THALIA

The next two days of the Summer Solstice celebrations were filled with laughter and mischief, decadent food that I at least got to sample, a lot more dancing, and some fascinating music, dance, and acrobatic performances from the various Lycan packs as well as the Karthians. Naturally, they had to display their physical prowess with friendly combat duels between packs.

If anyone would have told me about life here in Hundilinn, I would have called them liars. The Lycans were anything but savage beasts. Despite the undeniable hierarchy among their ranks, it wasn't overwhelming and crushing like in the vampire cities. Here, everyone felt like family. Therefore, it was with a heavy heart that I watched them all leave in order to return to their respective territories.

In the days and weeks that followed, I realized how little I had actually understood their way of life. With everyone focused on preparing for the Summer Solstice, their normally strict and highly disciplined daily routine had been temporarily set aside. Now that things were back to business as usual, my eyes opened to a much different reality.

While both adults and children had plenty of recreation time, they all had duties that they took on with impressive dedication. The first thing that struck me was the major focus on education for the young. Not only was school compulsory from an early age, but the topics covered were also heavily skewed toward giving the students strong scientific and technological foundations.

The second thing was that all physical activities for the young aimed at improving the mastery of both their wolf and Lycan forms. That wouldn't have been surprising aside from the fact that the training clearly relied on combat and not just proper use of their abilities in a general context. Even play time had a strategic and tactical aspect, a strong focus on teamwork, and obvious pitfalls that required at least one of the children to take on the leadership role to coordinate the others. Looking at them playing, I could already tell which ones would be potential pack leaders or Alphas.

It took me a moment to accept what my gut was telling me. Drogo was building an army. But why?

Every single adult, regardless of the career they ended up taking up, had gone through a thorough combat training. Service in the Iron Guard was compulsory for everyone until the age of twenty-two, after which it became voluntary. While all the traditional professions and services could be found in the city, most of the Lycans worked either in the gem mines, in the artificial blood lab and factory, or in one of the technological research and development facilities of the city.

To my great shock, I discovered that Hundilinn controlled the production of artificial blood. With so many plants around Verelinn where humans labored, I'd naturally assumed the vampires owned that market. Turns out that the base element to create it was an extract from the blood apples that grew on coral-like formations at the bottom of the Moon Well's pond. They processed the blood apples in their labs and sold a dehydrated compound to the vampires for easy storage. Humans rehydrated and bottled them. Some production plants went so far as to flavor the blood according to whatever was the latest trend.

No wonder Drogo—and the Lycans in general—were so filthy rich. They held the vampires by the balls. And yet, they didn't abuse that power. There was no price gouging and never any shortages of supply. Furthermore, Drogo had imposed a price cap to all the vampire distributors of artificial blood. He wanted it to remain accessible to all vampires in order to protect humans from being hunted to the brink of extinction. That had deeply moved me as I'd always believed that the Lycans simply didn't care about our plight.

Better yet, as we were visiting one of the blood apple processing plants, Drogo showed me the research section where the Lycans were studying ways of improving the product so that it even more closely emulated human blood and gave even lesser vampires the Day Walking ability.

Standing outside the glass windows of the sterile room where the researchers were working, I eyed my mate with a certain degree of confusion as I reflected on that information. From a compassion standpoint, it totally made sense. But from a strategic point of view, not so much. However, I liked the idea that Drogo wasn't a dictator trying to keep under his thumb those who were essentially cousins to the Lycans.

"Why would you give them that ability when it keeps them vulnerable to Lycans?" I asked. "What better way to keep them in check than with the knowledge that they could be obliterated during the long, vulnerable daylight hours? Or are you mainly doing that research for the Karthians?"

Drogo smiled with approval and caressed my cheek. "The Karthians are indeed my main priority," he confessed. "They have suffered enough… too much. But I also want to fix the vampires. The bloodlust is a curse. As long as we do not get it under control for everyone, there can never be a truly fair hierarchy. For them, the Apex isn't the fittest physically and mentally, but the one with the deepest pockets to enhance himself with the best blood. And that automatically means the Ancients like Konstantin."

"Yes," I said, nodding slowly. "I can see that, but it will destroy the human colonies. Our entire economy revolves around the blood trade."

"It is not an economy, my love," Drogo said gently. "It's just another form of slavery. Humans are chattel. If he doesn't have rare blood, as soon as a human child is able to walk and talk, he is trained into some type of manual labor. If he's lucky enough to be pretty, he might become a familiar, but in all cases, he's condemned to a life of hardship and misery. Too few have access to any type of real education. THAT is the key to the future. Once the blood trade stops being a way of life, but merely a delicacy for the rich and the occasional fancy treat for the masses, then the true human liberation can begin."

My eyes narrowed at him. I fully agreed with every single one of his words. My golden status had opened a vast world of knowledge to me. Most humans were just barely literate. Education was not only too expensive, but it ate away too much time that could be devoted to work and, therefore, to extra income. Only the rich schooled their children. Those were not only few and far between, they didn't stay in the squalor of the colonies, but settled instead in the heart of Verelinn.

"I have indeed noticed the important place education occupies in the life of Lycans," I said, choosing my words carefully. "Science, math, technology, and a great deal of combat and military training. Seems a tad heavy for a young child's curriculum."

Drogo intensely examined my features for a few moments, which almost made me squirm. He looked as if he couldn't decide *if* he wanted to fully answer me or *how* he would go about it. As far as I knew, Drogo had never kept anything from me whenever I'd questioned him. Had I just struck a particular nerve?

"Come," he said, taking my hand and leading me out of the plant.

While most businesses in Hundilinn were located in the heart of the city, the blood plant, science and technological research facilities were built directly inside the Ion Mountain, a short distance from the castle also embedded in it, and on the opposite side of the Wisdom Trail. In fact, I would have to visit the latter soon to see Vesna's progress on carving my scenes in its murals.

We hopped onto his hoverbike. While I'd learned how to pilot one over the past couple of weeks, and despite the vehicle being fully capable of operating on autopilot, I preferred riding with my Wolfy. He certainly didn't seem to mind. A series of underground tunnels connected the facilities. Although we could have walked, I was grateful for the less than five-minute ride as curiosity was gnawing at me.

"Do you know what's the main thing that keeps me up at night?" Drogo asked as he helped me off the bike.

"Whatever Selene locked behind that high-tech wall she built to seal in the Moon Well," I said with conviction.

Drogo's brows shot up, and he gave me an amused but inquisitive look, encouraging me to continue.

"That rock wall you showed me, blocking the entrance of the Well, may look organic, but it's not. Selene created it," I said, flicking my long, light brown hair over my shoulder. "Since Vesna started sketching me, I've been spending a lot of time looking at the murals. There were no Guardians before Selene came to 'rescue' the surviving original Sun Wolves. I think she planted some sort of cure in that cave that was meant to help heal the sick offspring of the Sun Wolves. But something went wrong."

Drogo tilted his head to the side, the intensity in his gaze told me I was on to something, even if it wasn't necessarily accurate. "What makes you say that?" he asked in a neutral tone.

"The Guardian doesn't make sense," I said. "When I looked at the entrance to the Moon Well, it reminded me of a secure door with some kind of biometric lock. I don't think the Well was meant to only open once every few decades or centuries, but at will by anyone possessing the right genetics—meaning a Lycan. I believe the Guardian is the result of either some alien organism accidentally introduced inside the Well, or the unexpected mutation of some organism that was already there."

Drogo pursed his lips and nodded slowly, visibly impressed. I puffed out my chest, proud that my speculations were proving to be accurate—or so I presumed.

"Go on," Drogo said, encouragingly.

I licked my lips nervously and rolled my shoulders to loosen the knots I'd not even realized had been forming between my shoulder blades.

"I think the reason the Well is taking more and more time to open is because the unlocking mechanism is defective," I continued. "I'm not sure what caused it to open last time, or why it's about to open now. But I bet Soren warned you because the other Spirits in the pond felt something change, be it in the chemical composition of the water, of the ground around them, or whatever else."

Drogo cupped my face in his hands and studied my features as if I were both a mystery and a wonder he wanted to comprehend.

"And this, my love, is why I want you to come work in our weapons development lab," he said softly.

I stiffened and recoiled slightly. Drogo had never struck me as a warmonger, and yet more signs seemed to lean that way.

"Generally speaking, you have the right idea about the Well. But it is *not* what keeps me up at night," Drogo said. "The Guardian will be terrible this year. But no matter the cost in lives on our end, we will eventually defeat the beast. What I fear are the next 'stars that will fall from the sky' like the Sun Wolves did, and then the slavers that came after them. Come," Drogo said in a grim tone, pulling me after him.

I followed numbly, my mind racing at this most unexpected answer. A double set of reinforced doors greeted us at the entrance of the tech research lab. Even though we were inside the mountain, the ingenious lighting system and high ceilings prevented the place from feeling claustrophobic.

A couple of guards nodded us in. We followed a short corridor to another set of reinforced doors. When they parted before us, my knees nearly buckled. In the massive hangar-like space, divided in various sections, hundreds of Lycans were working on what looked like extremely advanced weapons, defense systems, and other technologies I couldn't even begin to fathom what purpose they served.

"This is what you are training the children for," I whispered, understanding dawning on me.

"Yes," Drogo said. "To be able to handle all of this and further improve it. This way. I want to show you something."

My mate almost had to drag me after him I was so busy gaping at all the wonders surrounding me. My fingers twitched with the need to touch, to test all the amazing things within range. I wasn't a highly skilled technician, but I had some solid basic knowledge and a good head on my shoulders to solve prob-lems and learn. I definitely wanted to get my hands on all of these babies.

We headed towards a wide corridor on the left with a single garage door blocking our way. It automatically slid open upon our approach. The first thought that crossed my mind was 'museum' when we penetrated the room. Hundreds of carefully labelled objects, from small to massive, that I assumed to be ship parts, filled the room, some on large displays, others on individual pedestals or inside casings. Holographic displays of hand-scribbled notes also filled an entire wall.

"This is what my father, Viktor and a number of Ancients were able to steal or recover before the Sun Wolves left with Selene," Drogo said, gesturing at all the paraphernalia. "The Karthians were an extremely primitive species when the Sun Wolves first came here. They still cooked on coal and washed their laundry by hand in the lake. When Soren decided to settle here with the others, they had to renounce most of their technology to respect the Prime Directive. When things went sour, our ancestors did everything in their power to try and rebuild their technology to get the fuck out of here."

"But Selene's return spared them the trouble," I concluded for him.

"Exactly," Drogo replied with a nod. "Most of them tried hard to respect the Prime Directive, to the extent that they didn't share their alien origin or their advanced knowledge with the Karthians or even with their children."

"Oh God!" I exclaimed with sudden comprehension. "That's why your mother told me the Legend of Soren instead of simply telling me the facts."

Drogo nodded. "The legend is still taught to our young. Once they reach maturity—and often before that—they figure it out on their own, and we fill in the blanks. But my great-great-grandfather disagreed. He believed in passing down as much of his knowledge as possible to his children and grandchildren. The other Sun Wolves were mad at him, but they turned a blind eye because he wasn't revealing anything about their home world. He only taught theoretical knowledge that he had memorized, including math, physics, astronomy, and then more practical stuff like agriculture and architecture."

"Wow," I said, blown away. "I've studied plenty of math and some physics, but without proper teaching material, I wouldn't even know where to begin to teach someone else. Your ancestor was an extraordinary male."

"More than you know," Drogo said in an enigmatic way that poked my curiosity. But I didn't get a chance to question him further about it. "So, my forebears learned all that they could from him. Unfortunately, they had to recreate everything from scratch, including creating the tools to be able to create the things they wanted. How do you mine the hardest metals if you don't have the metal detectors or scanners to find the ore in the first place? And then what do you do without the tools to extract the ore?"

"Sheesh!" I said, looking at all the advanced technology surrounding us. "It makes all of this even more impressive."

"It took centuries just to get the basic infrastructure to allow us to do what we're doing now," Drogo said with well justified pride. "Initially, it was the desire to achieve the same enlightenment our ancestors' people had attained on their home world that had been driving us. But when Selene left with them, it finally struck us that we had no idea what other species existed out there that could come visit us with intentions unknown."

"And then the mercenaries attacked," I said, "confirming that you had been right to wonder."

"Our Lycan genetics saved us," Drogo said. "Our fast-healing abilities defeated their weapons. They didn't realize silver was needed to slow down our accelerated regeneration. In truth, we forced them to hand over the human slaves and we scavenged quite a bit of their technology. The next visitors we get could be a lot more powerful. Should that day come, I do not want us to be helpless. A united Karthia will be our only chance. I will start breathing more easily the day we achieve warp speed and are able to see what threats are out there."

"And that is why every Lycan is raised to be battle-ready, even the baker," I concluded.

"Even the baker," Drogo said with a smirk.

"Where do I apply for a job here?" I asked teasingly.

A broad grin stretched Drogo's lips. Closing the distance between us, he pulled me into his embrace, his silver gaze darkening.

"Rumor has it that you and the big boss are rather close… as in *really* close," my mate said, wiggling his brows in a suggesting fashion that made me chuckle. "I'm sure we can wave the whole interview process and just get you on the payroll."

"I knew there had to be some benefits to shagging the King," I said in a satisfied tone. "I guess I'll have to do much more of that in the future!"

"I assure you that the King will approve of such plans," he said before capturing my lips.

I melted against him, my hands slipping under his skin-tight shirt. I would never tire of the perfection that was Drogo. In the past four weeks since my arrival here, and just like he'd stated, my mate had filled in even more thanks to my blood and finally being able to eat normally. The Lycan King was a beast of a man, and all mine.

"So, when do I start," I asked when he ended our kiss.

"Soon, but not now," he said with a strange glimmer in his eyes. "As I recall, a certain Queen has been pestering me about getting bitten."

I gasped, my brain freezing for half a second, wondering if I'd heard correctly. "You're finally going to change me?" I asked, fighting the urge to squeal.

"If you still wish it," he said with a smile and a nod.

"Fuck yeah, I still wish it!" I shouted, squeezing him tightly.

Although I understood and appreciated Drogo's motives for delaying my transformation, I was beyond ready to start my true new life.

"Good, because my great-great-grandfather's Spirit misses you," Drogo said teasingly.

My jaw dropped. "Zabek? Zabek was your ancestor?"

"Mmhmm," Drogo said. "Just remember that *I* am your favorite Volkov."

I burst out laughing and let my mate lead me out of the facility.

CHAPTER 20

DROGO

I shifted on my feet, feeling both worried and restless as Dr. Tanner ran a final scan over Thalia. Three days had gone by since I'd infected her with the Lycan virus, two of which she spent unconscious in an induced coma. The change was painful. It didn't rewrite the person's DNA but modified it. The Lycan virus was actually a viral pathogen that messed with the host cell's DNA to form a provirus, which produced the viral proteins needed for the mutation.

Thalia wasn't the first human to be turned, but it happened very rarely. Despite Dr. Tanner's continued reassurance that all was well, until the change had been stabilized and sealed with the silver water, I would continue to fret.

She was so incredibly beautiful with her adorable little wolf ears, smaller and more delicate as was typically the case with our females. The short mantle of fur on her nape, and which tapered off in a V-shape between her shoulder blades, was beyond silky. I couldn't wait to rub my face all over it. In fact, there were many things I couldn't wait to do with her. Teaching her how to master her Lycan and wolf forms would be a riot in and of itself. Just the thought of how much Milos and Anya would provoke her into chasing after them in their wolf forms had me laughing in advance.

My mate had a natural talent for motherhood. It pleased me greatly that, like me, she wanted many pups. The contrary would have saddened, but not surprised me, considering the way she had been raised. Now that we were fully compatible, us knotting after lovemaking would be more than just an occasion of deep intimacy, but a true chance at starting our family.

"She's ready," Dr. Tanner said at last. "I can accompany you if you wish, but I do not expect any complications."

"Yes, I would appreciate that very much," I said to the doctor, not wanting to take any chances where the welfare of my mate was concerned.

This, too, was something I wanted to fix. Turning someone, be it into a Lycan or a vampire, should not require drinking from the pond to seal the change. For centuries, our technology and biological knowledge had been too limited to be fully capable of analyzing the chemical and biological properties of the pond. Now that we finally had advanced tools, our discoveries and technological development were growing exponentially. It was only a matter of time before the silver water yielded all of its secrets.

And so would the Moon Well and its Guardian.

We settled Thalia on a hover stretcher before taking her to the small shuttle we would travel in. Aside from the doctor, Ulia and Gavril accompanied us. There had been no new incidents since my visit to the Grand Council of Verelinn. I didn't expect any but, here again, I wouldn't take chances. A few more of my Iron Guards were roaming the surrounding woods, ready to intervene at a moment's notice.

We landed in the grassy clearing near the location where I had previously left the hoverbike. An eerie silence greeted us as we disembarked the shuttle. Only the shiny pebbles around the pond crunching beneath our feet and the discreet hum of the hover stretcher as it floated across the bridge disturbed our oddly quiet surroundings. What had happened to the usual chirping of the birds and singing of nearby critters and insects? Even the wind had stopped playing with the leaves of the trees.

While Soren didn't communicate any warning to me or any sense of urgency, I could feel his unease. Something terrible was coming, and nature was preemptively going into hiding. My gaze lingered on the doorway to the Moon Well. It remained sealed and unyielding, but a change had occurred. Although subtle, a slight discoloration had taken place on the stones forming it. The scent in the air had also shifted. It had a spicier, deeper aroma, that titillated long lost memories of danger... of battle. The Guardian was rising. The doorway would open soon.

Despite the sliver of worry at how bloody the battle would no doubt be, I also felt a great deal of excitement for what gaining access to the Well could mean not just for my people, but for all the inhabitants of Karthia. After three hundred years, we had lost hope it would ever open again. We'd been working on tools to help us hack our way into it, but now that it was reopening, even as the battle raged, we'd need to find a way to retain permanent access to it.

But that was for another time.

The hover stretcher settled on the main platform at the edge of the pond, with Thalia's head pointing at the water and her feet facing the doorway. Standing on her left side, Dr. Tanner removed the two little magnets stuck against Thalia's temples, which kept her unconscious. I crouched on her right, within range of the pond, and waited for her to wake. Her forehead wrinkled in a frown, and she slightly moaned in discomfort. Without the painkiller Dr. Tanner had administered, my mate would currently be writhing in pain.

Ulia handed me a ladle that I immediately dipped into the water while lifting Thalia's head with my free hand.

"Drink, my love," I said softly, bringing the ladle to her lips.

"It will make you better."

How ironic that only a little over two weeks ago, that same water had almost killed her. She gingerly sipped, her eyes still mostly closed. Thalia had barely drunk a third of the ladle's contents when a splashing sound in the water drew my attention. Although invisible to the human eye, my Lycan enhanced vision allowed me to see the outline of Zabek's form flailing impatiently in the water. I couldn't decide if I was amused or irritated.

"Patience," I mumbled sternly at the Spirit.

That seemed to irk Zabek who resumed his splashing in earnest. When I continued to ignore him, a sharp pain in my chest made me look at Soren in disbelief.

"For fuck sake, give her time to stabilize!" I exclaimed.

The wave of displeasure emanating from Soren hinted at another incoming zap.

"Zabek could accelerate the process for her," Dr. Tanner said timidly.

I hesitated, but the wave of approval from Soren convinced me to reluctantly cave in. Taking the ladle away from Thalia, I plunged it into the pond. The splashing immediately stopped. When I brought it back up to my woman's lips with Zabek inside, a sliver of worry flashed through me.

This entire process with my mate felt too rushed. No Lycan had ever possessed a Spirit from birth. It normally took many trips to the pond to drink for one of them to show any interest in a Lycan, and even then, only a minority of us hosted a Spirit. Granted, our research hinted that more than just personality impacted their choice to join with one of us, but biological factors as well. And there was no question that, like me, Thalia's genetics were unique. Such restrictions were yet another hurdle we hoped to solve in the future.

My mate began drinking again, only to jerk up with a brief cough when Zabek slid down her throat. She recovered in seconds and clung to me, panting for a second. When I brought the ladle back to her lips, my mate pushed it away, drawing me to her instead. I sat down on the stone platform and pulled her onto my lap. She snuggled against me and buried her face in my neck. I gently caressed her hair while casting a worried look at Dr. Tanner. Technically, she hadn't drunk enough water for a proper binding.

He hesitated, but it was my cousin that answered my concerns.

"Your mate's Spirit knows what she needs," Ulia said in a reassuring voice. "If she needs more, he will make her drink. He loves Thalia too much to allow any harm to come to her."

Naturally, I had known this, but the insecure part of me whenever my female was involved had needed to hear it. Soren further soothed me, as I rose to my feet with Thalia cradled in my arms. The slick surface of the pond stirred. It felt like they were waving goodbye to Thalia, or Zabek, or both. The Spirits had never made themselves so visible in the past. For a moment, I worried that the changes in the water were adversely affecting them, but once more, Soren reassured me.

By the time our shuttle landed back at the castle, Thalia had settled into a peaceful sleep. Her previously pallid skin had regained a healthier color. The delicate fur on her nape now had a lustrous shine that made my heart soar. I couldn't wait for her to be fully awake. Three days without looking at her beautiful eyes, hearing her delightfully throaty voice teasing me and calling me Wolfy had me piteously pining. I longed to have my mate back.

The day dragged on endlessly. Although I frequently checked up on her, Thalia continued to sleep like the dead. It shouldn't have surprised me as it normally took at least twenty-four hours, although closer to forty-eight for the entire process to be completed. You couldn't expect such extensive changes to someone's genetics to occur in a blink.

However, this was the worst time for me to be so distracted.

When I first felt the stirring of the Well, I'd believed we had between two and three months before the doorway opened. Now, one month later, I believed there were only a couple of weeks, three at most left. Worse still, if things were moving at an exponential speed—as I was beginning to suspect—the Guardian could be upon us even sooner.

On top of moving some of our heavy weapons near the Well to be able to react on the fly, we also multiplied the detection systems, including a seismic detector for even the most subtle of shifts that could indicate the impending opening of the doorway.

After a quick shower, I joined Thalia in my bed. Over the past couple of weeks, she had all but moved into my suite, which was bigger than hers. As my soon-to-be-official Queen, she would be sharing my quarters full-time. She would keep her suite, but I would make sure to never give her a reason to use it.

Drawing her naked body into my embrace, I closed my eyelids with the hope of seeing Thalia's beautiful green eyes in the morning. I couldn't tell how long I'd been asleep. I couldn't even remember dreaming. But my eyes snapped open as one would when sensing a clear and present danger. However, no threat had stirred me. The pleasant sting of my woman's claws on my side, and the rougher texture of her Lycan tongue teasing my left nipple had me fully awake in a heartbeat.

"Thalia," I whispered, my fingers slipping through the delicate fur of her mantle.

She shivered with pleasure in response to me caressing that sensitive spot for all Lycans. Unlike us males, whose mantles spread in a more or less wide patch of fur along the sides of our arms, our females' mantles stopped right before the curve of their shoulders. Aside for their fuller manes and slight fur on their ears, Lycan females essentially had no body hair. I still recalled how Thalia had squealed with pleasure when finding out that the change would spare her from ever having to get rid of unwanted body hair according to proper human aesthetic.

My mate lifted her head to look at me. She was glowing, so resplendent in her beauty it took my breath away. Her freckles seemed to stand out even more against her luminous skin. Her green eyes, now a lighter color, had clearly become wolfen. She grinned before lowering her face back to my chest. Thalia inhaled my scent deeply before rubbing her temples on my chest. My heart swelled with joy and pride to thus be claimed. My mate likely wasn't even aware of the reason that had prompted her to do that, but she was marking me with her scent, claiming me.

I loved the way she touched me, with a possessiveness and an eagerness that made me feel wanted and cherished, like she could never have enough of me. I had hated the illness that had brought me to an inch of my life. And now, I could only thank the powers that be that it had been the catalyst for me meeting the love of my life. Thalia exceeded everything I could have ever hoped for in a mate and as a Queen.

And right now, as a lover.

As much as the concept of the Seduction classes given to the Blood Maidens disturbed me, reaping its benefit almost made me reconsider. Thalia knew exactly when, where, and how to touch me. While my woman's 'training' no doubt played a role, I believed it was the generous and attentive nature of my mate that made her more sensitive to my responses to her. Having noticed how erogenous my nipples were, my female always knew just how to expertly tease them to make me rock hard in seconds. The way she gently raked her nails—and now her claws—along the V-shaped muscle around my pelvic area, had me moaning and trembling beneath her touch.

As a dominant, I'd never pictured myself willingly submitting to the lead of a woman in bed. But Thalia was no omega. I had expected to want a submissive mate, but Thalia's take charge attitude, her boldness in pursuing what she wanted and taking it was a fucking turn on. And right this instant, submitting to the possessive exploration of her hands and mouth had me melting from within.

I fisted the blankets when Thalia's tongue licked the entire length of my shaft before taking me inside her mouth. I hissed her name, my abdominal muscles contracting painfully as she began to bob over me. My mate had already driven me crazy with pleasure with her oral ministrations over the past weeks. But the rougher texture of her Lycan tongue was multiplying every sensation a thousandfold, driving me insane. In light of my considerable girth and length, I had not expected Thalia to be able to deepthroat me the way she was. And yet, every time we were intimate, she appeared to be taking even more of me.

Panting, I raised myself on one elbow to better look at my woman pleasuring me and caressed her hair with the other hand. Thalia seemed to interpret my touch as a signal to pick up the pace. It had not been. But the passion she unleashed on me, while stroking my testicles and massaging my knot had me begging for her to stop in no time. She ignored my plea, pushing me to the brink. Gritting my teeth to rein in my knot's untimely urge to swell, I grabbed Thalia by her small scruff and yanked her head back.

She yelped, startled. It had certainly given her a good sting but would not have hurt her. My woman looked at me questioningly, seeming a little offended to have me interrupting her feast. The savage expression on my face must have told Thalia what she'd been doing to me, because her light green eyes smoldered, and she licked her lips in the raunchiest fashion.

With a growl, I straightened and sat on my haunches. Moving at lightning speed, I pulled my woman up towards me before bending her backwards. Thalia yelped again and held onto the blankets when I lifted her legs up over my shoulders to return the favor. If not for the back of her head resting on the mattress, my mate would helplessly be dangling down in an upside-down position while I devoured her. With her ass pressed against my chest, and my arms wrapped around her midsection to keep her in place, it was my turn to feast on my woman.

The dominant in me loved having her helpless while I pleasured her. And now that she had been turned, I didn't need to rein in my passion anymore. My mate was no longer the delicate human easily broken by too much roughness, but my she-wolf, my Lycan Queen. And unleash I would.

As her legs began to tremble, I accelerated the movement of my tongue, focusing on the left side of her clit that always seemed more sensitive. At the same time, I fondled her breasts with one hand, loving the way Thalia was staring at me lapping at her. Lips parted, eyes smoldering, her cheeks flushed, her breath was coming out in short bursts interspersed with the sweetest moans.

When I gently raked my claws across her breasts, Thalia went off like a rocket. Even as she trembled with ecstasy, I moved back to let her legs off my shoulders and lay her body back down onto the mattress. I could have feasted on my woman forever, but the maddening scent of her musk and of her arousal had me on the verge of going feral. I kissed my way up her body, caressing and licking her tender flesh.

By the time I'd reached her face, Thalia's tremors had subsided. She stared at me with a naked hunger. Spreading her legs, my mate caressed my back from my shoulders down to my ass, before slightly digging her claws in. Ignoring the clear message, I captured her lips in a searing kiss while rubbing myself against her core. Thalia moaned, the sound a titillating mix of pleasure and a growl of frustration.

I couldn't explain why I was teasing her. My cock was painfully hard and all but yelling at me to take my mate and fuck her senseless. But I continued to hold back, deliberately provoking her.

Using her newly enhanced strength, Thalia pushed me onto my back with an angry growl. With dizzying speed, she got on top of me and reached blindly for my cock. But even as she was aligning it with her opening to impale herself on me, I reciprocated by pushing her off me. A very brief battle for dominance ensued. Despite her increased strength, Thalia would never be able to rival mine. There was something primal and exciting about subduing my mate in a playful setting, even though she did give it her best effort.

I flattened Thalia onto her stomach before lying on top of her. My legs immobilized hers while my hands pinned her wrists on each side of her face. My woman continued to wiggle in vain beneath me, her ass rubbing against my cock, driving me insane with lust. On instinct, I bit the back of Thalia's neck and held on. Obviously, I didn't break skin or put enough pressure to hurt, but my mate's newly acquired lupine instincts immediately kicked in.

Thalia froze, the fight bleeding out of her. As she relaxed beneath me, my woman lifted her chin, exposing more of her neck to give me a better grip. Widening my jaw, I tilted my head to the side, to take even more of her neck in my mouth. Thalia's whimper of submission resonated straight in my groin.

Something snapped inside of me.

With a swift movement of my knee, I swiped her legs open and rammed myself home. Thalia cried out. I tightened my hold around her wrists pinned to the mattress as I began to ride her in a frenzy.

"Yes!" Thalia said in a strangled voice, spurring me on.

She spread her legs wider, and slightly lifted her bum to allow me to sink deeper into her tight sheath. Ancestors… The way her inner walls gripped my cock, squeezing it from all sides in a blissful caress with each stroke was driving me wild. When Thalia asked me to go harder, I let go of the last shred of caution I still held on to. Without stopping moving in and out of her, I released her wrists, and got on my knees while holding on to her hips. Understanding what I wanted, Thalia followed my lead and got on all fours. She threw her head back and cried out my name as I thrust in and out of her with reckless abandon.

A pool of lava swirled around my nether regions as my growling moans mingled with those of my mate and the slapping sound of our flesh meeting in a savage crescendo of pleasure. Thalia met me thrust for thrust, a thin sheet of sweat forming on her slender back as she called my name in the sexiest of litanies. I shifted my angle until I began pummeling her sweet spot. Thalia climaxed with a sharp cry and all but face planted on the mattress, her arms going limp as ecstasy swept her away. I shouted as her inner walls clamped down on my shaft, trying to draw my own orgasm out of me. But I wasn't ready yet. I still wanted her too much.

Slipping an arm around my mate's neck and down her front so as not to strangle her, I forced Thalia to straighten. With her feverish back pressed against my chest, I frantically rubbed her clit while pounding into her. I gritted my teeth against the urge to come, determined on wresting another climax out of my woman first.

It came too soon, sweeping me away in the process. I roared my woman's name and rammed myself in deep. As my seed shot out inside of her, I yielded to my knot's imperious pressure to swell and lock me with my mate.

Thalia was boneless and trembling in my arms as I lay us both down on the comfortable mattress. Usually, I preferred to be face-to-face with her when we were knotted. But my protective and possessive instincts loved spooning her instead. I gathered her in my embrace, reveling in the searing heat of her body against mine, and the deliciously spicy-sweet scent that was all hers. I kissed her neck and the gentle curve of her shoulders while my seed flowed into her in blissful spurts.

"I love you, Wolfy," Thalia whispered while cuddling against me.

"I love you, too, my Thalia, my Queen."

CHAPTER 21
THALIA

The next couple of weeks flew by at dizzying speed. The very first day after completing my change, I finally understood why Drogo had wanted to delay it, and especially me becoming a host to Zabek. At first, I'd worried that maybe he hadn't believed me fully worthy of such an honor. Now, I could see how overwhelming it was to the senses.

Because of my sheltered—or rather controlled—upbringing, I'd never really tasted extreme foods, or been exposed to anything potentially dangerous except in a combat training setting that was also very controlled. Drogo had been slowly introducing me to spicier foods, fried preparations, sweets and desserts as well as alcohol. But I'd only consumed them in small doses.

Now, as a Lycan, every single one of my senses were enhanced. I'd gone from zero to one thousand overnight. Things that were once slightly spicy now had my throat on fire. The mere whiff of alcohol had me tipsy. The voices of the children playing at the other end of the garden sounded as if they were shouting right next to my ears. Even the dimmest lights felt like someone was stabbing my eyes with the brightest flashes.

Increased sensitivity was normal, but mine was compounded by Zabek enhancing me.

Despite the inconveniences, I didn't give a shit. I was a badass! During all of our previous training, I had known that Darya had held back. Seeing her spar with Raina and the other Iron Maidens had been indication enough. But now that I was no longer a delicate little flower, she had stopped pulling her punches.

While it was exhilarating to be able to move at the same crazy speed as the other Lycans, it wasn't without peril. On far too many occasions, I miscalculated the speed at which I was moving and almost ended up plastered on a wall that I hadn't expected to reach so quickly. Throwing things also was proving challenging. There was such a thing as throwing too hard. The children, especially that little brat Milos, were having a blast laughing at my clumsiness.

For all that, things weren't all peachy. With each passing day, Drogo was growing increasingly tense. I didn't have to ask why. Even the scent of the air blowing through the forest had changed. Many warriors from the Packs had returned to Hundilinn to camp in the clearing by the pond. The fauna, in all its forms, had left the area. I'd asked Drogo if the Spirits needed to be moved, but he claimed they would be fine. It still worried me, yet even Zabek seemed unconcerned.

Despite his busy schedule, my man made plenty of time for me. Early mornings always started with a little run in wolf form. My first few attempts had been pathetic. While I'd naturally inherited all of the lupine instincts of growling, whimpering, and expressing emotions with my ears and tail, learning to walk on all fours did *not* come naturally to me. And let's not talk about running. My bad Wolfy had howled with laughter—literally—while watching me trip all over my paws.

He'd then go to work, leaving me in the good care of Darya for my daily training—which qualified more as a daily spanking.

Whenever possible, he would come back to have lunch with me. Then I would spend the afternoon at the tech lab.

Ulia was a bonafide rocket scientist. As much as I also wanted to dabble in biological research, I had a stronger foundation in tech and weapons craft. My light shield technology was quickly adapted to the Wards—the small spheres Raina had thrown on the ground to create an energy wall between the vampires and us. It was also adapted to the Bakan—the Lycan version of the star-shaped blades the vampires had thrown at us. Initially, it disturbed me that they seemed to want to develop more technology to attack the vampires, but their true purpose quickly became obvious.

When my shield activated, it could slice through pretty much anything organic, aside from certain types of scales and bones. This would be extremely effective against most types of organic foe. Attached to the Bakan, that technology would allow us to erect defensive walls much farther than with the current Wards, and at more unusual locations.

But it was Ulia's latest project that held my attention. He had rebuilt a large maquette of the Moon Well, based on the recollections of those who had participated in the last couple of battles against the Guardian. Too much of it was vague approximations. The doorway opened onto a vast, natural-looking cave that spread out to the right of the entrance. The Well was located a few meters away from the right wall.

At first glance, the word 'well' had been used quite loosely. It looked more like a huge vat to collect the drips from some sort of organic-looking tubing hooked to it. Bioluminescent creatures or plants covered the entire wall behind it. Some kind of trough below them was connected to the tube. Whatever the Lycans needed to survive their strange illness had to be secreted by those bioluminescent things.

Straight in front of the entrance, about a hundred meters ahead, the uneven stone ground ended abruptly in a chasm. From the maquette, I couldn't tell how deep it dropped. My gut said the Guardian rose from those depths. At this time, this was pure speculation, but if the creatures were indeed filling that vat, after centuries without being harvested, the contents had certainly spilled over. And if so, it likely poured down the chasm, messing with whatever lived below.

But Ulia couldn't confirm it. When the doorway had opened, they'd been too focused on fighting to pay attention to their surroundings. During the last battle, the Well had closed again too quickly for them to investigate further. This time, they intended to be ready for all possibilities.

Drogo didn't think the Well would ever open again after this upcoming event. In fact, he wasn't convinced it would fully open. None of the process was happening normally this time around.

Just as that thought was crossing my mind, the shrill of an alarm nearly made me jump out of my skin. Time appeared to freeze for a beat, and then all hell broke loose.

"It's happening," Ulia said, his voice filled with tension.

All around us, the Lycans were running. Some of them were all but tearing their clothes off while shifting. Others were grabbing some of the advanced technological weapons they'd been working on before heading towards the shuttles or their personal hoverbikes—Ulia among them. As for me, complying with the instructions Drogo had given me, I hopped onto my hoverbike and raced back to the castle. Halfway through the Wisdom Trail, I ran into Raina who I was to remain with. Turning around, I followed her and the throng of other Lycans to the Well and the fate that awaited us.

CHAPTER 22
DROGO

Flanked by the Pack Leaders Viktor and Axel, the other Alphas and our packs behind us, we stood in front of the bridge at the edge of the pond. The doorway had shifted, showing a slight fissure wide enough to give us a tiny peek inside, but barely enough to slip in a hand. Like a gaping wound, a blackish-red liquid was pouring out, staining the pale stones of the platforms like old blood splatters. Except it wasn't blood, but the precious serum we desperately needed to get our hands on—among other things.

A terrifying, high-pitched roar resonated from within. Whatever had emitted it had to be beyond massive. As intimidating as it sounded, it was the countless smaller roars echoing it that made my stomach drop. There had never been more than a single Guardian inside. Then again, the Well had never remained closed for three hundred years.

Footsteps behind me drew my attention. Looking over my shoulder revealed Gavril approaching. I partially turned to look at him.

"The vampires are coming," he said. "Vlad and his brother are on their way with their troops. He claims he doesn't intend to interfere but will assist if needed. He also warns that Konstantin and the Red Guards are incoming. They should all arrive within thirty minutes."

"They have no business here," Viktor hissed.

"They have the right to try and claim it," I said dismissively. "Konstantin always refused to admit that he never stood a chance —not without a wolf. Thalia would have been his only hope. Let him come. He will find out the hard way that the power of the Well was *always* meant for the Lycans. Just be ready to take him and his guards out if they get in our way. Leave the Resnik brothers alone. I believe Vlad and Vasska are here to keep Konstantin on a tight leash."

Viktor pursed his lips but didn't argue further. Gavril nodded and went to inform the others of my decision. I signaled for Andrei to send the infiltrator to the doorway. The machine would not only allow us to peek inside the chamber of the Well, but it could also try to pry the doors open. The opening mechanism had apparently jammed after the doorway had begun parting. After more than a thousand years without maintenance, it wasn't surprising.

The infiltrator hovered over the bridge before landing directly in front of the doorway. Its retractable legs extruded, anchoring it to the top platform so that it would have better traction while forcing the doors open. The number of angry screeches rising from within seemed to increase exponentially, making me wonder if they had detected the infiltrator. A series of giant, holographic screens appeared around us, projected by all the unit leaders who were wirelessly connected to the infiltrator. The machine's telescopic camera extruded, poking its head through the narrow opening in the rockface.

Darkness first filled the screens. Andrei tapped some instructions on his armband, switching to night vision on the camera. A wall of carapace-like shells blocked most of our view of the room. Andrei attempted to change the angle of the camera, but the creature it belonged to was standing right in front of the opening.

Grinding my teeth in frustration, I exchanged a glance with Viktor. Under normal circumstances, I would have simply said to go ahead and pry the doors open. But the number of voices beyond them worried me that we might get swarmed by an overwhelming number of creatures. If that were the case, I would rather have the vampires here, too, to overwhelm the beasts with our own numbers.

But we never got a chance to come to a decision.

The creature shifted, giving us a glimpse first of a globular white iris surrounded by black sclera and dark-grey armored plate on the side of its head. It continued to turn to face the camera, revealing a huge mouth filled with sharp teeth. The creature reared, and the first thought that crossed my mind was that it resembled a giant, armored, grey prawn with five huge, spindly protrusions on its forehead that could have passed for the skeletal fingers of a nightmarish hand. At a glance, each finger appeared to be about two meters long.

Before we could get a proper look at the creature, it stabbed the infiltrator with one of its 'fingers.' If not for the legs anchoring it, the infiltrator would have been sent flying back. However, the strength of the blow demolished the camera and pierced right through the metal casing of the device. Curses resonated all around me, joining my own. Andrei attempted to retract the legs and move the infiltrator out of range, but the creature stabbed it again in quick succession, completely wrecking it.

Each strike from the beast damaged the doors. Even after the infiltrator had stopped being the target of its aggression, the creature continued to attack the doorway. More spindly fingers joined the fray. Judging by the different angles they were attempting to pry the doors open, more than one creature was at it. The doors suddenly gave way, sharply parting by about thirty centimeters on each side before locking up again. It was too narrow to allow a single creature through, but at least three heads were trying to force their way out at the same time, impeding each other.

The unit leaders dismissed the screens, while the rest of us armed ourselves with our heavy-duty blasters and disrupter rays. The latter would likely be the most effective, considering the foes we were facing. The disrupters caused damage by breaking or weakening the molecular bonds of their target, which often translated as an explosion at the point of impact. I didn't need to hit those giant prawns to know their carapace would be next to impossible to destroy unless we weakened it first.

I cast a glance over my shoulder, my gaze zeroing in on Thalia. I had caught her scent the moment she arrived a couple of minutes ago. She was way in the back with the rest of the non-professional combatants. A part of me wished my mother had kept her at the castle. But this was Thalia's place as much as any other Lycan's. She silently mouthed 'I love you' making me warm inside and further fueling my determination to obliterate the Guardian and its minions. I winked at her then turned back to our foe.

"LYCANS!" I shouted so all would hear me. "TIME TO HUNT!"

The few who hadn't shifted into their Lycan form did so while I aimed my two-handed disrupter on the creatures still trying to come out. In their eagerness, they had become stuck. The bluish white beam shot out of my weapon, striking the creature in the middle. It screeched and struggled even more. I couldn't tell if it was trying to come out or pull back inside the safety of the cave. Viktor and Axel imitated me, each male targeting one of the other two creatures.

As our companions joined their blaster fires to our disrupters, the beasts went into a frenzy. The struggle loosened the doors by a few more centimeters, allowing the top creature to wiggle free and get back inside the cave. Seizing this opportunity, the middle beast tried to force its way out, its frontal legs stepping on the head of the bottom creature. But the space was still too narrow. Using its facial fingers, it spread them on each side of the doors to try and propel itself free. Its front legs were all but crushing its companion underfoot.

My disrupter finally sufficiently weakened my target's carapace for the blaster fire of my guards to pierce through. The creature screamed and flailed in desperation and anger. Then a sudden violent push behind it snapped its carapace. Its armored shield caved in on itself as silver liquid poured out of the creature's mouth and fractured side carapace. Another brutal push propelled the creature onto the platform. Its broken body writhed as it screeched in agony.

The battered beast at the bottom never got a chance to stand as a larger beast tried to ram itself through the opening. This time, the doors groaned and emitted a huge clanking sound. The impact appeared to have snapped them back onto their rail as they smoothly slid open the rest of the way.

My blood froze in my veins at the sight of the multitude of monsters swarming out of the cave.

"SHIELDS!" I shouted. "Disrupters, fire at will!"

Wards were tossed and Bakan stars thrown, creating layers of shield walls around the platform. Simultaneously, the unit leaders formed a line along the edge of the pond, each of them armed with a disrupter like mine. The luminous property of the shields, thanks to Thalia's concept, further aided our cause. Being creatures of the dark, the extreme brightness was blinding them, forcing them to avert their eyes. A number of them covered their faces with their forehead 'fingers' making them look like a turtle's carapace. Only then did we notice the three long tails at their rear. While sheltered in this closed up position, they blindly whipped the energy walls with their tails, at least five meters long, breaking them down.

We could barely keep the defensive walls up so brutal was the damage their tails inflicted. In their impatience, some of the creatures at the front would use only three of their facial digits to protect their faces and stab the walls with the other two. But the disrupters were doing their job, with more and more beasts at the front forced to retreat as the blaster shots pierced through their weakened armor.

For a moment, hope soared within me. We had found a functional rhythm with two disrupters focusing their fire on the same creature to weaken it faster while blasters were obliterating it. We were successfully thinning the herd. Maybe the horrible battle we had feared wouldn't be so bloody—for us—after all. The vampire vessels starting to land in the other clearing, a short distance from here, meant even more help—potentially.

All the critters piling up made it harder for the others to try and navigate their way to us. However, they also made it harder for us to target the new ones coming out. Showing an ingenuity I had not expected from such primitive-looking creatures, a few of the beasts remained hidden behind the corpses of their kin to safely whip at the wall. The vampires poured in at that exact moment, Konstantin in the lead and Vlad shadowing him. But I couldn't waste my attention on them.

The Lycans firing the disrupters on the left side of the pond were forced to move from their current position to target the beasts. By the time they managed to find a proper angle, the energy shields collapsed. To my horror, one of the creatures taking cover whipped its tails forward. They appeared to lengthen, like the tongue of a frog, and wrapped around two of my men. The tails yanked them back over the pond and towards the platform. Thankfully, my Iron Guards thought on their feet and used their vicious claws to slice through the thick membrane of the tails holding them. They both fell into the silver water while their would-be captor screamed in pain.

And then chaos reigned.

Using their long front legs and shorter back ones, a dozen or more creatures jumped prodigiously high over the piles of corpses, landing almost at the edge of the pond to rush us. At least three meters long and close to two meters high, the wretched creature could run at lightning speed. Moving as one, Viktor, Darya, and I jumped on the beast before it could attack Axel, who was still firing his disrupter at it.

I caught its two left facial fingers, while Viktor caught the two on the right, stopping the beast barely a meter in front of Axel. Its massive mouth could have easily bitten his upper half. Simultaneously, Darya jumped onto the creature's back and grabbed its middle finger. She yanked it backward with all her might, exposing the vulnerable spot at the base of the joint. The creature screeched so loudly that my ears rang. It surprised me that they didn't bleed.

Lightning fast, Ulia rushed behind the beast and sliced off its tails with a long sword even as it was about to whip us all. It bellowed again, violently struggling to free itself from our hold. My feet were slipping on the pebbled edge of the pond. I had to dig in the claws of my left foot to somewhat anchor me then signaled Viktor to imitate me. We simultaneously kicked its front legs, making it fall on its belly.

"Darya!" Ulia shouted.

The Iron Maiden—who was still stabbing at the joint with a dagger, looked at my cousin over her shoulder. Her silver white hair flew around her beautiful, dark-skinned face as she gazed upon him. Without a word, Ulia tossed her the sword he'd used to chop off the tails. Moving at dizzying speed, Darya shoved her dagger back in its sheath, caught the sword, and in one swift motion, stabbed it into the creature's vulnerable spot. It made a crunching as the weapon sank in all the way to the hilt. A violent tremor shook the beast before it froze then went limp.

All around us, Lycans and vampires alike were working in teams to take down their own monstrous critter. Everyone was fighting, including my mate—thankfully surrounded by Gavril, my mother, and three other of my high-ranking Iron Guards. Even Vlad and Vasska were battling, assisted by their personal guards. Everyone except Konstantin, who was nowhere to be seen.

As I looked around for another target, a savage roar turned my blood to ice. Loud thuds made the ground shake as the sound neared the entrance of the cave. I felt faint at the sight of a much bigger version than the critters we'd been battling—at least four times the size—as it came crawling out.

The Guardian hadn't only grown bigger, it had reproduced.

To my shock, the mother devoured the corpses of her offspring even as she attempted to worm her way out of the cave. Then again, it shouldn't surprise me. What did they feed on over all those centuries if not each other? Despite the huge size of the opening, the Guardian barely fit. Unlike her young, who only had four legs—two longer ones in the front and two shorter ones in the back, her longer body, at least six or seven meters long, had multiple spindly legs similar to the unusual 'fingers' on her forehead.

"We must take her down before she's fully out," I shouted.

If she was allowed to move about freely, it would be a massacre. Casting aside any thought of Konstantin, I rushed the beast with my loyal companions.

CHAPTER 23
THALIA

When I first saw the giant legged prawns emerge, I'd been on the verge of passing out. On top of them being terrifying, massive, and ridiculously fast, I didn't feel anywhere near competent enough to battle one. And yet, here I was slashing tails off and stabbing joints with the best of them.

Maintaining the shields from a safe location had significantly helped easing me into the right mindset. Being surrounded by the badass and unfazed aura of Raina and Gavril had done wonders to boost my own confidence. Witnessing Darya's badass moves as she spanked that first critter had awakened my hunger for battle. With the adrenaline pumping through my veins and Zabek's emotions cheering me on, I'd grown increasingly bolder in my contribution to the battle. Knowing that Raina and Gavril were keeping a close watch didn't offend me, quite the contrary. As a newbie, knowing such competent fighters had my back made me feel safe.

My man was a beast in a category of his own. Where the others were fighting to pin down a single one of the facial fingers of the creatures—very few managing to hold two—Drogo made it look effortless. On a couple of occasions, he held two of those

268

giant fingers with one arm while stabbing at the joints with the other. I'd never thought I'd say this but watching him massacre monsters was sexy as fuck.

To my relief, the vampires joining us turned out to be very helpful. Although I didn't doubt that we would have prevailed without them, instead of the mild to severe injuries our people had sustained so far, we definitely would have sustained some casualties.

When Konstantin saw me in my Lycan form, the hatred in his eyes almost felt like a physical blow. Intrigued by the source of such venom, Vlad had followed his gaze, seeing me for the first time. The shock and pain on his face—although quickly dissimulated—had broken my heart. I hated that I had hurt him. Vlad didn't know me much, and yet his feelings for me were real. Saying I wasn't strongly drawn to the Vampire Lord would be a lie. But Drogo was my soulmate. I could never regret choosing him. No man would ever complete me the way he did.

But this moment of distraction nearly cost Vlad his life. Without Vasska's timely intervention, Vlad would have gotten impaled by one of the spindly fingers of a beast. Cursing myself inwardly, I returned my focus to the battle at hand. Catching Raina's frown as her gaze went from Vlad to me made me squirm. Nothing slipped past the Queen Mother's notice.

In the endless minutes that followed, my growing belief in an impending victory was shattered by the appearance of the true Guardian. My blood turned to ice when I saw my man rushing towards it with nothing more than a sword hooked on his back, and both a dagger and a blaster on his hip. The Guardian's feeding frenzy on what I presumed to be her own offspring, allowed Drogo and his team to get the drop on her.

Except, repeating the same strategy as with her young didn't work out as well.

While Drogo barely managed to immobilize a single leg along her body, the other Lycans who tried to hold onto one on their own got tossed with a single flick of her leg. As the others defeated the remaining young, they ran in to assist their King, as did we after killing our last one. Three or four people were required to pin down a single leg. We resembled an army of ants swarming a prey. Seeing mixed groups of vampires and Lycans working together to subdue the Guardian moved me in the most unexpected fashion.

Oddly, I really wanted peace and friendship between the two breeds despite spending my entire life more or less hating the vampires. They treated us like chattel and maintained us in a state of poverty that ensured we continued selling ourselves as blood cows. But I genuinely wanted a truce, and I wanted Vlad to be their ruler.

Even with everyone attempting to shackle the Guardian, using her facial fingers and free legs, the Guardian managed to drag herself out of the cave. Along with a number of other Lycans, I threw myself at one of the tails as she tried to whip them forward to knock off those trying to restrain her. Thankfully, the frame of the doorway prevented them from fully lifting up. Clinging to the tail like a monkey to a vine, I furiously slashed at it with my claws until it tore off. I fell back down to the ground along with the severed appendage.

Just as I was turning to look for either another tail to sever or a leg joint to stab, a familiar scent struck me hard. It was close. Too close. I spun around, eyes wide, my gaze flicking this way and that, looking for Konstantin. Although he was nowhere to be seen, his scent kept moving past me and began fading as it headed into the cave.

Camouflage.

My stomach dropped as I realized the bastard was going to sneak in to steal control of the Well while everyone else was busy fighting. On instinct, I followed him in.

Contrary to my initial beliefs, the cave had not been natural but fully man-made—well, alien-made. A series of wall carvings similar to those in the Wisdom Trail drew my attention. But I forced my gaze away from them. Now was not the time to be distracted. The stone floor was badly damaged, like someone had repeatedly battered or stabbed at it. The same was true of the edge of the chasm. Despite the size of the cave, it couldn't have housed that Guardian and all of her offspring. The damaged edges confirmed the creatures lived further down and had climbed up.

The Well—or rather the massive vat—overflowed with an amber looking fluid, although it had looked like very dark blood outside. At least five centimeters of the liquid covered the floor. My heart constricted at the sight of the barren, pockmarked wall where the bioluminescent critters should have been. The protective glass that had kept them trapped lay in shattered pieces on the floor. If the Guardian and her young had eaten them all, once this current reserve of serum was used up, there would be no way to make more.

And Konstantin was in here trying to fuck with that very last batch. Even as a Lycan with a Spirit, I could never take that bastard on my own. I turned my head towards the entrance, looking for my two babysitters. At the same time, perched on the back of the Guardian, Raina was looking for me. I opened my mouth to call out to her, but rapidly approaching splashing sounds had my head jerking back towards the cave.

I never got time to raise my blaster in the general direction of the splashes. A living, invisible brick wall smashed into me, sending me flying backward. I crashed against the cave wall with such force, my teeth rattled. Something shifted on the wall behind me as I collapsed to the ground, stunned. Had I still been human, every bone in my body would have shattered. Winded, I watched with horror as the doors began closing again.

"Thalia!" Raina shouted, with a horrified expression when she finally spotted me sprawled on the floor inside the cave.

She jumped down from the back of the Guardian, multiple

heads turning to watch her as she raced for the entrance. The same horrified expressions descended on every face when they realized what was happening. But none managed to reach the doorway in time. That last brutal push from the offspring trying to exit the cave had visibly fixed the doors' misalignment.

Coming out of stealth, Konstantin towered over me. A profound disgust settled on his face as he took in my Lycan appearance.

"You were so perfect," Konstantin said, his voice dripping with contempt. "Now, you're just a fucking animal. You could have ruled by my side. Instead, I'm just going to take what little you still have to offer."

He grabbed my hair and yanked me up. Using his body, he sandwiched me against the wall and held both of my wrists pinned above my head with one hand. I tried to fight him off, but even with my enhanced strength, I might as well have attempted to move a mountain. There was a reason no one dared to challenge the ancient vampire. He pulled my head to the side, exposing my neck with such brutality, I all but expected it to tear right off.

"No!" I shouted when I saw his fangs descend.

Not only did the thought of him drinking from me feel like a violation of my body, but I also knew he wouldn't stop until he had killed me. Naturally, he ignored me. Outside, mixing with the enraged screeches of the Guardian, multiple voices were calling my name, and countless hands were attempting to open the doors slightly ajar in places where they had been damaged by the young.

Just as Konstantin was leaning in to sink his teeth in my neck, a terrible heat rose from my chest and then lightning struck my aggressor, the electric tendrils running all over his body and his face. The vampire shouted in pain and stumbled back, freeing me. Without missing a beat, I brought down one of my liberated hands, slashing my claws across his pretty face, before kicking him square in the chest. I addressed a silent thank you to Zabek for saving me. Despite his wave of affection for me, he was seething with anger at Konstantin.

The Vampire Lord fell on his ass into the orange fluid, putting one hand on the floor to stop his fall. He was back on his feet so fast, if not for the liquid dripping from his hand and his clothes, I would have believed I'd imagined it. He touched his cheek and felt the deep wounds my claws had inflicted on him. Enraged, he charged me with murder in his eyes. I dodged at dizzying speed, applying Darya's training as I effectively kept out of range, avoiding most of his blows, and parrying those I couldn't.

I began gaining confidence as he chased me around the room. However, each time I tried to move back towards the location where my blaster had landed after Konstantin smashed me against the wall, the bastard would force me in a different direction, towards the back. God only knew how long that little dance would have lasted if the badly damaged floor hadn't tripped me. I never saw the blow coming. The sole of the vampire's foot struck my chest with such violence, I thought my sternum would cave in.

As I flew backward, the brief thought that Zabek might have been squashed crossed my mind. But even as he reassured me that he was fine, I struggled to get a grip on the floor. Carried by the momentum, I kept sliding all the way to the edge of the chasm. My claws failed to hang on to the mangled edge, and I fell. I screamed with terror as I tried in vain to stop my fall, but each time my claws seemed to find purchase, my weight and excessive speed nearly tore them out. Drogo's face flashed before my eyes moments before I crashed onto a hard surface and darkness swallowed me.

I regained consciousness wondering how long I'd been out. However, the pain in my limbs felt like no more than the light soreness after an intensive training. Did that mean I'd been unconscious a long time or had my Lycan accelerated healing done wonders? Either way, it didn't matter. I'd landed on a deep plateau that visibly served as entrance to the lair of the Guardian. Many unhatched eggs could be seen inside little nooks in the walls. But now wasn't the time for exploration. Worse still, I didn't want to run into a hungry hatchling.

Looking up at the rock face above the plateau, I almost panicked at the sight of the long way to climb. Thankfully, the creatures' frequent climbs had left deep grooves that made it easy for me to find purchase. Using the claws of my hands and my feet, I made quick work of hoisting myself back to the edge as quietly as possible. Once more, I marveled at the power of my Lycan abilities. As a human, I'd be panting right now, my muscles burning from the effort.

My heart ached as Drogo's desperate voice shouted my name. From the absence of painful screeches, I presumed they had defeated the Guardian. I peered above the edge located straight across the room from the doorway. The Lycans were multiplying their effort to pry open the doors. At first glance, they didn't seem to have made the slightest progress.

I cast a glance at Konstantin. He was cursing under his breath while glaring at the small receptacle hooked on the vat. He bit the side of his left hand and let some of his blood drop into the receptacle. I nearly panicked when I realized he was trying to set the serum to serve the vampires, but he cursed again and stomped his foot on the floor with helpless rage.

He can't do it. He can't make it work.

Drogo's words to the effect that Konstantin had no chance of claiming the Well without me came back to mind.

He's missing something that my blood would have given him.

Zabek's reaction confirmed I had guessed right. While figuring that out was all fine and dandy, it didn't tell me how the fuck I would get my sorry ass out of here. I believed there was a switch to open the door near the area where Konstantin had smashed me against the wall. But I'd never reach it, let alone find and activate it, before Konstantin caught me. I couldn't fight him without getting my butt handed to me.

My shield!

As a Daywalker, my light shield wouldn't kill him, but it might keep him from touching me long enough to find the switch. I looked at the interface of my bracelet only for my heart to sink at the sight of its shattered screen. It probably broke during my fall.

Just when I was beginning to despair, Konstantin cradled his right hand to his chest, his face constricted with a painful expression. His hand was red, the skin appearing to have melted off as if it had been exposed to excessive heat or dipped in acid. I frowned, wondering what could have caused it. Using his blade with his left hand, he clumsily fished something out of the receptacle and tossed it to the floor. It looked like a small, black rock. I then noticed about seven or eight more similar rocks at his feet.

Is that his blood?

Zabek once more expressed his agreement with my thought. The serum wasn't accepting his blood. He wasn't a Lycan and didn't have a Spirit—anymore. Selene had built this place for the children of the Wolves, for those loved by the Spirits. Soren would have made Konstantin's blood acceptable to the Well had he stayed with him. And my golden blood was compatible with the Spirits, even more than the Lycan one.

The vat would accept my blood.

This time, Zabek's agreement was beyond powerful. In that instant, I realized he wasn't just agreeing but was actually saying that *I* should be the one binding the Well. However, this was a discussion for later. First, I needed to get out of my current predicament.

I shifted slightly from my position. Konstantin looked defeated, his gaze going from the vat to the doors. Unfortunately for him, his only way out was currently crowded by people who would want to butcher him for 'killing' me. What I wouldn't give to hear the thoughts crossing his mind right this instant. Was he cursing himself for the greed and ambition that had put him in this situation?

His wincing in pain again while flexing his right hand brought my attention back to that issue. And then, it finally hit me. Unlike his left arm, the sleeve of his right one was wet. When I'd kicked him earlier, and he'd fallen to the ground, he'd parried part of his fall with his right hand. It had been submerged by the amber serum covering the floor.

Could it be?

Once more, Zabek gave me a resounding yes. Not for the first time, I wished my Spirit and I could speak using actual words instead of me having to interpret his emotional reactions. However, feeling confident enough that I had understood him correctly, I kicked my feet and pushed myself up with my arms, making myself jump on top of the floor.

Konstantin jerked around, a shocked expression on his face. Without wasting a moment, I ran towards him. Using my momentum, I crouched down to swipe some of the serum on the floor and splash it at his face. The vampire raised his hands before his face and shouted in pain. He tried to rush me, but I continued splashing the liquid at him in a frenzy, forcing him to back away. His shouts turned into screams when the serum touched the open wounds my claws had left on his cheek. They wouldn't close until he drank blood again.

A sliver of pity flashed through me when he ran to a back corner of the room, his back to me, and made himself into a ball, failing to silence his grunts of agony. To think I had wanted to belong to that man. How the mighty had fallen.

Ignoring the vat, I ran to the wall near the entrance.

"Drogo, I'm fine!" I shouted, running my hands all over the wall in a frantic search for the switch. "Hang on!"

"Thalia!" Drogo yelled back through the narrow opening. "Can you open the door?"

The relief and love in his voice almost undid me. I cast a nervous glance at Konstantin who, thankfully, had not moved from his fetal position.

"I'm trying. There's a switch. I can't find—"

CLICK

I stared at my hand with disbelief as the small section of rock depressed. The doors immediately slid open. Drogo rushed in and pulled me into a bone crushing embrace as well as a brutal a kiss. He released me only to start examining me from head to toe for any signs of injury.

"I'm fine, my love. I'm fine," I said, trying to calm him.

But the angry growls and shouts coming from the back of the cave snapped me out of my happy reunion with my mate. Drogo's face took on a murderous expression as Ulia and Viktor dragged Konstantin before us. His entire face and hands were covered in blisters where the skin hadn't flat out peeled off. Vlad gestured for the Red Guards to stay put when they made as if to intervene. From the look on their faces, all of them were torn at the thought of allowing a Lycan—even though he was their King—to slaughter the High Lord they had considered as the vampire king.

"I'm going to tear you to pieces," Drogo hissed, his vicious claws coming out.

"No!" I exclaimed, placing my palm on his chest to hold him back. Every face turned towards me with flabbergasted expressions. "Konstantin came here with the intent of claiming the Well. He has failed miserably. The price for his arrogance can be seen on his body and his face. He now knows his place. Let that be a lesson to any who wishes to challenge the rule of the Lycans."

Drogo stared at me in disbelief. I held his gaze unflinchingly, hoping and praying he wouldn't override my request. My mate clenched his jaw and scrunched his face as if he'd bitten into something foul. He turned to Konstantin with a world of hatred burning in his eyes.

"I would have cut you limb from limb and left you to die of Blood Starvation," Drogo said, his voice dripping with contempt. "But my Queen has spoken. Don't you ever return to Hundilinn. The next time our paths cross, there will be no mercy. Take that vermin out of my sight."

Ulia and Viktor dragged Konstantin out of the cave and dropped him on the platform at the feet of the Red Guard. Vlad gestured for the guards to handle the fallen High Lord. They picked him up and started heading towards their shuttles. I shifted back to my human form—although default form would be more accurate as I wasn't quite human anymore.

Vlad signaled for all of the vampires to head back to their ships. Instead of following them, he approached the entrance of the cave but didn't step inside. The clever man cast a glance at the serum and immediately figured out it had messed up Konstantin. I closed the distance between us. The stares of the Lycans, especially my mate's and his mother's, were burning holes in my back.

"Mercy?" Vlad asked as his sole comment.

"The vampires would never have forgiven the Lycan King for executing their leader when he was already too injured to put up a fair fight," I said matter-of-factly. "But more importantly, your reign as their new leader will be challenged if you merely inherit the role. You must win against Konstantin fair and square, then no one will oppose you."

A slow smile stretched Vlad's sensual lips even as the sliver of sadness quickly crossed his features.

"The pawn checkmated the would-be king and became a queen," Vlad mused out loud. "Well played."

I curtsied. "You flatter me, milord."

He snorted and examined my features for a few seconds. "Be

happy, Thalia," Vlad said at last before extending a hand towards me. I placed mine in his without hesitation, despite the frowns of the Lycans surrounding us. The vampire raised my hand to his lips before gently kissing my fingertips. "My Queen."

He released my hand then slightly bowed his head at Drogo's mother. "Raina," he said in farewell, "Drogo," he then said, repeating the gesture towards my mate before turning on his heels and leaving.

Vasska came to stand in front of me with that eternal irreverent smile plastered on his gorgeous face. "Cute ears," he said to me after glancing at my wolf ears.

I burst out laughing. Vasska embodied the bratty little brother I wish I'd had. There was something irresistible about him.

He looked at Drogo and his mother. "Greetings, and all that," he said with a flourishing curtsey.

I snorted and shook my head at him. He winked at me before hurrying after his brother.

"Interesting friends you have," Viktor said, pursing his lips.

"More like she makes smart alliances, as a proper Queen should," Raina said while looking at me with pride. She leaned forward and kissed my forehead in a maternal fashion that had my throat tightening with emotion.

"While I agree with your reasoning, I still wish you had let me fuck him up at least a little," Drogo mumbled before pulling me into his embrace.

I chuckled, rubbed my nose against his, then kissed him. Rising to my tiptoes, I drew his head lower and pressed my mouth to his ear. "You can fuck *me* to your hearts content later," I whispered.

EPILOGUE
DROGO

Despite the rage that still bubbled inside me, relief to have my female safe in my arms supplanted everything else. Pride also filled my heart as I stared at Thalia. She was a true Queen. With her keen analytical sense, she had seen what my anger had blinded me to. As much as Vlad's obvious deep feelings and longing for my mate made my hackles rise, I didn't fear any impropriety between them. My mate had freely chosen me, and her affection for the vampire lacked the passion she bore me.

However, her reasoning about Vlad handling Konstantin had been sound. I wanted to unite the vampires and Lycans under one rule, but the vampires needed to feel like they would retain their autonomy. If they believed I'd installed my pawn as their ruler, Vlad would forever be undermined. Without a peaceful alliance between our peoples, it would be impossible for me to elevate the life and living conditions of the humans without becoming a dictator.

As we turned to look at the Well, my heart soared to find it full and untainted. However, Thalia's fascination with a mural drew my attention. I'd entered this cave once before. Unlike now, the doorway had been attempting to close too quickly. My father had poured some of his blood into the receptacle to bind the serum. We'd then rushed to haul as much of it out of the cave before we could no longer hold the doorway.

For the first time, we were finally able to explore the space with relative confidence in our ability to exit should the doors close again. The carvings on the walls emulated the Karthians' storytelling style of wall sculpting. It didn't have the same artistic finesse but was clearly meant to be understood by a primitive species. Selene had left this for our forefathers to manage the place once all the 'educated' Sun Wolves had left.

Despite the extensive damage they had sustained both from time and the creatures that had rampaged here, they remained legible. This was a clear operation manual for the biometric lock, the switch, the Well, and the bioluminescent bugs on the wall. Contrary to Thalia's fears, the glowing critters that produced the serum had not been devoured by the Guardian and her offspring. They had hidden inside the creases pockmarking the wall where they dwelled. While we observed the carvings, Ulia's team 'vacuumed' the serum on the floor. It was too tainted with everyone traipsing in it to be used for medicine, but our researchers would nonetheless use it for study purposes. They also filled a couple of flasks of pure serum from the Well.

As I turned back to approach the receptacle of the Well to pour my blood into it, Soren tightened around my chest. The discomfort wasn't painful but sufficed for me to know he didn't want me to proceed. I frowned in confusion. Not only did I have the most powerful blood of the Lycans, but my dual vampire-Lycan nature meant vampires who received the serum would benefit even more from its healing powers.

I placed my hand over Soren and cast a baffled glance at Viktor.

"It's refusing you?" Viktor asked, stunned.

"He doesn't want me to. Could it be because of my illness?" I asked, taken aback by this unexpected turn of events.

"No," Thalia said softly, her hand caressing my back in a soothing motion. "I believe the Spirits want *me* to pour my blood in the serum."

I recoiled, rendered speechless by her comment. And then it dawned on me. "Of course," I whispered before looking at my mate with awe. "You've got golden blood; the universal blood that every breed craves. Spirits, Lycans, *and* vampires are strengthened by it. You could be the key!"

My mate's shoulders relaxed, and she gave me a sweet smile. I realized then that she'd been tense, worried about my reaction. Silly female. I wielded the Well as a weapon to keep Konstantin in check. The Well didn't make me the Lycan King, my strength did.

"Go on, love," I said with an encouraging smile.

She stepped up to the receptacle and nervously slashed her wrist with her claw right above it. The delicious aroma of her blood made my mouth water. The memory of its divine flavor on my taste buds and its smooth silkiness as it slid down my throat made me ache to sink my fangs into her. But I held myself in check.

I held my breath as some kind of chemical reaction was taking place. Stunned, Thalia made to pull her wrist away from the receptacle but the way she clutched her chest, Zabek clearly told her not to. My mate cast a worried glance my way, but I nodded for her to proceed. That earned me an approving nudge from Soren. The serum rippled, taking on a scarlet color. Its maddening scent had every Lycan in the room salivating.

"Fuck," my mother whispered. "I've never experienced bloodlust before, but right this instance, I want to gulp down that entire vat."

"You and me both, my friend," Viktor grumbled.

Just as he finished speaking those words, a series of lights lit up around the edge of the Well, and a mechanical sound resounded as if some mechanism beneath it had activated. Thalia pulled her hand away from the receptacle. This time, Zabek didn't seem to argue with that decision.

"What the fuck is that?" Viktor asked. "This has never happened before."

"DROGO!" Gavril's voice called out from outside of the cave.

Thalia and I exchanged a look before we rushed out of the cave. My jaw dropped at the sight of the pond's silver water slowly turning crimson. I cast a questioning glance at Ulia, still partially inside the cave.

"The vat is emptying," he confirmed.

"The red waters are back," Viktor whispered in disbelief. "If this is what I think, it isn't just the cure for Blood Starvation, but it's also the cure for the Karthians' photosensitivity."

"Like in the days of old, after the Bloody Wedding, when drinking from the red pond allowed them to live a normal life," my mother concluded, a look of wonder on her face.

The Spirits, all but dancing at the surface of the pond, and Soren's joyous waves of emotion seemed to confirm those speculations. I pulled my mate into my arms and crushed her lips with love and gratitude under the victorious roars of my people.

In the days and weeks that followed, we took extensive pictures and videos of everything inside the cave. Ulia and his team spent the next eternity studying the locking mechanism. Our goal was to completely dismantle the current doors and install new ones that we would have full control over. Now that we had seen the switch, we ensured there was *always* someone assigned to remain inside the cave in case the doors decided to close again.

We also kept a close eye on the creatures that dwelled in the chasm and that spawned the Guardians. We'd named them mollix as they more or less reminded us of mollusks. Our observations determined that as the time between openings of the doorway lengthened, the serum overflowed and dripped to their lair, and modified whatever small critter had originally dwelled there. Although we couldn't quite explain how, we believed the mollix played a role in the unusual nature of the water in the pond. The creatures' silver-colored blood shared too many similarities with the water for this to be a pure coincidence.

But the best part was being able to confirm that, thanks to Thalia's blood, the new serum constituted the cure to both Blood Starvation and photosensitivity. Then again, 'cure' was too strong a word. Effective treatment would probably be more accurate as a monthly dose was required to keep those conditions in check in the people affected by them. However, for me, a single dose of the serum wiped out the lingering traces of my illness within a couple of days. And more importantly, it fixed the issue that prevented so many of my people from hosting a Spirit.

After a few successful tests to be certain, the Karthians wept when the serum effectively gave them back access to a normal life without instantly burning under the sun. Their pallid skin still required them to wear sunscreen to avoid sunburns over extended periods of time outdoors, but it was a minor discomfort for reclaiming their lives.

As for the vampires, for the first time, not only did the water from the pond no longer increase their bloodlust, but it also resolved their light sensitivity issues. As we didn't trust them to freely roam on our territory, they were required to place orders with restricted quantities per individual, which were delivered to Verelinn by the Karthians. Needless to say that this 'treatment' completely messed with the vampires' economy and social status. I almost felt sorry for their High Lords and Grand Council. The foreseeable future would be a massive headache for them to juggle.

But their hands were also full with power plays and shifting alliances. Konstantin's status had been beyond hard hit following his series of defeats. Worse still, according to rumors, the wound inflicted by Thalia's claws had permanently scarred him. While the rest of the serum's damage to his skin had healed, its effect on the open wounds had essentially cauterized them. As his beauty had been a non-negligible part of his charisma, I didn't doubt how much his hatred for us—and especially for my mate —had grown.

In the months that followed, not a single pregnancy or birth was derailed by any blood illness, be it among Lycans, Karthians, or vampires. In one fell swoop, my mate had taken us leaps and bounds closer to achieving all of our goals. Studying the technology within the cave was also broadening our horizons on both the defensive and offensive fronts.

Although I no longer needed to drink blood, Thalia insisted I continue doing so once a week. Her reasoning was that I needed to remain the strongest Lycan of all the packs. While valid, I believed she also enjoyed that it inevitably resulted in us having some wild, unbridled sex—not that I needed an excuse to chase after my mate's fluffy tail.

We stood inside the Wisdom Trail, surrounded by our friends and loved ones for the final reveal of the latest murals. On the right, Vesna had made a magnificent carving of the two stages of the Guardian's battle. On the left wall, multiple scenes depicted Thalia's incredible journey since we'd met and her impact on the fate of the Lycans and the people of Karthia as a whole. My heart swelled with love for my mate and for our two pups kicking inside her swollen belly.

Only a few months ago, I'd been at death's door, fighting a losing battle without any real hope for the future. Now, a delicate human seeking a better future had turned an entire planet upside down and laid the world at my feet. No words would ever be able to express all that she meant to me.

She was my light, my love, my Queen.

THE END

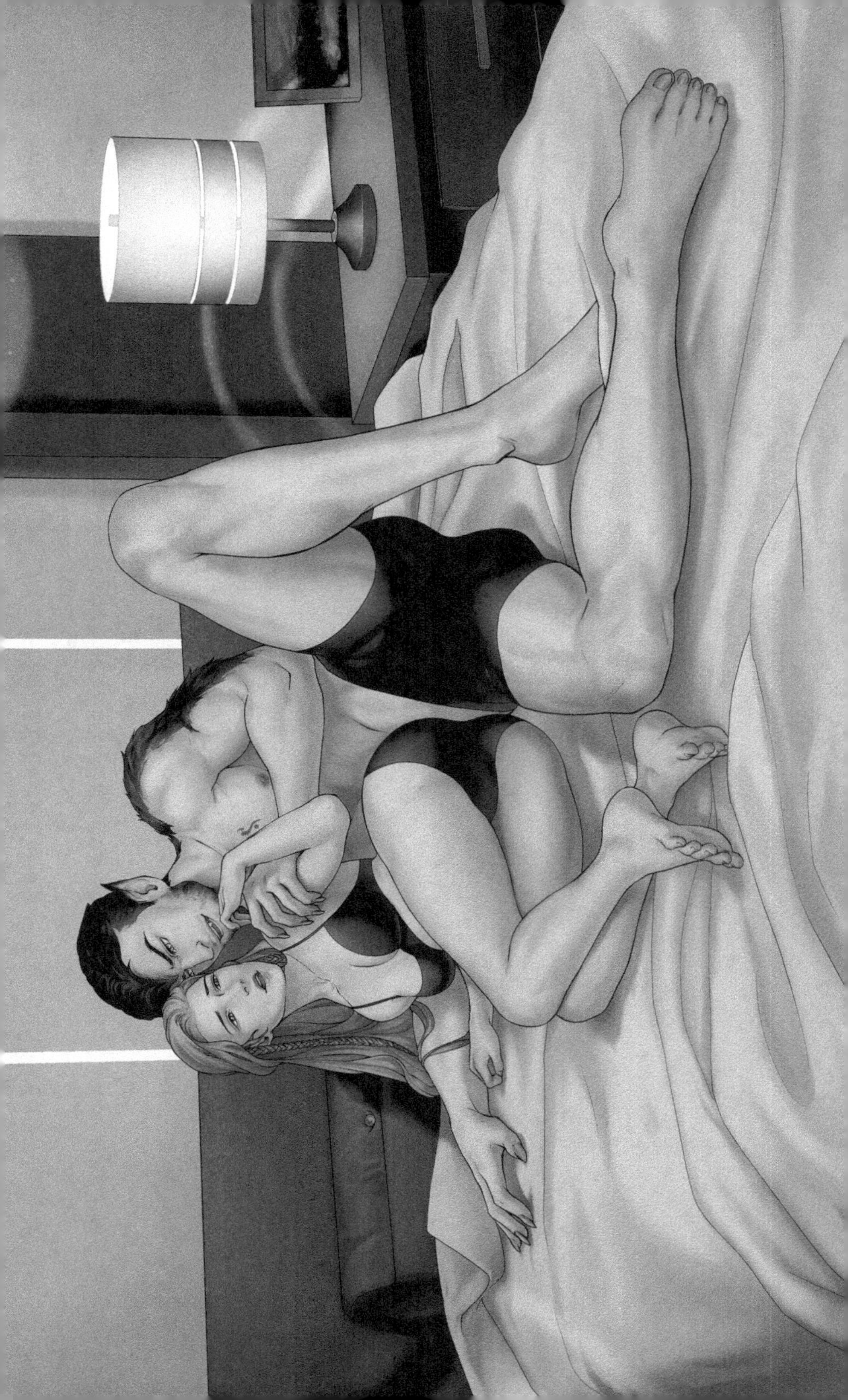

ALSO BY REGINE ABEL

THE VEREDIAN CHRONICLES
Escaping Fate
Blind Fate
Raising Amalia
Twist of Fate
Hands of Fate
Defying Fate
Imperial Fate

BRAXIANS
Anton's Grace
Ravik's Mercy
Krygor's Hope
Keran's Dawn

XIAN WARRIORS
Doom
Legion
Raven
Bane
Chaos
Varnog
Reaper
Wrath
Xenon
Nevrik
Rogue
Doom: A Graphic Novel

BLOOD MAIDENS OF KARTHIA
Claiming Thalia

PRIME MATING AGENCY
I Married A Lizardman
I Married A Naga
I Married A Birdman
I Married A Minotaur
I Married Wonjin
I Married A Merman
I Married A Dragon
I Married A Beast
I Married Krogal
I Married A Dryad
I Married An Incubus
I Married A Mothman
I Married A Catman
I Married Amreth
I Married Kayog

THE MIST
The Mistwalker
The Nightmare

DARK TALES
Bluebeard's Curse
The Hunchback

THE SHADOW REALMS
Destined to the Wraith
Destined to the Reaper
Destined to the Lycan

VALOS OF SONHADRA
Unfrozen
Iced

EMPATHS OF LYRIA
An Alien For Christmas

OTHER
True As Steel
Alien Awakening
Heart of Stone
Oops! I Summoned a Liderc

ABOUT REGINE

USA Today bestselling author Regine Abel is a fantasy, paranormal and sci-fi junkie. Anything with a bit of magic, a touch of the unusual, and a lot of romance will have her jumping for joy. She loves creating hot alien warriors and no-nonsense, kick-ass heroines that evolve in fantastic new worlds while embarking on action-packed adventures filled with mystery and the twists you never saw coming.

Before devoting herself as a full-time writer, Regine had surrendered to her other passions: music and video games! After a decade working as a Sound Engineer in movie dubbing and live concerts, Regine became a professional Game Designer and Creative Director, a career that has led her from her home in Canada to the US and various countries in Europe and Asia.

Facebook

https://www.facebook.com/regine.abel.author/

Website

https://regineabel.com

Regine's Rebels Reader Group

https://www.facebook.com/groups/ReginesRebels/

Newsletter

http://smarturl.it/RA_Newsletter

Goodreads

http://smarturl.it/RA_Goodreads

Bookbub

https://www.bookbub.com/profile/regine-abel

Amazon

http://smarturl.it/AuthorAMS